KILL LIST

Richard L. Hatin

For Karen
Enjoy!
Richard L Hatin

Publisher Page
an imprint of Headline Books, Inc.
Terra Alta, WV

Kill List

by Richard L. Hatin

To order additional copies of this book or for book publishing information, or to contact the author:

Headline Books, Inc.
P.O. Box 52
Terra Alta, WV 26764
www.HeadlineBooks.com

Tel: 304-789-3001
Email: mybook@headlinebooks.com

Publisher Page is an imprint of Headline Books

ISBN 13: 9781882658978

Library of Congress Control Number: 2017936320

PRINTED IN THE UNITED STATES OF AMERICA

*To all whose life is a struggle over
choices; both good and bad.
Whatever challenge you may be
encountering, be it physical, mental,
emotional or spiritual or even a
combination of these, know this;
God is with you, waiting for you, and
is there for you!*

"God is not willing to do everything, and thus take away our free will and that share of glory which belongs to us."
—Niccolo Machiavelli

"Life is like a game of cards. The hand you are dealt is determinism; the way you play it is free will."
—Jawaharlal Nehru

"I live in sin, to kill myself I live; no longer my life my own, but sin's; my good is given to me by heaven, my evil by myself, by my free will, of which I am deprived."
—Michelangelo

Chapter 1
Manchester, New Hampshire
December 12

Stephanie Monroe hurriedly pulled into the driveway of her single family home on Chestnut Street, just a half block away from busy Webster Street in Manchester's affluent north end neighborhood. Her car's tires screeched slightly as it came to a stop.

She hurried out of the car, opened the trunk and retrieved three bags of groceries. She slammed the trunk closed.

It was December 12th and she was running late. Her newest boyfriend, Doug, was coming over for romantic pre-dinner visit cocktails before they set off to go to her office holiday dinner party. Twice divorced and nearly thirty years old, Stephanie had been cruising the dating scene as of late and Doug was her latest catch. She didn't have deep feelings for him but that hadn't stopped her from being intimate with him. For Stephanie sex was a tool, an instrument towards whatever end suited her. Doug was handsome, available, and successful. He also had above-average career potential. That was good enough for Stephanie. She had turned up the heat index and was thus hoping for a holiday proposal from her latest heartthrob.

Stephanie rushed inside her house and kicked her side door, closing it with the back of her right shoe.

She checked her watch and noted she had, at best, twenty minutes to get ready.

Damn traffic, thought Stephanie, *bunch of old ladies out there always slowing things down for the rest of us.*

Kicking off her shoes, she made a beeline for the shower. She started the hot water and stripped hurriedly out of her clothes.

She was about to climb into the shower when her front doorbell rang.

"Damn it!" she grumbled.

Throwing on a bathrobe she padded through the house to the front door.

If the sound of her footsteps conveyed anything, it was clear she was annoyed, big-time annoyed at the unexpected interruption.

"**Who is it**?" shouted Stephanie.

The tone was another tell regarding her mood.

"Delivery for Stephanie Monroe," said the voice of the person on the other side of the door.

"Just leave it on the porch," she replied.

"I can't ma'am. I need someone to sign for it."

"Can't you sign for me? I'm in a hurry."

"No can do! I could lose my job if I did that."

She pulled back the small lace curtain to the narrow window alongside the front door. She could barely make out the dark shape of a man standing on her front porch holding a small package.

"Oh, what the hell," she said as she unlocked the front door and pulled it open. She then opened the glass storm-door just a crack.

She could see the man holding a small box wrapped in plain brown paper. She couldn't make out any details of the man because he was back-lit by the streetlight which was at the edge of her front curb.

Pulling at her robe, she tightened it around her neck.

"Where do I sign?"

The man dropped the box on the porch and quickly pulled the storm door open with his powerful left hand. He raised his right arm up pointing it at her.

Everything was happening so fast.

Why is he pointing at me? thought Stephanie.

The correct question should have been **what** was he pointing at her?

She never saw the gun.

The man aimed for her forehead and pulled the trigger once.

The muzzled gun made a small **"whump"** sound.

Stephanie fell backwards onto the foyer's hardwood floor. Her bathrobe flew open. She was dead before she hit the floor.

"Merry Christmas, Bitch!" said the man. He kicked her feet out of the way and bent down and picked up the package. Next, he reached around the front door and engaged the door lock. He closed the locked door and then he closed the screen door.

He had already scouted the street and knew no one was out and about. He was confident he had blended in sufficiently.

"Act like you belong and no one will remember you," he repeated to himself as he slipped the muzzled gun back into his jacket's left inside pocket.

Moments later, he reached his car which he had parked at a Cumberland Farm store less than two blocks away. Now he removed the rubber gloves he had been wearing and carefully placed them in the trunk of the car inside of a small canvas bag. He tossed the small brown box into the trunk, too. Settling into his car seat he unscrewed the silencer from the pistol and put both in the glove-box of his car. Finally, he removed a small spiral bound, flip-over notebook from the glove-box.

He flipped the pages until he came to page numbered thirty-nine.

He took out his red ink pen from his shirt pocket and wrote across the Stephanie Monroe information on the page: Died December 12, 5:35 p.m.

He then initialed the latest entry, S.B.

As he settled into the driver's seat a voice from the back seat sang: "It's beginning to look a lot like Christmas!"

The driver looked up into the rear-view mirror at the dark faceless shape sitting in the backseat of his car and broke into a smile as he started up the car.

Chapter 2
Hooksett, New Hampshire
Six Days Earlier

Stanley, 'Stan the Man,' Bolinski was in a hurry. On the spur of the moment he decided to pick up some last minute groceries at the Market Basket Supermarket at Market Drive, just off of Exit 10 of Interstate 93 in Hooksett, NH. It was nearly five o'clock on December 6.

Stan knew that the store would be very busy. It had been busy ever since it opened earlier in the fall. Now, it was the busiest time of the day and with December and all, it would be more than just busy. It would be jammed. He didn't care. He needed some milk, some coffee, coffee creamer and a few other things. Since he now lived alone he had no reason to rush home and no one else to do his grocery shopping for him.

Stan was sixty-four years old and nearing the end of his working career. He already had delayed his retirement once. He was the Senior Manager at a regional branch of Coast-to-Coast Trucking. He had worked in a variety of jobs in the interstate trucking industry since he was nineteen. Now, as he was nearing his mid-sixties, he found himself working for the owner's newest son-in-law. His supervisor was the twenty-three year old, 'know-it-all and all around pain-in-the-ass,' Ramon Ordonez.

Ordonez always bastardized Stanley's name by pronouncing it, "Meester Bulinky." No matter how many times Stan-the-Man would correct him; the little piss-ant would still mangle his name. For that, Ramon now stood on Stan's special list at number thirty-six. His time would come, sure as there was a sun, a moon and stars. When that time came, Stan would insist on one last thing from this miserable excuse for a human being. He would get him to pronounce his name correctly, at least one time before he dies.

Stanley Bolinski drove his 2010 sky-blue Ford Focus up Market Drive to the front of the store. He slowly turned to the right and drove along the front of the store. He looked to his right, along the rows of parked cars, and spied a woman pushing her grocery cart towards a small sedan half way down the row on the left side. He pulled into the row to the right. He put on his left blinker signaling his intention of pulling into the soon-to-be vacated space. He put his car into neutral as he waited his turn to pull into the parking space.

The woman soon backed her car out of the parking space, pulling her car to the right, positioning her car to face his. As she pulled forward Stan put his car back into gear. Just as her car cleared the vacant parking space, another car came careening around the end of the parking row and swerved into the vacant space before Stanley could.

Stanley was outraged at the parking vulture who had just pounced on the parking space he had patiently and courteously waited for.

A woman got out of the newly parked car and righted her scarf by throwing the falling end around her neck.

Stanley powered down his driver's side window and bellowed at the woman, "Bitch, you have a lot of nerve!"

Without pausing or flinching at his outburst she looked causally at him, flicked him the middle finger of her left hand and said, "Back-off old man. You snooze you lose."

He watched the young woman in his rear-view mirror head through the parking lot towards the grocery store entrance.

Stanley Bolinski was furious. In fact, he was heading straight past furious to blind rage. Sitting in the back seat of his car was a dark, human-shaped form. There was no visible face, only an ink-black shape.

"So, Stan the Man, she blew you off. That little bitch needs to be taught a lesson. No one screws with you, no one. Right Stanleeeeeeeey?" huffed the shape in the back seat.

Stanley looked up into his rear-view mirror. Stanley's eyes were nearly bugging out of his head. His lips were pursed tightly and spittle was running out of both corners of his mouth.

"You're goddamn right she needs to be taught a lesson. I'm going to fix her up real good, just you wait and see," said Stanley.

"*She belongs in the book, belongs in the book. Ladies and Gentlemen just step right up and watch the magical wheel spin. Around and around she goes, where she stops nobodies knows!*" The dark shape was mimicking a carnival barker's voice.

Stanley reached for his glove box and opened it. He removed a spiral bound flip-over notebook. He thumbed through the heavily trafficked pages and stopped at the first blank one. It was previously thirty-seven. He glanced over at the "Bitch's car." Using a pen which had been inserted into the spiral binding, he jotted down her license plate number along with the color and make of her car. Once the information was recorded he stowed the pen and tossed the notebook onto the passenger seat. He looked up and sure enough, three spaces down from her spot was an open and available parking space. He pulled into the space and turned off his car.

Stanley reached into his car's still open glove box and pulled out the nine millimeter Glock, Security Special. He checked the gun's clip and found it fully loaded. He slapped it back into position with the palm of his hand. He next rummaged around the glove box and found the noise suppressor he always stored with his gun. He carefully screwed the attachment into position, being especially careful to not cross thread the suppressor.

"*You can't take her here. Too many witnesses. Remember, we have got to remain invisible, you and me,*" said Stanley's ever present passenger.

"Don't you worry, okay? I have it covered. I haven't ever screwed up and I won't now, so get off my damn back," growled a highly agitated Stanley.

To anyone looking at Stanley it might appear he was talking with himself or perhaps with an out-of-sight cell phone.

The open notebook sitting on the passenger car seat was partially flipped open to page number twenty-five. Written in heavy red ink over the information inscribed on the page was the following: Died, July 20, 2008. 1:50 p.m. followed by the initials S.B.

Stanley looked to his left and caught a glance of the "Bitch," his newly targeted, number thirty-nine, hastily running to her car. She cautiously glanced around before she unlocked her car door and slipped quickly inside.

She next pulled her car out of her parking space with a sudden lurch. She tried to quickly drive away but was blocked by an elderly couple moving slowly across the roadway between rows.

The "Bitch" leaned on her car's horn startling the older couple.

Now distracted, she didn't notice Stanley had pulled his car up directly behind hers. His immediate plan was to follow her and see if an opportunity presented itself. Once someone was in Stanley's notebook, he could become a patient and a highly focused man.

"Stan is the Man," said his companion with obvious glee.

Chapter 3
Chestnut Street
Manchester, New Hampshire
December 13

There were five police cars parked outside of Stephanie Monroe's house on Chestnut Street. Three cars were marked police cruisers and two were not. The unmarked cars belonged to homicide detectives. The officers from the other police cars were blocking off the ends of the street and standing guard outside the residence. A large, black, box van marked MPD - Crime Scene Unit was parked at the curb in front of her house. Bright yellow "Police – Do not Enter" tape was stretched across the front of the property.

Detective Michael O'Toole was a fourth generation cop. He had twenty–three years on the force, the last nine of those in Homicide. He stood six-foot three and had bright red hair, cut close and flat. He was trim and serious. Michael strode out of the house and approached his partner of five years, Edgar Horton. Horton, sipping a coffee, was also chatting up one of the uniforms standing on the sidewalk.

With a nod of his head O'Toole motioned for Horton to approach him.

"So what do you think?" asked Horton.

"Point blank range, single shot to the head, almost looks like a contract job." Shaking his head he continued, "Crime scene people aren't finding anything either. The uniforms and I got nothing from the neighbors. No see - no hear. Windows closed. Based upon body temp the ME estimates time of death at between five and six p.m. Boyfriend is the one who called it in.

He's sitting in the back of the squad car," said Horton gesturing to the marked car parked at the curb.

"What's his story?" asked O'Toole.

"He says he was coming over to have cocktails before they were to head out to a holiday dinner party. She didn't answer the door bell. He saw her car in the driveway, so he says he figured she was showering or something. He lets himself in with the key she had given him. He finds the deceased spread-eagled in the entrance and calls PD right away. Claims he didn't touch or move the body. He's puked twice in the last ten minutes. We've patted him down and he gave us permission to inspect his car. No sign of a weapon. Oh, and CU techs wiped him down for GSR and found nothing."

Just then a small luxury sports car pulled up to the opposite side of the street and the County Attorney stepped out of her car. She pulled a faux-fur coat tightly to her as she strode towards the detectives. Her high heels emitted the usual "clicking" sound as she crossed the street heading for the detectives. Her name was Julie Feinstein, she was a slender brunette, never smiled and was as tough as nails. No one dared to argue with her. After several minutes of chatter the County Attorney called the New Hampshire Attorney General's secure telephone number and asked for the major crime unit to be brought in. It was standard procedure on all homicides in New Hampshire. The investigation and prosecution, if any, would be handed off to the State.

Chapter 4
New Hampshire State Police
Cold Case Unit
Concord, New Hampshire

Mark Atkinson sat down at his desk in the offices of the New Hampshire State Police, Cold Case Unit. Mark was a relative newbie cold case investigator who had signed on to the unit during the preceding fall. He had previously served in the New Hampshire State Police and retired with the rank of Sergeant Major, Commander of District E. He had tried his hand for two years teaching US History to high school students in Concord, New Hampshire. He left his teaching job soon after the Governor had signed into law HB 690 on July 29th, 2009. That bill created, in the NH Department of Justice Attorney General's Office, a formal relationship to a new cold case unit to be located within the state police to investigate the nearly 188 unsolved murder cases which had accumulated over the past forty or so years.

Mark was a sixty–one year old, ex-Marine, and yet he looked not a day over forty. He was six feet tall and weighed not an ounce over one hundred and sixty-five pounds. He was fit, trim, and worked out three times a week. Mark could still run a mile at a six minute pace. He shaved his head bald. He was one of the best shots in the state police during his years of active service. Back in 1999, he had been wounded in the left side and left leg by a deranged boyfriend during a domestic incident he was called to in Peterborough, NH. He had returned fire and killed the man with two center mass shots in the man's upper torso. The man's girlfriend and two children were found safe. Later, Mark was unsuccessfully sued by the woman. Mark's actions up to and during the shooting were investigated by the Attorney's General's Office. Mark was found to have acted properly and bravely. His shooting of the man was found to be justified.

Mark had decided to return to law enforcement and join up with the cold case unit (CCU) because it allowed him to still be active in police matters. With the CCU there was no mandatory retirement rule and since he had a strong investigative background, the Attorney General thought Mark would be a good fit for the CCU.

Mark looked down at the new file sitting on his desk. It had been recently sent up to the CCU from the Manchester, NH, PD and the Hillsborough County Attorney's Offices. It was accompanied by a file clearly marked as being transferred to the CCU from the NH DOJ-Major Crime Unit. The file was marked, and entered into the CCU data base. The victim's name— Stephanie Monroe.

He took a sip of coffee and proceeded to open the Stephanie Monroe cold case file. He began to carefully read all of the material in the folders.

Three cups of coffee and a late lunch later, Mark closed the file and sat back in his office chair. He folded his fingers behind his head and stretched his back out. Both his chair and his back creaked.

He needed to take a break and so he picked up a magazine from the pile of out-of-date law enforcement magazines. He thumbed through one of the law enforcement magazines. He skipped through several articles as he tried to untangle from the massive amount of information he had read through in the Monroe murder file.

Something was teasing at his mind. *Was it something in the Monroe file? Was it something in one of the other files he had already pored over?* It felt like there was something he should see but yet he couldn't. He stood up, grabbed his coat and headed for the door. He signed out of the office on the white-board and avoiding the elevator, jogged down three flights of stairs. Soon he was outside. It was early January. The sky was bright blue and the air was a cold and crisp twenty-one degrees. There was no wind, but there was over three feet of snow banks piled high along the road sides and sidewalks. He turned to the West to walk along the sidewalk of the state police headquarters located on Hazen Drive in Concord, New Hampshire. His walk took him along a series of sidewalks meandering around various State buildings situated in the Meldrim Thompson State Office Park. Within forty minutes he had covered over three miles. Refreshed, he returned to the office and his desk.

He reopened the Monroe file and began to take careful notes.

Chapter 5
St. Johnsbury, Vermont
Summer of 1967

The old and heavily used transistor radio was tuned to station 670 on the AM dial. It was a popular music radio station broadcasting out of the State's Capital, Montpelier, Vermont. The reception was good and Stanley Bolinski, a fourteen-year-old freshman at St. Johnsbury, Academy, was listening to the Doors latest hit song, "Light My Fire."

He was so focused on listening to the music with the radio ear piece plugged into his left ear he had no idea that his nemesis, Ed Willow, was following him home from the school bus stop.

Ed was a junior who played on the offensive line of the high school's football team. His friends nicknamed him, "Big Ed," because of his immense size. He was six-foot seven inches tall and weighed over 280 pounds. His detractors nicknamed him, "Igor," after some character in a monster movie. His victims, of which there were many, had worse nicknames for him. He was the school's serial bully and for the past week his target of choice was one, Stanley Bolinski.

Stanley was an outwardly timid boy. He suffered from acne and was mostly shunned by the other kids in school. He didn't have any brothers or sisters, and to the best of his knowledge, there were no other relatives to be found in the immediate area. His mother was an alcoholic, his father, a long distance truck driver who also drank too often and too much. Both of his parents would beat on him rather than each other. He was a virtual whipping boy for their many personal inadequacies.

He lived on a small, failed farm at the end of a dirt road of off US Route 2 just west of town.

Big Ed lived a half mile further west, where his family's dairy farm sat on 500 acres of cleared, prime pasture alongside US Route 2. His family's farm had a herd of over 200 head of prized Holstein "milkers" and a single, middle-aged bull, named "Bob."

Ed was furious at Stanley because he had the audacity to scratch his face when Big Ed had tried to pull Stanley's dungarees down in the school's cafeteria during lunch period yesterday. The gouging of his face left three red lines down both sides of his face. Many of the girls who had witnessed the episode giggled and pointed at Big Ed.

A teacher had intervened and separated the two boys.

Big Ed was planning to finish the job and even his score with "puke-face Bolinski."

He quietly followed the distracted Stanley into the run-down Bolinski barn.

When Ed entered the barn, Stanley was inside the back of the barn in the shadows moving some boxes around looking for something. He had his back to the barn's front doors.

Stanley was looking for his box of murder mystery magazines he kept hidden in the barn. He was planning to finish reading an article in this month's *Detectives Greatest Stories*, which he had begun earlier in the week.

Suddenly, Stanley was pushed from behind. He crashed hard into the wooden boxes and then was pushed again, this time slamming into the back wall of the barn.

He hurriedly managed to turn around. His squinting eyes settled on the hulking silhouette of "Big Ed Willow."

"Hey pussy, you fight like a girly-girl. I'm here to teach you a lesson. No one, and I mean no one, messes with me and gets away with it."

Stanley stood himself up by sliding his backside along the barn wall. His legs were shaking and his nose was bleeding.

He wiped his nose with the back of his right hand.

"When I'm done with you, you little bastard, you're gonna wish you were never born."

"You can go screw yourself," replied Stanley. He could taste the coppery tang of his own blood still running from his nose, and now, down to his mouth.

Ed's eyes bulged as his fury rapidly maxed out.

He lunged for Stanley, but the younger and smaller boy ducked under his closing arms. Stanley spun away and was standing in the middle of the barn with his fists clinched.

Ed turned around and looked at Stanley. Ed now noticed a large, black human shape standing immediately behind Stanley. Ed couldn't see any facial features, or for that matter any details since the shaped was back-lit by the bright late afternoon sunlight bursting through the open barn doors.

"Who in the fuck are you?" asked a now slightly cautious Ed.

"He's my friend," said Stanley.

"Figures, a pussy like you won't fight me, man-to-man," said Ed.

"You're wrong," said a grinning Stanley.

Ed began to circle Stanley as the dark shape moved to the side of the barn to take up a watching position.

An unfamiliar voice, spoke out loud so Ed could hear him. "Stan, you have got to dance with this freak and teach him some manners. Maybe cut him a new asshole. What do you say, Stan, my man?"

The eerie voice, emanated from the dark shape, unsettled Ed.

"Shut your girly mouth," demanded Ed as he began to circle the center of the barn moving ever closer to Stanley.

"He's the pussy now, Stan. Watch out, cause he wants to get you in a big, old bear hug, maybe even give you a big wet kiss. Ain't I right Igor?"

"Shut your pie hole because I am coming after you next," growled an angry Ed.

The boys continued to circle. Suddenly Ed made a quick move towards Stanley but Stanley moved out of his reach.

"This is so boring," said the shape. "I think we need to jazz things up."

The shape move behind Ed and pushed him hard. Ed stumbled to the floor of the barn.

Ed jumped back up. He was sweating heavily now and his eyes were not as full of confidence or anger. In fact, his eyes revealed a trace of fear. He looked around for something to use as a weapon. Ed quickly spied an old axe handle without its axe head leaning against a side of a stall. He scooped it up and now held it like a baseball bat.

"Now you just try some of that cheating shit again, pushing me when I wasn't looking is just chicken-shit."

Ed decided then and there that he would make one big move on Stanley, whack him with the axe handle and then tear-ass out of the barn. He thought, *There was something wrong about that shape, it wasn't right, it wasn't human. It was ...... what's the word, evil."*

Ed made his move. He rushed forward with the axe handle gripped tightly in both of his hands. He began to swing the axe handle back and forth as he stood side-on to Stanley.

From the near side of the barn a pitch fork flew across the empty space and slapped into the outstretched hands of Stanley. Instead of extending his arms and hands up to defend himself Stanley suddenly found himself gripping the pitch fork handle with the sharp pointy tines extended outward.

In a blink of any eye Ed began his planned mighty swing of the axe handle. Just as he did, Stanley countered with a thrust of the pitch fork forward and upward. Ed's hoped for crushing swing stopped in mid-motion. Stanley pitch fork was now fully thrust into his chest, just below his rib cage.

The axe handle slipped free from his hands and fell onto the floor of the barn.

Ed looked down at the pitch fork buried into his lower abdomen. His body was now rapidly descending into a state of shock.

Stanley pulled the pitch fork out and thrust it once again into Big Ed.

Blood began to run out of the left corner of Ed's mouth. He fell to his knees. His eyes were pleading for release from the all-powerful pain.

"Who is the pussy now, huh? Who? Answer me," half-shouted an emboldened Stanley. His face twisted from a murderous rage now fully spilling over. He fought to twist the pitch fork as he pushed it deeper and deeper.

Big Ed never provided him an answer. He keeled over onto his right side, trying to cover his wounds with his hands. There were not enough hands for this.

Stanley withdrew the murderous weapon and threw it aside. He bent over trying to catch his breath. His knees were shaking.

From across the barn emitted the sound of hands slowly clapping. "Smack, smack, smack….."

The dark shape seemed to be applauding Stanley.

This time the shape's voice was heard only in Stanley's mind.

"Yip, yip, yippee, Stanley. You just bagged your first. I'm proud of you son. But now the hard part begins. You can't just leave him there to be found or your career will be over before it really gets going. C'mon son - Think! What are you going to do?"

Stanley ran his fingers through his hair.

"I don't know, okay. Just let me think."

"Tick tock, tick tock," said the dark shape with a mocking tone.

Stanley ran out of the barn and went over to the old International Harvester tractor sitting alongside the barn. He looked at it for a moment than ran back inside the barn. He grabbed some rope and tied it around Ed's feet. He ran the rope over a pulley hanging from a nearby rafter and began to pull on the rope with all his might. It took him a couple of minutes before he was satisfied he had raised Ed's body high enough. He then went out of the barn and backed the tractor over to a small wagon. He hitched the wagon onto the tractor's trailer hitch and then maneuvered the wagon inside of the barn. He lowered Ed's lifeless body into the wagon. He threw the rope and pitch fork into the back of the wagon. Stanley then climbed back onto the tractor and managed to get it out of the barn. He turned to the right and drove off.

Fifteen minutes later, he had driven across the rear of his parents property and then across a neighbor's large field. He stopped the tractor and climbed down. He opened an old gate for cattle crossing. Stanley next drove the tractor and attached wagon across a small wooden bridge. Now he was on another neighbor's pasture land. This farm was abandoned. It had been abandoned for over ten years, ever since the owner had died at the age of seventy-three. His children were still squabbling over his assets ten years later.

Stanley turned the tractor to the right and followed the fence line for several hundred feet. He stopped at a small swale and began to use the tractor's front end loader to dig a hole. Moments later, Stanley dragged Ed's body into the bottom of the freshly dug hole. Stanley threw the rope and pitch fork into the hole and then buried everything with the tractor.

Sweating heavily, he drove the tractor and wagon back, being careful to put them back where he had found them. He spread gasoline over the blood stain on the barn floor and then set it on fire. He let it burn for a couple of minutes then he kicked dirt over the fire putting it out.

Stanley then went looking for his transistor radio and found it on the barn floor next to the back wall. It was scratched but still playable. He hurried to the house. When he came through the backdoor entering the kitchen, he found his mother passed out sitting at the kitchen table with her head lying flat on the table. An overflowing ash tray was beside her left hand while a half-finished bottle of gin sat just beyond the reach of her right hand. She was wearing a stained and tattered bathrobe that reeked with her body odor.

Ignoring his mother, Stanley made a peanut butter sandwich and went to his bedroom. Closing the door behind him, he sat at his small desk. He wiped the sweat from his brow with the back of his left arm.

Stanley then reached for a small spiral bound flip over notepad and opened it to the first page. It had some notes scribbled on it. He tore the page out and tossed it on this desk. Taking up a pencil he wrote on the now blank notebook page: "Ed Willow, died June 4, 1967, #1."

The dark shadow shape was sitting on Stanley's bed.

"Stan, you are the man, now. No one messes with my Stan, the Mannnnnnnnnn!" bellowed the evil voice.

"Yesireee, Stan is now my man. Who can set things right? Stan, can. Why, who has my vote? It's my good buddy, Stan."

Stanley Bolinski broke into a smile. He closed his notebook and tucked it away in his hideaway place underneath a loose board in his closet, right next to an old, well-thumbed copy of the magazine, *True Crimes*. Just as he closed his closet door, he heard his father's big rig pull up outside the house. There was a couple of *"hisses and whooshes"* as the air brakes were applied and the truck then turned off.

Stanley waited in his room. He was expecting the usual. First, there would be a big fight between his father and mother followed by things being thrown at one another. Then, they would separate for a while to drink and stew. Before long they would look for Stanley to lay some hurt on the boy, their personal whipping boy.

But not for much longer.

Chapter 6
New Hampshire State Police
Cold Case Unit
Concord, New Hampshire

Cold Case Investigator Mark Atkinson had finished with the Monroe case file. He put the file away and sat back down to look over his case notes. He couldn't see anything in his notes which might point him towards a person of interest, a motive, or any sort of *"modus operandi."*

From experience, he knew most murder cases are solved because of one or more of several things. Sometimes there are direct witnesses to the crime itself. Other times there is hard forensic evidence like blood, fingerprints, DNA, etc. Some cases are solved because many murders are crimes of passion and the victim and murderer knew one another. Once police zero in on a prime suspect, police interviews can begin to break down alibis and soon a case is able to be built around mounting evidence.

Then there are other cases where murder is a crime of opportunity. No connection is apparent between victim and perpetrator. No witnesses and little in the way of forensic evidence. Police have to work these types of cases especially hard to find the one thing, the key piece of evidence, which they can use to unravel the mystery and solve the crime.

Finally, there are the murders for which there is no apparent thread to pull, no surprise witness, often times not even a body to examine, along with no obvious motive and no suspects. These kinds of cases typically get moved to the cold case unit, where investigators keep tenaciously searching for the one, elusive thing which will break the case.

For the past couple of weeks, Mark worked the Monroe case. It had been newly assigned to the NH Cold case unit at the beginning of the year.

Mark had set up re-interviews with all the investigators who had worked the case and the few "so-called" witnesses who were listed in the case file. He added to this list of people the surviving parents and the victim's two sisters.

His first interview was with one of the victim's co-workers. The victim had worked as a claims processor in the office of a large national insurance company.

The person being interviewed was Lydia Muncie.

Mark had agreed to meet her for lunch at a downtown Manchester, NH restaurant named Sizzle.

He arrived early to get a table seat facing the front door. It was an old police habit. He spotted her when she walked in. He recognized her from her driver's license photo he had pulled earlier. He stood up and caught her eye. He waved her over to join him.

She appeared to be quite nervous. When she sat down she didn't remove her overcoat.

Mark reached out his right hand offering to shake hands.

"Hi, I'm Mark. Thanks for agreeing to meet with me."

She took his offered hand limply with only half of her hand.

Lydia Muncie pulled her coat tight as if she was experiencing a chill.

She looked down at the small table in an effort to not meet his gaze.

Mark was used to this behavior. Most of the civilians he interviewed were nervous for many possible reasons. He always made an effort to put them at ease in an effort to get at the tiny grains of information he was seeking.

"I'm sorry to have to bother you again about Stephanie's case," said Mark.

Referring to the victim in a personal way, by using her first name, was an interview technique. It usually could be counted on to emotionally reconnect the interviewer with the victim. Some people will compartmentalize their feelings about the deceased and no longer see them as real, but rather just a fading memory.

"Lydia, can I get you coffee, a sandwich, anything?" inquired Mark in a soft and somewhat intimate voice.

"No, no thanks. I'm kind of in a hurry. I don't have time to eat. I only have a few minutes, okay?" said a nervous Lydia.

"I see, well I only have a couple of questions. Nothing complicated."

"I already was interviewed four or five times by the detectives. I really don't know anything that can help you." Lydia pulled at a paper napkin from the table dispenser. She began to shred it into a pile of tiny pieces.

"I understand, really I do. Look, as I told you over the phone. I'm an investigator with NH's Cold Case Unit. It's my job to re-interview everybody. I'm just doing what I am supposed to do in these cases. You know, right now Stephanie's murderer is still walking the streets. I don't know about you but that really pisses me off. She didn't deserve to die. Right now I'm the only one trying to do what's right by her. I want her killer found and locked up. To do that I need the help of good people like yourself, to let me revisit your memory, your recollection of things—to help me maybe, just maybe, find that one piece of information which can point me in the right direction. So, what do you say? Wanna help, or not? It's up to you. I can't make you talk with me but I sure would appreciate anything you can give me."

He waited for some kind of reaction to his sermon.

Lydia swept the shredded napkin aside with the backside of her right hand. She pulled her coat off and let it fall across the back of her chair. Now she folded her hands on the table and raised her eyes to look up at him.

"Okay, you have my attention. So, what's your first question?" asked Lydia.

They talked for several minutes. Up until now Mark had not taken any notes.

"So, Lydia, talk to me about what kind of person she was. Was she happy, fun to be around? Was she moody, mean? Was she a gossiper? Did she ever get angry? What would piss her off?" asked Mark.

"Hold on there. Those are lots of questions. Okay, let's see," said Lydia, looking up at the restaurant ceiling. She continued, "Stephanie was generally a happy person. She was fun to be around but yeah, you could say she was moody. She was twice divorced as I am sure you know. So she was a poor judge of men. No, she wasn't a gossiper. Did she get angry, oh yeah. She had a big-time temper. She was a very assertive type. She was always pushing men's buttons, ticking them off; unless she was looking to get them in bed and then she was a pure sex kitten."

For the first time Mark took a note in his small field note pad. *Assertive, pushes men's buttons.*

"Can you give me an example of how her temper might flare up?" asked Mark.

"Okay, I can give you example. Steph and I were going out shopping one day. We headed out to the mall in her car. Steph pulled into a parking space cutting off an elderly couple who were obviously waiting for the spot. The old man hollered at her and Stephanie went off on the old guy. I though he was going to have a heart attack or something. It was really embarrassing with the two of them swearing at each other. I pulled her arm to get her to leave and she gave me the biggest, "don't screw with me" look. It scared me. Then all of a sudden she just turns around and walks into the mall like nothing happen."

Mark took another note: *short fuse, bully, confrontational.*

Moments later Mark thanked Lydia and the interview was over.

After Lydia left, Mark looked at his scant notes and knew he had uncovered something about the victim that wasn't in the current case file.

Was it important, was it significant? What might it indicate? thought Mark.

Over the next couple of weeks Mark conducted all of his re-interviews. He noted that many of the interviews of friends, family and co-workers seemed to provide variations on the theme Lydia had painted. Yet, the investigators hardly picked up on her personality and how it may have played a role in her murder.

The investigators had pursued the usual lines of inquiry, looking at her boyfriend, ex-husbands, neighbors, etc. They were following the "likely motive" angle and their efforts came up dry.

Chapter 7
Barre, Vermont
January of 1958

Young Stanley Bolinski sat quietly in the back seat of the car. The family was on its way to visit Stanley's dying paternal grandfather. Stanley's younger brother, two year old Walter, sat across from him propped up on the car seat between a pillow and a rolled up blanket. Walter had fallen asleep within minutes of leaving St. Johnsbury, Vermont, earlier that morning. The family car was a black, heavily rusted, 1949 Plymouth coupe which had seen more than its fair share of the harsh winter back roads of northeast Vermont. The drive to the grandfather's home would normally take close to an hour and a half but with last night's snow storm having dumped seven inches, the driving had become more difficult. Today's trip would take over two hours.

Adding to the difficult travel conditions, the old Plymouth's heater and defroster were not working at their best.

"It figures, the old bastard would choose to die in the middle of winter. Look at this damn windshield, I can barely see out of it. Damn piece of junk," said Stanley's father as he pounded the steering wheel.

"Please keep your voice down or you will wake up Walter," admonished his wife.

"Look you and I both know the old man hates me. Hell, he probably hates you and the kids too. He ain't leaving us anything when he dies."

"Honey you don't know that. You have got to be on your best behavior and let bygones-be-bygones, you know, for your boy's sake. Your sisters and brothers will be there paying their respects and it won't look right if his oldest boy isn't there."

Stanley's father gripped the steering wheel so hard his knuckles were turning white. He was clearly fighting with the car and the road conditions.

"That son of bitch beat me and my mother from the time I can first remember. He broke both of my arms and one of my legs. My ma would always make excuses for him but I hated him so bad I would pray at night that he would die. I hated my ma too for standing up for that bastard. When I was old enough and big enough I finally knocked him on his ass. I was putting a good old fashion whipping on him when ma pulled me off of him. She was bawling and you know what, that old son-of a-bitch was smiling at me through his bloodied lips. Smiling at me! Damn him to hell!"

Stanley's father pounded the steering wheel with his right hand.

They drove on in silence for a short while.

Stanley took in every gesture, every nuance and every word spoken and unspoken. Even at five years old he could relate to the story.

Stanley's mother looked back at Stanley and tried offering a reassuring smile, but it faded so fast that Stanley would have missed it entirely if he had blinked.

Stanley's parents didn't speak another word until they arrived at Stanley's grandfather's home. There were several cars parked in the driveway and on the street in front of the old, mansard roofed two-story home. The house was once painted light blue with white trim but the paint had badly blistered and peeled these past few years. Behind the house sat a barn with a metal roof, along with faded red barn board sides. It was padlocked. It was always padlocked.

Stanley's father got out of the car and slowly walked over to meet up with one of his brothers who was standing outside on the front porch. Stanley's mother pulled him out of the back seat and sternly told him to "wait right here."

He watched his mother as she gently woke up his younger brother. Before she lifted him out of the car she opened her purse and tried to shield herself from view as she took a long pull on a small greenish colored flask of whiskey. Stanley took in the incident as nothing more than the usual. His mother always had her "medicine" within reach.

His mother nudged Stanley along as she made her way towards the front porch.

It took several minutes before Stanley's parents finally decided to enter the house. The rest of the family didn't rush up to greet them. The chill from the extended family was almost a match for the outside January weather.

Stanley spied three other children similar in age to him who were seated at a small table drinking milk and nibbling on cookies. The three children simply looked over at Stanley and his brother Walter who was being carried by Stanley's mother, and then resumed their shared, silent consumption.

Stanley heard he had cousins but he had no idea how many or what their names were. He barely understood they were related somehow but just what this truly meant was beyond him.

The house smelled of stale cigarette smoke mixed with the odor of wood burning coming from a wood burning stove not yet in sight.

Stanley didn't remove his winter coat or boots. He was waiting to be told to do so. Removing them before being told was a sure invitation to a heavy smack on his backside.

The men were gathered in the living room, or parlor as it was called, while the women gathered in the kitchen. Stanley's mother finally removed his winter coat and left to put it on a huge pile of coats stacked nearly four feet high on the couch. She gave no hint as to what to do about the winter boots so Stanley just kept them on. His mother took his brother with her and left Stanley to fend for himself.

The adult conversation from the women was hushed while the men spoke with more volume and what seemed like rising anger.

Stanley decided to wander around a bit. He moved down a hallway to a small room stocked with food and other things.

This must be the pantry, thought Stanley.

To the left side of the hallway was another door which was cracked open. Stanley stuck his head up against the opening and took note it was obviously a bathroom.

He went back up the hallway towards the front of the house. He looked to his right and noticed a set of drapes pulled closed across a doorway. This seemed strange and curious at the same time. Stanley pulled back the edge of the drape and looked inside the room.

There was a small table lamp light on a table next to a bed. Lying upon the bed was an old man whose long, tangled, white hair and skin matched color. The man was propped up on some pillows and appeared to be asleep.

Stanley stepped into the room.

He could hear muffled voices coming from elsewhere in the house, but now he could also hear the heavy, raspy breathing of the old man.

Stanley slowly crept towards the bed. He looked over at the nightstand. It was covered with vials and bottles of every sort of medicine. To the young boy the room smelled of pee and vomit. He now was next to the bed. Stanley forced himself to look at the "old bastard" who had beat his dad and later took a whipping from him.

Stanley was about to turn and leave when the old man's eyes blinked wide open. The man's bony, blue veined, right hand reached out like a snake and seized Stanley's left arm.

"Who are you?" asked the old man with a wheeze.

"I, I'm Stanley," stuttered the boy.

"Who's your mom and dad, boy?"

"My dad is Joe, I mean Joseph and my mom is…"

"Never mind I know who she is," interrupted the old man.

"Your father is a useless asshole. Why did he bring you here?"

"They said it was because you are dying and we needed to pay our respects," said a growingly defiant Stanley.

"Pay respects. That's a bad fart and a laugh. Him, paying his respect. He doesn't know the meaning of the word."

Now straining to turn more fully and look at the young boy, the pupils of the old man's eyes turned large and black.

"Do you respect your father, eh?"

Stanley couldn't bring himself to answer.

After a pause the old man said, "Humph, just as I thought. You hate your old man. Probably hate your mother, too. I bet he's given you plenty of reasons to hate him. I'm right about this sure as I am that I'm going to die soon. Take that to the bank."

"Let go of me. I want to go," protested Stanley.

"Not before I give you something to remember me by."

Suddenly a shape, a human form stepped out of the far shadows at the end of the makeshift bedroom. It was faceless and black as night. The form silently crossed the short distance towards Stanley and stood beside him.

Stanley's grandfather looked at his grandson and smiled a sick and deadly smile.

"He's yours now. You take him and use him when you need to boy. I can see you were meant to, so now git out of here. Let me die in peace and quiet. Go, go!"

His grandfather released his grip on his arm and sank back into the pillow closing his eyes as he did so. A serene smile washed over his countenance.

The dark form, now invisible to anyone except Stanley, followed along with Stanley as he left the room. Moments later Stanley's grandfather passed away.

Stanley's father was wrong. His own father, Stanley's now dead grandfather had left him something after all. From the young boy's point of view, the old man had left behind a part of himself, left it to Stanley.

Later that winter, Stanley's younger brother, Walter, died from pneumonia.

Stanley was now an only child, but he wasn't truly alone, not anymore.

Chapter 8
New Hampshire State Police
Cold Case Unit
Concord, New Hampshire
Late January

Mark Atkinson had worked the Stephanie Monroe case from every possible angle he could. His research and interviews had produced nothing at all, not one workable lead.

Yet he couldn't bring himself to let go of the case. He had a feeling he wasn't seeing something he should and that thought kept pulling at him. He had even conferred with the other three Cold Case Investigators in the office. Collectively they came to the conclusion that unless something like an eyewitness came forward, there wasn't anything there to use to work the case.

Mark grabbed his coat and left the office. It was later Friday afternoon and he had tickets for a show at the Palace Theatre in downtown Manchester. He calculated he had just enough time to make it back to the house, shower, shave, change his shirt and then head out to meet his girlfriend for a pre-show dinner. He looked forward to taking the night off from his work.

Later, Mark and his date for the evening, Marcy Cousineau, settled into their seats at a small table for two at Ragi's Restaurant. It was a favorite of theirs. The cuisine was Thai, the service and food were simply excellent. They placed their orders and settled back.

Marcy was a teacher at a private high school. She taught biology and physiology. Marcy was beautiful, smart, enjoyed the arts equally with all things sports. She had never been married but was engaged once before. She had only recently decided to begin dating again. A friend introduced her to Mark at a social function last October they both happened to attend. They enjoyed each other's company so much they had a follow up date one week later. Soon, they began to date regularly. Their mutual friends considered them a couple even though they themselves hadn't formally agreed they were a couple. It was just sort of understood.

Marcy was making small talk about an incident which had happened earlier in the day with another teacher. When she delivered the punch line about the embarrassing event Mark didn't even laugh or smile. He was attentively looking at her but his mind was in another place.

"Mark, Mark, you didn't hear a word I just said?"

Mark didn't reply.

Marcy extended her right hand to place it on his left hand. She gave his hand a gentle squeeze.

"What is it Mark?"

"What's what?" answered Mark.

"You're here but you're not. What is it? What's wrong? Talk to me, maybe I can help."

Embarrassed, he averted his eyes.

"It's just a case I have been working. It has me stumped, that's all. I'm sorry about not listening. That wasn't polite of me, to say the least."

Marcy knew where he worked and what he did. She admired him for trying to speak for the dead and bring closure to the victim's friends and family. However, this job had its burdens, too. See could see in Mark the emotional and mentally draining consequences the job held for those who spent the day working on unsolvable puzzles involving dead victims.

"Why don't you talk to me about it?"

"Naw, I don't want to ruin our dinner."

"Nonsense; if there is information rattling around in your head, let's bring it out into the light and take a look. You never know what we might think of."

With some reluctance he began. For the next hour, straight through dinner and the walk to the Palace Theatre, they discussed the case. She asked many questions which impressed him.

As they were seated in the Theatre Marcy turned to Mark and said, "Have you considered Occam's razor theorem? It is a theoretic principle which generally poses that, from among competing hypotheses, selecting the one which makes the fewest new assumptions usually provides, or leads, to the correct one. The simplest explanation will be the most plausible one until evidence is presented to prove it false. Scientists use it all the time. It often helps them break through blocked thinking whenever they get hung up on a problem."

"I frankly don't see how it could help me with this case."

Marcy touched his left arm and said, "You are looking for a witness or hope to find missing evidence to help break your case, right?"

"Yes, so?"

"So, what does the evidence you have, tell you? If, as you say, it tells you nothing, isn't that a clue by itself, or possibly a pattern? Have you seen this sort of thing before?"

Just then the Theater house lights went down and the musical began.

Mark never heard a word of the show as his mind began working in high speed overdrive.

Chapter 9
New Hampshire State Police
Cold Case Unit
Concord, New Hampshire
Late January

On the last day of January, Mark arrived early for work in the Cold Case Unit of the New Hampshire State Police Office.

After throwing his coat on a side chair he quickly sat down at his computer and pulled up the list of unsolved homicides. He used the data base to sort the status sheets for all 160 plus cases of currently unsolved homicides under review by the NH-CCU. He flagged each case which had forensic evidence, eye witnesses, and "person or persons of interests."

His work took him nearly two and a half hours. When he was through, he directed the computer to run a sort program, which would tell him which cases had none of the factors he had used to filter the cases.

In a blink of an eye the screen listed eight files including the Stephanie Monroe case. Of the eight, three involved "suspected" homicides with no body found.

Mark moved on to the hard files and pulled all eight files and took them back to his desk.

Mark didn't take lunch. He poured through the records he had pulled and took notes on a legal pad.

After returning from lunch, one of the other investigators walked over to Mark's desk and leaned over the desk while putting his two hands on the front edge of the desk.

Mark was busy flipping through his notes and hadn't noticed his colleague's approach.

"Mark, it looks like you caught a hot one. "Hot One" was inside police speak for ,a workable lead.' What are you up to?" asked Tom Sisti.

Tom had been a CCU Investigator for close to nine years. For the past two years, he served as the Investigator-In-Charge for the CCU. He had started as a volunteer back in the day when there was no formal investigative unit. He had worked in Naval Criminal Investigative Service for twenty-eight years before retiring and returned to New Hampshire where he had been born and raised. He eventually volunteered to investigate unsolved homicides after reading about a case in a local newspaper story published on the fourteenth anniversary of a victim's murder.

"Mark, did you hear what I said, what are you up to?" inquired Tom. This time he used his right hand to reach out and gently push down on the yellow legal notepad Mark was busy reading.

"Oh, sorry, I didn't hear you," said Mark.

"So what's on your radar? What angle are you analyzing this time?"

"It may seem weird."

"In our business, we specialize in weird. Now let me in on this!"

"Okay, look, I was out having dinner with my girlfriend and later we took in a show at the Palace Theatre. Well, anyway she tells me about Occam's Razor."

"I've heard of it. So, what's the point?" asked Tom as he sat down in Mark's side chair which still had Mark's coat draped over it.

"Well, I decided to look at all of our cases from a different perspective. Look here, I weeded out all the cases which had forensic evidence, or eye witnesses, or persons of interest. I did this to see what was left and this is what shook out. Eight cases spread out over close to twenty years, located in eight different communities but having one thing in common. No forensics, no eyewitnesses, and no suspects. Could it just be that these cases represent a pattern in and of themselves?"

"Keep going," said Tom.

"Look, I'm thinking, what if there is a killer out there who is so cunning, so careful that he or she doesn't leave any trace evidence and manages to avoid being seen at the crime scenes or even any time before with the victims? Could such a killer be that clever?"

"Okay, Mark, suppose there is such a killer. Let me play devil's advocate here and ask, what would be the motive for all of these murders?"

"I don't know yet. However, I did pick up something from the Stephanie Monroe case. Her case is the last one on this list. What I found from my interviews with people who knew her is this, she could be pushy and confrontational at times. She apparently enjoyed really pissing people off. I'm thinking maybe she might have pissed off someone who decided to rid the world of her."

"Do all the other victims have the same propensity to annoy people?"

"I don't know yet. I would have to do a bunch of re-interviews in the other cases to find out," said Mark.

"What about the three cases without a body? How do they fit your theory?"

"I am not sure. Right now I can't rule them in or out."

Standing up, Tom said, "Well, this all sounds interesting, to say the least. I say follow it through and see where it takes you. Just keep me in the loop as you work it."

"Sure, will do," said Mark.

Tom turned and left.

Mark pulled out the oldest of the cases he would be working. Next, he then took out his appointment book and ran down the list of people who had been interviewed during the original investigation. He picked up his cell phone and made his first call.

Chapter 10
St. Johnsbury, Vermont
November, 1969

High School Junior, Stanley Bolinski stood at his school locker. He was having trouble dialing the numbers to open his combination lock. He was growing frustrated with each passing second. In an angry outburst he punched his locker. The resulting loud "**bang**" could be heard up and down the school hallway.

Distracted by his problems with the combination lock he hadn't notice a very pretty girl standing slightly behind him to his left side.

He finally opened the lock and quickly threw open his locker door.

The girl reached out and touched Stanley on the left shoulder and half-whispered: "Stanley, would you be my date for the Sadie Hawkins' dance this weekend?"

The girl, Abby Cobb, was a senior at St. Johnsbury Academy and widely known to be the steady girlfriend of another senior, Larry Fitzgerald, the very popular captain of the basketball and football teams.

Stanley suspected a set-up, a prank to be pulled at his expense. He was in no mood for this.

"Leave me alone," he said. Stanley turned his back on her and proceeded to put another book into his locker before closing the locker door.

"C'mon Stanley, it will be fun."

She reached out to Stanley in an effort to put her right arm under his left.

Stanley reflexively threw back his left arm to ward her off. As a result, he accidentally struck her in the nose with his left elbow.

She let out a screech and threw her hands up to her face. Blood began to drip through her fingers.

"You shit head, look what you've done!" she shouted. Tears began to run down her cheeks. She turned to run to the school nurse's office. Distracted, she ran smack into the chest of her boyfriend who came running when he heard her shout.

He took one look at her and gently pushed her aside. Three girls immediately clustered around her and led her away. A couple of the girls looked back at Stanley with scowls on their faces.

"What did you do dick-wad?" asked Larry Fitzgerald who stood nearly a foot taller than Stanley.

"It was an accident. She wouldn't leave me alone. She was asking me to go to this week's dance with her and I wasn't going to fall for her bullshit. I was just trying to get her to leave me alone."

Grabbing Stanley by his shirt Larry nearly raised him clear of the floor as he pulled Stanley's face closer to his own.

"Look, you stupid shit, she was just trying to be nice and you went and hit her. Maybe you broke her nose. Now I'm going to have to break something of yours. "The dark shape appeared to Stanley. The shape was standing right behind Larry.

"Tell him to back off or you're going to have to teach him a lesson. Tell him you know about the two lovebirds humping in his car behind his dad's gas station last night. Go on, tell him," said the dark shape with a gleeful lift in his voice.

Stanley just looked at the shape and didn't respond or react.

"Stan, you can't let this goliath bully you. Do something or tell me what you want me to do. Let's rock and roll!"

"She was trying to be nice my ass. You think I don't know what you two were trying to do? You were trying to lure me there to pull some stunt and make me the laughing stock of the dance and the whole damn school. Well, screw you and your little whore!"

Larry released his grip as he pulled back his right hand, now clenched into a tight fist, ready to deliver a painful punch to Stanley's face.

Larry miscalculated on one front. He was too close to Stanley which gave Stanley the opportunity to strike first and he did. Stanley's mind had flashed a signal. *"Kick him in the balls, yes, kick him hard. Make him drop like a bag of shit and then side kick him in the head. Yessir, take him down, all the way down.*

Stanley delivered an incredible upward kick to Larry's groin.

Instead of delivering a punch to Stanley's face Larry quickly grabbed for his crotch and dropped to his knees. His eyes were quickly tearing up as the paralyzing pain took hold.

Stanley bent slightly and leaned forward so that his face was nearly touching Larry's.

"Nobody fucks with me, remember that asshole, nobody." He was now readying a fisted right hand to deliver a roundhouse punch to the defenseless bully.

Just then, Math Teacher Fred Couture and Physical Education Teacher Sam Ross pulled Stanley back.

The two teachers grabbed Stanley by his arms and hustled him off to the Principal's office. Later, Stanley sat quietly and listened to a lecture about fighting in school and juvenile delinquency.

Stanley was suspended from school for three days.

The Principal, known as "Old Man Benson," escorted Stanley to the end of the sidewalk in front of the Academy.

"Look, Stanley. I think I know what was going on this morning and perhaps you're probably right, they were trying to embarrass you. Yes, I could even see it was probably an accident you bloodied Miss Cobb's nose. But look, perhaps they were not looking to embarrass you but to provoke you into doing something along the lines of what you did. Unfortunately for you young man, your temper is becoming a problem.

"The kids know it, the teachers know it and I do, too. Now son, let me offer you some advice."

Stanley began to walk faster trying to pull away from the Principal.

The Principal pulled back on Stanley's right arm and turned him around.

"Look at me, Stanley, look at me, I say," demanded the sixty-four year old Principal.

Stanley slowly raised his eyes and forced himself to look like he was interested in what the man had to say.

"That's better, now Stanley, I know things are tough for you at home. Normally I would be calling your parents about your suspension but I know it would only cause you some problems. I shouldn't do this but I am going to make an exception in this case and not call your parents. I want you to promise me you will stay out of trouble and work on that temper of yours. Come back to school next week and show everyone you're a changed young man. Can you do that son?"

"Yes, sir and thanks for not calling my parents. I will try, I promise, I'll try and get along better and stay away from trouble."

With a clap on Stanley's shoulders Principal Benson released Stanley and watched him walk down the street, presumably heading home. Stanley had his hands in his pockets and carried his head low.

What Principal Benson couldn't see was Stanley's hands were closed into tight fists inside his pants pockets. He couldn't see Stanley engaged in a conversation, a conversation with something dark and evil. To the elderly Principal, it simply looked like Stanley was into talking to himself. Odd, but not a signal the Principal could sort out as wrong.

"Stan, my man, I am so proud of you. You drove Larry's gonads nearly into his throat. That sent a message all right, but it ain't going to stop him, Stan. No sireee, it won't stop him. He will be looking for you and will want to hurt you real bad. Now, what are we going to do about that? Huh, you got a plan?" After a pause he said, *"If you don't I have one!"*

Stan didn't answer at first, he just keep walking, picking up his pace until he was nearly jogging along.

Once he turned the street corner and was completely out of sight of the high school he slowed down. Finally he stopped entirely.

He looked to his right where the ever present dark shaped was hovering.

"I'll fix them both. They think they're so adorable, high school sweethearts and all that bullshit. I promise you. I will get them both."

Stanley began to walk again. When he reached the next street corner he reached out and punched the stop sign with his right hand. There was a loud "clanging" sound while the sign twisted back and forth several times.

"There will be payback. Count on it," grumbled a very angry Stanley.

When he reached home his mother was already passed out drunk. She was sitting and half-lying on the living room sofa. Stanley's father was away on a long haul for the interstate trucking firm he had begun working for a year and a half ago.

He wouldn't be home until next Tuesday at the earliest. The long distance trucking driving job gave his father the excuse to not be home too often or for too long. That suited Stanley just fine.

Chapter 11
New Hampshire State Police
Cold Case Unit
Concord, New Hampshire
Early April

Mark Atkinson had finished all the interviews he thought he needed in the eight unsolved murder cases that fit his elementary profile. He was especially looking to see if the victims might have something in common with his alpha case, the Stephanie Monroe murder.

The results were thin.

Only three victims were reported to be strong willed and obstinate. The other people were not deemed to be pushy or aggressive by any of their family, friends or co-workers.

Mark sat at a table in the "Poor Man's Diner." He sipped his coffee while staring at his notes and tapped his pencil on the table. It was a nervous habit of his and he often didn't realize he was doing it.

Two elderly women meeting for brunch sat at the table next to Mark and were busily engaged in conversation.

Mark continued to flip through his notes and tap away on the table.

Finally one of the women leaned over to Mark's table and said, "Young man, do you mind? Please stop tapping that pencil. It is distracting and annoying." Her tone was delivered in a lecturing fashion.

Mark was so very deep in thought he hadn't heard a word she had said.

"Humph," said the woman who had spoken up.

In a huff she continued addressing her friend, "To not only continue tapping but to completely ignore me is just plain rude, don't you think so, Margaret?"

This time she would get his attention.

She reached across the small space that separated the two tables and gave Mark's table a small shove.

Mark regained his focus and looked over at the women.

"Can I help you ladies?"

"Yes, indeed," said the outspoken woman. "My dear friend and I are trying to have a conversation here and your constant tapping of your pencil is, well frankly, annoying. Do you mind?"

At the end of her remarks she raised both eyebrows for added emphasis.

"Oh sorry, I didn't even realize I was tapping. It's a bad habit. Sorry, I'll stop."

"That will do," said the woman who then turned to her friend and resumed their hushed conversation.

Mark sat back in his chair and drifted back to his thoughts about the cold cases when a veritable light bulb went off in his head.

That's it, he thought to himself. *It's not what their personalities were like, it was what they did that probably set off their killer.*

Now he went back through his notes with renewed energy and anticipation.

Moments later he had developed a list on the eight cases.

One victim had been a toll booth worker on I-95 in Hampton. Another worked at a drive-through window at a fast food restaurant. A third victim was a dentist. The fourth and fifth victims both worked at an auto-body shop in Dover. The sixth victim was a part-time police officer who frequently worked the Deerfield and other local fairs. The seventh victim ran a convenience store in North Conway and the eighth victim was a traveling salesman whose body was found outside of Keene alongside of Route 101.

Somehow, each victim had a prior encounter with their murderer and that encounter provided the murderer the motive.

Mark began to thumb through his notes in frantic search for the common thread.

The dentist had had a recent encounter with a man who was angry about apparently not receiving enough Novocain. Back in the eighties, this old-school dentist worked alone on occasion but mentioned the incident to his wife. The police tried to follow the lead but the dentist apparently kept poor records. The toll-both worker complained about threats she would receive from people coming through her booth. The convenience store employee's body was never found but the store's video surveillance system was stolen the same night he disappeared.

The fast food drive-through window employee had mentioned to a co-worker she had spilled hot coffee on a customer during her final shift. Her body was never found.

Mark was now excited. His working theory might just hold up, a pattern may be there after all.

He had more to do. Much more work. He needed to get back to the office to discuss this angle with Tom Sisti.

Mark hurriedly gathered up his notes and paused at the table of the two women.

"Ladies, I want apologize once again. I want to make it up to you so let me but pick up your tab."

"Oh dear," said the outspoken lady.

"That is so nice of you young man," said the other lady with a slight blush filling and tinting the cheeks of her face.

"It is the least I can do." He dropped three dollars tip on his table and took his receipt to the register. Along the way he stopped the waitress who had served both tables. She walked over to the register with him so he could work out paying for the two women's brunch just as he had promised.

As he was about to leave he glanced back at the two older women. They hadn't taken their eyes off of him since he left their table. He gave them a friendly wave and one of the women smiled and waved back.

Finally, he hurried out the restaurant's front door and half-jogged to his car.

Chapter 12
St. Johnsbury, Vermont
November, 1969

Stanley went to the Sadie Hawkins dance after all. Only he didn't actually attend the dance. He hid in the shadows along the tree line next to the school parking lot. He knew which car belong to Larry Fitzgerald. He had watched the black 1966 Chevy Chevelle SS muscle car as it rumbled into the parking lot.

He knew the car well. It was the envy of every hormone-driven boy in the school.

Abby and Larry exited the car. Larry made a grab for her bottom which she playfully swatted away. She ran ahead to the school. Larry slapping his hips jogged after her.

Stanley had worked on an alibi for tonight. He had made sure his mom was fast asleep. She would be useless as an alibi. His dad was out of town and wouldn't return until early next week. So his father was out as a possible alibi. Stanley's alibi was going to see and being seen at a movie. He left the school and headed into town. He made a beeline to the downtown theater which was a one-screen theater. He would be taking in the movie "Gamera versus Guiron," a grade "B" Japanese sci-fi flick at the Star Theater. He had sat through it yesterday so he could be acquainted with the film just in case the cops asked questions.

He had skated by with his previous murder of high school bully, Ed Willow. The local cops knew he and Ed had been fighting, they had suspicions, but they never found the body. Stanley had weathered some questioning but nothing he couldn't handle.

This time he wanted to be extra careful so he had decided on going to the movies and making a scene there so someone would remember him.

He had the family car stashed one street over from Larry's father's garage where he knew Larry would be taking Abby well before the school dance was over. Stanley was a good observer of his fellow students. He paid careful attention to all rumors.

He walked hurriedly to the theater.

Less than a half an hour after the movie began he left his seat in the theater. There were only five other people in the theater. He quietly slipped out the rear, fire exit door. He stuck a piece of cardboard in the lock jam so that when the door closed the bolt could not fully engage. He next ran up the alleyway and hurried off to find his parent's car. It was parked around the corner from Northeast Kingdom Sunoco, which was Larry's father's gas station and auto repair shop.

Stanley started up his parent's car. It was a Studebaker Commander, old, rusty, not pretty to look at, but it ran like a top thanks to his father's mechanical skills with the engine and transmission.

Stanley drove it over to the Sunoco Station and backed it slowly to the side of the garage. He shut off the lights but left the car running. He quietly slipped out of the car and edged along the side wall of the garage.

Sure enough, Larry's car was parked there and the windows were already steamed up. The car's radio was playing which would provide Stanley with added cover. He had brought his mom's brownie camera with one flash bulb in the flash attachment. He had also brought along a pair of side cutters from his father's tool box.

Now Stanley crept down low to the ground and moved alongside of the Chevelle SS. He moved to the front passenger side of the car and set the camera down on the gravel. Lowering himself to the ground he slipped himself under the car. Using a penlight held in between clenched teeth he quickly found the car's brake line. He reached over to the brake line with the side cutters and carefully pinched the side of the brake line causing a small hole in the line. Fluid didn't pour out, it merely began to drip. Stanley knew that when Larry applied the brakes the pressure in the line would cause more and more fluid to leak out. Soon the car would be without brakes.

He slid himself out from under the car. He brushed the gravel from his clothes and put the side cutters into his back pocket. Now he picked up the camera, ready to put his plan into action.

"Stan, my man, this is brilliant, I tell you just brilliant. You're a veritable master in planning and execution. I can't wait. I can't wait!" said the hulking, ink-black shape.

Stanley knocked on the passenger side window.

The rocking of the car stopped.

There was no answered from within.

Stanley knocked again. This time the knock was more insistent. He used the penlight to shine it on the steamed up window.

"Get up immediately. I know you're in there!" growled Stanley.

Inside the car, Abby and Larry were stunned by the intrusion and neither recognized Stanley's voice. They were hurriedly engaged in trying to get their clothes back on.

Stanley took a chance the car door wasn't locked. He was about to reach for the door handle when the dark evil shape intervened. He felt a push on his left hand pushing it away from the door handle. He was not going to be allowed to leave any finger prints.

The car door swung open as if Stanley had opened it himself. He quickly swung the camera up and clicked the shutter. The flash bulb went off temporarily blinding the teenage couple.

"Got you, the whore and her whore-master, doing the dirty deed in the back alley of the garage!"

Larry at last recognized Stanley's voice.

"You son-of-a-bitch Bolinski - I'm going to beat your useless ass bloody for this!" screamed an outraged Larry Fitzgerald. Abby was completely distraught.

She was sobbing but when she picked up on Larry identifying Stanley as the peeping tom, she screamed out her own outrage.

"You little ugly monster, Bolinski!"

Stanley ran to his waiting parent's car. He threw the camera on the back seat. The camera didn't have any film. He didn't want to really take their picture, only to make them think he had. The deception seemed to have succeeded. He waited for the sound of the Larry's car being put into gear. The plan was to have him chase Stanley and use up his brakes.

When he heard their car being put into gear he dropped his own car into gear and pulled out of the gas station side parking lot turning left on Railroad Street heading south on Route 5.

Stanley paused for a moment, watching his rear view mirror. Suddenly he spotted the fishtailing Chevelle SS pulling out onto the street. The race was now on.

Stanley stepped on his own gas pedal and began to pull away. He knew the Chevelle SS was too fast for his own car but not by much. The Studebaker Commander had a big six-cylinder engine. His father had also ramped up the horsepower by installing a larger carburetor. Stanley turned to the right, down a small street and then took another left at the next corner. Next, he drove through a downtown stop light, took another right and was soon back on Route 5. Larry was following and with each cornering move he had to apply his brakes.

Brake fluid squirted from out beneath his car.

Larry spotted Stanley's car about a quarter mile ahead. He raced south after him, out of Town onto Route 5.

Two miles out of Town the long straightaway of Route 5 turned to the right and followed a tight s-curve pattern before picking up another half–mile long straightway. At the end of this second straightaway the road turned to the left. Larry cleared the s-curve and pushed his car to catch up to the back bumper of Stanley's Studebaker. Larry and Abby had no idea they had now lost all their brake fluid while the car accelerated from forty to fifty and on past sixty miles an hour.

Stanley fought the oversized steering wheel but easily made the curve. He chanced a glance back into his rearview mirror and saw the Chevelle SS shoot off the roadway into a thick stand of trees.

Stanley slowed his own car down and quickly executed a U-turn. He slowly drove past the wrecked car. Suddenly it exploded into flames. Stanley simply stared at the burning car. His eyes caught the approach of another car from the headlights in his own rearview mirror.

He drove away carefully not wanting to attract attention.

He soon noticed the car in his mirror had stopped near the burning car.

Stanley smiled as he drove along.

His best friend and constant companion, the always present dark shape, sat in the passenger car seat alongside him.

Stanley could feel his passenger was pleased.

"Stan, that was just incredible. Stan you are the man! Together, we can do a lot to rid the world of assholes. By the way good buddy, I brought your notebook along so you can record the victory."

The glove box door fell open.

"I knew you could pull it off. Panavision spectacular, Stan! It worked just like in the movies."

Stanley parked the car near the movie theater. He pulled the notebook out of the open glovebox. He wrote down Abby and Larry's names and the date and time of their deaths. He etched the number symbol followed by the numbers 2 and 3.

Stanley slipped the small flip notebook inside his coat pocket. Moments later he reentered the Star Movie Theater and sat down just as the movies credits were beginning to roll. The house lights went up and Stanley stood up.

As he exited the theater he went over to the concession stand and loudly demanded his money back for what he described as "skank" popcorn.

The concessionaire was just a kid like him. He knew Stanley from school and was intimidated by him but he couldn't open the cash register since it was locked by the manager thirty minutes before the scheduled end of the movie. The young man offered to track down the manager who doubled as the projectionist but Stanley waved him off.

Stanley left the theater, accomplishing what he had set out to do which was to make just enough noise someone would remember he had been there. Stanley retrieved his parent's car and headed for home. He left the driver's window down as he listened to the sirens resonating from somewhere south of the Town center along Route 5.

Stanley had the best night's sleep.

Hovering in the corner of his bedroom was the stealthy dark shape. The figure never, ever slept. It watched over Stanley as he slept. He used the time and opportunity to enter Stanley's sub-consciousness in order to tweak a few things. Stanley needed to become a finely tuned killing machine. He had all the necessary ingredients. He had passed the test, so to speak. But to take on the role envisioned for him, his supremely evil companion needed to make sure his little ambassador of evil would deliver whenever called upon.

"The others will be so proud of me. Stanley may be my best yet!" thought the dark shape.

Nighttime was now beginning to slip away as the first hints of daylight began to blossom on the eastern horizon.

Chapter 13
New Hampshire State Police
Cold Case Unit
Concord, New Hampshire
Early April

Tom Sisti was on the phone when Mark Atkinson entered his office.

Tom gave Mark a signal, the index finger pointing upward on his left hand, which meant, "I'll be just another minute."

He gestured to the well-worn leather office chair in front of his desk inviting Mark to take a seat.

Mark sat down with his notebook and some files.

Tom's telephone conversation dragged on a bit longer than his earlier informal estimate of just "another minute."

To Mark's trained ear, although he wasn't trying to eavesdrop, the conversation was with the parent of a murder victim. These types of calls were always the toughest. Tom was very skilled in taking such calls. He has always honest and sincere and never tried to sugar coat anything. The deceased victims always left behind other victims who all too often carried the burden of the tragedy with them for the rest of their lives.

Tom finally was able to say goodbye after promising to call back in a couple of months. He hung up the phone and let out a big sigh.

"Tough one?" inquired Mark.

"Yeah, it was the grandmother of Maggie Turner, the fifteen year old who vanished after CCD class, back in "85." Sweet lady. I have been working that case since I started and I don't have squat to show for it. The file is thin as thin can be. There hasn't been any new leads in years. Next week is the anniversary of Maggie's disappearance."

Tom paused and looked up at the ceiling before continuing."Mark, I want this one real bad, real bad, you know? But I'm afraid wanting and solving are not within reach on this one. Oh, well, do you want a soft drink?"

Tom slid his chair overt to the small office refrigerator he kept in the nearby corner of his office. He flipped open the door and pulled out a can of diet coke and offered it to Mark. Mark reached out for it and Tom gently tossed it over. He pulled another can out for himself and then slid his chair back into place.

"So, Mark, what's up?" said Tom as he popped the top of the soda can and took a generous draw of the refreshing cold drink.

"I think my hypothesis is coming together. It's not tight yet but it feels right, you know what I mean?"

"Yeah, yeah I do," said Tom. Continuing, he said: "So let's have it!"

Mark had to deliberately slow himself down as he laid out his analysis. He spoke uninterrupted for nearly thirty minutes. He was careful and meticulous, often referring to his notes and case files for the exact reference or quote.

Tom would nod occasionally but otherwise he kept his body language in check.

When Mark was through Tom picked up his empty soda can, crushed it with one hand and tossed the crumpled carcass into the recycling container next to the file cabinet across the room.

The successful toss made Tom break into a smile.

He then turned his full attention once more on Mark.

"Okay, my honest assessment is this theory of yours still has some holes in it. Not all the cases line up, yet. Notice, I said not yet. I would give your theory about a seventy on my confidence scale. That's more than you had before, I'll grant you."

"But, Tom," pleaded Mark.

"Not yet, I'm not done. You already know this as much as I do. It needs more work before we can task-force it. You're getting close, just dig a little more is what I am telling you. Now, for whatever it is worth, if these cases are linked, then it is possible we have a serial killer on the loose. As we both know these perps don't always respect the boundaries of our states, right? So I want you to reach, out to CCU in Maine, Vermont and Massachusetts and see if you can get them to run your analysis against their cases to see if they have anything similar. Don't push too hard though, because this theory of yours requires a lot of digging and their resources may be even more stretched than our own. Just give it a shot and keep me in the loop."

Mark was very pleased. Tom, in his own way, was validating Mark's theory and giving permission to expose it to other professionals in the other states. He wouldn't have done that if he didn't think there was anything to be gained or that the theory was hair brained. Mark thanked Tom and headed off to his own desk to begin the process of coordinating with the other states.

Before he began to reach out to his colleagues in Maine, Vermont and Massachusetts he decided to call his girlfriend, Marcy Cousineau, to make arrangements for going out to dinner tonight. He was eager to share with her Tom's reaction. This whole breakthrough was made possible by her persuading him to work the Monroe case in a non-conventional way.

Later, after hanging up with Marcy he firmed up dinner arrangements. Now he began the process of calling the three states as Tom had suggested.

The rest of the afternoon just flew by.

He glanced at his wristwatch and noticed it was now nearly five o'clock. He had been on the phone with his contacts in the Maine and Vermont's CCU offices for nearly two hours. He promised to fax them his spreadsheet along with a working outline of his theory for their reference. The Maine investigator was very intrigued by the theory and even commented it was similar to some rough thinking she had kicked around their office during a retreat months before.

It also turned out the Maine investigator had mentioned they had a criminal justice intern working in their office who was a computer geek. This theory, when applied to their own case log, would be a perfect fit for the intern who had recently run out of things to do.

Mark decided the Massachusetts call would have to wait until later. He closed up his computer, put the files together with his notes into his desk and locked it. He grabbed his coat and headed out for the evening, really looking forward to tonight's dinner date with his girlfriend.

Chapter 14
Manchester, New Hamsphire
Mid- April

Stan Bolinski was with a couple of guys from his trucking company. At first he had resisted, but they had persisted in getting him to join them for the opening home game of the New Hampshire Fisher Cats, the Double AA baseball affiliate of the Toronto Blue Jays. The game was a night game scheduled for April 14th. The weather was promising to be cool and windy. The opponent would be the New Britain Rock Cats.

Stan didn't like baseball and he really wasn't into the "guy's night out" thing but he had a lifelong habit of doing just enough to blend in. So he reluctantly agreed and now found himself sitting in Section 104.

His colleagues from work were having a great time. They were razzing the opposing team, the umpires, and just about anyone else they could think of.

Stanley, on the other hand, was miserable. He was cold, his co-workers were too loud for his tastes, and he was bored by the game.

In the top of the second inning he left his seat, which was at the end of the row, and trudged up the stairs to the mezzanine level where the food concessions and souvenir stands were located along with the bathrooms.

He had to relieve himself and he needed to stretch his legs.

Just as he began to move through the crisscrossing stream of baseball fans, a tall man carrying a flimsy cardboard serving box filled with four cups of hot chocolate bumped into Stanley. He ended up spilling one cup of hot chocolate all over Stanley's windbreaker and his khaki-colored chinos. The dark-colored beverage began to quickly settle in and stain Stanley's clothes.

Stanley pursed his lips and growled in a deliberately low, but threatening voice, "Look at what the hell you've done, you blind, careless bastard!"

"Sorry, I'm really sorry. I didn't see you. I was so worried this damn box wouldn't hold up. I really am sorry," he repeated. "Look, let me give you my business card. You get your clothes cleaned and send me the bill. I'll reimburse you."

The man put the box filled with hot chocolate drinks down on a condiment table and hurriedly fished out his business card and offered it to Stanley who hadn't budged an inch.

"Please take my card. It's the least I can do and please accept my apology."

Stanley snatched the card from the man's outstretched hand. "You better not try and stiff me," said Stanley as he glared at the man.

"I wouldn't think of it. You'll see, I'm a man of my word."

The men stared at one another for another few seconds and then the tall man said, "Well I have got to get back to my seat."

With a nod towards Stanley he picked up his remaining drinks, turned away and headed off to his seat.

Stanley looked down at the card and read it.

"Superior Court Judge Harold W. Ambrose, Hillsborough County Superior Court North, 300 Chestnut Street, Manchester, New Hampshire 03101." His telephone and email address were also listed on the business card.

The oily, dark shape, hovering just two feet away to Stanley's right leaned in and whispered into Stanley's ear: *"Hot damn, we have landed ourselves a big one this time. The old fart has no idea what kind of hurt is going to rain down on him and his for tagging you like this. Am I right, or am I really right-as-rain, Stanley?"*

Chapter 15
Manchester, New Hampshire
Third week of April

It was late in the afternoon on Wednesday the 22th of April.

Earlier, Stanley Bolinski had been inside of the Hillsborough County North Courthouse to conduct some reconnaissance. He was able to quickly confirm that Superior Court Judge Harold W. Ambrose was engaged in court sessions today.

Stanley moved outside the courthouse. He took up a spot sitting on a bench on the South side of the adjacent Veteran's Park. The park was located to the West side of the courthouse. It was also separated from the courthouse by a small parking area reserved for senior staff members along with a service corridor used to transport and deliver prisoners inside of the underground holding and transfer facility. Underground were secured parking spaces for vehicles operated by the judges and the Clerk of the Court.

Stanley already knew where his target, the Honorable Superior Court Judge Harold W. Ambrose lived. Stanley had driven by the house several times. He had passed by twice during the daytime, three times during the early evening and once more in the middle of the night. He had learned the Judge was a widower and lived alone in a large brick colonial house located at the end of Oak Street in the City of Manchester's desirable North End neighborhood. Stanley had spotted exterior surveillance cameras on the home. He had no doubt the interior had an alarm system as well as more cameras.

The Judge's habits were another matter. He went to bed early and rose early as well. He liked to take an early morning walk in and around his neighborhood. He often walked alone. His walking pace was casual. With his long legs and long strides he generally appeared to enjoy the general solitude of his walks. To Stanley's advantage, the Judge did not appear to have a dog to walk. The Judge would be completely alone and vulnerable.

Stanley's ears picked up the distinctive sound of the garage door leading to the underground parking of courthouse beginning to open. His companion, the dark shape was near, sitting on the park bench beside him.

A dark green Mercedes Benz exited the garage and turned southward. The driver of the vehicle, Judge Ambrose, gave a wave to the lone guard stationed inside the glass-enclosed control station. The guard, a female Sheriff's Deputy, waved back. As the car slowly made its way to the gated exit to the adjacent street, Stanley risked a direct glance at the Judge. The man looked directly in Stanley's direction and never so much as hinted he noticed, or for that matter, recognized him.

Stanley stood up and watched the fading tail lights of the Judge's car as it turned to the right onto Elm Street and headed north.

Stanley looked over at his partner and smiled.

"He's all mine. Tonight's his last night," said Stanley.

"This one's going to bring on a firestorm of cops. I've got your back. I always have. You can count on me. You just do your thing," said the dark shape.

Stanley knowingly nodded his agreement.

Twelve hours later, Judge Ambrose stepped outside of his home after setting the intruder alarm and locking the front door. He slipped the house keys into his nylon jacket pocket. His hands were cold. Over the past few years his hands seemed to always be cold. His circulation wasn't what it once was. At sixty-four years old, he didn't look anywhere near his age, but at times, he surely felt it.

He slipped on the light walking gloves which helped provide some warmth to his stiff and cold hands. He adjusted his nylon jacket and then took a deep breath taking in a full serving of the early morning springtime air. It was just couple of minutes past 5:00 a.m. Judge Ambrose now set out a slow pace to warm up before he would quicken his pace two blocks later.

Ten minutes later, he was walking down Madeline Road. At the bottom of the road he would be turning left onto North Bay Street next to the small wooded park set into deeply sloped woods. The park was across the street from Webster Grammar School. It was filled with wooden playground equipment.

As the Judge made the turn he noticed a man down on one knee beside the park side of the road. The man had his back to him. The man seemed to be in some sort of distress.

The Judge hurried over to the man calling out to him as he approached.

"Say, are you okay? Do you need some help?"

The Judge reached inside of his left side jacket pocket and pulled out his cell phone, ready to dial 9-1-1 if necessary.

As soon as he reached the man he bent down next to the man's left side. As he did so he placed a hand gently on the man's back.

"Tell me what's wrong. Are you sick, do you need an ambulance?"

The Judge didn't feel or see the silencer-equipped end of the gun now pointing at his chest.

Stanley jabbed the gun forward and upward to make sure the Judge could feel it.

The Judge now looked down at the gun pointing directly at him.

His first instinct was to flee but the thought lasted for less than a second. He immediately knew he didn't have the agility to outrace a bullet.

The unknown man now stood up and turned, facing the Judge.

He was smiling in a dark and menacing way.

The Judge eyes nervously looked him over, then there was the moment of recognition.

"You, you, you're that guy at the ball game, the guy...." stammered the Judge in a whisper.

"Shut up, now move!"

"What, what do you want?"

"I said move, now move," said Stanley.

He shoved the gun into the Judge's midsection. He had no fear the Judge would make a move for the gun. He could see it in his eyes. He could see the Judge knew, if he tried, his fate would be a certain death.

"Move where?" asked the Judge.

"Down there, in the park," noted Stanley with a nod.

The Judge began to put up his hands but Stanley slapped them down with his left hand and a stern comment: "Keep those fucking hands down or I'll shoot you right now, now move your bony ass!"

The Judge shuffled along and slowly made his way into the park.

His logical legal mind began to engage and so he decided to try and talk his way out of this situation.

"Look, whatever you're planning to do, I urge you to think it through. I am just one judge. I do my job as fairly as I know how. I enforce the laws others make. Tell me what angers you. Maybe I can help, maybe, offer some advice. Just tell me. I'm willing to listen," he pleaded.

"Turn around!" Judge Ambrose did as he was directed.

"You think this is all about your job?" laughed Stanley. "You're such an arrogant son-of-bitch. This isn't about your damn job. It's about respect. It's about your attitude. It's about how you look at the rest of us as if we are all just little fucking ants you can step on whenever you feel like it. Nobody steps on me, nobody."

Stanley was working up to a full blown rage.

"No, no, I am not like that. I care about people. I do, you have to listen to me. Please. I don't even know your name."

Spittle was forming at the corner of his mouth. He wiped his left sleeve across his mouth.

"You never asked me my name when you spilled hot chocolate all over me. No, you couldn't be bothered. Just hand me your friggin business card and promise to pay for the cleaning. No sir, you were in too much of a hurry to even ask me my name. Just another good-for-nothing ant on your sidewalk is how you saw me and now you want an introduction? You want to talk? You think I am some dim bulb you can just bull shit?"

"No, that's not correct," he protested. "I'm sorry if I disrespected you. I am truly sorry."

The Judge was beginning to shake all over.

"Look here Judge, my name is Stanley. Let me introduce you to someone. Meet my best friend, I call him, Buddy."

The dark shape materialized to the left of Stanley. The human form was inky black. Sort of like an empty hole of complete darkness swirling inside of a humanoid shape.

The shape moved forward and was now right in front of Judge Ambrose. The form's head with its undefined face was close enough so that the Judge believed he could make out a mouth and even two black-on-black eyes. The evilness of this face pressed against him. He could feel icy coldness from the darkness. He could also smell a foul odor which made him want to retch. The evil, dark shape spoke to him with a voice that dripped with hatred.

"You...will...soon...know," he paused, "due to your complete lack of respect for my friend, as your judge I hereby sentence you to death by firing squad."

The dark shape instantly snapped back beside Stanley.

While the Judge's attention was still transfixed upon the evil shape, Stanley raised his pistol and fired it once into the center of the Judge's forehead.

At the last possible moment the Judge noticed the gun being aimed at his head. His eyes widened in shock just as his mouth began to form the word "Oh...."

"Phttt!"

His body convulsed once as he fell backwards onto the playground slide. There he landed, splayed out upon the bottom stretch of the slide. Stanley bent over and picked up the ejected shell.

Stanley carefully smeared the footprints he had made in the playground sand.

Moments later Stanley and his evil dark companion, Buddy, carefully left the park. Stanley soon reached his car. He carefully stowed away his gun and the silencer. He removed the light blue rubber gloves he was wearing and tossed them into a plastic bag. He tied up the bag and slipped it under his driver's seat.

Stanley carefully drove away. As he left the area he spotted the newspaper delivery person cruising along her route in the neighborhood. He also noticed an elderly couple out walking along with a couple of joggers. He ensured his driving would not draw any attention to himself.

He looked up into his rearview mirror and smiled at his evil partner. The shape seemed even more defined than ever before.

Several blocks later Stanley pulled over. He didn't turn off the engine. He opened the center console and took out his killing list spiral notebook. He flipped it open to page thirty-one.

He wrote the following: "Judge Harold W. Ambrose, #31 died April 22th, 2015."

"Well done, Stanley. You continue to exceed my expectations! You're still one bad ass. I can't wait to see the fall out on this one. My friend, the shit is surely going to hit the fan on this!"

"I can't wait either. His pompous ass is now history," said a proud and fully satisfied Stanley.

Chapter 16
Manchester, New Hampshire
April 19

The frantic 9-1-1 call came into the Manchester Police Department dispatcher.

"Oh my God, oh my God, please hurry! There's a man's body in the playground."

What followed was muffled conversation and a short, loud shout, **"Molly, get the children out of here, hurry!"**

"Ma'am please......."

The dispatcher was interrupted by the caller, "It's a man, an older man. I think he's been shot. He looks dead."

"Where is this person located?" asked the police dispatcher in a calming, professional voice.

"In the small playground park on the North side of Webster School, he's on the slide. Please, send someone right away. We've cleared the children out of the playground. Oh my God, Do you think the killer is still around, oh God?"

The dispatcher was both listening to the caller as well as sending out a text dispatch call to a patrol unit located in the area, by way of another radio channel.

Coming back on with the 9-1-1 caller, the dispatcher said, "Ma'am, I need you to stay on the line with me. I have a police unit already responding to your location. You should hear them shortly. Try and stay calm. Move to the park entrance if you are not already there and do not touch anything. Got all that?"

The dispatcher also alerted emergency services with a code call to respond to the park with report of a male with serious injury - possible gun-shot victim. Through coordinated emergency communication an ambulance and fire truck were also immediately linked into the response. These services would reach the scene within a couple of minutes.

"Yes, I got it, I haven't touched anything. I hear them. I hear sirens," said the excited and nervous caller. "Over here, here!" shouted the caller to the arriving police officer.

The dispatcher now declared, "Okay, ma'am, they will take over now."

"Thanks," replied the caller as the dispatcher broke the connection.

Within thirty minutes the street beside the park was cordoned off. An ambulance, fire truck and several police cars were parked inside the cordoned off street. The adjacent school decided to invoke emergency procedures to "shelter in place."

Later, with police agreement, the school invoked an early dismissal. Text messages, and automated phone calls went out to all parents informing them of the early dismissal and the chosen pick up point which would be south of the school's location, on the east side of north Elm Street. The school announcement indicated they would release the children at 12:15 p.m.

The body had been initially discovered during the 9:45 a.m. recess break for first through third graders. Several children, upon seeing the body ran back to their teachers. The adults normally trailed the students into the playground.

The teachers who were initially involved were interviewed by detectives. Nothing new was discovered through these interviews and so everyone was released back to their classrooms to await dismissal. The school was already making plans to bring in a crisis team to counsel their staff and students.

Events were moving quickly. A local television news truck pulled up down the street from the secured and restricted area. A reporter and a camera technician hurried to set themselves up outside the end of the school building so that the camera shot would allow the video feed to show both the school as well as some of the police activity in the adjacent park. While they were setting up a second and then a third broadcast news trucks arrived at the crime scene.

A large, dark-colored, extended van pulled up to the cordoned off street and was quickly waved through. It was the New Hampshire State Police Major Crime Unit, Mobile Crime Lab. The lab was followed close behind by a dark, late 2011 BMW sedan driven by New Hampshire Attorney General, thirty-four year old, Constance Fuller-Morton. Her friends called her Connie while her enemies nicknamed her "the Pile Driver." Her reputation was to work tirelessly and to not allow anything to deter her prosecutorial fervor. She stood only five feet three inches tall. She weighed slightly over 100 pounds and favored smartly tailored business suits. Her petite appearance never deterred her from going toe-to-toe with law enforcement types and defense lawyers or simply anyone who got in her way.

The mobile crime lab pulled to a stop behind the Manchester Police Cruiser parked alongside of the small pocket park. The Attorney General pulled her car up alongside of the police cruiser. Seeing her car pull to a stop, Manchester Police Lieutenant Peter "Pete" Burlingame hurried over.

As the Attorney General exited her car, Lt. Burlingame reached the side of the open driver's door.

"Pete how's the new wife?" asked the Attorney General.

"Things are great. Thanks for asking," responded the lieutenant. He had recently married for the fourth time.

"So is it true? Judge Ambrose is our vic?"

"Oh yeah, it's him for sure," he replied with a confirming nod.

"I want to see the crime scene first and then you can fill me in."

"Okay, he's down inside the park. The ground is a little soft," said Lt. Burlingame as he cast a quick glance down at her three-inch spiked, patent-leather, high heel shoes.

Ignoring his hint and glance she rushed past him and headed towards the park's entrance.

She stayed outside of the bright yellow crime scene tape as she made her way alongside the oval shaped area. The ground along the perimeter of the park was densely packed with bark mulch while the area immediately around and underneath the playground equipment was deeply covered in filtered playground sand.

She stopped at a point approximately thirty feet from the body. Manchester City Police Detectives were now being joined by three state police detectives along with two State Crime Lab Forensic Investigators.

The Attorney General watched silently for several minutes.

Finally, she turned to the lieutenant and said, "Okay, tell me what we've got so far."

"Well, first of all, the body doesn't appear to have been moved. We've done canvassing of some of the neighbors. So far no one reports hearing any gunshot or shots. He was known to walk or jog the area regularly in the early morning hours. He usually did so unaccompanied. He was visually identified by arriving patrol officers. We think we have his footprints in a couple of places but as you can see, the playground sand is soft and heavily trampled by students and staff so I doubt we will find anything of use. The gunshot to the head appears to be a close-up with stippling tightly packed around the wound. My guess is that the shooter's gun was very close. Our CSI personnel are working the scene in coordination with your CSU's. Maybe something else will turn up."

"Why here, why now?" asked the Attorney General while not taking her eyes off the processing of the crime scene by the investigators.

"As I said, he liked to take early morning walks in the neighborhood. He was sort of a fitness fanatic. This park is apparently along the route he usually took. If one or more perps knew his habits this would have been a likely place to jump him."

"What is your gut telling you Pete?"

Pete Burlingame took in a deep breath before offering his answer.

He leaned in a bit while lowering his voice and said, "As a judge he had his share of pissed off criminals, litigants and lawyers. But this guy was fair and better liked than most. To my way of looking at this, the killer or killers planned this out and set a trap for the Judge. They waited for him and when he was in sight they grabbed him and forced him down here somehow, plugged him once. It sure looks like a job pulled off with the precision of a hit man, but that part just doesn't hang right for me. Why take a chance of killing him in a public place? That's just way too chancy for a pro."

"Okay, for now, I see it the same as you."

The lieutenant was about to offer more when he spotted Manchester Police Chief Patrick J. Kennedy and Manchester Mayor Christopher Fotopoulos heading their way.

Now the political bullshit begins, thought Pete.

The Attorney General spotted the two men approaching as well. She looked at Lt. Burlingame, smiled and said, "Stay here and talk with the investigators. Get me everything you can. I've got the Chief and the Mayor."

She separated herself from Lt. Burlingame and headed towards the approaching Chief and Mayor. Attorney General Fuller-Morton subtlety walked them back up the small hill to the street where they stood together and huddled for several minutes.

The Mayor eventually left. The Chief accompanied by the Attorney General approached Lt. Burlingame.

The Chief spoke up first. "Burlingame, the Attorney General speaks very highly of you. She shares with me a great measure of respect and appreciation for your skill and discretion."

Nodding in the direction of the Attorney General the Chief went on to say, "She has informed me she will be putting together a task force on this case and she wants you to serve on the task force as liaison for MPD. I've agreed with her request. Lieutenant - as of this moment you're assigned as requested. Let's solve this thing and catch the bastard who did this to Harry," referring to the deceased Judge. "Now if you will both excuse me," said the Chief as he nodded at both before turning around and heading out of the park.

Chapter 17
Montpelier, Vermont
Early July

NH CCU Investigator Mark Atkinson pulled his state vehicle into the small gravel parking lot alongside of a small red brick building which outwardly looked like an early 1900s single family home. The building was located on 443 Elm Street, four blocks away from State Street and Vermont's Capital Complex. The two story building had seen service for many years as a household residence. In 1999, it was purchased at a tax title auction by the State. It is now the home of Vermont's Cold Case Unit. Vermont's CCU is positioned in the State's law enforcement organization chart as a sub-unit to the Vermont State Police.

Today, Mark was returning to Vermont for his second visit with Investigator Douglas Wetstone. Douglas has been working for the State's CCU since 2002. He was a former state police corporal who was badly injured on the job in 1997. He was working undercover on a drug case when the gang he had infiltrated somehow figured out he was an undercover cop. They lured him to a meeting deep in a remote area in the Town of Middelsex where he was beaten and left for dead. The gang left him to go and find some shovels with which to dig his grave. He managed to regain consciousness from his beating and crawl on his elbows for nearly a hundred feet through thick brush, where he reached a rural dirt road. He managed to flag down a passing pickup truck driven by an old time Vermonter who took him to the hospital in Burlington, Vermont.

Douglas Wetstone suffered a punctured ear drum, punctured left-side lung, two broken legs, severe head trauma, along with kidney and liver damage from his attack. He lost his sight in his left eye. He would permanently limp on his right side for the rest of his life. He testified at the trial of the gang members over the course of the summer of 1998. The four men who had beaten him and left him for dead were each sentenced to life in prison without a chance for parole.

After enduring three years of therapy and five surgeries he was found to be not fit enough for duty with the state police. Instead of taking a disability pension he pleaded with his superiors for a chance to join the CCU. In 2002, they reluctantly agreed on a trial basis to let him try-out for a job as a CCU Investigator. He has been in the job ever since.

Mark's shoes crunched as he crossed the gravel parking lot. It was an unusually hot and humid day. The temperature was approaching ninety-four degrees with the humidity rising well above sixty percent and climbing fast.

When he reached the front door he entered but before he could announce himself to the receptionist he heard Douglas shouting out his name from somewhere in the back.

"Mark, back here, I'm out back!"

The young woman receptionist said, "Go on down the hall, last door on the left. He moved in there just this week and he is so.....ugh!" she said with a look which easily conveyed her opinion Douglas was not one of her favorite people.

Mark smiled at her and then headed down the hall.

As he entered the office he could feel the heat. The office was considerably warmer than the front office or even the hallway. Mark immediately noticed the window air conditioner was off and the other two windows in the room had their lower windows raised wide open.

Mark tossed his sport coat on a coat rack next to the door. He moved the huge, overstuffed briefcase he had brought along to the front side of the desk where he settled it on the floor.

Mark reached out and shook Douglas' hand.

Douglas shook Mark's hand with considerable vigor. He hadn't stood up to greet his friend and colleague because his legs were causing him considerable pain as of late and the act of standing was the most painful of all.

"Sit down, please sit down. If you need a drink I've got some cold ice tea in the mini-fridge over there," he gestured with a nod towards the compact fridge. "Made it myself. Feel free to help yourself."

"Thanks, I'm fine for now."

"Before we get started, is there any news on the Judge's murder?"

"Nope, not a thing! No prints, no forensics at all, no witness, no suspects. Lots of persons of interest, but the Task Force has been pressing for weeks now and they've come up empty handed. The political types are now sticking their noses in it as well as the local paper. It's becoming a big blame game. I hear, the man's kids are frustrated as hell and I can't say as I blame them."

"Holy crap, batman, do you think it might end up in your unit's lap?"

"I sure as shit hope not. You asked for this meeting and I hope it wasn't so we could catch up on the latest homicide gossip."

"You're right on. Look, after your last visit I started pouring over our open cases just like you did. I sorted them out until I had a list of sixteen murders, excluding missing person cases where the only thing they had in common was the absence of any physical evidence which might present a workable lead. I picked out five cases and re-interviewed by phone or in person over one hundred people. Following your hunch about how the victim might have pissed off somebody, some unknown and anonymous perpetrator, I looked for some signs which might point us in that direction."

"And what did you come up with?"

Before Douglas could answer he hurriedly pulled the eye patch which he wore off. He scratched heavily at the eyelid covering up the empty eye socket.

"Damn thing has been itching like crazy lately." He scratched at it for a few seconds before he replaced his eye patch. Years ago, he had declined the chance to wear an artificial eyeball.

"Okay, so what I found is this, in four of the five cases there are indicators matching up with your theory."

"Incredible!"

The two investigators extended high-five's to one another.

"Wait, it gets better. I spoke with Alice Poindexter over at Maine's CCU. She and I have been talking about once a week on this theory of yours ever since you went to Augusta. It seems her intern, Bruce Wyte, that hot-shot computer whiz kid, developed a spread sheet on their open cases. After doing a probability analysis he cited twenty-two cases which potentially fit the working profile. They conducted interviews on some and they have some news. I'm going to call them right now and put them on speaker phone."

"I'm all ears," said a smiling Mark Atkinson.

The phone rang three times and then the voice of Maine CCU Investigator, Alice Poindexter came on the line. Her voice had a sort of seductive quality to it which was not lost on the Douglas and Mark.

"Morning, boys," said Alice.

"Morning, sweet thing," said Douglas with a smirk on his face.

"Douglas you do have a certain way with words. Let me see, its' sort of like a warm bagel filled with steaming horse shit."

"Ouch, that hurts. So is the Wonder Boy in your office, too?"

"Yeah, Bruce is here."

"Good morning, Mr. Wetstone and Mr. Atkinson," offered the intern.

"Alice you've got him trained just right, don't she Mark? Listen Bruce, better watch out or she'll have you wearing one of those doggie collars."

Douglas let loose with a huge chuckle at his indelicate sense of humor.

Mark smiled at Douglas' line then he jumped into the conversation in effort to move things along to a more professional topic.

"Hey, Alice and Bruce, this is Mark. If you don't mind I would like to move past this exceptionally entertaining banter to business. Doug here tells me you folks have made some progress going back through your cases and you might have something. Is that correct?"

"Finally, a real man's voice of reason presents itself."

Douglas was about to launch a rejoinder but Mark hand signaled for Douglas to hold off.

"So what have you got?" asked and eager and hopeful Mark.

"I'm going to let Bruce run you through what he did in setting up our analysis. Bruce?"

The young Intern noticeably cleared his throat before beginning.

"Ahem, okay, well what I did was to first create an editing and selecting Macro, then I developed a list of parameters to help sort through our CDP, that's shorthand for our internal Crime Data Profile."

"What in the hell is a Macro?" asked Douglas.

"It is a computer term which allows a programmer or user to use the design or data controls of a task to establish limiting parameters to help extract or interpret data. It helps speed up analysis and reduces errors provided the parameters are properly defined."

"Oh, okay, go on," said Douglas as he looked at Mark and shrugged his shoulders.

"The Macro I developed helped crunch our CDP. It snagged over two dozen cases in our inventory."

Douglas mouthed the word *"inventory"* at Mark who just waved him off.

"Then what?" asked Mark.

"I then brought the results to Ms. Poindexter."

"Thanks, Bruce," said Alice. Continuing she said, "We looked at the list of possibles and identified six cases for in-depth sampling review. I tossed one case as being too dated. In the remaining five cases we first scrubbed the files, second we interviewed detectives who worked the case and then finally we went back and interviewed as many solid citizens as we could. As you pointed out Mark, we were looking for the one thing which wasn't in the file. We were looking to see if there was any hint the victims had recently had an accidental encounter with someone where there may have been an argument or something like one which might have set off the un-sub."

Alice's voice grew just a bit louder as she leaned into the conference call speaker.

"Mark and Doug, we found in three cases folks recalling instances of an argument or something happening with an unknown male within a month or less of each homicide. Now I know this may sound a little thin, but three out of six in our sample would give us around twelve cases which fit your profile. And that's before we dig further. One case would not be unusual, two a coincidence but three or more, well boys, I would call that a pattern."

Mark leaned back in his chair and contemplated what he had just heard. With his list of three identified cases, Douglas' list of four cases and Alice's having identified at least 3 more confirmed; that made at least ten cases, with a pattern matching up with his theory. The pattern wasn't enough to yet identify a suspect let alone bring a case but based upon this data and the sample size there could easily be twenty or more cases without any outward common link except for an unsubstantiated encounter with an unknown suspect or suspects with the possibility the victim may have provoked a suspect and thus provided a motive for murder.

Damn, it's just not enough. It's way too thin to be able to justify spending more investigative time, thought Mark.

"Mark, Are you there?" asked Alice. "Talk to me."

"I appreciate everyone's work on this; but the theory is still a theory and neither of us has been able to identify any hard evidence which would help us pry open these cases. I doubt my supervisor or yours will allow us to invest any more time on this. I guess we now report back to our superiors and wrap this up as just another theory which didn't hold up. Thanks guys, I really appreciate the time you each put in on this. I owe you."

"Now just wait a damn minute," said a clearly irritated Douglas as he nearly bolted from his chair. "There's something here, we all know it. We just need to find the end of the string and see where it takes us. I say we have that string. We have victims which appear to have pissed off some guy who may have stewed over the encounter and worked himself into a rage before he hunts them down and kills them. He's good because he doesn't leave trace evidence or witnesses, but hey, we all know perps make mistakes. They all do. We just have to find the one mistake which will lead us to the perp. I, for one, am convinced we have a serial killer on the loose. I want to get the son-of-a bitch."

Mark was stunned by Doug's reaction. Before he could respond Alice chimed in.

"I second that," said Alice. "Don't you dare think of tossing in the towel on us honey, cause if you do, I will personally come down to New Hampshire and kick your ,*Live Free or Die*' ass. Do you hear me?"

Her reference to New Hampshire's State Motto, "*Live Free or Die"* amused Mark. He knew Alice, although as a sixty-eight year old grandmother, she could be feisty. He had never before experienced her umbrage. The woman was intense. That was what he liked most about her.

"Look guys I guess I really didn't want to keep working this angle alone. I figured you would have a hard time selling this to people up the line and Lord knows, we have enough cases to work already with families waiting for some closure. I earned the chewing out so thanks for not pulling the punches."

"Pulling the punches, my ass," said Douglas. "We've all got our hooks into this stinking fish. So any ideas on what we do next?" he asked to no one in particular.

It was Alice's turn again.

"I don't know about you two but I say we work the other cases we all originally identified. We should look at them all. The samples gave enough justification and our cross agency collaboration only reaffirms the validity of the theory. I think one of the other cases is going to break this thing."

"What is it?" It was Alice speaking.

Doug and Mark exchanged curious glances.

"Bruce you don't have to raise your hand. They can't see it. You have something to say just say it. There is no right or wrong here; we're all just tossing out ideas!"

"Uh, okay, well I was just thinking, I could develop a time line on the cases to see if there is a pattern. Are the cases clustered around one area during a narrow period time? That sort of thing might give us a clue into the movement of the killer or killers."

"I like it," said Mark. Go for it. Doug and I will send to you our overall case records of the ones we've identified for you to use. We'll send the others once we've screened them."

Doug jumped in and said, "Kid, you raise a good point. The location and dates may disclose another angle, another lead, another direction. This killer or killers moved around, that much we can already see. But we don't yet know if the area is bigger than just our three states. The next question is how does he or they move and why? Is there a link to a job like a traveling salesman, or a person with a route they have to service or perhaps even a truck driver?"

"Another good point," said Mark. "We might be a ways off yet in being able to work that angle, but I like the thinking."

Bruce spoke again only this time he didn't raise his hand.

"Has anyone worked up a profile of the killer or killers?"

Doug and Mark looked at one another and realized that needed to happen, and soon. As bits of evidence are uncovered it will need to be filtered against a profile. The evidence, the victimology, the dates, travel patterns, everything will need to be looked at to help paint a portrait of the suspect or suspects.

"I know up here in Maine we haven't. We usually bring in the FBI itself when we need one. Have you guys done one? Do you have someone you guys use?" said Alice.

Mark answered first. "We use the FBI too. But right now I don't think we have enough to work with and I wouldn't want to have them kick it back to us because it's too thin. My supervisor would be all over me just on the embarrassment factor alone."

Doug leaned in close to the speaker phone and spoke.

"We have a former FBI profiler who has retired to live in Vermont. Maybe we could have this guy take a look and tell us if there is enough to try and kick it up to the Bureau. It can't hurt, right?"

"Sounds good to me," said Mark.

"Works for me, too. I say do it!" said Alice.

"Okay then, I'll set up a meeting with him. I want Mark to be in on the meeting if you can. Alice and Bruce, I don't expect you two to travel all the way over from Augusta, so we could conference call you in, if you're okay with that?"

"That works for us. We have an embargo on out-of-state travel, so a conference call will do just fine. What's this guy's name?" asked Alice.

"It's Crosby K. Baylor. He goes by Kit Baylor, or just plain Kit."

"What's his rep?" asked Alice referring to his reputation.

"It speaks for itself. The man wrote the book on profiling."

Mark thought today's meeting and conference call was an important breakthrough, a huge step forward. He was more optimistic than he had been in a while. It had seemed there was so little to work with and yet today, it seemed there was more than he had allowed himself to see. Deep down, he was grateful for the help from his fellow investigators in Maine and Vermont.

For the time being, he put off plans to reach out to Massachusetts or any other state.

Chapter 18
St. Johnsbury, Vermont
June, 1971

For a short while, Stanley Bolinsky had been a suspect in the deaths of high school cheerleader Abby Cobb and her boyfriend and captain of the high school basketball team and football teams, Larry Fitzgerald. The popular couple's tragic car accident and subsequent car fire had devastated the Town of St. Johnsbury and their fellow students at St. Johnsbury Academy.

Police had picked up Stanley and interviewed him. It was widely known in school Stanley had an argument and fight with the two young high school students. However, there was no evidence to link him to their deaths. The police examination of the car didn't turn up any useful information, since the fire had pretty much destroyed any possible physical evidence. The police did note the teenager's vehicle hadn't left any skid marks in the roadway which would have indicated braking to slow the car down. An eyewitness remembered seeing the well-known Chevy Chevelle apparently speeding in the downtown area moments before the deadly crash. The eyewitness hadn't remembered any other car speeding at the same time. How very fortunate for Stanley.

Stanley's alibi checked out. The young man who staffed the Star Theater concession remembered Stanley. He remembered him, not just because he raised a ruckus over the quality of the popcorn, but because he knew him from around town. He described Stanley as "creepy and always angry."

When Stanley returned home after the Police released him, his father beat him with his belt for having brought shame on the family. Apparently his father excluded himself and his soddened wife from the circle of shame.

Stanley's mother cried for two days over the incident. She cried for the two dead teenagers, she cried for the embarrassment of having her son held for questioning as a possible suspect and the cried out for more booze. Every so often she would stagger into Stanley's room where his father had confined him and give him a good fist pounding. She couldn't really physically hurt him but her blows nevertheless left marks, both emotional and psychological ones.

Stanley had silently taken all the abuse his parents could hurl upon him. His dark and dangerous partner, the evil human-like shape, had repeatedly exhorted him to retaliate; "*to rain some pain on these two pitiful excuses for human beings.*"

For the moment, Stanley's mind was closed to even the evil urgings of his dark guardian.

Stanley had decided early on to just wait, and wait, then wait some more.

He would know the time when he would strike. His parents would receive a payback in due time. They would be paid in full, of that he was most certain.

Finally payback time had arrived. Stanley was eighteen now and recently, though barely, graduated from high school. His parents didn't even attend his graduation. That didn't matter much since Stanley had skipped his graduation anyway. He had gone to the local Army Recruitment Office and signed up for the Army. The Vietnam War was still ragging and the Army was engaged in casting a wide net for enlistees.

Stanley was scheduled to head out to basic training on July 10th. He had passed his physical and was looking forward to the change. But first he needed to "*rain some pain.*"

It was time for payback.

His plan, worked out with some very useful suggestions from his evil shadow, involved killing them by making their deaths look like an accident. He would have no alibi this time. He needed to be there to witness his handiwork. Once they were dead, he could create a pseudo alibi and it would hold. He was confident he could play the part of the distraught son with enough creditability to deflect suspicion. And so he began to put into action his deadly plan.

On the evening of June 30th he arrived home just before dinner time. His mother was lying face-down drunk across her bed. She was still in her night clothes and bathrobe. His father was due home from a recent long distance haul at any time. He would already have had several beers before he even walked in the door. His old man would often claim he could hold his own with alcohol, but Stanley knew better.

Stanley now heard his Father's rig, a Diamond REO truck, pull into their driveway. He heard the familiar hiss, as the air brakes were applied. The truck idled for several minutes as Stanley waited in his room. Since he was off the roadway, Stanley knew his father would be switching his drink of choice from beer to whiskey. He was likely taking a couple of good long pulls off of a bottle he kept secretly stashed in the cab of his truck.

The quiet of the early night air was suddenly disturbed by the shutting off of the truck's engine and the slamming of the truck's driver side door.

It wouldn't be much longer now, thought Stanley.

"He's coming Stanley. I'm here for you good buddy. Together we are going to right the wrong, even the score, collect some dues, and deliver some news!"

The dark shape appeared to be clapping with glee.

The side porch door creaked open then slammed shut as Stanley's father entered the house.

Stanley had grown nearly seven inches taller in the past two years. He had added another thirty pounds of weight, most of which was muscle. Stanley had organized a sort of exercise area in the barn. He lifted everything he could find and had set up a rope from the center beam that he would climb again and again. He did sit-ups and pull-ups by the dozens and now he was not only taller, heavier he was much stronger than his father. His father hadn't really noticed while he continued slapping his son around on a regular basis, always while heavily intoxicated.

Stanley tolerated the abuse to keep his father thinking he had the upper hand over his son. But as of tonight the abuse would all end.

Stanley moved to stand behind his bedroom door.

His father threw open the bedroom door and bellowed for his son.

"Where in the hell are you, you good for nothing son-of a bitch?"

Stanley stepped up behind his father and threw his left arm around his father's neck. Using his right hand he pulled on his own left wrist tightening the choke hold.

At first this father tried to fight back but, impaired by alcohol, his efforts amounted to little but useless flaying about.

Stanley's father was soon unconscious. Stanley then hauled his father into the living room where he was placed sitting up on the beat-up, vinyl recliner.

Next Stanley retrieved his mother who stank of cigarettes and booze from her bed and sat her up on the opposite end of the couch.

Stanley unscrewed two previously unopened whiskey bottles and set them down, one next to his father's on the side table and the other on the end table next to his passed out mother.

Now Stanley took two cups of water and tossed them into his parent's faces.

They both woke up startled by the splash of ice cold water.

His father was the first to spot Stanley.

"Why you little bastard, I'm going to beat your ass!"

His father was about to get up off of the recliner when a powerful force pushed him back into the chair with such energy that the entire recliner skidded on the hardwood floor several inches before slamming into the wall.

His father still struggled to get up but found his arms pinned back by some unseen force.

Meanwhile Stanley's mother began sputtering and wiping at her face.

"What time is it?"

"That's a good question ma!"

"Stanley, I'm all wet. Did you pour water on me, you little shit?"

"No Ma, I pissed all over you and you can't even tell, can you?"

His mother shrieked, "I am going to beat your ass for this, do you hear me, beat your little ass until it bleeds. You can't talk to your mother like that. I'll show you...."

Now shouting Stanley erupted, "**WHAT WILL YOU SHOW ME, YOU USELESS PIECE OF SHIT?**"

Stanley had in his right hand a pistol he had taken out of his father's closest weeks before. He had bought several boxes of bullets and practiced in the nearby woods for two weeks. He now felt very comfortable with the gun in his hand. In fact, he felt confident, powerful and in control.

Stanley pointed the pistol at his mother.

She gasped and raised her hands to her face.

Meanwhile, Stanley's struggling father, slowed by the consumption of alcohol, had found his strength sapped. His efforts subsided for the moment.

"That's my gun you little shit. You stole my gun out of my closet. Do you know what this means, Stanley? Damn little pecker-head. It means you're in for some straightening out son. Yessir, you are in for it now! When I get out of this chair, and you can bank on that, oh yes indeed, I'm going to beat you so fucking bad you're going to wish you were never born."

Spittle dribbled down from his father's foul and angry mouth.

"That's a joke, Pa, me wishing I was never born is a damn bad joke. Before tonight's over, you're the one who's going to wish I was never born. The beating shit is over. In fact, it's time for me to deliver some payback to you useless human beings. My good friend and I have something special planned for the two of you. Mom, Dad, meet my guardian angel!"

The dark shape seemed to grow to twice its usual size as it revealed itself to Stanley's parents.

Stanley's father muttered two words.

"Sweet Jesus!"

His mother didn't say anything but a look of absolute terror seized her. Her eyes were now nearly bulging out of their sockets.

Stanley waved his pistol at his parents and said, "Take a drink. Take a good, long drink. You're going to need it."

He gestured to the nearby whiskey bottles. His mother reached for her bottle immediately, took a long draw on the slippery contents and wiped her mouth with the back of her right hand. She set the bottle down in her lap between her legs while fiercely clinging to it with both hands. Her eyes were still wide open with terror.

Stanley motioned to his shadow partner and the whiskey bottle meant for his father was lifted off of the side table. It now hovered in front of his father's face. His father refused to reach for the bottle. He somehow knew he needed to sober up if he was to survive. The shape reached out to him, forced open his mouth and poured nearly a third of the bottle straight down his throat. He gagged and sputtered as he tried to catch his breath.

"Dad, before this ends tonight you should know something. Remember how you always pissed and moaned that Pep Bolinsky, your dad, never left you anything when he died? Well, you were wrong. He actually left the family something. He left it to me. You see, he left me his shadow partner. Pep said he was all mine and would look after me. My special friend and I have decided it's now time to balance the scales a little bit. So drink up and celebrate the special present Pep left me."

No one made a move to drink. The evil shape had to force another drink down his father's throat. When his mother saw that she quickly took a long pull on her own bottle. The two bottles were now less than half full.

Stanley could see the effects beginning to settle in. His mother's eyes were becoming unfocused and her movements were slowing down.

His father was fighting to stay sober but the total effect of all the alcohol he had consumed on an empty stomach was beginning to take hold of him as well. His eyes were glassy and his mouth fell open and stayed open for long periods.

"You two have made my life a total hell. For years I was your whipping boy. You wouldn't beat the shit out of each other, instead you used me. Your damn drinking, your abuse never stopped. I prayed since as far back as I can remember that I wanted to die just to get away from you two. Then I prayed you would die. I prayed and prayed and prayed. Then this gift from

Pep come along and changed my life. No one was going to push me around anymore. Not if I could help it. Not if it could help it! Now take another drink, **TAKE ANOTHER DAMN DRINK, BOTH OF YOU!"**

This time his father didn't need any force to get him to take a drink. He grinned at his son and reached for the bottle. He took a swig and gestured with the bottle as if he was toasting his son.

"Sssssso you finally developed some ssssssteel ones, eh? Well, here's to you! It's about time youuuuu became a man!" His words were delivered with a heavy drunken slur.

His mother took a drink as well and sullenly, without uttering a single word plopped the bottle back between her legs. Her face was now slack, expressionless.

"Yeah, Dad, I'm a man now, and you especially deserve what's coming for you. May you rot in hell for what you did to me," said Stanley as he waved the gun around.

His whole body was tense; he felt his adrenaline burning up quickly. He needed to finish what he had started.

"Finish up the whiskey. It's time to celebrate my revenge and freedom from you two. **NOW DRINK UP!"** he roared with venom drawn from somewhere deep down.

His mother swiftly drained the bottle. The empty bottle slipped out of her hand and fell to the floor at her feet.

His father slowly drained his own bottle and sneered at his son as he did so. When he was done he tossed the bottle to the floor and gave the dark shape the proverbial finger. He extended the same gesture at his son.

"I may end up in hell sssssson, but you won't be far behind me. That's aaaah fact!" said his father as his own head rolled around a bit. He was having obvious trouble with his muscle control.

"I've got to pee, please honey, your momma has to pee!" pleaded his mother.

"Too bad," replied Stanley.

His mother's head dropped down, her chin now rested on her upper chest. She slipped into a deep alcohol stupor.

His father sat there with a sneer on his face. His eye lids were getting heavier and heavier even while he fought to remain awake.

A couple of minutes passed and then his father was likewise out, stone-cold drunk.

Stanley slipped the pistol into the waist band of his jeans. He then went to the kitchen and returned with another couple of bottles of whiskey. He poured most of the contents all over his mother and father.

He then poured the remaining contents all over the top of the end table next to his mother along with a generous amount in the ash tray that sat on the table top. He positioned the nearly full ash tray next to the lamp base. He tore out of a match book several matches and laid them out in the whiskey soaked ash tray. Next he lit one of his mother cigarettes and carefully and laid it out in the ash tray so that as it burned down it would come into contact with the unlit matches and the whiskey vapors.

With everything in place Stanley hurried out of the house. He tossed the gun into the wheel well in the rear of the trunk of the very beat up Studebaker Commander. He slipped in behind the wheel, fished the car keys from his pants pocket and quickly sped out of the driveway. He turned the car towards downtown St. Johnsbury. Within two minutes he was parked at a parking space outside of the local diner. He headed to the diner's front door and took a seat at the counter. He ordered a hamburger along with an order of onion rings and a cold, extra-large, triple thick, strawberry milk shake. The diner was fairly busy. There were nineteen customers enjoying the comforts of the diner along with one evil, ink-black shape which sat in the empty counter seat alongside of Stanley.

Stanley's food was soon delivered. He took a bite out of his hamburger when he heard the familiar sound of the fire station alarm going off. The Town's fire station was located across the street from the diner. The diner customers along with Stanley and his companion had a good look at the fire trucks as they raced out of the station turning south. The patrons all began to speculate where the trucks were headed except for Stanley. He knew, and the knowing put a smile on his face. His companion elbowed him and uttered a snicker as well.

Stanley looked at his companion, leaned over and said, "Do you think they're dead?"

"*I know they are.*"

"Are you sure?"

"*Sure as shit, Stanley. They are both toast, if you get my drift!*"

"I like that, toast eh?"

"*Yup.*"

Stanley reached for an onion ring and savored the crispy, salty taste.

Food never tasted so good.

He pulled his small spiral bound notebook out of his back pocket. He drew a pen out of his shirt pocket. He next flipped the notebook to the first blank open page. Calmly and with a great deal of satisfaction he entered the names of his parents along with the notation "Died on" and today's date. He also added the numbers four and five next to their names. He flipped the notebook closed before slipping it back into his right rear jeans' pocket. He clipped the pen to his front shirt pocket.

He took a sip of his milkshake and savored the cold sweetness.

A police car sped by heading south followed soon after by an ambulance. The crowd in the diner began to buzz over the sight of the racing emergency vehicles.

A few citizen fire-chasers were soon seen driving after the caravan of town emergency vehicles.

The town will be talking about this one for quite some time. Unfortunately, Stanley would be far away in the US Army.

He thought about that right then and wondered, *How long it might be before he would be in "Nam" taking care of business and killing him some of those whiny sounding Communist Vietnamese.*

He and his dark companion couldn't wait for the opportunities which awaited them. They were a team, an unstoppable team of death.

Chapter 19
Island Pond, Vermont
Second Week of July

One week after the meeting in Montpelier and the conference call with Maine's CCU staff, NH CCU Investigator Mark Atkinson found himself driving to Vermont once again for another meeting.

He was going to meet up with Douglas Wetstone at the former Buck and Doe Restaurant located in the center of the small community of Island Pond. The new restaurant was called Pride and Joy. The small rural town was located in the very center of the area of Vermont known as the Northeast Kingdom. This area of the state was the most rural, most poor and least developed of any part of Vermont. Folks in this region were known to be fiercely independent and private. The Pride and Joy was located directly across the street from a large railroad switching area used by assorted regional rail carriers. There were 16 pair of tracks concentrated in this small area which bisected the town. Just behind the restaurant was Island Pond. In its heyday, the Pond was a haven for fresh water fishing. It had been making a comeback in recent years, but the Pond still suffered from run-off pollution problems.

Mark pulled his state car into one of the available spaces which lined the developed side of the block in which the restaurant was located. It was the last available pull-in parking space. He exited and locked his car. He pulled out of the trunk a boxy shaped lawyer's style brief case filled with paperwork. The contents supported his serial murderer theory which was now being examined by the CCU's in three states. He was here to meet retired FBI Criminal Profiler, Crosby K. Baylor. He had been forewarned to use the nickname "Kit" in place of Crosby by his Vermont CCU counterpart, Douglas Wetstone.

Mark walked halfway down the block and up the four front steps before entering the Pride and Joy Restaurant. It was a little past eleven o'clock in the morning and the place was already three-quarters full. The brightly lit restaurant was noisy, as each occupied table appeared to be heavily engaged in conversation. Mark's eyes searched the room. At a table along the right wall, Doug stood up and waved him over.

Mark began to weave his way over to the table. He spotted a man sitting with Doug. The man was wearing a V-necked blue tee-shirt, khaki colored chinos and a forest green John Deere cap. He also wore some sort of tinted glasses. He was sitting with his back to the wall.

When Mark arrived at the table he set his brief case down on the floor next to the table. Doug stood and shook his hand.

"Kit this is my friend ,Mark Atkinson, from NH's CCU Office. Mark, this is Kit Baylor."

Mark noticed Doug did not mention the man's past career with the FBI. That was certainly odd.

Kit Baylor stood up and took Mark's outstretched hand. His grip was very firm. He stared at Mark through his shaded sunglasses the whole time without revealing any expression of his own. As it turns out, Kit was a very short man and quite trim. He was not more than five foot four inches tall. He possessed a carefully shaped, grey colored goatee. His posture was Marine like. The man sat down.

Doug tried to keep the conversation moving.

"Mark, have you ever been here?"

"Nope, never," said Mark.

"Let me tell you, the food is great, right Kit?"

Mark looked at Kit Baylor for his reaction and the man offered a slight shrug.

"Check out the menu," said Doug.

Doug opened one of the tallest menus he had ever encountered. The four sides to the menu had to have more than two hundred items. Noticeably, none of the sections of the menu were labeled breakfast, lunch or dinner. He finally spied a footnote at the bottom edge of the menu which proudly declared *"Anything – Anytime – We Are Here to Serve You!"*

Mark folded up the menu and said, "I'm not really hungry right now. Maybe I'll just have a coffee, if that's okay?"

"Sure, sure," agreed Doug.

Clearing his throat Kit finally spoke.

Turning towards Doug, he said, "From the looks of things this must be a business meeting? When you invited me here today, you mention your friend was a fellow unsolved murder investigator from NH and in turn, I reminded you I am out of the business Doug."

His tone was not offensive but authoritative.

Doug looked at Mark and then Kit before he said, "When I called you the other day I told you we are up against the wall on this complicated case we've been working. I know you're retired and all. Yeah, I also know you have repeatedly refused to be brought in to profile cases. You've made it clear to me and others you're no longer in the business. I also recognized you moved to Vermont to get away from all the hideous and violent things you had to investigate in order to look after your mom. By the way, I hope she's well." Kit didn't react.

Nervously, Doug continued hoping to somehow persuade Kit they were in desperate need of his help.

"Well, anyway, uh, Mark here developed an interesting serial killer theory while working some of his Cold Cases. He approached Alice Poindexter over in Maine's CCU and me with his theory. He thought maybe it might have some relevance to our cases. Well, we each conducted some analysis and damn if there aren't some clear parallels to some of our own cases."

"But now we've hit the proverbial brick wall. The problem is, we don't have enough to send to the Bureau. It's too thin. We really need some help to, you know, point us in some direction to help us put some weight behind our work to induce the Bureau to give our work a hard look. Mark is here to explain......."

Kit raised his right hand up with a gesture for Doug to stop.

Kit said, "I guess you have developed a serious listening problem. So listen to me now, not interested, period."

"Wait you haven't heard us out. Kit look …….."

"Since you've dragged this man up here all the way from Concord, NH let me reiterate for both of you, I'm retired. I do not consult on cases. You both know there are plenty of other profilers out there you can call upon. You don't need me and I don't need the work or the notoriety."

He folded his hands before him. His body language screamed, *Leave -me -the -hell -alone!*

Mark felt a swirl of emotions. He had arrived hopeful and nervous about meeting an FBI profiling legend. Now his hope was shattered and he felt the bile of anger rising in his throat.

Doug tried once more.

"C'mon Kit. This is a serious problem for us and we don't have anyone in our three states we can turn to. Will you at least think about it?"

Before Kit could respond a voice boomed in their direction.

"Well, well, will you look who's here! It's my man, Kit. How in the hell you doing?"

An older black man wearing a white shirt, white pants, white shoes and a white, slightly stained apron was now approaching their table. The man resembled Sammy Davis, Jr. both in looks and in stature. He arrived at the table and slapped Kit on his back.

"Kit, How's your mom?"

"Good enough and thanks for asking. Our neighbor, Ester is looking after her while I meet with these two gentlemen."

"You give her my best, will you? Now before you leave you let the waitress know I have a takeout order on hold for your mom. I'll put some squash, mashed potatoes and some chicken tenders aside for her. Might even add a brownie or two."

"Thanks, Tonne, thanks, I know she'll like that very much."

Mark noted the man's name tag which was spelled Tonne. It was clear from Kit's response the man's name was pronounced Ton.

"Tell your mom we all miss seeing her. My wife and I have been meaning to stop by but we didn't want to be a bother."

"It wouldn't be a bother, Tonne, it would please her very much."

"Then you can count on our stopping by this coming Sunday."

Tonne looked at the other two men. He pointed at Doug and said, "You I recognize. Can't ever forget that cool eye patch. How you doing? It's Doug, right?"

"Good memory, yeah, I'm Doug. I work Cold Cases for the State. This here is Mark Atkinson. He works Cold Cases for New Hampshire. We were just telling him about your restaurant. This is Mark's first time up here."

"Ah, so you're an out-of-state flatlander," said Tonne with a knowing nod.

Tonne tried to look skeptical but he immediately slipped back into a big smile.

"Don't you dare leave here without trying some of our home-style cooking. You won't find better anywhere, even in that weird state of yours. He chuckled. I'll send over some coffee and some sweet rolls for you hard-working men."

Tonne then looked back at Kit and said, "Kit you have got to loosen up my man. Look at you sitting there with that hat and those shades. If you're trying to not be noticed, I have got to tell you, it ain't working, my brother. Don't you have any manners? Come on, lose the hat and glasses and just chill. You're in my house now, so just kick back."

Kit looked up at his friend and slowly removed his hat and glasses.

"You happy now?" said a serious Kit.

"Shit man, put that hat and glasses back on ,cause you are, one, ugly, white man," said Tonne, laughing so hard he nearly doubled over.

Mark noticed the scars on the right side of Kit's shaved head. He had one scar near the top of his head that was circular in shape and another jagged scar which extended across his head from back to front immediately above his right ear. The scar stopped just short of his right eye. Kit's eyes were light blue/ grey in color.

Mark made a sudden decision. He stood up and picked up his briefcase.

Looking at Tonne he said, "Thanks for the kind offer of coffee and rolls. I really have to get going." Nodding in the direction of

Kit Baylor he said, "Sorry to have wasted your time. Doug, I'll give you a call later, okay." Mark turned and headed to the door.

Tonne stood there with his jaw hanging open.

He looked at his friend Kit and said, "You better go and git that man. I know how you can be Kit. Catching bad guys is what you do and the same for Doug here. It appears to me you're brushing the man off. That isn't the Kit I know. You may be retired but I know your momma would want you to use all that God-given-talent you have to help these men catch bad guys. Now do the right thing Kit. Do the right thing, you hear!"

Tonne turned and left the two alone

Doug didn't dare speak. He didn't want to alienate Kit.

This has been a total cluster.... thought Doug. His thought went unfinished as he was interrupted by Kit.

"Damn it, go bring him back. Go!"

Doug bolted from his seat and limped across the room and out the front door. He looked to his right and then his left where he spotted Mark nearly at the end of the street. He whistled and Mark turned around. Doug gave him a wave to come back.

Mark turned and started walking back to the restaurant as Doug walked towards him. They met up about a hundred feet from the front of the restaurant.

"What is it?" asked a skeptical Mark.

"He told me to bring you back."

"Who, the man named Tonne, or the retired legend, Kit?"

"Look, I know you're pissed off and I am, too. But the man said to get you and bring you back. It looks to me, like he at least might be willing to listen to your theory."

"Big deal!"

"Look, what the hell have we got to lose here? Maybe, just maybe he might help steer us in the right direction. Anything has to help since we are short on angles on this. One shot with this guy is all I am asking you for Mark. So what do you say?"

Mark was thinking and not answering.

Doug put his left arm around Mark and said, "Coffee and sweet rolls, come on Mark. These sweet rolls will take you back to when you were a five year old, trust me."

With that said, he eased Mark back towards the ever popular Pride and Joy Restaurant.

"One thing," said Mark. "How did Tonne come by his name? It is unusual to say the least."

Doug smiled at Mark before replying.

"Tonne is the man's nickname. His real name is Gabriel Hazzard. He's originally from Atlanta but grew up in Detroit. He was a highly ranked flyweight prize fighter. It was said his punches felt like getting hit by a "ton of bricks." Anyway, he killed a man with his fists when a man robbed him and tried assaulting his wife. During the robbery/assualt the scumbag shot both of them. Tonne's wife was shot in the abdomen. She was three months pregnant. Tonne was shot twice in the chest but his wounds were through and through. Tonne was charged with manslaughter and sentenced to twenty-five years. He was released early after serving ten and half years. He and his wife and three kids packed up and moved here where he's been a solid citizen ever since. His wife made him add the ne letter's to his nickname. She said it sounded sexy! Can you believe it?"

"I like him," said Mark.

"He's cool, right? Good, now let's see what Kit thinks of your theory before he changes his mind."

The two men re-entered the restaurant and headed back to their table.

Chapter 20
Tay Ninh, South Vietnam
Late November of 1971

Stanley had just received his mail from the camp's courier. He had only one letter to open while his fellow soldiers had several and a few packages, too. The letter had been postmarked nearly three weeks earlier from his attorney back in St. Johnsbury. The envelope was legal size and heavily wrinkled. It had signs of having been opened. Incoming mail was occasionally scrutinized by the US Military while outgoing mail was much more often examined by military censors with the Defense Intelligence Agency or even the Central Intelligence Agency. Stanley didn't feel threatened by any of this.

Stanley tore open the envelope and quickly read the three page formal letter through and then read it again more slowly.

It appeared local authorities had finally ruled his parent's deaths were an accident "due to the unsafe disposal of lighted material."

Stanley chuckled over the terminology.

The lawyer who represented Stanley during the brief police investigation also represented Stanley in the matter of his parent's estate. Since each had died intestate, that is, without a will, the Vermont Estate Laws were clear on such matters. Stanley, as the only child stood to receive the proceeds and assets of whatever his parents may have had at the time of their deaths. Those assets would have to be handled through Probate Court proceedings. The lawyer's letter laid out his conservative estimate of their assets along with a projected timeline for the Probate process.

The assets include the value of the land and buildings of their former residence. Since the house was previously inherited by Stanley's mother there was no mortgage to pay off. The house was underinsured in the amount of $10,000. The remaining barn and the land were valued at $207,000. The family car, the tractor and other miscellaneous items were valued at $12,900. His parents surprisingly had life insurance policies still in effect which would pay out another $20,000. His father's big rig truck was valued at $30,000. After deducting his estimated fee and the burial costs for his parents the attorney approximated that Stanley would receive approximately $200,000 more or less. The final amount would be settled before the Caledonia County Probate Court sometime in the spring of 1972. The lawyer's letter went on to say he would be sending along some documents for Stanley to sign and get notarized. The lawyer closed his letter by expressing his condolences for Stanley's loss along with his best wishes and prayers for Stanley's continued safety while honorably serving his country in the Vietnam War.

Stanley folded the letter and put it inside a pocket in his rucksack.

His unit was moving out in fifteen minutes for an "unofficial incursion" into nearby Cambodia in search of North Vietnam Regular Forces traveling down a supply route on the western shore of the Mekong River just inside of Cambodia's border.

Stanley's Unit was on a black-ops mission to interdict the supply route and engage the enemy. Stanley, while only in the South Vietnam combat theater for less than six months, had already been on five missions, four of which involved heavy fire fights. He had excelled in those fights as a fearless and an exceptionally effective fighter. His kill count, that is, the number of confirmed enemy kills, had already exceeded twenty. This number alone was more than twice that of any other member of his unit during this same period.

"Stan, your lawyer is screwing you, through and through. Something has to be done about that," said the ink-black human shape that stood next to him.

"Yeah, I know. I'll take care of business when I get back, that is, if I get back."

"Not to worry, I'm here."

Stanley had volunteered for this new mission. He headed to the front of the unit and took the "point." His fellow camouflaged "hunter-killers" as they referred to themselves, soon headed off along a trail which would take them deeper into Cambodia. They were moving from a village known locally as Krek, thirty-five clicks northwest to another village called Chup. The Bravo Company used the jungle to their concealment advantage. They marched silently in single file, spaced out every twenty feet or so, using hand signals to communicate.

Four days into the incursion Bravo Company broke up into two units, Bravo-One and Bravo-Two. Bravo-One silently crossed over the suspected NVA supply route and took up a position on the West side of the trail. Bravo-Two set up explosives along the southern edge of the trail, two hundred feet past their position. These pressure mines, when detonated, would cause the NVA forces to turn back. They set up five machine gun positions pointing along the trail, taking care to create a kill zone between the two Bravo Units. The plan, developed with reliance upon intel developed from previous infiltrations, was for Bravo-One and Two to open fire once half of the NVA regulars crossed their position. It was expected that once half of the NVA's split, their discipline would collapse and the battle would smooth out with plenty of opportunity to rack up some confirmed kills.

There was no back-up air cover in place for this trap since the intel had indicated the likely NVA numbers would be manageable. The extraction point for Bravo Company was five kilometers back down the path they had come and one kilometer east from that point in a three acre clearing.

With the trap was set - the waiting began.

The next day, during the pre-dawn period, at precisely five minutes past five in the morning, Stanley could hear voices, barely a whisper, but voices nonetheless approaching his position. He looked down his line and gave a hand signal with his right index finger pointed upward. He circled the gesture a couple of times.

His fellow soldiers acknowledged the signal and silently passed it down the line to the others set in their positions.

The approaching men were NVA scouts.

Three small young men heavily camouflaged and armed crept along the trail. Their eyes were darting in every direction, their guns at the ready-to-fire position. They silently moved past Stanley's position. As the scouts passed the second hidden Bravo position one of them stopped and knelt down. He began to closely examine the soft ground. He silently signaled to his fellow scouts he had found something. They too knelt down. After a moment one of them broke away and began a hurried half-run back north along the trail.

He passed Stanley's position and disappeared into the dense jungle.

They must have detected footprints despite efforts to conceal Bravo-One's crossing the trail. There was a slight possibility it could be something else but not likely. Stanley and his fellow soldiers silently held their positions. There was a chance the mission could still succeed and so they waited. The two remaining NVA scouts waited as well.

Suddenly, Stanley's ears picked up a metallic clicking sound coming from somewhere north of the trail.

Stanley listened carefully.

The evil black shadow leaned in close and whispered into his ear, one word: "*Tanks!*"

Stanley carefully left his position as he began a hasty but silent move towards the concentration of Bravo-Two's position. He finally reached his sergeant and whispered, "They're mechanized."

The Sergeant's eyes bulged wide with the news. He signaled to the radioman in contact with Bravo-One to signal mechanized enemy approaching. The signal was a soft set of four clicks on the radio.

This news could only mean one thing, they were about to engage a mechanized armored enemy, probably in large numbers. This battle would be a bloodbath for Bravo Company which was already divided across the trail. They could recall Bravo-One to join up. They would have to kill the two scouts, evacuate the area and hurry to the extraction point, if they could survive.

Before even that decision could be made Bravo-One and Two were suddenly in the middle of a fire fight. They had been outflanked by NVA infantry who had stealthily moved through the jungle and moved behind their positions. In addition, two NVA tanks and two Armored Personnel Carriers moved along the trail and opened fire with their heavy caliber machine guns on the US soldiers.

The radioman tried to call for air support, even knowing the mission wasn't to expect any. Before he could hear the response to his request he was torn in half by 50 caliber fire from the second tank.

Stanley rushed the first tank, an old Soviet T-55. He managed to get close enough to toss a grenade under the tank near the left rear track wheel. The explosion blew apart the tread disabling the tank. Stanley next opened fire on the guy operating the tank's machine gun.

The man's head exploded. Stanley now using the tank for cover, crept up along its side and took aim at the driver of the second tank who had pulled it to a stop behind the first tank. Stanley could only see the top half of the driver's head as he kept a low position. His helmet and only his eyes were exposed.

Before Stanley could fire off a shot his evil partner rushed the tank and suddenly the tank's driver was pulled upward by an unseen force. He was now exposed from the waist up. Stanley killed the driver with one shot to the face.

The occupants of the two tanks began to try and evacuate their tanks to join in the fight. As they climbed out they were picked off by some of Bravo Company's men. The turrets of the tanks still swung about looking for targets. The second tank let loose with a volley that was deafening. The shell ripped through the jungle and exploded harmlessly about four hundred yards to the South. Stanley handed two grenades to his dark partner. Soon the grenades were dropped down the hatches of the tanks bringing an end to the remaining occupants.

Meanwhile, the two NVA BTR-50 old Soviet Armored Personnel Carriers began to back up the trail while firing their 50 caliber machine guns defensively.

The NVA ground troops were soon the only enemy left. They were formidable and committed to the fight. The battle waged on for another thirty minutes. Casualties were mounting on both sides.

With the tanks neutralized and the NVA's APC's retreating, the gap between the divided Bravo units was soon safe enough for the units to hook up. Once remaining members of Bravo-One managed to join up with remnants of Bravo-Two, a decision was made to pull back and try and make it to the extraction zone. They were concerned the NVA would be soon calling in reinforcements if they hadn't already. The wounded who could be moved, were moved along. There were some wounded who couldn't be moved. They were given a three full ammo clips for their weapons. They were told as soon as possible they would be rescued once air support could be called upon.

Since no one had a working radio this assurance was seen for what it was, an empty promise. The only means of signaling for extraction would be the prescribed colored flares they would use to mark their position at the extraction point. Four men volunteered to guard the rear and the immovable wounded. One of those was Stanley. As the survivors moved out, the four assigned rear guard spread out. This was done to give the enemy the appearance that larger numbers of Bravo Company were still engaged in the fight. Their orders were to hold back any pursuit as long as possible before evacuating the fire zone themselves.

The jungle drew suddenly very quiet. Every now and then there was a yell and a couple of shots or a grenade exploding as Bravo Company's immobile wounded valiantly fought to the last. Stanley signaled to his fellow rear guard to pull out. He would cover their escape. They each shook their heads and signaled, all would leave or none would leave.

Then at once there was an explosion of voices as nearly fifty NVA screamed and charged Bravo's rear position.

Stanley was not looking to be a hero; he just wanted to kill as many as he could. He stood up and began to fire his weapon. He had it on full auto and his shots ripped through the onrushing enemy ranks. He emptied his weapon and dropped a clip and inserted another in a one swift motion. He pressed forward and continued shooting. Suddenly his fellow rear guard also stood up and did the same thing. This fierce up-close battle lasted for less than a minute. In that short span of time all the NVA were killed. One of Bravo's Company's rear guard, a nineteen year old soldier nicknamed "Bull Dog," had also died. Stanley and the other two rear guard soldiers were wounded but their wounds were survivable and would not hamper moving out to rejoin the remnants of Bravo Company.

Stanley was physically drained but on a huge high. His personal kill count was up to forty-seven, give or take a few.

His evil guardian, the secret counselor, was jubilant.

"This was a good day, Stanley. This is one to remember. Look at all those bodies. You did mighty fine, yessir, mighty fine indeed."

"Yeah, it felt sweet. It was like shooting mother-fucking fish-in-barrel. I could do this all day."

"Hey, Bolinski, who're you talking to?"

The soldier gave Stanley a look over and then said, "You know you are one crazy son-of-a-bitch," said Bobby Ortiz.

The other soldier, known by the nickname of "Sweet Jesus" because he was always praying and reading his Bible whispered, "Guys, we have got to move!"

None of Bravo's seriously wounded had survived the NVA rushed attack.

Stanley, Ortiz, and Sweet Jesus picked up spare ammo from among the dead. They soon melted into the jungle, but not before Stanley looked back one last time to imprint a final memory of today's harvest.

Chapter 21
Island Pond, Vermont
Pride and Joy Restaurant
Second Week of July

Doug and Mark re-entered the restaurant and headed back to the table along the wall. Kit left off his baseball hat and dark colored glasses. The coffee and sweet rolls were waiting.

After finishing off the rolls and refilling their coffee cups, Kit broke the ice by asking Mark to describe the theory he had developed, including the genesis of the theory. He said, "Start at the beginning. I need to understand your thought process, what led to what. Everything. Don't leave anything out no matter how trivial you may think it is."

Turning to Doug he said, "And as for you, I need you to just sit back and listen for now. I will get to your cases and your analysis after I am through with Mark."

"Fine, fine with me," deferred Doug.

With a gesture to Mark, Kit sat forward in his chair and settled his head into his hands while he placed his elbows on the table.

Mark reached down and opened his brief case and removed his notebook, the notebook he had started when he first developed his theory.

Referring to his notes, Mark systematically laid out his rudimentary profile theory. He worked through his analysis of the flagged cold cases and the redo-interviews. He anxiously explained his thinking concerning the hints of hostile encounters by the victims with some unidentified male in close time proximity to the victim's murders.

Kit hardly asked any questions. When Mark was through it was nearly three o'clock. They had gone through several more cups of coffee and bathroom breaks.

Recognizing the lateness of the hour and the expected long drive back to New Hampshire Mark offered to come back up to Vermont at another time to continue the discussion.

He was about to offer to leave copies of his notes and the case files when Kit interrupted him and said, "No, I would prefer you stay. I still need to hear from Doug and Ms. Poindexter in Maine. I propose we adjourn to my house. We can continue there. You will be my guests for the evening. We have plenty of room. Doug, I want you to call this Ms. Poindexter and tell her I need to have her available for a conference call say around six o'clock. Tell her to have her notes and case files available as well. Now if you will excuse me for a moment I need to pick up the order Tonne has prepared for my mother. I will be right back and then we will leave."

Kit stood up and tossed money on the table and said, "This is on me."

Once Kit had left Doug and Mark looked at each other.

After a moment Mark said, "I don't know about this, Doug. Stay at his house, I mean really, are you comfortable with that?"

"Mark, we gotta do what we have to do to move this along. I've got to call Alice. Jesus, I hope I can reach her."

Doug pulled out his cell phone and began calling Alice.

Mark thought, *this guy has done a one-eighty on us and now he's inviting us to a sleepover. I don't get it.*

Kit was now back just as Doug ended his call.

"Alice was going to have dinner with some friends tonight but she's going to cancel out. She said she would be available and looked forward to the call."

"Good," said Kit, "now if you will follow me."

Chapter 22
Tra Poh, South Vietnam
Delta Base – Pheonix
Mid-December 1971

Army Special Forces Chaplain, Father Daniel G. Linwood, had just turned thirty years old on December 2. His rank was a lofty Second Lieutenant, but he commanded no one. He was simply a Roman Catholic Priest who wore combat boots and a combat helmet.

It was mid-week, a Wednesday. He was conducting what he termed "Soul Chats" with the men coming and going from this forward base. He mainly focused upon the men returning from combat. These weary and torn men, most under twenty years of age, saw more gore and horror in a single day than most people might experience in a lifetime. These young men tried to hide the emotional scars as best they could. They each developed their unique brand of coping skills. Still, the poison of the horror of combat ate away at their humanity with each passing day.

Father Linwood's nickname was "Woody." He was generally popular with the men. His job wasn't to convert anyone but to minister to all, regardless of their faith, even when some might profess to have no faith whatsoever. He was a good listener without passing judgment.

Woody had just finished chatting it up with Bobby Ortiz from the badly decimated Bravo Company. There was only one man left from that unit he hadn't yet connected with. Chaplain Woody went looking for Stan "*the Man*" Bolinski.

He finally tracked him down. Stan was sitting outside his tent cleaning his weapon. Cleaning one's weapon was a lifesaving daily ritual for the "grunts" here in Nam.

The hot, humid environment along with the mud, jungle, and frequent torrential rain storms took a heavy toll on both men and equipment. Keeping a gun clean and well-oiled helped ensure it would work when called upon. That fact alone could mean the difference between living or dying.

Stan spotted Father Woody heading his way. He had managed to avoid him ever since he was based at Delta's Phoenix Base.

Stan kept his eyes lowered while he diligently wiped down his rifle.

"Stan, Do you have a moment to talk with me?"

"I've got nothing to say."

"You have been dodging me. Why's that?"

"I mean no disrespect, Padre. I just don't see a need to listen to Bible crap."

"I'm not selling Bibles, Stan. They would throw me in the brig if I tried that."

"Yeah, yeah, whatever you say!"

"I hear you took some major heat along the NVA supply trail a couple of weeks ago. The guys say you're a tough son-of-a bitch in combat. Their words were, now let me think, because I want to get it right. Oh yeah, they said you "tango with some supreme prejudice." I had to have that translated for me. It apparently means that you're fearless, a real killing machine."

The dark evil shape, always nearby spoke to Stanley, "*This useless piece of shit is just trying to get inside your head. He's probing like a gook scout. Don't let him play his little game on you, Stan. You don't want to lose your edge do you?*"

Stan cocked his head slightly as he listened to his buddy, his shadowy companion.

Woody noticed the slight turn of the head, the shift of the eyes.

"Stan, you're from Vermont, right?"

Returning his attention to the priest, Stan said, "Yeah, the Northeast Kingdom. So, is that news?"

"Not really. As for me, I'm originally from Crossfield, Connecticut, a real small town. I think there were only about three hundred people in the whole place. My family moved to New Hampshire when I was nine. We lived in Claremont then later moved to Laconia. I miss my family and friends back home. How about you, are there any family or friends that you especially miss?"

The evil companion was ready to erupt with rage. The constantly morphing shape growled at Stanley, *"You're letting him get too close. That's what he does, he creeps under the door like a winter chill. He's trying to open you up like a damn can of beans. I can't believe you're letting him."*

Again Woody perceived he saw a slight tilt of the head and the shift of the eyes. He even noticed a flicker of anger from Stanley, which passed in the blink of an eye. Something else was going on here. Father Woody felt some uneasiness. A chill settled over him even though the temperature was ninety-eight degrees with over ninety percent humidity.

"Look I'm busy here. I don't have any time for your useless bull shit. Just leave me alone. Go save somebody else, okay?"

"No problem, perhaps another time, you know, when you aren't so busy. Stan, if you ever want to talk about anything, anytime, I will be around. I'm always available."

Stan didn't respond, he just went about wiping down his rifle and reassembling it with a precision that was incredible to see.

As Father Woody stood looking down at Stanley Bolinski, he felt someone or something close by. This presence felt monstrously evil and menacing. The priest didn't sense the evilness was coming directly from Stanley, only that Stanley was somehow at the epicenter of this force. Out of the corner of his eye, Father Woody suddenly and clearly discerned a dark malevolent entity glaring at him. He didn't turn to face this ink-black shape because he sensed it would fade from his view if he did so. He kept it at the very edge of his vision as he backed away from Stanley.

Once he had turned away, a dark and clearly hideous voice entered his mind. The eerie voice said, *"I know you can see me. I wanted you to see me and so I revealed myself to you. Stay away from him. He's mine. If you speak to him again, I will have him kill you. If you as much as look at him, I will rip your heart out. Don't doubt for a minute that I can't do this because I already have and so has he."*

Suddenly the chill which had gripped Woody for the past few minutes lifted just as the evil voice melted away.

Chaplain Woody was shaken by what he had just experienced. Precisely when he began to walk away he tasted something coppery in his mouth. He tasted blood. He spat on the ground to rid himself of the foul taste. Looking down he noticed in the small blood mass he had just disposed of, there was something small, but alive, writhing in the bloody mass of phlegm. Shaken, the Chaplain ground his boot on the bloody material and hurried away.

He vowed to keep an eye on Stanley Bolinski but only from a safe distance. The evilness which surrounded this soldier frightened him. Nevertheless, as a Priest, he knew what he had to do. He had to find a way to stop him, but how?

Chapter 23
Island Pond, Vermont
Kit's Home
Second Week of July

Kit waved Mark and Doug to come in. They stepped inside the mud room, just off of the small kitchen, in a modest looking New England "Salt Box" style home. An older woman wearing faded jeans, a blue cotton T-Shirt with a huge sunflower on the front was in the kitchen washing some vegetables.

She grabbed a towel and wiped her hands. She turned around when the men entered the kitchen.

The woman, in her late sixties immediately extended her hand and said, "Hi, I'm Ester, from next door. I was just washing some vegetables I brought over from my garden."

From somewhere in the rear of the house came a strong and clear voice.

"Ester, is that Kit?"

"Yes, Nana," said Ester while turning herself slightly towards Nana's voice.

Kit hurried through the introductions and Ester excuse herself to return to her own home now that Kit was back.

Kit gestured for Mark to put his overstuffed briefcase down in the far corner.

"Follow me. I need to introduce you to my mother."

Doug and Mark trailed along behind Kit as he walked through the surprisingly cool house. They headed to the rear where they stepped out into a fully screened-in porch which ran the whole length of the house. Seated in a wicker rocking chair was a tiny white haired woman with the brightest blue eyes Doug or Mark had ever seen.

Next to the wicker chair, on the left, was an aluminum walker. On the right side was a small side table whose legs were apparently cut down to accommodate her shortness. Underneath the table sat a basket filled with knitting material along with an unknown unfinished project.

Upon seeing the men, Kit's mother broke into a wonderfully warm smile.

"Please, Kit, tell me who are these handsome young men?"

Introductions were made. Kit's mother seemed genuinely pleased to have some company in the house. She invited them to sit down on the porch and chat a bit. She had Kit bring in some lemonade along with some oatmeal cookies he had baked just the day before.

She was a very alert and eager conversationalist. Kit finally had to interrupt the chatter.

"Mom, we have a conference call to make and a lot to discuss. Our discussion may go on for quite a while so I have invited them to sleep here for tonight."

"Oh dear, I am so sorry I'm taking up your time. Your work is way too important to be sidetracked by the likes of me. Of course you both are most welcomed to stay the night or for as long as you need. I have my knitting and books to read, so scoot, get to work!" she said with a slight wave of her left hand.

The three men left her on the porch and headed back inside of the house. Kit showed them where they would be sleeping. The corner bedroom was not too small. It had two beds, windows on two walls and an overhead ceiling fan. It was also next door to a full bathroom.

Doug and Mark settled in.

Next Kit led them back to the living room where he placed the wireless phone unit on the coffee table located in the center of the room. Later the call would be placed from here to Poindexter.

Kit invited Doug to lay out his own work on this serial killer theory. Doug went through all of his analysis, interviews and Vermont case files. At the end he added his own interpretation of what he saw in the data. Kit once again didn't interrupt Doug. He asked only one follow up question.

Kit left them briefly while he warmed up the take out order from Pride and Joy for his mother and took it out to her for her dinner.

He offered to make sandwiches but both Mark and Doug declined.

Mark had listened to Doug, but his attention was more on watching Kit's body language. He tried to get a read on what Kit's thinking may be on this whole effort. His efforts so far resulted in no sense of what Kit may be thinking. Next up was the conference call with Alice. Her intern Bruce wasn't available for the call. As the call went along Alice needed to be prompted a few times. This was mostly a consequence of the conference call as opposed to a more typical face-to-face discussion. The call lasted nearly two hours. Once again Mark mostly listened as he studied Kit.

After the call was over Kit's mom made her way slowly and carefully into the house using her walker. She said goodnight to all and then proceeded to head to her bedroom.

Kit spent some time helping her after which he returned to the living room.

"You guys want some coffee? I could brew up a pot!" asked Kit.

Neither Doug nor Mark wanted any.

Mark said, "I could use some fresh air and a stretch of my legs."

"Ditto," echoed Doug.

"Okay, let's step out back."

The three men headed out of the house, through the back porch and into the back yard. It was a beautifully designed and decorated space. Flowers and shaped shrubs were arranged in an eye-appealing way. The vegetable garden was abundant with produce. It was located next to a small, well kept, glass greenhouse.

At the very center of the yard was an open air gazebo.

The men strolled around the yard while Kit pointed out the varieties of plants. They eventually settled in the gazebo.

Mark was growing impatient with each passing minute. He needed to learn what Kit's reaction to all the analysis was.

He finally broached the all-important question.

"Pardon me for asking but after all the discussion, what do you think about the theory we presented, our analysis, everything? We're all adults. Personally, I won't be offended if you think it's all a bunch of horse shit.

Kit looked from Mark to Doug and back again, and paused.

Kit stood up and leaned against a post. He folded his arms and said, "Your analysis, your leg work on this theory is sound but limited. The data still needs work but I believe you do have a serial killer on the loose. What I can discern from the data so far is that it's an individual, a male. I believe he works alone. This person has lived in or most likely worked in all three states. That may sound encouraging but it is not enough by a long shot. The data doesn't point you in any direction. This killer is very calculating and above all, careful. This is all I can extract from what you have developed so far. If you are going to catch this guy, assuming he isn't already dead, incarcerated, left the area or is incapacitated; you will need to develop much, much more from your cases."

Doug was stunned. He had just heard confirmation on the theory he had developed. Things were pointing towards a probable serial killer case.

Mark was stunned by the news, too. It only served to confirm to him the core element. There was, or is, a killer on the loose. Mark's gut instinct led him to believe the killer was still active especially since the Alpha case, the Stephanie Monroe murder in December of 2010, was relatively recent.

Mark and Doug had many questions. They began unleashing them upon Kit.

Kit held up his hands and said, "First, let's have some dinner. I can make us some sandwiches; some veggies and I have some beer. Okay? I know you didn't want to eat earlier but I assure you I make a pretty good sandwich and we'll all be better able to think on a full and satisfied stomach."

They agreed and followed him back inside of the house.

Over the light dinner they peppered him with questions, most of which he couldn't answer.

"Look guys, it isn't because I don't want to answer your questions. I do. It's just that the data needs to be developed more fully before we can put together a profile which will be of some use."

"How do you mean?" asked Doug.

Leaning forward Kit placed his coffee cup down on the table. He folded his hands together and began, "As you know, most serial killers have some sort of signature. For example, the way they may pose their victims or messages they leave behind or send to the police. Sometimes the signature is the method of the crime, repeated and repeated with precision. Another telltale indicator is the choice of victim such as a killer always choosing the same sex, age, hair color, that sort of thing. Sometimes the pattern is more subtle like the murders or bodies are concentrated in one area or along a certain highway.

But this one is different in a way I haven't seen before and I doubt anyone else has either. This killer picks random victims, with no apparent connection to one another. Different ages, occupations, different communities, no narrow or discern-able location pattern, different kill methods and spread out over a large number of years."

"So if I hear you right, this killer is too clever for us. He isn't leaving us anything we can use to trip him up and catch him. So we've got butkus!" said an exasperated Mark.

"Not exactly," said Kit.

"Okay, I'm listening," responded Mark.

"I have a theory, for now, that is all it is, just a theory. Your case work has uncovered a possible pattern. Your pattern suggests these victims all had a previous encounter with their killer. That encounter was hostile in some way. There was most likely an argument or some sort of conflict between the killer and victim. Mark was right, that's a place to start. I also believe this killer has a high opinion of himself. He has a long and so far undetected record of success. He may well be overconfident and overconfidence can, and will, lead to mistakes."

Mark and Doug were now busy taking notes.

Kit continued, "It also appears to me the killer is motivated by a sort of revenge factor. Revenge is usually driven by highly emotional impulses, yet this characteristic is missing here.

While he may have an encounter with someone which leads him to target that person as his next victim, he doesn't let himself get out of control. He waits, bides his time and then strikes. This indicates a high degree of self-control. This killer plans his attack down to the last detail. He may even stalk his victims, but I somehow doubt that."

The question now comes to motivation. Why kill people he might argue with or have a brief dispute with? The circumstances you have uncovered so far don't suggest the arguments or disputes were significant except in the mind of the killer. This killer is driven by something which is deeply rooted in his personality. It most likely goes way back to his childhood. Something caused a switch in him to be turned on, something big. I would stake my reputation on it. This guy has been killing since he was a child. His external demeanor is cool, or perhaps cold but always in control. Inside is where the action is. Inside, he is a volcano of anger, hatred and rage which erupts when conditions are right."

"Wow, that's a lot. Sounds like we have the makings of a profile," said Doug.

"Yeah, but a profile with no substantive markers to guide us to our perp," said Mark.

"Mark is correct. Right now all I can give you is a sketch without detail. Your cold cases need to be sifted to see if more cases pop up with hostile encounters by the victims with a unsub close to the time of their murders," said Kit.

"One mistake, just one mistake is all it will take and we will have the lead we need to begin to unravel this killer's modus and allow us to dial in on him," said Mark. "But we have been on this for a while. We have many other cases to work and frankly I need something to be able to justify up the chain of command why this needs to be expanded not just in New Hampshire, but in Maine and Vermont, too."

"I hear you. You can use my name if it will help. I'm willing to continue to help you on this case for as long as I can."

"For as long as you can, what does that mean, are you planning on moving or something?" asked Doug.

Kit unfolded his hands and leaned back in the chair. He looked away and then meeting their eyes he said, "I have been diagnosed with pancreatic cancer. The doctors tell me I have six months or maybe a little more to live. They want me to do chemo and radiation, try some experimental drugs, you know, stuff like that. I said no."

"Man, I am sorry to hear that, Kit," said Doug.

"Me, too," added Mark. "We shouldn't be bothering you with this shit, not now."

Kit raised his hand in protest. "Thanks for your concern, but I'm now okay with you bringing this problem case to me. Up until today I was trying to shut things down, you know? I was avoiding friends, not going anywhere. My mother encouraged me to go through with meeting you guys for lunch. She knows about my cancer. She's strong about it. But deep down I know it's eating her up. I'll be gone before her."

Sighing Kit continued, "Look, I need to be involved. It will help me keep my mind off of other things for a while. So count me in."

Chapter 24
Concord, New Hampshire
New Hampshire State Police
Cold Case Unit - July 26th

It was late in the afternoon and Mark had just returned from another witness interview. He was working the case of Calvin Schaub. Calvin was murdered thirty-six years ago. In the summer of 1981 he was shot once in the back of the head while he was sitting in his car alongside a dirt side road just south of Whitefield, New Hampshire. The gun used in the crime, a 22 caliber pistol was found on the ground about a hundred feet from the vehicle. It had been wiped clean of any useful fingerprints. His friends, family, acquaintances, colleagues were interviewed many years before without any success. Just like so many other cold cases being re-examined by the Cold Case Units of Maine, Vermont and New Hampshire, there were no reported eyewitnesses to this crime. There were unsubstantiated rumors of an affair which had ended badly, a gambling debt and even a rape. Nothing turned up during the initial investigation to corroborate these rumors. Mark's cold case investigation had proceeded slowly through the case records and now was moving through the re-interview phase for this case. He had uncovered some inconsistencies with prior statements by two close friends of the victim.

Today's interview was with one of the two friend's girl friend from back in the day. The revisited interview proved very revealing. Her recollection of her boyfriend's alibi was materially different. This was the sort of opening Mark was hoping to catch. This case may yet be solved. It just needed more work.

As Mark organized his notes and plotted his next move a shadow swept across his desk. Mark looked up. He immediately recognized Lieutenant Peter Burlingame from the Manchester Police Department standing in front of his desk.

The lieutenant extended his right hand. The two men shook hands. Mark gestured to Lt. Burlingame to take a seat which he did.

"Good to see you, Pete. Can I offer you a bottle of water, a soft drink, some coffee maybe?"

Waving him off Pete said, "No thanks."

"So, to what do I owe the pleasure?"

"I was in the neighborhood and I just thought I would stop in, you know, catch up with things. Just a friendly visit, that's all."

Mark eyed him and said, "Sure and I'm supposed to believe that. You street badges never come here unless you're looking for something. We usually have to chase your asses down if we want something. So what gives? Cut to the chase."

"Okay, okay, I'll level with you. You probably know I've been working the Judge Ambrose Case. I'm on the Task Force. So far our investigation has hit a wall. Mark, we have zero eyewitnesses, no forensics, and no motive angle. We don't have any legit suspects, or persons of interest. Bottom line is we haven't got butkis. Plenty of the usual suspects, you know pissed off lawyers, criminals, stuff like that. Even our confidential informants have nothing for us. We're grinding it along but it doesn't look promising. I was meeting with the Deputy AG this afternoon and she said to look you up. She said you're working on a breakthrough for some cold cases. She said you have a good eye and can see through crap. The Deputy AG said to tag you and see if you could maybe lend us a hand."

Mark was initially going to tell him no way, he was too jammed up with his own work but then the run through on the status of the Ambrose case set off a light bulb.

"Let me get this straight, you're telling me you have no eyewitnesses, no forensics, no motive?"

"That's right; all we've got so far is an empty bag of shit.'

"Look, Pete. I'm really jammed here but I'll tell you what. I have a hunch, just a hunch, okay? See if you can re-interview his family, friends and neighbors for the two week period prior to his death. Look for an argument with a stranger, a disagreement, something were the Judge might have unintentionally pissed off someone. This is most likely to have taken place away from his courtroom. If you turn up anything, anything at all, no matter how small, I want you to get back to me. Then I'll see what I can do to help. Don't get your hopes up too much, after all this is just a hunch."

Pete stood up and shook Mark's hand. "I got it, Mark. I'll work this angle right away. I'll let you know what we find. It sure can't hurt, right?"

As Lieutenant Burlingame left his office, Mark sat back in his chair. He hoped his hunch about the Judge's murder paid off. If it did, it would clearly point to a fresh case in the trail of the mysterious serial killer he and the others had been working on. More importantly, it would also be the second murder in Manchester. That would mean the killer is close by and possibly not on the move.

Mark picked up the phone and began to make calls to his CCU colleagues Alice in Maine, Doug in Vermont and to retired FBI Profiler Crosby "Kit" Taylor.

Let's see what they think, thought Mark.

Chapter 25
IMAX Movie Center - Screen Eight
Route 3, Hooksett, New Hampshire
Sunday July 29

Stanley Bolinski decided to take in a movie. He wanted to see the latest sci-fi adventure film, the supposed summer blockbuster. He bought a ticket for the 10:30 p.m. showing of the film in screen eight of the sixteen screen theater. He expected the show wouldn't be too crowded, after all it was a Sunday night.

Stanley had misjudged the widespread appeal of this film. It had been a widely anticipated movie release. The movie was based upon a graphic novel which was hugely popular with teenagers and young adults. When Stanley entered theater eight on Sunday night to watch the film on the IMAX screen the place was nearly filled to capacity.

On those rare occasions, whenever Stanley opted to see a movie, he never bought anything to drink or eat when he went to a movie theater. He only wanted to enjoy the movie without distraction. Now Stanley's eyes searched for a seat where he might be undisturbed. He spotted a couple of seats in the third row from the top, four seats in on the left. He soon settled into the reclining seat.

Behind him sat four teenage boys, ages 14 and 15. They had seen the earlier show and had managed to sneak back in to see it again. One of the boy's older brother, who worked at this theater complex, was checking tickets for this show. He had simply waved them through. It turns out these boys were a noisy bunch.

Stan expected things would settle down once the movie began.

Sitting directly in front of him were three teenage girls, ages thirteen and fourteen who were busy texting on their cell phones. On either side of Stan were young adults who were loudly discussing the graphic novel upon which the movie was based.

Stan felt himself rapidly getting on edge. He tried to control his temper, but his shadow friend spoke to him.

"Stan, you paid thirteen bucks to see this movie. These shit heads are hell bent on making you miserable. I bet they'll keep up their shit ass behavior once the movie starts. Mark my words good buddy, these punks need to be taught a lesson."

"Relax, I can handle this."

"I'm not so sure. You seem to be fading on me, Stan."

"I said I can handle this!" said Stanley loud enough to be heard by those around him.

The teenage boys sitting behind Stan looked at one another. One of them made a twirling gesture with his index finger in the universal sign that Stan was a "crayon short of a full box."

The boys broke out in boisterous laughter.

The lights in the theater began to dim.

The theater sound system came up as the previews for coming attractions began on the giant IMAX screen.

Stan couldn't help but notice the girls sitting in front of him still had their cell phones on as they continued texting friends. The light from the three cell phones was an annoying distraction. The girls would hold their phones up so their friends could each see the recent text message and then they would giggle.

Stan leaned over the seats in front of him where the texting teenage girls sat and firmly said, "Do you mind, your phones are a distraction."

The girls didn't turn off their phones. They instead resorted to holding them closer to shield the emitting light.

Stan sat back. The boy sitting directly behind him put his feet up against Stan's seat back pushing it unexpectedly forward.

Stan turned and glared at the boy who sarcastically smirked at him and said, "Sorry man, my foot must have slipped."

His friends laughed.

Once the previews were over the anticipated feature film began.

Two minutes into the film one of the teenage girls shrieked and held up her cell phone to show her friend a new text message.

Stan shot forward in his seat. He bent over the seat backs in front of him and poked the offending girl's seat back angrily with his index finger. "I asked each of you before to stop your rude behavior. You obviously are ignoring my request. Turn the damn things off, now."

The girls were suddenly scared of this hulking man. The teenage boys behind him saw things differently. They saw the stranger as an opportunity for some fun.

"Hey old man, sit your ass down and shut up," declared the boy who had earlier pushed Stanley's seat back.

Stanley slowing turned and glared at the boy.

The boy emboldened by overactive testosterone said, "You're blocking our view old man. Sit your ass down."

His friends laughed nervously.

Before Stanley could react other patrons began "shushing" everyone. Some mumbled, "sit down," while others said, "everyone shut up."

The dark evil shape whispered into Stanley's ear.

"Let's get out of here. We can deal with the assholes later. Don't want to make too big a scene, not here, not now!"

Stan stood up and began to make his way from his seat to the aisle. He made his way down the darkened stairs accompanied by his evil partner.

"Do you think the old man is going to the manager?"

"Nah, that old fart doesn't have the balls. If he tried that I would jump his ass once he left the theater and lay one on that old dude, give him a personal clinic. Yo, you know what I mean?"

The boys laughed again and fist bumped in mutual celebration.

Stanley did not approach the theater manager, who was a teenager himself.

Stanley headed straight out of the theater to his car. He looked at his watch and estimated what time screen 8 would be emptying out once the film was over. He exited the car and opened the trunk. He rummaged around until he found just what he wanted. He climbed back inside of his car and began to fashion a garrote from the heavy wire he found in the trunk along with two wooden handles.

The shadowy ink-black figure sitting beside him sat silently as he contemplated what his protégé was planning.

Five minutes before Stanley estimated the movie would be ending he started up his car and pulled out of his parking space. He pulled it into the fire lane which extended the length of the front of the movie complex. He parked at the right side end of the fire lane so he would have a clear view of the exiting patrons from either the front or north side of the building.

A few minutes later a stream of moviegoers began to file out of the exit doors. As the stream of exiting patrons began to thin Stanley spotted his targets. The three wise-ass boys were laughing and leaning into one another as they stepped of the curb in front of the movie complex. The boys began to head into the parking lot in search of the car owned by the older brother of one of the boys.

Stanley started up his car and put it into gear. He kept an eye on the three troublemakers as they walked off in a southerly direction towards the outer edge of the parking lot. He spotted them standing next to a small, four-door sedan. They were lighting up cigarettes and leaned up against the sedan while they continued to smoke.

Stanley pulled his car into and through a vacant space in the row across from where the boys were hanging out. His car was now facing their position but was at least eight spaces to the left of their location. Stanley surmised they were waiting for the driver of the car to take them home.

He turned off his car and sat in the darkness watching, just watching, and waiting.

His evil passenger huffed and said, "*You could take them out right here. What are you waiting for?*"

"You should know the answer to that by now. Grabbing all three at the same time would be like trying to catch cats. They'll run all over and I'm in no mood for chasing these punks around. Besides, there are still too many cars in the parking lot. That means too many eyes and ears."

"*Big deal*," responded his evil soul mate. "*I can help you know. C'mon, let's do this together. It will be fun. You'll see.*"

"I'm not even tempted," answered Stanley.

The smoky black menace slipped out the car's window and reformed beside his car. Now it began to drift towards the three boys.

"Damn," grumbled Stanley. He reached up, turned off his car's dome light and got out of the car— gripping the garrote he had fashioned.

He hurried across the parking lot and swiftly went behind the remaining parked cars in the same row as the one the boys were waiting in. Stanley began to carefully make his way down the row to bring himself up behind his targets.

As he advanced his position, Stanley nervously scanned the parking lot for signs anyone was looking in his direction or possibly heading this way. So far, the coast was clear.

The evil spirit had arrived next to the boys. He was ready to make direct contact.

"Smoking is bad for you, don't you know it can kill you?" declared the evil presence in a menacing guttural voice.

The three boys were startled and hurriedly looked around. However, in the near darkness, they couldn't discern anyone.

The black shape pushed one of the boys backward against the car.

"What the shit?"

The other two boys looked at each other and then suddenly their heads were banged together.

"Ouch," muttered one while the other said; "Damn it, why did you do that?"

"I didn't do anything!" declared the other boy as he rubbed the side of his head.

"**I did it!**" growled the shape.

The three boys began to back up behind the car. They were instantly afraid, even though they couldn't yet know what or who was threatening them.

Stanley was in a preferred position, waiting. Now he pounced on the ringleader. He swung the garrote around the boy's neck and pulled him against his own formidable body. Stanley pulled harder.

The other two boys' eyes widen in terror as they watched their friend being strangled to death. They turned to run away.

The still invisible ink black menace enveloped them. They couldn't break free. They tried to scream but their lungs were filled with a putrid, foul aroma. All they could manage to do was gag and cough.

Stanley pulled so fiercely his wire garrote tore through the boy's right side jugular vein. Blood squirted out and covered the other two boys. Stanley released the boy he was strangling and hurried to do the same with one of the remaining two boys. Soon, the second boy was dead, too. His body was cast down beside his dead friend. Finally, the third boy was dispatched by way of an equally intense strangling. His carotid artery was also severed. His blood gushed against the car they were planning on riding home in and the car beside it. Now, his drained body was dropped to the pavement beside his dead buddies.

Stanley's adrenaline rush was intense. His heart was pounding so hard he could hear every beat thundering in his ears. He rolled up the garrote and slipped it into his pocket. Covered in blood, Stanley planned to burn all of his clothes later. But first he had to move the bodies.

He dragged them behind the car and onto the grass edge. The three bodies were now in slightly deeper shadows at the very edge of the mercury sodium vapor parking lot overhead lights.

Stanley returned to his car and opened his trunk with his car keys. He removed a box of industrial disposable towels. He quickly wiped himself down. He put on rubber gloves to cover his stained hands. He next draped a heavy blanket over the driver's side front seat. Stanley wiped down the surface of the trunk in the area around the latch. He would later carefully wipe down his car keys in bleach.

Stanley slipped behind the steering wheel of his car and soon drove off.

Thirty minutes later a young couple exited the theater and walked arm-in-arm back to their car which was parked along the South edge of the parking lot.

The young man opened the passenger car door for his girlfriend. She smiled up at him and let him have a good look at her long and shapely legs as she swung into the seat.

The young man was hoping to get lucky later.

He walked over to the driver's side of his car. The pavement felt sticky underfoot.

He immediately thought someone must have spilled something next to his car. Then he noticed the dark streaks alongside his car. He touched one of the streaks. It was sticky to the touch. He was not happy with the situation. At this point he believed he would have to wash his car off before he took his girlfriend home. He couldn't take the chance that the sticky stuff would damage his car's paint. Fortunately, he knew of a Do-It-Yourself car wash which was less than a mile away.

He opened his car door and slipped behind the wheel. He left his car door open so that the car's interior dome light would remain on. He took a tissue from the center console and was about to wipe his stained fingers when he noticed that the sticky material looked like blood.

"Eric, what is that?"

"I think its blood."

"How did you get that on your hands?"

"It's all over the side of the car!"

The two looked at each other and realized the implication.

The young woman began to frantically look around as did her boyfriend.

He decided to close his car door and turn on the car. He locked the doors just in case.

When he started the car, the automatic feature of his headlights engaging kicked into effect. His girlfriend threw her hands to her face and emitted a scream of complete terror.

He looked where she was pointing, which was directly in front of the car. The bright headlight sheen helped illuminate the bodies of the dead boys. Their heavily stained clothes along with a purple streak around their necks were visible, as were three pairs of staring, unblinking, dead eyes.

The young man and girlfriend frantically tried to exit their car but couldn't since the car doors were automatically locked. Their minds were seized with fear. They couldn't think of unlocking the doors. They were both screaming, driven and consumed by their mutual, absolute terror.

Chapter 26
IMAX Movie Center
Route 3, Hooksett, New Hampshire
Early Monday Morning, July 30

It was 1:45 in the morning. Four racks of portable generator powered lights had been hoisted earlier high above the crime scene. Hooksett, New Hampshire Police, along with the New Hampshire State Police Major Crime Unit were working the crime scene at the IMAX Theater Movie Complex on NH Route 3. Possible evidence had been marked by yellow, numbered tags. Digital crime scene photos were snapped earlier by two crime scene technicians. The County Prosecutor for Merrimack County was in transit along with the State Attorney General.

A wide area was marked off by yellow crime scene tape. Police officers were also busy interviewing and re-interviewing the young couple who discovered the grisly murder scene. Several other people were also huddled together in several small groups as potential witnesses. The brother of one of the victims, whose car was now in the middle of an active murder investigation, sat on the curb in front of the movie complex. Police had been dispatched minutes before to notify his parents along with the parents of the other victims. He was hunched over, head on his knees, in shock and alone.

Two ambulances, with their sirens off and emergency lights flashing, slowly pulled off of NH Route 3. They were waved through by the police officer controlling access to the parking area. The vehicles formed a two vehicle caravan as they proceeded down the movie theatre's entrance into the parking lot to the lighted crime scene and parked.

Two people from each ambulance walked over to a cluster of detectives standing outside the crime scene tape.

A crime scene technician, who was part of the mobile major crime unit with the state police, motioned to one of the state police detectives. He broke away from the pack of police officials and approached the camera totting technician who was standing next to the yellow barrier tape.

"Scott, I have some really good photos of foot prints trailing both in and out of the blood pools. I also took some shots of the vics' shoes along with the shoes of a guy who owns the car the vics expected to use. I also took photos of the occupants of the adjacent car, you know, the one who called in the 911. All four shoe prints appear to match some of the bloody ones, but there are another couple of prints which don't. There is a partial near the grass and another full, right-foot print in front of it. Might be your un-sub. These two prints are positioned in such a way which suggests the un-sub was dragging a body from the pavement to the grassy area. I also shot photos of the blood trail from alongside the car to the edge of the pavement and then to the bodies."

"Thanks, Mike, let me know what else you come up with."

The police officer slapped the technician on the back as he turned back to continuing examining the crime scene.

As the state police detective turned away his radio crackled, "Scott, this is Ed, you have got to see this security video."

"Be right there," replied the detective.

Before he headed over to the cinema building he grabbed a Hooksett PD Detective and brought him up to speed on photos the crime scene investigator had taken. The state police detective invited the local detective to follow along to see the security video. The two detectives soon entered the inside of the building. They were immediately waved over to an office just off the lobby.

Ed Fillmore, an electronics criminalist with the state police, greeted the men with a head tilt.

"Look at this. This is just weird, Scott. I have never seen anything like this before."

The two detectives leaned over the shoulder of the state police criminalist who is operating a computer. The computer is linked up with the facility's two dozen digital security cameras. The computer screen is in pause mode displaying a single camera view of the parking lot which covered the area of the deadly attack. The static image is time stamped in the upper left hand corner of the screen."

"I'll run this first in real time and then again in slow-mo for you guys. Pay particular attention to the right side of the screen."

The tech clicks the play button. The screen image begins to run for nearly five minutes. The camera clearly shows a man exiting a car nearly opposite the eventual crime scene. It shows him hurrying across the parking lot and then moving behind the parked row of cars to a point just behind the car where the three teenage boys are outside of a vehicle smoking cigarettes. Suddenly, the image of the boys and the car they are standing beside, along with the man standing in the grassy area in the shadows, is obliterated by a moving mass of dark swirling material. The screen distortion is limited only to the critical area where the murders are taking place.

The distortion evaporates when the unknown man is back standing beside his car apparently cleaning up. The camera doesn't allow for a clear image of the man or even the license tag on his vehicle. The best they can determine is the vehicles dark color and possible make of the vehicle from its shape. The limited light in the parking lot combined by the distance of the camera from the crime scene severely limits what the police can clearly see.

The video is replayed in slow motion and then repeated a couple more times.

"This isn't going to help us much. Can you tweak it, you know, clear it up?" asked the Hooksett detective.

"Was this video tampered with somehow? Could someone have added the shadow thing after the fact, to block out what the camera was recording?" inquired the state police detective.

"The short answer is no and no. I will take a look at that angle once I run this video through our own equipment. Right now, my read is this isn't edited or tampered with. Like I said, I'll take the disk drive back to our labs, but right now I would have to say I doubt I can do much with it."

"Well, it's looking more and more like we're going to have to pursue this the old-fashion way. Perhaps the brother can tell us which movie they were here to see and what theater they were in. My bet is these kids pissed off the perp and he waited for a chance to bag them. What I don't get is why they didn't see him coming so they could run away or even range up on the perp. You can't tell a whole hell of a lot from this video. To me, it looks like they stood there and waited their turn to be killed. Maybe we'll get lucky, maybe find a witness who can tell us if these boys had a confrontation with anyone tonight or anytime earlier. We're going to have to track back their whereabouts and movement for at least the past three days, maybe more," said State Police Detective Scott Zimmer.

***

When Stanley arrived home he took his blood-stained clothes, shoes, rubber gloves, the garrote, the blanket he draped over the driver's front seat along with the industrial wipes, and placed them all in a couple of paper bags. He would toss them in with the garbage for pick up the next day. His trash would be compacted by the City's trash services truck and then hauled directly to a regional trash collection center which served over fifty NH cities and towns. There would be no way to trace his garbage bag to him out of the thousands of tons of waste processed there every day.

He showered, went to bed and enjoyed a deep and restful sleep.

Stanley awoke shortly after 8:00 a.m. The first thing he did was turn on the television to the local station. He also turned on the radio in the kitchen. He was looking for any news on the murders. Hearing no news, he quickly dressed and went outside to retrieve the newspaper. There was nothing in the newspaper. This didn't surprise him since the newspaper was being printed around the time of the murders. He was surprised about the television and the radio not covering the story.

Perhaps the police had issued a news blackout, he thought. He quickly dismissed the idea. Then, before he went searching the internet, the television flashed a yellow colored "Urgent News Update" symbol on the lower edge of the screen.

The morning news anchor next came on screen and began to discuss the late breaking news story. He turned the story over to a field reporter who was standing somewhere in the parking lot of the IMAX Theater movie complex on NH Route 3 in the town of Hooksett. The stand-up report was filled with crime scene images displayed over the left shoulder of the young reporter.

Stan listened carefully to the report. He wasn't interested in the sensational aspects of the report. He was interested in any major loose ends he may have created in this matter. Before long, the police would be looking for witnesses. It would be easy to pin down which movie the boys had been in just before their murder.

They would be looking into where they were seated and who might have been nearby. The young girls who sat in front of him were now a very real threat. He needed to know how much time he may have to eradicate this lose end, this threat.

He listened and heard what he needed to know. Police were appealing for any witnesses who might remember seeing the boys at the last show in theater 8 last evening.

Stan knew he would not have more than a day to track down the girls. Other nearby patrons would be of no particular use to the police since Stanley did not speak directly with them or even make direct eye contact. The girls were an entirely different matter.

Stanley's dark companion spoke up. *"The girls must be silenced. My man Stan, we don't know who they are or where they are from."*

"Not a problem," replied a confident Stanley. "Those girls were twittering and emailing their friends. They're all addicted to that social media junk. I have several Facebook and Twitter accounts I created under bogus names some time ago. I'll put them to good use now. Looks like I've got some trolling to do. It should be easy enough to find them. Just watch and learn."

"And if you can't find them?" asked his companion.

"Then you can use your magic and monitor the cops. When they know, we will know. At that point, the girls will be all yours."

Within the next thirty minutes his various alter egos had dropped into several messaging applications. He soon picked up on hot rumors about three girls from Londonderry, New Hampshire who had seen the victims at the movies last night. The rumors and message traffic revealed the girls had an encounter with "some old dude who creeped them out." Now they are "totally freaked out" the old man might be the killer. The girls are telling their friends they're each afraid to go to the police with what they know. The social media was white hot with messages offering all sorts of bizarre and useless advice on what to do.

It only took Stanley a few minutes before he had their names and addresses.

Before he could act on the information his evil partner spoke out. *"Good work, good buddy. You just go on with the usual stuff. I'll take care of these three. I'll make sure these loose ends are eliminated."*

Before Stanley could respond the dark force vanished.

Stanley proceeded to casually make his breakfast and read his newspaper. He left both the television and radio on so he could catch the latest news, after all, something bad is always happening.

As he waited for his coffee to brew he pulled out his small spiral flip notebook, his Kill List, and entered the three kills from last night. He wouldn't take credit for the girls since they technically were not going to die directly at his hands. He had standards after all and he would not claim that which wasn't rightfully his.

Chapter 27
New Hampshire State Police Office
Cold Case Unit
August 3

Lieutenant Pete Burlingame climbed the stairs two at a time. He was in a hurry to catch up with CCU Investigator Mark Atkinson. Lt. Burlingame had followed up on the angle Mark had provided him several days ago in the Judge Ambrose Murder Case and now he wanted to confer with Mark once more.

After pushing his task force team of investigators to conduct re-interviews of everyone on their original list he had struck gold. The Judge's baseball buddies, who had attended a Fisher Cats game with him, recalled the Judge had mentioned he had accidentally spilled hot chocolate on some guy whom the Judge had to calm down with an offer to pay for his cleaning bills. His friends hadn't actually witnessed the encounter, but they all agreed the Judge did seem to be a little rattled by the encounter.

Burlingame then checked to see if the baseball stadium video footage taken by security cameras might still be available. There had been no reason during the initial investigation to check the video. It turns out the video records were re-recorded over after 30 days. No useful video data was available. Next, he obtained the list of employees who had worked the concessions at the game. He had them interviewed. One young lady working a cash register across from the area where the Judge was sitting remembered the Judge. She also remembered seeing the Judge speaking with a heavy set man whom she described as *"old but not too old, like in his fifties or maybe sixties."*

She agreed to be put under hypnosis. When hypnotized, she was able to remember that the man wore a dark green nylon windbreaker with some kind of company logo on the upper left chest. She described him as angry looking with his fists clenched tight. She also recalled seeing the Judge hand him something before the two men parted. She never got a straight on look at the man. She only saw his profile during his discussion with the Judge.

It wasn't much but it was something. Right now Lt. Burlingame and the Judge Ambrose Task Force needed a breakthrough. The political heat on this case was huge and only getting bigger. There were rumors the FBI and the US Attorney's Office might take the case over.

The only thing holding up the progress of the Judge's case was the recent triple homicide of teenage boys in Hooksett, NH, followed by the startling and shocking disappearance of three teenage girls from Londonderry, New Hampshire. The link between the two cases had been leaked to the media late yesterday.

Consequently, today's newspapers, television, and radio were filled with the reports the missing girls were initially sought by the police as possible eyewitnesses who may have had an encounter with the suspected killer of the three boys.

The whole state was in an uproar over this revelation. Regionally, the reaction was much the same. National media were now rushing to New Hampshire to follow this extraordinary story.

Breathing heavily, Lt. Burlingame hurried to find Mark in the CCU Offices.

Mark was at his desk. He was listening to a talk radio discussion of the murdered boys and missing girls.

Mark acknowledged Pete's arrival but held up his index finger to his lips in s sign for quiet while the radio discussion raged on. Pete slid into a chair and dragged the chair closer to the front of Mark's desk.

After a couple of minutes Mark used a remote control device and turned off the radio.

"Damn shame," said Mark.

"Yeah, I know," replied Burlingame. "The County Attorney's Office along with the State Attorney General's Office has formed another joint task force to work the case. The FBI is being brought in on the possibility the girls may have been kidnapped and taken across state lines. There has been no contact from any un-sub regarding ransom demands. The nut jobs are cranked up over this and everyone is being flooded with false claims and wild tips. That's the story for now but no one in law enforcement expects to find them alive."

Mark nodded his concurrence with Burlingame's speculation.

"So what brings you here?"

"I want to tell you, your hunch proved to be right on target. It seems the Judge had an argument with some burly dude at a baseball game after spilling some hot chocolate on the guy. We think the Judge offered to clean his clothes. He may have given the man his business card. The description of the man is weak. What we have so far is heavy set, mid to late fifties or older, white male, perhaps six foot tall and he was seen wearing a green nylon jacket with some kind business logo stamped on the upper left chest. That's it."

Mark sat back in his chair and folded his fingers. He rocked back and forth in his office chair staring over Pete's shoulder at nothing in particular.

"Talk to me, Mark. What're you thinking? Is there anything else you can point me to that might help?"

Mark leaned forward and leaned his elbows on his desk.

"I want to explain something to you. Keep an open mind, okay? For the past couple of months I have been working with my counterparts in Maine and Vermont on a series of cold cases which we believe are linked."

"You mean you guys are on to a serial killer, shit!"

"We think so and we have been conferring with a retired FBI Profiler who happens to live in Vermont. He sees it the same way.

"For the longest time these cases all had no apparent connection, no eyewitnesses, no forensics, no overt pattern. All the vics are different and unrelated and get this, no apparent motive."

With a raise of his right eyebrow he continued.

"Except, we think we have found a motive. The un-sub appears to have had some kind of hostile contact with the vics days or weeks before their murders. These events were never picked up during the initial investigations but when we did re-interviews looking for this link, we found it in nearly twenty cases. We are still working other cases to see if the connection shows up."

"If I get this straight, the hunch, your hunch, my Judge's case may well have this same pattern. This would like Judge's case to your possible serial killer. Holy shit!" exclaimed Pete. "Wow, this means your un-sub and my un-sub must be the same bad ass, right?"

"Bingo!" said Mark.

The two detectives exchanged fist bumps.

"So how do we work this?"

Mark responded, "Carefully, very, very carefully. It means we have likely had a serial killer on the loose in Northern New England and possibly the rest of region for many years. This guy has managed to fly under the radar of many law enforcement agencies for quite a long time. This won't sit well with the public once that connection is made. Now, if we say this guy is still a player and he took out the Judge then the political gloves come off and the politicians will be looking to dump the blame on someone. Right now, I don't see any upside to publicly linking my investigation with yours until we catch this bastard. Another possible upside I can see here is this, the freak is operating from somewhere in our backyard. We need to nail him, the sooner the better!"

"It all makes sense to me. But we both don't have much to work on. What does your profiler friend say? Any useful suggestions?"

"Not yet; by using the retired profiler we have managed to avoid bringing this straight to the FBI. I am not sure we can hold off much longer. The CCU offices in Maine and Vermont, just like here, have supervisors who are pressing their investigators to expand this investigation and bring in the Feds. One other thing, our retired profiler is battling pancreatic cancer. As of now, probably has less than four months to live."

"Damn, this can't get any worse. What do you suggest I do with this information in connection to my case?"

"I think you see if there are any other possible witnesses. See if your witness can work with a sketch artist. Maybe you get enough from that to work other possible witnesses.

If I remember correctly, some of the Fisher Cats ball games are broadcast on cable TV. Maybe that game was one. If so, the video record of that game might still be available and if so perhaps they have some crowd shots. Who knows, you might get lucky?"

"Yeah, we need to catch a lucky break here just like our guys working the triple murders and the missing kid's cases. So far, with all the resources being thrown at the two cases nothing has turned up except for a couple of bloody footprints. They don't have anything to work with. It's like …………."

Pete stopped speaking in mid-sentence. His jaw hung half open. He looked at Mark who had a frozen look on his own face.

"Mark, is it possible? Do you think that our un-sub is involved with those cases?"

Before Mark could react Pete slumped down in his chair and shook his head.

"Pete, we can't rule anything out or in at this point, but I would hate to think our suspect could or would be involved in all of that. Right now there isn't anything in the two cases which suggest someone was pissed at those kids."

Pete looked ashen.

Pete looked up and began, "Mark, in a briefing two days ago we were told the girls were being sought for questioning because they witnessed the boys arguing with an older, heavy set man inside one of the theaters earlier in the evening. Apparently the girls argued with the same guy. The information wasn't made public. This sure looks like a connection to me!"

Mark ran his fingers through his hair. He was angry, frustrated and most of all disappointed in himself. This whole theory of his was supposed to help brake a backlog of cold cases and hopefully bring a killer to justice and closure for the victim's families. Instead, while he was hunting a cold case killer, this same shit head was still out there killing, killing and killing. Mark felt the blood of these recent victims was partially on him.

What needs to be done now? The answer was simple. He and Pete needed to take this to their respective bosses and through them to the AG. This whole mess would likely result in the Feds being called in. It was the right thing to do.

Mark told Pete what he was thinking and Pete immediately disagreed.

"Look Mark," said Pete, "I see this is way too thin to kick up the food chain. We need more than your theory to sell this. As much as I'm on board with your analysis, and my gut tells me you have nailed this, we both know there isn't much to work with. What about the profiler you're tied in with? Can he give this another look-see and maybe help us build a case we can take up the line? What do you say?"

Mark was feeling the weight of the string of cold cases he was working and now he felt even more squeezed by the probable tie in with the recent homicides and missing person cases. He signed and said, "Okay, I see your point. I'll give him a call and see if I can set up a meeting. But understand this Pete, right now we are dancing on the edge of the blade. If higher ups think for a minute we sat on this angle while more shit happened, they will gladly sacrifice our asses, do you understand?"

"I have already thought about that. Our careers and retirements are on the line so, yeah, I know the risks."

Mark picked up his phone and placed a call to Kit Baylor.

No one answered at Kit's residence.

Mark tried Kit's number several more times that late afternoon and evening with the results being the same.

Around 10:45 that evening Mark called his Vermont CCU buddy, Doug Wetstone.

Chapter 28
New Hampshire State Police
Cold Case Unit
August 4

Mark was nervous. He hadn't heard back yet from Doug since he called him late last evening and left a message he needed sent along to Kit. He sat at his desk tapping his pencil on the desk as he stared blankly at his computer screen.

It was now 9:45 in the morning. Mark's morning coffee soured in his stomach.

Suddenly his phone rang.

He grabbed it before the first ring was complete.

"Hello," said Mark.

It was Doug.

"I located him."

"And?"

"He's in Burlington, at the Fletcher-Allen Hospital. Apparently he had some sort of attack or something. He was taken there by ambulance two days ago. His mom is being looked after by the neighbor lady we met. Anyway, I spoke with him and he said he expects to be in the hospital for a couple more days while they do some tests on him. He said for you to come up there and visit him. So I told him I would pass along the message. What do you say? Do you want to come up and visit him in the hospital?"

"I'm leaving right now. I will be there as soon as I can."

"Shit, hold on buddy. You really want to pop in on him this afternoon?"

"Damn right, I don't have time to explain everything right now, just have your ass there too."

The line went dead. Mark had hung up his end of the call.

Doug hung up his phone too. He looked at his afternoon calendar and saw he had three appointments. He began making calls to postpone the appointments.

Something had lit a fire under Mark and Doug was curious to find out just what it was. He also placed a call to Kit's hospital room. He spoke with Kit and gave him a heads up about Mark coming up that very afternoon to meet with Kit. He shared his impressions with Kit that something big must be up but he had no details to pass along. He ended the call by asking if he needed anything.

"I'm fine," answered Kit. "Tired and weak. I don't have much of an appetite. Could use a beer. It seems they aren't licensed to sell alcohol in this fancy place."

"I hear you. See you this afternoon."

It was twenty minutes past one o'clock in the afternoon when Mark parked his state car in the Fletcher-Allen Hospital visitor's parking garage located just off of Colchester Avenue directly in front of the hospital.

He jogged to the hospital entrance and on through the doors to the information desk. Mark went to the patient information kiosk and picked up a phone. Following the telephone prompts he eventually learned Kit Baylor was in Room 426, East Wing. He looked around for more directions and soon spotted an overhead sign pointing towards the location of the visitor elevators. Mark moved off in the indicated direction. After exiting the elevator he soon found himself following a series of signs and arrows painted on the floor which eventually took him to the correct wing where cancer patients were located. He thought he might have to flash his badge but in didn't become necessary as he navigated his way to Kit's hospital room. When he stepped into the room he could hear Doug and Kit whispering.

When Mark stepped around the privacy curtain he immediately spotted what the whispering was all about. Kit and Doug each had a bottle of beer in hand along with a big grin on their faces.

Doug whispered, "You want one?"

"Are you kidding me? It's just a little after one guys, of course I'll have one," said Mark with a grin.

Doug opened the front door to the patient's cabinet next to Kit's bed and removed a bottle of beer from a brown bag.

Mark twisted off the top and took a pull on the cold beer.

Just then a nurse silently walked in and now stood beside Mark. She had managed to sneak up on them without being noticed. She didn't look too pleased to see the three men drinking beer on her floor in the middle of the day no less.

She exhibited a stern look at each before she said, "I will be back in five minutes and I don't want to see any more beer drinking, am I clear?"

"Yes, ma'am!" said Doug.

"Whoever brought the beer, please make sure you remove the bottles when you leave. I do not want to see them in the trash."

Without another word, but with one last stern look around, she left the room.

The guys burst into laughter once she had left.

Kit said, "She's cool. Doug, make sure you take the empties, okay! I don't want to get her in any trouble!"

"Will do," said Doug.

Mark noticed Kit appeared gaunter than when he last saw him. The cancer was taking hold on his weakened body, yet his spirit seemed good.

Once the beers were finished off, Kit got out of bed and pulled the tall med-rack with his IV along with him. He maneuvered over to a recliner in the corner of his side of the room.

The other side of the double room was empty.

Doug asked, "You don't have a roommate?"

"I did at first. It was a man down from Canada. He died yesterday afternoon. He had brain cancer and no family to speak of. One of the staff said he never had any visitors, pretty sad."

Changing the subject Kit said, "Anyway, you guys raced all the way up here to see me, so what's up?"

Doug looked at Mark and said, "It's all you, buddy!"

Mark used Kit's bed to spread out some notes.

While he was doing this the nurse who had caught them drinking beer earlier poked her head in to check on things. She just smiled, nodded and left the room.

Mark said, "Doug, can you close the door please. I don't want any citizen accidentally listening in."

Doug stood up and closed the hospital room door.

Mark began to brief Kit and Doug. He remained standing next to Kit's bed throughout his presentation. He shuffled on his feet, nerves and stress pee building up inside him. Doug and Kit recognized the symptoms.

For the moment, neither Kit nor Doug interrupted him with questions.

Mark finally finished. He rubbed his temples with his right hand.

Then lifting up both hands, palm side up he asked, "So what do you think?"

Doug whistled through his teeth. "You have one big-ass problem. If your theory holds true, this guy's now working your neighborhood and his kill numbers are exploding. Mark, you have got to kick this up the chain. Your AG and the FBI need to be brought in ASAP."

Mark ran his fingers through his hair.

"I don't want to do that yet. I don't think there is enough here. They might blow me off or worse yet, they run with and if it's a dead end then I've wasted their time."

Kit spoke up, "I agree with you Mark, at least for now. The thread you fellows have been pulling is still thin. You want to pass this up the chain when there is some meat on it. There is no time to waste. This killer's fuse seems to be real short and ornery. He's showing us he can kill anyone, anytime and anyplace just because he can. Doug, don't forget, this killer has left bodies here and in Maine. Nothing yet precludes him from returning here or ping ponging over to Maine."

Doug exhaled and sank back in his chair.

Kit continued, "Mark you need to catch your breath on this. A case like this will wind you up way too tight and that's not good. It can make you more likely to miss something. Can't afford to miss anything, especially with a hot lead to work."

Mark spoke next, "Advice duly noted. Kit do you see anything new in the info I brought today, anything at all?"

Kit paused before answering. He seemed to be dealing with some discomfort and it had his full attention.

"Kit, do you need to get back in bed? Do you need the nurse or a doctor?" asked Mark.

"Nah, I'll be okay. I think the beer has given me gas, that's all."

After a moment Kit began once more.

"From what you have now, it would seem this un-sub is single. At least that is my best guess. He is seen alone in places where spouse, children or grandchildren might likely be expected to be accompanying him, yet none are noted. Also, I have a hunch he's getting help from someone, maybe after the fact. In addition, he is making mistakes which up until now he has managed to avoid doing. So what accounts for this? My best guess is he is under some kind of pressure. The pressure is affecting his thinking, his concentration. If this continues it increases the chances he will be caught. Another thing, his kills do not follow a time table so we're not looking at a rhythm whereby we can reasonably predict the timing of another strike."

"That still doesn't give us anything solid to work with," observed Doug.

"I know."

"So what's next?" asked Mark. "We can't just sit and wait for him to kill again."

"I'm afraid it is all you can do. For now, I would only monitor murders in Northern New England. It seems his territory has narrowed, perhaps due to age," said Kit.

Mark asked, "What about missing persons?"

"The same, monitor them, too."

"There has to be something we are missing, something which could point us in the right direction!" said a frustrated Doug.

"Believe me, I wish there was but for now there isn't," said Kit.

"I should call Alice Poindexter and bring her up to date on what we have," said Mark as he stuffed his papers back into the mud brown colored accordion folder, he then stuffed it inside of his briefcase.

"Good, now if you guys could excuse me, I need to get back in bed. My stomach is cramping up real bad."

Kit stood up and shuffled gingerly to his hospital bed. He eased his legs up and under the covers.

Mark placed the call to Alice.

While he and Alice caught up on the serial killer discussion, Doug and Kit talked about sports and other things. Doug could see Kit was tired and in some discomfort. Yet, when he suggested Kit call for the nurse to get something for his pain, he refused.

After Mark hung up the phone he turned back to Doug and Kit.

"Alice and her intern, Bruce Wyte, the wiz kid, had a hunch. They have been working it for the past couple of weeks. Using our inventory of suspected cases they started a clock going back to 1980. They were working the angle that our un-sub is, or at least was, a long distance truck driver. So they went through the DMV records of Maine, New Hampshire and Vermont for all the federally controlled Class "CDLA" [Commercial Driver License – A] licenses issued by those states which are currently active drivers. This list included all drivers who were previously issued State only "C" licenses under the old system when States issued and controlled commercial licenses. It seems there are at least two hundred and ninety-two licenses which were active throughout this entire period. Based upon what Kit said, "the un-sub is not likely married" I asked them to see if they can trim the list down to those who have been single throughout the period or who are presently single. She said she would get back to me as soon as they could. They were not sure their DMV records could be filtered this way but her whiz kid intern might have a way of cross checking the data with vital statistics, birth, death and marriage info maintained by another State agency. So what do you think?"

"It makes sense to me," said Doug.

"Brilliant, just brilliant," said Kit as he closed his eyes while wincing from obvious pain.

Continuing, he said, "Let me know what she turns up."

"I will," said Mark. "I know the un-sub could be a salesman or have another occupation we haven't been able to guess, but at least this gives us something to work with for now."

Chapter 29
New Hampshire State Police
Cold Case Unit
August 8

The phone rang in Mark's office. He wasn't there to take the call. It was Kit Baylor calling.

At the beep he left the following message, "Hi Mark. Kit here, I uh, wanted to call you and let you know I will be having surgery later today. It seems the doctors want to remove a few things. I should be good as new after that, just a few pounds lighter. I'm sure we will talk soon. Bye."

Mark didn't remotely check his messages. He had been in court all day. One of his cold cases had come up for trial and he was expected to testify for the prosecution. He sat in the courtroom all day and was not called to testify. Procedural maneuvers had considerably slowed down the pace of the trial. At the end of the day he was told he wouldn't be called to testify until the following week.

Mark dragged himself into his office and spotted the blinking message light on his office phone. He had eleven messages. Kit's message was the second one in the message queue. Mark called the hospital but due to patient confidentially they would not discuss Kit's status. Mark then called Doug who relayed that he, too, had been left a similar message from Kit. He also had tried unsuccessfully to get an update on Kit's condition. Mark suggested Doug try and reach out to the woman who was looking after Kit's mother. Perhaps Kit had arranged for his mother to receive an update.

Twenty minutes later Mark's phone rang. It was Doug. He had reached the woman looking after Kit's mother. She confirmed Kit's mom had received a call from the hospital regarding Kit's status. It seems Kit had come out of surgery sometime in the mid-afternoon. He was being transferred to ICU where he would remain for at least the next 24 hours. This is all that they were told.

Mark thanked Doug and then hung up.

He checked the rest of his messages. There was one from Bruce Wyte, Alice's intern who reported he hoped to have wrapped up his efforts to cull the list of CDLA licensed driver's by tomorrow afternoon. He was filtering the list to identify only those who have been unmarried for the past thirty years and those who are presently unmarried. He reported he had found a way to filter the data with a merge and sort bridge integrated with marriage records maintained by Maine, New Hampshire and Vermont. The intern was proving to be an increasingly valuable asset to their work.

The research and analysis side of police work was always tedious and more often than not took longer than he expected. Waiting was all he could do.

The last message left for him was from Lieutenant Peter Burlingame from the Judge Ambrose Task Force.

The message was brief and urgent, "Hi, this is Pete Burlingame. Call me as soon as you get this."

What could he want? thought Mark.

Mark used his cell phone and dialed up Pete.

When Pete answered the phone he immediately told Mark, "I'll call you right back in a couple of minutes."

Moments later Mark's phone rang and he picked it up on the first ring.

"Hello."

"Mark, it's me, Pete. Sorry about putting you off. I was in a meeting and I couldn't talk. Listen, I have some news. The FBI was brought in on the Ambrose case and the US Attorney is also now working the case. They took control of the case earlier today. They are pushing hard and are working fast. They believe they have a suspect. A guy named Deshaun Washington. His street name is "BooBoo." Years ago he was a low level dealer in illegal substances. He quickly moved up the criminal food chain until Judge Ambrose sent him away for 6 to 10. He's been out for the past few months and has been bragging he would even the score with our good Judge. The Feds think he figures this would up his street "creds." Now a CI is telling our people BooBoo has admitted he did the deed. Right now he is under surveillance while the search warrants are being processed. I thought you would want to know."

"Thanks Pete. Keep me posted. I doubt he's your man, but you never know! Good luck with the bust."

"Yeah, I'll pass along what I can!"

The call ended.

Mark felt certain the Ambrose Task Force was wasting their time. Only time will tell.

Mark was tired and decided to call it a day. He called up his girlfriend and asked her if she would be up for a drive. She agreed but asked where they would be going.

"I don't know right now, but I'll think of something."

He would pick her up at 6:30 at her place.

Chapter 30
Outside of Kon Tho
Region IV, South Vietnam
Early April, 1972

Just a little over ten "clicks" northwest of Kon Tho was the small village of Pu Wha. It was a tiny village of around eighty to ninety people. The villagers were farmers who grew rice along with a couple of other basic food staples. They were barely able to get by. The war between North and South Vietnam had taken a heavy toll on people. All the young boys had been either dragged away at gun point by raiders working for the North Vietnamese Army, or by the forces of the South Vietnam Army. The population of the village had devolved to consist of elderly men and women, a handful of disabled young men who had managed to escape conscription and numerous young mothers with children.

Situated in the Mekong River Delta area meant the villagers were caught in a deadly crossfire between Communist North Vietnam forces and the allies of South Vietnam.

The North Vietnam Spring offensive had begun ten days before. Just north of Pu Wha a large, heavily-armed division of the North Vietnamese Army or NVA was sweeping southward. Thus, far opposing forces had not yet mounted a counteroffensive. The tiny village was in the direct path of the southward advancing NVA forces. They would reach the village in less than two days' time.

Several allied squads were air dropped by helicopter into the area. The allied forces were from New Zealand, Australia and the United States.

Their mission was to sweep the area ahead of the advancing NVA forces and deny the NVA safe cover and support by all locals. The orders were to move the locals out of the area to "temporary" refugee camps. Their villages and any resources such as cattle, or food were to be destroyed thus denying the enemy a comfortable environment. Once the area was cleared it was going to be blanket bombed with Napalm to defoliate the jungle and expose the NVA. This was the "hold and crush" strategy developed by the Joint Force commanders in Region IV operating under US military command.

Stanley Bolinski had been sloshing through the jungle for the past two days without any sleep. His squad of eight men was split up into two fire teams. The squad was led by an NCO Sergeant from San Diego by the name of William "Willy" Tanner. He was a battle-hardened veteran who had already done two tours in 'Nam. He was tough and respected by the men in his squad. Even Stanley gave the man his due.

It was approaching nightfall. The squad was less than a kilometer away from the village of Pu Wha.

Sergeant Tanner circled up his men. They squatted down in deep, dense jungle cover. The men were on edge. Their eyes were darting in many directions and their ears were on high alert. Stanley and another man kept their backs to the rest of the squad as they kept a watch on the perimeter to their position. They were able to listen to Tanner from this position.

Tanner spoke in a low whisper, "We will break into our separate fire squads from here. Bolinski will take his team and sweep in from the right and my team will move in from the left. We will move in at 0200 hours. We want to round up everyone and explain to their elders helicopters will be arriving at 0530 to ferry them out. No one is to be left behind. No matter how much they protest, they must leave. Be alert for any harbored NVA forces and extra careful about booby traps. Don't touch anything unusual or out of place. These bastards can turn damn near anything into a bomb."

"What if we get any resistance, you know, what if they fire on us?" asked a rookie soldier from Delaware.

"We shoot to kill but let's keep the shooting to hot targets only. Is that clear?"

The men nodded, but Stanley didn't.

He had seen it before. The fucking rules of engagement always wanted to spare the civilians. As far as Stanley was concerned, it was the civilians who were the problem. If they weren't getting in the way, they were busy switching sides on a daily basis. The enemy moved about the civilian population dressed as civilians by day and soldiers by night. What's a soldier to do when you can't tell who the "frinkin" enemy was? Stanley had long ago come to the conclusion the best thing for this damn country was to nuke it.

Naturally it was hot and humid. Stanley's clothes clung to his body like a second skin. Sweat poured off him. His grease camouflage paint felt slick. His palms were sweaty. He drank from his canteen carefully. He had the usual quinine pills so he could drink ground water they came across but Stanley knew it would just be a matter of time before his body would be racked with cramps and diarrhea from drinking bad water. Water in Nam had the reputation of being the worst, stinking, polluted water anyone ever encountered.

Stanley gave a silent hand signal and moved his fire team out to set up their entry positions. The Sergeant did likewise with his men.

The jungle was a cacophony of sounds. Tree frogs were noisily calling out into the deepening night. Birds made small noises. An occasional monkey cried out. From somewhere in the distance a low throaty rumble was heard, most likely made by a water buffalo. The soldiers moved as stealthily as possible into positions around the village and waited.

At precisely 0200 Stanley gave a hand signal and his men slowly moved forward into the village. The village was completely silent. On the other side of the village the other fire team encountered a dog which began to bark.

There were several small fires in fire pits which were close to being completely burned down. Numerous huts were arrayed in small clusters.

Orders were now shouted in Vietnamese to wake up and assemble in the center of the village. Soon, a small flood of sleepy eyed villagers exited their huts and moved towards the village center next to a small well. The Sergeant asked one of the elders who was in charge of the village. The frail man pointed at another equally frail man. The Sergeant was somewhat fluent in Vietnamese. He asked if the village harbored any NVA. The man shook his head no. He asked the man if the village had any weapons. The man's eyes flickered before he answered. Once again he shook his head no. The Sergeant knew he was lying by the hesitation and eye movement. He got right up in the man's face and spoke very quietly for a moment. The old man bowed his head and shook it affirmatively. He then spoke in the high sing-song voice of his people and pointed to a nearby hut.

The Sergeant had two of his squad take one of the other old men over to the hut. They had him enter first. They then followed him inside. Moments later the men returned with a small, long wooden bamboo box. The old man walked in front of them. The box was put down and when opened revealed its contents. It contained three, old, French made rifles that were not in working condition.

While the Sergeant was engaged in a short conversation with the village elder Stan was eyeing the villagers. His evil partner was at his side. The ink-black shape leaned into Stan and whispered into his left ear.

"Something doesn't feel right about this place. Your Sergeant is doing too much talking. These people have always supported the NVA. Their damns kids even joined the NVA and are now killing your brothers-in-arms. They're just scum, Stan, just scum. I say waste them all!"

Stan was half-listening, he was more into watching the villagers. One very old woman was nervously watching Stanley. Her eyes were locked onto Stanley. Her face revealed the woman was puzzling over something about Stanley which had her full attention.

Suddenly she started wailing in a high sing-song voice. She started to push her way towards the village elder. She was wagging one finger and pointing at Stanley.

Stan watched her movement but something else caught his attention. Soon after the woman began to act out, a young boy around eight years old began to separate from the other villagers.

His mother tried to whisper to him to come back but the boy wasn't having anything to do with her increasingly urgent whispers. His eyes were wide. One of the other squad members also noticed the boy trying to pull away from the others. He sternly gestured for the boy to get back in the group.

The boy now bolted.

The other squad member chased after the boy who soon disappeared around a hut with the US soldier in close pursuit.

Meanwhile, the old woman's rant was only getting louder and more accusatory. She was now screaming as she fell to the ground at the foot of the village elder.

A single shot loudly rang out.

All the villagers and remaining squad members turned their attention in the direction of the hut the young boy and soldier just ran behind.

Suddenly, in the soft and shifting light of one of the remaining fire pit fires appeared the soldier. He walked backwards three steps before he collapsed, dead.

Without waiting for a command Stanley lifted his assault rifle and began opening fire on the villagers. This caused his squad mates to reflexively do the same. The Sergeant was about to command the men to cease fire when in the ongoing clatter of rifle fire, a single round from Stanley's rifle penetrated his forehead and exploded out the back of his head. He died immediately. Villagers tried to run, to get away, but the squad was relentless. Inside of one minute nearly all of the villagers were dead or dying. A few villagers had thrown themselves to the ground covering their heads as they wailed for mercy.

Stanley wasn't having any off it. He pulled out his sidearm and shot several crouching survivors in the head. The smell of gun fire and death hung in a haze over the village. The only survivor to this carnage was the lone young boy who had first run. His attempted escape was a cover for an effort to reach a hidden cache of weapons. He had managed to successfully turn one of the weapons on the squad member who was chasing him, killing him. The boy didn't wait around to witness the fallout of his efforts. He melted into the jungle hurriedly running northward to meet up with approaching NVA forces.

Stanley broke the silence. "It was them or us. You all saw what happened to Jimmy over there," said Stanley as he pointed at the dead body of his squad member. "These little bastards would have picked us all off one-by-one if they could manage to reach their weapons. Now that gook boy is hot tailing to his NVA buddies to bring down their special pain on us. We have to get out of here pronto. I say we set fire to the huts and get the hell out. We can radio for an extraction once we move south of here. We had better place some separation between our asses and those NVA bastards or they will be pissing on our bodies before the sun is high!"

It sounded to the other squad members Stanley was assuming command and no one objected. What he said made sense to them. They could see their Sergeant was dead. No one had seen Stanley fire the shot which killed him. The other squad members couldn't be sure one of them might have accidentally delivered the fatal shot during the heavy fire they each had delivered in close quarters at the center of the village. For all they knew it could be the shot was fired by the same person who shot Jimmy.

Resigned to follow Stanley's direction the men broke up and began to set fire to the huts. One of the men even shot the dog which had first barked at them when they entered the village.

Less than ten minutes later, with the burning village at their backs, the remaining members of the squad melted into the dark jungle.

They brought the Sergeant's and Jimmy's bodies with them taking turns carrying the dead men. Thirty minutes later they radioed a report they had come under fire from the villagers and had to returned fire. They also reported there were heavy casualties on the ground which was a euphemism for dead civilians. They cancelled the civilian extraction and instead arranged their own for mid-day extraction at landing zone Z-14.

Chapter 31
Forward Base Zulu
Region IV, South Vietnam
Early April, 1972

Army Chaplain, Father Daniel G. Linwood was walking through forward base Zulu in Region IV of the Mekong Delta. He had asked to be sent to this forward staging base. From here Army Ranger squads were being dispatched into the jungle in an effort to slow down the advance of several North Vietnam Divisions pressing into the South as part of their surprise "Spring Offensive."

A counter attack was being assembled elsewhere, but it was at least another two days before the allied forces would be ready. Meanwhile, the NVA was making deep and successful incursions into South Vietnam seemingly attacking from several directions at once.

Father Woody was recognized by all. He stopped and talked quietly with everyone he met. He slapped a few on the back and shared a laugh with others.

Nearby, a couple of helicopters landed at the edge of the camp. Father Woody headed over to see who was arriving.

He spotted two men rushing to one of the helicopters. He soon saw they were carrying a body on a stretcher. Another stretcher team arrived and off-loaded another body. Two other men exited the same helicopter while another four men were now exiting the second chopper.

Woody recognized one of the men, it was Stanley Bolinski. He went straight to the first stretcher. He knew the dead man. He had known the Sergeant who was a stern, but effective man who was thinking of becoming a teacher after his current tour of duty was over.

Woody said a brief prayer over the Sergeant's body. He would revisit the body later for more prayer and blessings. He did the same for the other body. He didn't recognize the young soldier. He reached for the dead soldier's dog tags and read the name. James D. Carlisle. He said a silent prayer for young Carlisle. In war, chaplains always keep their focus on the living. This approach was necessary to steady the young chaplains so they could carry on their work. He went to each arriving man and without making any forgone judgment he offered his blessing and a warm greeting. There would be time to hear their stories later.

Working up his courage Woody approached Bolinski. When he reached Stanley no greetings were exchanged. The two men walked on in silence for a short while.

"Stan, if you need to talk about what happened out there you can come to me." The priest was still trying to reach Stanley even though deep down he knew what Stanley was. More importantly, he knew Stanley traveled and harbored a dark and evil partner.

"Don't waste your time, Padre. I'm not interested."

The priest stopped walking alongside of Stanley. His eye caught something unusual. Stanley had two shadows on the ground. One was clearly his and caused by the afternoon sun. The other shadow was much, much bigger. This shadow had its arm around Stanley's ordinary everyday shadow. It was leaning in seemingly having a chat with Stan's shadow. Once more Father Woody was seeing pure evil in the presence of Stanley.

Within days Father Linwood had learned through the confessional what had happened in the Pu Wha. The dark secret tore at his conscience and his very soul. His faith required him to extend God's forgiveness to the men who had been on that ill-fated mission. However, these men would be carrying a haunting burden with them for the rest of their lives.

Stanley Bolinski was the exception. He didn't use the Act of Confession to heal his soul. He seemed unfazed by what had transpired. In fact, he seemed buoyed by the experience. He was already clamoring for another assignment.

Father Linwood felt the need to do something about Stanley and his evil partner. But what could he do? He feared confronting Stanley head on. The extent of the power of the evilness which surrounded him was unknown. Woody Linwood decided to reach out to the second in command at Delta Base, which was the command and control center for this forward base of operation. He arranged for a ride on a supply helicopter back to Delta base. He was going to have a private chat with Army Ranger, Colonel Daniel G. Liddy.

Chapter 32
Forward Base Delta
Region IV, South Vietnam
April, 1972

Father Woody stepped off the supply helicopter and was immediately escorted to the command barracks. He sat down and waited in the outer area of the Commander's Office.

Nearly an hour later, Colonel Liddy came through the door with his right hand extended. He had a warm smile on his face and moved quickly to shake the hand of his good friend, Chaplain Woody.

The base commander was away at a briefing and Colonel Liddy was the Commander of the day.

He enthusiastically pumped Woody's hand. "Good to see you, Woody. Yessir, real good," said the Colonel, continuing he said, "C'mon in!

The two men walked into the small, sparsely-decorated office. Everything in the office was colored some variation of Army green. The Chaplain took a seat and the Colonel sat behind the metal desk. His swivel chair creaked as he sat down.

"Do you want something to drink? I have some cold cola available. I could even rustle up a beer if you want one."

"No thanks, Colonel."

"So what brings you here? I know you have been up at Zulu. The dailies I've seen tell me the boys are doing a bang up job of sweeping the area. We're nearly ready to launch our counterattack. The NVA is going to get their butts hit and hit hard, I promise you that."

Woody leaned in towards the desk. He looked around and then spoke in a hushed tone.

"Colonel, you have a problem at Zulu that isn't being reported in your daily action reports. There is this one soldier that's, ah, that's a serious problem."

Now it was the colonel's turn to lean closer. He dragged his chair up close to the desk and set his elbows on the desk as he leaned forward. All joviality disappeared from his face and voice.

"Talk to me," said the Colonel.

For the next several minutes the two men talked in a whisper.

Woody ran his fingers through his hair and said, "Frankly, the man scares the shit out of me. I know it's a bad time to bring this to you. You and I both know what the newspapers would do with this. I have tried to get the others to speak up but they won't turn their back on a fellow soldier. Some consider him a hero for God's sake. Colonel, this man is as close to pure evil as I have ever seen and believe me, I've seen a lot. Surely there's a way to remove him. I'm praying you will help me stop this man."

The Colonel leaned back in his creaky chair.

Nothing was said for over a minute.

Finally the Colonel spoke.

"I have seen his personnel file but from what I know of him he has a reputation as a fearless fighter. By all accounts he's a soldier's soldier. I can't wreck a man's career on your opinions, no offense, Woody. I would need hard evidence before the Army would consider putting an active duty soldier up on charges, especially when we're in the middle of this damn war."

"Please Colonel, I beg you."

"Sorry, Woody. Bring me some hard evidence. Bring me a couple of witnesses. I promise you then something could be done. I appreciate you taking the time to come in and bring this to my attention. I promise you I will keep an eye on this soldier and if I so much as smell anything wrong I will come down hard on him. Count on it."

The Colonel rose signaling that the meeting was over. He extended his hand. Woody accepted it and shook it with little effort. Woody was clearly disappointed. The Army had helped create a highly effective killing machine, they were all in the middle of a war zone, and the war could go either way. The last thing the military needed right now was the distraction of an investigation or trial of one of its own. It would affect morale.

Woody felt helpless and defeated.

He caught a return flight to forward camp Zulu just as dusk was settling in over the steamy Mekong region.

Woody prayed that night for an answer. His prayers were not answered that night.

Chapter 33
Hampton Beach
Hampton, New Hampshire
Early Evening, August 7

It was a warm night. The tide was heading out and it was a quarter to eight in the evening. The beach was crowded with vacationers walking the long sandy beach. In the East, the cloudless sky was just turning a deep purple color. A lone star twinkled in the transitioning sky.

Mark and his girlfriend, Marcy, walked in the tidal wave in their bare feet. They carried their shoes in one hand and held hands with the other. They had stopped along the boardwalk before and had an ice cream. Neither had much of an appetite for a regular meal and so the ice cream worked just fine.

They exchanged small talk about their work and mutual friends.

They soon ran out of things to talk about. Marcy knew Mark was wrapped up in a huge case and he wasn't particularly sharing of late, so she gave him his space.

His cell phone vibrated in his pants pocket. He pulled it out and looked at the caller ID. He was about to slip the phone back into his pocket when Marcy spoke up, "It's okay, take the call. I'm sure it is important."

Her eyes said much more. She understood and knew the burden he carried and she accepted she had to share his attention.

He released his hold on her hand and stepped quickly to the dry edge of the beach. He dropped his shoes down just as he swiped the phone and selected redial.

"Hello. Yeah. So what happened? You have got to be joking. Is that right? So what now? That's just incredible! Yeah, let's meet tomorrow. I'll give you a call in the morning and we can set something up. That might work. Okay, yeah, I will. Bye." Mark tapped his cell phone ending the call. He dropped it into his pocket.

Marcy didn't ask about the call. She waited for some kind of cue from Mark as to what his mood was going to be like, the call didn't sound like good news.

Mark picked up his shoes and took her hand once again. They walked in silence for several minutes. Reaching the southern end of the beach they turned around and began the long, slow walk back up the beach. The sky was now nearly completely dark and filled with twinkling stars and a crescent moon. The sound of music drifted down to the beach from the nearby boardwalk. The beach was still populated with many walkers but the numbers had dwindled considerably.

"That call I took earlier was from a fellow officer with the Manchester PD. He's serving on the Judge Ambrose Task Force. He and I have talking lately, you know comparing notes."

"And?" responded Marcy, hoping her response would illicit more conversation.

"It seems the Task Force caught a lead on the case and had a suspect lined up. They were planning on arresting the guy tonight. They had search warrants. They also had a SWAT Team along to bring him in for questioning."

Another brief pause.

"What happened?"

The guy must have spotted something because he had time to barricade his place. Shots were fired. The SWAT guys busted in and found the guy had shot himself in the head. He died on the way to the hospital!"

"So was he the guy, you know, was he the one who killed the Judge?"

"I really don't think so."

"That's not good is it?"

"Yeah, you can say that again."

They finished their walk without talking any further.

Marcy could tell Mark wanted and needed to sort things out. She had fallen deeply in love with this complicated man. She would wait and be ready for him, for when he needed someone to love.

Chapter 34
Manchester, New Hampshire
Headquarters of East Coast Trucking
August 8

Stanley headed through the front door of East Coast Trucking. He gave a wave to the receptionist and moved past her to his office. As the company's Route Director, he was responsible for all delivery assignments. He had risen through the ranks. He had accepted this RA Director job back in 2002. One of the reasons he took this job was strategic to him. He could, on occasion, still jump in and take a haul himself. He served as the ultimate back-up driver. He had taken four or five day trips to make routine deliveries in Northern New England during the past year alone. On those occasions he often used the opportunity to dump evidence of his crimes.

Whenever he was out on the road, Dennis Morton, another employee in the office would handle any assignment issues which might arise. Stanley routinely declined his vacation time. He loved trucking and hated being away from it. Eventually, Stanley pushed for an employee's leave bank. Employees were encouraged to donate a certain amount of unused sick or vacation time to a leave bank. This would allow employees facing a sudden need for extra time off due to illness to have a resource to help them out. In 1997 Stanley was recognized as the "Employee of the Year" for this idea. His motive in pushing for the leave bank wasn't altruistic. He simply was annoyed by the Personnel Office badgering him about his unused vacation and sick time. It seemed the company frowned upon an employee accumulating too much of either.

Stanley now closed the door to his office and immediately turned on the small radio he kept here. He had it dialed into the local news station.

Unlocking the right side desk drawer to his desk, he removed a can of special blended coffee he enjoyed. He measured the correct amount out and set it in the one-serve container for the brew machine located just across from his office in the break room. He grabbed his favorite mug and headed off to the break room to brew himself a cup of coffee.

Dennis Morton was in the break room mixing his own cup of coffee.

"Morning Stan - how are you doing?"

"Okay, Dennis, how about you?"

"So-so. My arthritis is really bothering me right now. It sure sucks getting old."

"Yeah, I hear you," responded Stanley as he set his one-serve-container in the brewing machine.

Once the coffee had finished dripping, Stanley removed the serve-one container and dumped the coffee grounds in the adjacent trash can. He poured in creamer from the refrigerator along with a small amount of sugar.

As he stood there stirring his coffee Dennis spoke once more.

"Say Stan, my birthday is near yours, right?"

Stanley nodded.

"Anyway, I received my notice to get a physical for my CDLA license. I'm thinking of giving it up, seeing as I haven't driven in nearly three years. I doubt I'll drive again. Frankly, I am not sure I can pass the physical. What do you think?"

"It's your life. Do what you want, just don't let someone else make the call for you, is all I can say."

Dennis was about to say something else when Stanley turned his back on him and returned to his office.

Stanley closed the door once more. He sat down and began to open his snail mail. The second item in his mail was a notice from the New Hampshire Department of Motor Vehicles. It seems Stanley was also being tagged for his biannual physical in order to maintain his CDLA license. He needed to produce for

NH DMV evidence of a valid physical taken on or within sixty days before September 30th.

Stanley noticed the envelope included the latest notice on the need for the physical as well as highlights to any changes to his health since 2013. The notice provided instructions to the doctor or qualified nurse who would complete the physical-taken form. It also required them to sign the notice which must be also brought to NH Motor Vehicles by the operator seeking a CDLA license renewal.

Stanley picked up the phone and called his doctor's office.

Moments later he had his appointment for a physical. As luck would have it they could take him on Monday of next week. He would need to come into the lab for blood tests before the office visit. He was also told to fast beforehand as well as provided the details on how long to fast depending on the time of his appointment.

Stanley made a reminder note to himself about his appointment and stuck it on the cork board next to where he hung his coat.

His office phone began to ring. Caller ID revealed the caller was one of his driver's on a run to New Jersey.

He took the call.

Chapter 35
Manchester, New Hampshire
Red Line Diner
August 8

Mark met with Lieutenant Peter Burlingame for some coffee at the Red Line Diner. It was just a little past 6:00 a.m. Office Burlingame had pulled an all-nighter while working the Judge Ambrose case. He had been in on the raid the previous night to arrest a possible suspect. The suspect had killed himself during the raid.

Pete and other detectives had worked throughout the night searching the suspect's home for evidence which would have linked the man with the Judge's murder. Other than copies of newspapers which carried the story of the Judge's murder nothing of any investigative value was uncovered. The tip leading to the planned arrest had seemed promising. Now, in hindsight, the tip was thin at best.

The Task Force was beginning to exhibit signs of infighting. Leaks to the press and unsubstantiated rumors were becoming an everyday occurrence. Pete felt like a target was painted in his back.

After a brief exchange of greetings the two men sat in silence. Peter didn't drink his coffee. He stared off out the window at the brightening day. He kept stirring and stirring his coffee.

Finally interrupting him Mark said, "Pete, if you don't mind my saying so, you look like shit. You need to get some rest."

Without looking at him Pete responded with a weak, "Yeah!"

After another minute of silence, Pete pushed his untouched coffee cup aside.

"I can't drink any more damn coffee."

"Okay, no coffee. How about some food? Why don't you grab some breakfast?"

"Not hungry."

"So, why did you ask for this meeting?" asked Mark.

Exhaling, the lieutenant replied, "I've been thinking about what we talked about in your office the other day. The judge's case, the tie in with a long time serial killer who may still be on the loose is getting to me. Professionally I know I should be kicking this up the line but it's still too thin. Look what happened last night. That was just as thin. The guy is dead and the AG and FBI are squeezing everything and everyone. It's all one big cluster f......"

Mark held up his hand signaling for Pete to stop as the waitress paused beside their table.

"Can I get you guys anything?" said the middle-aged woman. Her name tag identified her as 'Stella.'

"Nothing for me," said Pete.

"Same here" responded Mark.

"Okay," said the woman who pulled out her order pad. She tore off their order slip and left it on the table between both men.

Mark took the bill.

"What about that profiler you've been working with?" asked Pete.

"Right now he's in the hospital recovering from emergency surgery."

"Shit."

"But I am working with the CCU office in Maine. They're taking the lead on working up a list of long distance truck drivers who would have been actively working northern New England in the time period we are investigating. We are also looking to reduce the list down to those who are now single or who were single for a substantial period doing the time frame. Kit, our profiler, thinks our guy is single. It's not much given what we can extract from our cases and recent events."

"So how soon do you think you'll have the pared down list?"

"I don't know for sure, maybe today, maybe on Monday."

"Then what are you going to do?"

"I don't know yet. I haven't figured out that part."

"Mark, the clock is ticking here. We both need to catch a big break!"

"I know, believe me, I know!"

Chapter 36
Manchester, New Hampshire
Headquarters of East Coast Trucking
August 9

Stanley arrived at work a few minutes later than usual. He had stopped at the Dartmouth-Hitchcock clinic for his scheduled blood work as part of renewing his CDLA truck driver's license. He wanted to get it out of the way early.

The phlebotomist who had extracted his blood was a pretty young woman from some East Asian country. He didn't know which and he didn't care. As far as he was concerned she talked way too much. She also seemed nervous. She couldn't have felt the presence of his buddy, the dark shape. At things like this, his evil partner kept himself well hidden inside of Stanley.

She had trouble getting a good stick in his vein. It took her three tries before she was successful. Stanley had to restrain his partner who wanted to kill her.

Now back inside of his office he closed the shade on his office door so he could have some privacy.

Sitting in his office chair Stanley pulled up his shirt sleeve and ripped off the tape and gauze the phlebotomist had applied earlier. He tossed the items into the trash can across from his desk. He swiveled his chair around and turned on the radio.

He began to listen to the early morning news. His ears piqued up when he caught the story about the man who died from an apparent self-inflicted gunshot wound during a police raid on his home. According to the radio report, the man was supposedly wanted by police in connection with the Judge Ambrose murder.

Stanley started to laugh out loud.

His dark and evil companion separated from Stanley and hovered in the far corner. He too enjoyed the report of the apparent botched police raid as much as Stanley.

The report then went on to say the US Attorney's Office and the FBI would be conducting a press conference later in the day.

"Can you believe it, they're like frickin' keystone cops?" chuckled Stanley.

"*Yeah. You gotta also like the news your former friend, Judge Ambrose's murder, has drawn the attention of the big ass Feds. Ain't that sweeeeeet!*" exclaimed the ink black shape.

"You bet your smoky ass I like it. If they get too close, we can teach them a lesson and maybe tee up ourselves an FBI investigator or maybe the US Attorney. That would make for some hot headlines for sure," said Stanley.

"*Your grandfather would be proud of you.*"

"You think so?"

"*I know so.*"

"I wish I had had a chance to get to know him. I bet he would have had some stories to tell. Too bad my drunk-ass father and bitch of a mother kept me away from him."

"*But you at least hooked up with him anyway. That's all that matters.*"

"You know, you never told me how long you knew my grandfather."

"*I knew him since he was eleven years old.*"

"Did he conjure you up? How did you two meet?"

"*I was passed on to him just as he gave me to you. I was given to him by a woman who lived up the street from his family. She liked little kids. She liked doing things to them. I helped her kill quite a few. She liked your grandfather. She saw potential in him. She taught him all she knew before she died. Your grandfather was the one who killed her.*"

"Damn, I can't believe it."

"*Believe it, partner, believe it.*"

"So I guess the question is, where did it all start for you?"

"*Excellent question, Amigo. Let me tell you, I have been around for a very long time. To shorten it up let me just say;*

in terms of modern times I was first sent to serve Reverend Benjamin Calef in 1691. He lived in Gardiner, in the colony of Massachusetts."

"Sent by whom?"

"Who do you think?"

"Not him?"

"Yeah, him, he's the boss, has been for a very long time, like forever. So, this Reverend conjured me to appear and to help him do his bidding. He thought he was praying to the other side but deep down he really wanted our help. I am very good at what I do so I was sent to him. Together we had a great time leading investigations into witchcraft in and around the Town of Salem. I've got to tell you those Puritans were something else! They were so easy to screw with. It wasn't long before they were holding trials and hanging or drowning suspected witches. The Court of Oyer and Terminus held in Salem was at the center of our work. By the time I left, 19 women were hung, along with one priest. Another 8 were condemned and were scheduled to be drowned. Not too shabby for a couple of years work."

"You've been around since then, wow, that's amazing."

"Actually, as I should of said, I have been around for much longer. That was just the beginning of my latest string of adventures. That's what I call them when I get handed down to others. I like keeping the string going just to see how long it will go."

"So back in Salem you were helping to make history?"

"You could say that."

"Do you think we've made some history?"

"I know we have and we aren't done."

"Damn right!"

Chapter 37
New Hampshire State Police
Cold Case Unit
August 11

Mark was out of his office at a meeting in the Attorney General's Conference Room. He was presenting his findings on a case he had worked for the past year and half. It involved a divorced mother of four who had gone missing back in 1988. Her body was found in a roadside bog off of I-93 in Windham, New Hampshire. The autopsy had determined she had been strangled. Her ex-husband had died the previous year in a motorcycle accident. She was a known drug user and was suspected off helping to transport drugs between Massachusetts and New Hampshire.

Mark had spent a great deal of time on this case and had turned up a witness who confirmed the victim, Sarah Lee Bakker, had gotten into a car with the prime suspect less than three hours before her disappearance. The suspect, a member of a local biker gang, had denied being with her that night. He had an alibi which placed him in Maine at that time. Armed with the new witness' details Mark was able to break the alibi. The woman who had provided the alibi had agreed to recant her previous sworn statement and instead had reported the suspect had threatened her and her children if she didn't agree to give him the alibi.

The case was still too thin for the Deputy Attorney General's comfort but she agreed to reopen the case and assigned her investigators to rework all the evidence.

Mark left the conference room and headed back to his office. Arriving at the state police office, he heard his office phone ringing from the hallway. He ran into his office and picked up the phone.

"Hello."

"Hello, Mark, this is Alice."

"Hi, Alice, have you got anything?"

"Wow, no how are you doing, nice day, how's the weather up your way, you know stuff like that?"

"Alice..!"

"Okay, okay. Bruce has pared down the list to thirty-one individuals. Twenty-five of which have never been married, at least according to the records we could access. Of the twenty-five, twenty-three are still driving and two only drive on occasion since they are mostly doing dispatch duty assigning other truckers to their routes. I sent you and Doug this list of names, addresses and their place of business via email a few moments ago. So what do you want to do next?"

"I want to get Doug on the line with us first. Hold on while I dial him in."

Moments later all three CCU investigators were joined together on the call.

After a short conversation they agreed to take the list and work the names on the list in their respective states. They also decided to work the list of thirty-one individuals who are at present not married, rather than the shorter list of those who were never married. As a result of this decision, Alice had nine names to work on. Doug had seven while Mark had fifteen.

Mark asked his CCU friends to make this a priority and they agreed. They would pull whatever information on these individuals they could get their hands on and then approach them for an interview. The pretense they would use was they were looking to solve an old case and they wanted to talk to truckers who had been around awhile. They would pitch this as seeking out anyone who might have heard something or seen something which could be useful to their investigation. Doug, Alice and Mark agreed to have another conference call on Friday to see how things were progressing unless something broke before then.

After hanging up, Mark called the hospital to speak with Kit. After three rings Kit answered the phone.

"Kit, this is Mark. Are you able to talk with me right now? I could call back later if this isn't a good time."

"I'm fine, Mark. I am glad you called. You actually saved me a call. I'm being discharged. Right now I'm packing up my stuff. They are going to wheel me out of here any minute now."

"So, you're well enough to go home. That must be good news, right?"

"Sort of."

"What do you mean?

"I have recovered enough from the surgery. The doctors think they removed the cancer that had developed in my colon and stomach. But now I have to permanently wear a damn bag to handle my waste. I really hate that. But, I've got no choice. They did another biopsy on my lymph nodes early this morning. They want me back here in a week for some more damn tests. I told them, no more tests. I'll deal with the shitter bag but that's it. I'm not coming back. Whatever happens, happens when it happens. That's just the way it is, you know?"

Pausing, Kit continued, "Sorry to vent on you Mark. I just have been…."

"Holding it in?" said Mark completing Kit's sentence.

"Yeah, that's it, holding it in and that's no pun. Sorry."

"Hey, Kit, there is nothing to be sorry about. If it were me, I would probably have torn the hospital room up by now."

"Believe me, I've thought about it."

"So how are you getting home? I can call Doug, I'm sure he would love to come and get you."

"Thanks, but no thanks. A neighbor friend is already on the way here. So how's the case going?"

"We don't need to talk about that right now."

"Yeah, we do, and you know it, so what have you got?"

Mark hurried through a summary of where things stood with the list Alice and Bruce had developed. Mark described their approach to working the list of names. Mark also mentioned the suicide of a possible suspect during a recent police raid. He noted that the US Attorney's Office and the Boston Regional

FBI Office had taken over the reins of the Judge Ambrose investigation. He also mentioned they were also looking into the murder of three boys outside of a movie theater complex along with the disappearance of three teenage girls who may have been witnesses in connection with the boys' murder investigation.

"That is a whole lot of crap going down all at one."

"So what do you think?"

"I think we all need a miracle."

Chapter 38
Pleasant Cove Retirement Center
Laconia , New Hampshire
August 11

Father Daniel G. Linwood sat in a wheelchair in his room at the Pleasant Cove Retirement Center. The retirement home was only two years old. It had all the latest in amenities. It actually served as a retirement home as well as a rehabilitation center. It was located off of Steele Hill Road on a bluff overlooking Lake Winnipesaukee.

Woody was admitted several weeks ago to the facility. A grateful parishioner had passed away three years ago. The man had unexpectedly bequeathed to Woody a trust fund to be used for his care. At the time, Woody was astounded to learn of such a generous gift. The church generally frowned upon pastors personally benefiting from their assignments, but in this instance, the Diocese had looked into the matter and proclaimed it acceptable.

Woody sat patiently waiting for someone to wheel him down to the community dining room for breakfast. Six months ago Father Woody's diabetes problem took a turn for the worse. Regardless of what he did, what treatment he received, he nonetheless loss both of his feet and his vision.

He was nearly eighty-two years old. His mind was sharp. His other faculties were fine. He was still relatively robust, but now he was crippled to the point of being confined to a wheelchair. Later this week, he was going to meet with his doctor and rehabilitation specialist. He was hoping they could offer him some good news. He had asked them to look into seeing whether he could be outfitted with prosthetic feet. Woody hoped and prayed they would come back with some good news. His blindness was irreversible. For that he would just have to make do.

Woody was a fighter and fighters never quit. He woke up early each and every day and made it a practice to not stay in bed and feel sorry for himself. Today was no exception. One of the staff had helped him into the wheelchair. He had practiced to the point he could handle the bathroom all by himself. He was proud of having mastered this task in near record time. He had also mastered the art of dressing himself.

Part of his morning ritual was to tune in to the morning news on his television as soon as he had completed his morning prayers. He dressed while listening to the news.

Father Woody was especially attentive to the Judge Ambrose murder investigation and now the newest investigations concerning the murder of three teenage boys and the missing three young girls.

Woody was fascinated by crime stories. He enjoyed reading everything he could get his hands on regarding crime and police stories, fiction and non-fiction alike. After serving as an active duty chaplain during the Vietnam War he left New Hampshire and for twelve years lived in Washington, D.C while teaching at Catholic University of America. He taught courses on Ethics and Philosophy. He loved his time in Washington but soon an offer to return to New Hampshire came to him. He was offered the opportunity to become the chaplain at the New Hampshire Men's State Prison in Concord. He accepted the assignment and served in the challenging job for the next thirteen years.

Over time, he came to know not only the prisoners and their families but countless numbers of lawyers, victim's families, prosecutors, investigators, judges and law enforcement types at every level.

As he listened to the morning news and the updates on the investigations his mind drifted back to a time just three years before.

Woody and a parishioner from the Wolfeboro Church of the Assumption where Woody was pastor were pulling into the Interstate rest area alongside I-93 northbound in Hoosksett, New

Hampshire. The parishioner and Woody had gone to Boston for a Saturday afternoon Red Sox baseball game. The parishioner wanted to pick up something in the State Liquor Store and they both needed to use the restroom facilities.

As Woody exited the rest room he nearly bumped into a burly man who was rushing inside.

Reflexively Woody said, "Sorry."

The man didn't acknowledge the priest's apology.

Woody had a powerful feeling of "déjà vous!"

I know that guy, thought the priest.

It was the man's eyes which triggered a deep recollection from somewhere in Father Linwood's past. He felt certain he had known this man.

Woody lingered next to a map kiosk. His patience was rewarded. Moments later the seemingly familiar man exited the bathroom and walked purposely towards a parked 18 wheel tanker truck.

The memory hit Father Linwood in a flash. The man was Stanley Bolinski.

Just seeing Stanley brought back a flood of memories of time back in Vietnam. He couldn't take his eyes off of Stanley. He watched him climb inside the cab of the big rig. Then he watched as Stanley moved through lower gears and slowly drove the truck past the spot where he stood.

Looking up for the last time Father Linwood eyes locked on a dark human-like form sitting in the passenger side of the truck's cab. The shape was ever shifting and dark as coal. From his vantage point Father Linwood could feel the evilness. The evil shape's head seem to turn and look with even blacker eyes in his direction. The truck passed by and headed for the on ramp and I-93 north.

Ever since that day at the rest stop, Woody had been consumed with memories of Stanley and his evil partner. With every murder that hit the news, the priest wondered and pondered the possibility his old nemesis, Stanley Bolinski, and his menacing shadow somehow had a hand in the affair.

He deeply regretted not paying closer attention at the rest stop. He racked his mind trying to remember the name of the trucking firm's name boldly displayed on the side of the big rig.

The memory eluded him.

He also regretted not trying harder to learn where Stanley worked.

Deep down Father Linwood knew the evil killing duo were not just together but were undoubtedly still active.

Could the murder of the Judge be the handiwork of Stanley? What about the three young boys? Killing in numbers was something almost natural to those two. The missing young girls, now that was almost too much to ponder!

I have to tell someone, I have to, thought Father Woody.

Chapter 39
Dartmouth-Hitchcock Clinic
Manchester, New Hampshire
August 12

Stanley was escorted to examination room 16 in the Internal Medicine Department of the Dartmouth-Hitchcock Clinic in Manchester, New Hampshire. The Department was located on the second floor of the busy facility.

He was in a sour mood. His toaster oven had broken this morning. It gave off an ozone type odor before it short-circuited and died.

On the way to the clinic some "asshole" cut him off without using his turn signal while the idiot cut across two lanes to get into the turn lane to take the I-93 southbound entrance at exit 8, just off of Bridge Street.

If Stanley wasn't already late for his physical at the clinic he would have pursued the fool, taken his license plate number and later hunted him down.

Today happened to be the idiot's lucky day, only he never would know it.

At the clinic, Stanley had waited twenty minutes past his appointment time. He was almost ready to boil over when his name was finally called.

As he walked down the hallway to examination room number 16 the nurse mentioned to him his doctor had an emergency and for now his patients were being seen by Physician Assistant, Tamara Sacha.

"Right in here," said the nurse as she gestured to Stanley.

Stanley had not taken the news well. His regular doctor was someone he could barely tolerate but at least they had an understanding when it came to Stanley's physical. Do the minimum and sign the damn forms.

Stanley stomped into the exam room. He went to sit in one of the two small office chairs.

"Mr. Bolinski, before you sit could you please remove your shoes and step on the scale for me.

He did as he was told.

She weighed him and measured his height. "Thank you, you can be seated."

The young nurse's name tag declared her name to be "Trudy." She sat down on a round stool and opened a laptop computer. She clicked keys on the key board and then spun around to look at Stanley.

"How are you feeling today?"

"Why?"

"I have to ask."

"Okay, I'm feeling okay."

"Now let's see, I need to review your meds with you. Are you still taking ....?"

She went down the short list of drugs that Stanley more or less took.

His answers to her questions were short and emotionless.

Deep inside, he was seething. *This is all a big friggin waste of my time,* thought Stanley.

His evil partner had accompanied him to the exam room. The shape leaned against the wall in the corner of the room where the patient usually sat.

Nurse Trudy felt a cold chill and shuddered. She rubbed her arms up and down.

The evil shape moved and now hovered over her shoulder peering at the computer screen.

The nurse next took Stanley's temperature, pulse and blood pressure.

She entered the data into the computer. The young nurse closed her laptop and stood up.

"The Physician's Assistant, Ms. Sacha will be with you a

few minutes," said the nurse as she made a beeline for the door.

"Do I have to sit on the table or change out of my clothes?" asked Stanley. I usually have to do that for my regular doctor."

"That won't be necessary today."

She exited the room leaving Stanley and his unseen evil companion behind.

"I don't like this" said Stanley.

"Something's up, Stan, I can feel it, can't you?"

Just then there was a gentle knock on the exam door as Ms. Sacha entered the room.

The young Physician's Assistant also carried a laptop computer. She set it down on the small table next to the round stool and turned to Stanley.

"Good morning, Mr. Bolinsky," she said as she extended her hand to shake his hand.

He shook her outstretched hand.

She could sense he was irritated.

"Sorry about the mix up today. Your doctor is delayed in surgery. We're all helping out this morning. Now, I see you are in for a CDLA Physical."

"Yeah, that's right."

"You drive trucks for a living?"

"That's what the CDLA is for," said Stanley. "I mostly assign routes now, only once in a while, I have to take a job myself."

The bitch is clueless, thought Stanley.

"Most are, my man," responded his evil shadow.

"Mr. Bolinski, I have been reviewing your blood work and your records. It's been nearly two years since your last physical. Have you felt light headed lately? "

"No!"

"Have you felt any tingling in your legs or feet?"

"No, so what's this about?"

"Could you sit up on the table? Also, please take off your socks? He did as he was told.

The PA took a look at his feet especially the bottom of his feet. She poked his feet and asked him if he could feel her touching various points.

"You can put your socks and shoes back on."

Stanley did so and sat back down in the small chair once again.

"Mr. Bolinkski, it seems from your blood work you are now a Type II diabetic. Please know that this is a perfectly manageable condition. Conversely, if left untreated or unmanaged it can lead to many serious problems. I am going to prescribe a drug for you to help you manage the early phase of this disease. I'm going to put you on Metformin which will help you stabilize your blood sugar levels. I want you to also meet with our Diabetic Counselors and with a Nutritionist as well. I'll also write you an order for a blood meter and testing strips. Your regular physician will want to see you in another three months and you will need to have another blood work up scheduled before that.

"Before you leave, I want to give you some pamphlets on Type II Diabetes. The material should help answer any questions you may have."

Stanley sat there in stunned silence as the PA's words cascaded coldly over him.

Finally Stanley said, "What about my CDLA license?"

"I have made a note on your application regarding your diabetes."

Regaining his focus he said, "Did you sign it?"

"Yes, I did, but from what I understand the State will not extend your license once you have diabetes. The risks are too great."

"What damn risks? You mean I'll lose my license. Is that it?"

"Please, Mr. Bolinski. Please try to remain calm. You need to focus on your health right now. The State Motor Vehicle Officials will explain things to you if you wish. It is their rules. We only conduct physicals and report results to the State. I am sorry. Let me get you the pamphlets and the prescriptions. I will be right back."

She grabbed her laptop computer and hurried from the exam room.

Stanley's evil partner leaned close to Stanley and said, "*You just got stomped my man. This is a major screw job if I ever heard one.*"

"**Shut up,**" shouted Stanley just as Ms. Sacha returned.

She was startled by Stanley's outburst.

"Here, uh, here are the pamphlets and the prescriptions. Please stop at the check out desk on your way out to schedule your follow up appointments."

Stanley's chest was heaving. He was really worked up. She could plainly see his rage was still building. Rather than saying anything further she elected to leave.

She placed the paperwork on the exam table and left the room.

Stanley stood up and began to pace the small room. Suddenly he turned and grabbed the pamphlets and shredded them. He threw the torn papers all around the room.

He stuffed the prescriptions into his pants pocket. He stuffed the CDLA paperwork into his opposite pants pocket. He then flung open the exam room door and stormed out of the exam area. Staff who had heard his angry profane outburst stared at him as he rushed past them on his way out of the clinic.

He never stopped at the check-out counter before leaving.

Chapter 40
New Hampshire State Police
Cold Case Unit
August 13

Mark was spending the morning working his list of unmarried, long-distance truck drivers. The review of the married drivers offered no probables as far as he was concerned. For the past two days he had pulled the driving records of all of the New Hampshire driver's on his list. Nothing on the list jumped out at him. For the fifteen drivers on his list he turned up the usual speeding tickets, overweight citations, faulty equipment citations and two DUI's.

Next he did a Lexus-Nexus search for any interstate violations as well as any criminal or civil legal actions involving the drivers. Three of the drivers had once filed for bankruptcy. Other than that there was nothing of any significance which emerged from the search.

His efforts were going nowhere.

He did a credit search and found that eight of the drivers were heavily over using their credit cards. Thus far, Mark was frustrated with the fruits of his efforts.

He decided to move to the next phase of his investigation. He would make appointments to meet each and every driver. He would conduct only preliminary interviews at this point.

He picked up the phone and began to call each of the drivers to make arrangements. He decided to put the two drivers who only infrequently drove at the bottom of his interview list. He had noted one of these men was a route supervisor while the other was a substitute driver. He considered them both as low risks.

It took the rest of the day to finally connect with the thirteen currently active drivers. Things had gone smoother than expected. He had been able to make arrangements to interview all thirteen of the active drivers.

He grabbed his coat and headed out the door. He was going to meet up with the first of the drivers at a local diner at 4:00 p.m.

He arrived at the diner a few minutes late for the interview.

He entered the diner located on Airport Road in Concord. The place was brightly lit and noisy. The sounds of dishes clashing along with utensils falling on the tiled floor were only overpowered by the cacophony of voices filling the aromatic air,

Mark looked around the diner and then spotted an older man sitting off to the end of the diner's lunch counter.

He walked over to the man who was wearing a dark grey jacket and matching baseball cap emblazoned with a trucking company name. The company name was simply "Orton."

"Hi, are you Sam Turtuo?"

"Yeah, you that investigator?"

"Yup! I'm the guy who called you. My name is Mark Atkinson," said Mark as he extended his hand. The man shook his hand and then turned his attention back to his coffee mug and half-eaten piece of pie.

"Do you mind if I sit down?" said Mark as he gestured to the empty counter seat next to the man.

"Suit yourself."

Mark slid into the seat. He deliberately didn't bring any notes or even a notepad. He didn't want these preliminary interviews to be seen as threatening.

"Thanks for agreeing to meet me on such short notice; I appreciate it very much."

"Ayuh!"

"So I hear you have been doing big rig driving for a long time. I expect you've driven all over New England."

"Could have."

The man eyed Mark out of the corner of his eye while he took a bite of the piece of pie. He slowly chewed the piece of pie and then asked, "Where did you say you work?"

"I work at the New Hampshire Cold Case Unit out of State Police Headquarters."

Turning in his seat the man stared directly into Mark's eyes. He was taking the measure of Mark.

"So why are you chatting me up?"

"It seems you're someone who doesn't like to have his time wasted so I'll come straight to the reason I called you asking to meet."

"Don't bullshit me mister. I'm not concerned about wasting time. If I thought you were wasting my time I would leave you sitting here on your sorry ass all by your lonesome. No sir, what I want to know is why me? You think I did something? Is that it?"

Mark had to be careful with this guy. He was sharp and deeply suspicious.

"I'll be honest with you. I need your help. I will be talking to several other drivers over the next few days. In my job I try to solve unsolved murder and missing person cases. The victims' families deserve an answer. I try to get that for them as well as find justice for the victims. I have a huge backlog of cases I'm working with colleagues in Maine and Vermont. We have a theory some of the cases may be connected. These cases seem to be close to major roadways. Naturally we want to look at the possibility of long distance truck drivers since they would be driving along these routes. I'm hoping that since you have been a driver for many years maybe you saw something or heard something which maybe didn't feel right to you! You know, something which didn't fit."

Sam Turtuo silently eyed Mark. His hazel-colored eyes searched Mark's face.

Sam turned in his seat and took a sip of his coffee.

A waitress approached Mark and he ordered a decaf coffee.

"Well?" inquired Mark.

"Well, what?"

"Have you seen anything that looked wrong to you?"

"Are you asking me to rat on other truckers?"

"Look, Sam, I need help. I'm looking at everything I can. That's my job."

Sam finished his piece of pie. He turned in his seat and once again faced Mark.

"I have seen a lot over the years, guys drinking, drugs, women and cheating on their log books. I ain't going to rat on anyone just because you ask. Unless you got something specific you want to know you're just blowing smoke. This feels like you're fishing and I ain't biting."

Sam stood up and threw some money on the counter. He picked up his check and headed to the cashier.

Mark watched the man leave.

That didn't go very well, thought Mark. He reached into his pocket and removed a plastic bag and carefully put Sam's coffee mug inside of it. Mark would later drop it off at the state police lab for DNA testing and prints. Mark paid for his coffee and for the mug he was taking.

Chapter 41
Dartmouth-Hitchcock Clinic
Manchester, New Hampshire
August 14

Physician Assistant, Tamara Sacha, hurried out the side door located on the North side of the Dartmouth-Hitchcock Clinic. It was nearly 6:30 p.m. and she was already late for dinner. Today had been an exceptionally long day for her.

Her day had not started off well. The first patient of the day was a refugee from the Sudan who couldn't speak English. The patient, a young mother, had brought her three young children into the examination room with her. The children were between the ages of three and six years old. They too were not conversant in English. The youngest child cried constantly while the other two children clung nervously to their mother.

The patient held several papers in her hand and thrust these at PA Sacha. The papers seemed to indicate the woman and her children had arrived in New Hampshire eight days ago. Among the papers were one which listed the name of an assigned mentor and translator. PA Sacha used her cell phone to call the person whose name was on the piece of paper.

After three rings a woman's voice came on the phone and the PA introduced herself and the reason for her call. The person on the other end of the call could barely speak English herself. After a while the woman asked to have the phone handed over to the woman patient. The patient listened for a moment and then broke into a rapid fire conversation. Suddenly, she handed the phone back to PA Sacha.

The mentor who doubled as a translator then explained the patient had felt ill during the night. Another guest of the host family, a fellow refugee, a Sudanese woman, had told her she needed to see a doctor right away. She told her to take a cab to the clinic. The other Sudanese woman had also been treated at the clinic a few weeks earlier and had kept a business card with the address which was given to the cab driver. Somehow money was obtained to drive the woman and her children to the clinic.

With all this history and with enormous language challenges she was able to somehow pass through the registration desk and ended up being Sacha's first patient of the day.

Eventually by passing the cell phone back and forth between the patient, her mentor and translator, and PA Sacha, an examination was completed. It seemed the patient had a painful and swollen area in her upper left pelvis area. The area was abnormally hard and was inflamed. More tests would need to be done. PA Sacha made plans for the tests and for the translator to be available. The tests were going to take place later in the day. The nervous patient needed to get back to the sponsor's home and so PA Sacha paid for a cab ride out of her own pocket.

The entire episode of dealing with this first patient had set back the day by nearly forty minutes. It only got worse as the day progressed.

As she rushed out of the clinic building to the employee parking area, she dropped a bundle of papers she was carrying. She had to bend down to pick up the papers before they scattered about.

Sitting in a small compact car at the end of the parking lot was a lone figure. The occupant of the car was a man, none other than Stanley Bolinski. He watched PA Sacha pick up the papers. His face was unrevealing.

His eyes moved slowly while he focused upon her movement. His eyes continued to follow her as she proceeded to her car. He started up his own car and slowly backed out of his parking spot before he cruised slowly down the row. He passed behind her car and proceeded to the end of the row. There he paused. He looked back in his rearview mirror as her car backed out of the parking space. She turned her car in the opposite direction.

Stanley now hurried his car forward in order to drive around the building. He drove around the perimeter road to the clinic's many other parking lots. In a moment he came to the intersection which exited the clinic property. He spotted her car turning out of the parking area and heading down the exit road. He pulled in behind her car and followed her all the way to her home.

He already knew where she lived. He had followed her home every day since she had told him during his physical he had Type II diabetes. He pulled his car over to the curb and stopped a half block away from her driveway.

While she exited her car two small children ran to the car and swarmed about her. She bent down and gave each a kiss on the cheek.

Stanley watched.

His fellow dark traveler also watched.

Soon everyone went into the house.

"How many times are we going to follow her home?" asked the ink black shape.

"As many times as I want," said Stanley.

"Seems like a waste of time, if you ask me."

"Like you have something to do or somewhere to go," mocked Stanley.

"Get it over with."

"I will when I decide I am ready."

"When will that be?"

"Soon, real soon."

Chapter 42
Home of retired FBI Profiler, Kit Baylor
Island Pond, Vermont
August 14

Kit sat on the back porch while his mother and a neighbor talked in the kitchen. His mother so enjoyed the company of the woman who lived two houses down from theirs. Kit worried about his mother and what would become of her once he was gone. She needed looking after. They didn't have the money for live-in-care.

His federal benefits were good, but he had made a poor choice several years before when he elected not to select purchasing additional group life insurance. His mother was the beneficiary of his estate and he was in turn her beneficiary. He never imagined he might go before her. The opportunity to purchase additional life insurance was a good deal. At the time, no prior health examination was needed. It was too late now.

Kit felt exceptionally weak today. He hadn't been able to eat very much since leaving the hospital. His clothes hung on him. Eating had devolved into a pill popping exercise almost to the point of one pill after every bite of food. He had to take fourteen pills with each meal, another three pills when he awoke each morning and finally, another five pills at bed time.

After eating, he would experience long and painful cramping. He reached the point that the mere smell of food would sour his insides. The operation had removed half his stomach and over half of his small and large intestines. His oncologist wanted to take half of his liver and remove a nodule on his pancreas. The doctor's had strongly recommended he submit to chemotherapy and radiation treatment. He didn't hesitate at all when he declined. He knew his condition was fatal and he was resolved to avoid as much as possible so as to not unduly delay the inevitable. The only thing which made his days bearable was his being intellectually consumed by the search for the serial killer which had been brought to his attention by the joint CCU investigators from Maine, New Hampshire and Vermont.

This case challenged him like no other before. He wanted to help catch this guy before he died. He wondered if he had enough time left.

Kit decided to pick up the phone and call Mark Atkinson, the New Hampshire CCU investigator. Mark was the de facto leader of the investigation. The man had good instincts. He was dogged and determined to get this killer. Kit saw a little of himself in Mark. Most of all he admired the man for not being a prima donna type but one who was focused on getting justice for his victims and closure for the families. Mark was walking a career tight rope with this case. It could well make him or bury him.

After two rings he heard Mark's now familiar voice.

"Hello, this is Mark Atkinson."

"Mark, this is Kit calling."

"Kit, great to hear from you."

"I was calling you to see how things are going."

Mark paused, "I've got to tell you it is damn frustrating. I don't know how Doug and Alice are doing with their interviews but mine aren't going so well. I just finished my third one and it was like pulling teeth. Long distance drivers are a tough bunch. They don't like talking with the law enforcement types, I can tell you that. I've got nothing to show for my effort and the clock is ticking. This bastard is probably hunting someone right now."

Kit remarked, "Mark, success in this kind of work doesn't happen quickly. Murder investigations, especially cold case investigations, don't get solved in an hour like people see on television shows. You know this better than most."

"Yeah, you're right. Thanks for reminding me. So, how are you feeling?"

"I have good moments and not so good ones. I'm trying not to think about it."

"Are you able to eat?"

"Yeah sort of, I don't have much left in me to process anything I might eat. Right now, all I can stand is a protein shake.""Damn, is there anything I can do for you?"

"Yeah, I need to stay up on this case. I've got to tell you I need the focus, you know a place to put my mind. It's all I've got left to be honest with you"

Mark was moved to tears listening to this once incredible investigator, a man who stood for victims in a way that Mark admired.

"Kit, man, I am so sorry."

"Don't worry about me. I'm at peace with this. I really am. I just want this guy before, you know, before I check out."

"I want him too, for the vics and for you. How's your mom holding up?"

"She is doing okay, considering. We've talked things through and she understands my decision. She's buried my dad and my sister who died when I was just eleven. She died from the flu. She's also buried one of her three sisters. She has found her own way to cope. She has her own health issues, so she might not last much longer either."

Mark was dumbstruck by Kit's stoicism. The man was fearless and apparently his mother was as well.

Kit turned the conversation back to the case.

Listen, I was thinking, could you and Doug and Alice send me your list of drivers? I have an old buddy in the FBI who I trust who can check some things for us. They have access to some data which you guys don't. I want to have him also take a look at any military records these drivers may have. Who knows, something could pop up."

"That would be excellent. I'll make sure to get you the list right away. Can we email it to you?"

"Sure, here's my email address."

Kit provided his email address to Mark and then ended the call shortly afterwards.

After Mark sent out the information Kit had requested he grabbed his sport coat and headed out the door to another interview meeting with yet another truck driver from the list.

Chapter 43
Home of Physician's Assistant Tamara Sacha
Londonderry, New Hampshire
August 15

PA Tamara Sacha kissed her two daughters goodbye. The babysitter had arrived moments before and was ready for the day. Tamara's husband had left for work nearly an hour before. He had a long commute to work and on most mornings left before 7:00 a.m. He worked in Boston for First New England Investments as a financial planner.

Tamara reminded the babysitter the children's grandmother would be stopping over in the afternoon to take everyone to the movies. Tamara grabbed her car keys and headed out the side door to the garage.

She slowly backed the car out of the garage and down the driveway. After checking the street for any oncoming traffic she backed into the street and headed down the quiet neighborhood street on her way to work.

As she drove down the street she passed a small car parked on her side of the street. She had seen the same car parked on the street each morning this week. She mentally noted it was always parked in a different spot. She pulled alongside the car and glanced into the car and noticed the driver who quickly looked away from her. In that split second she caught a glimpse of the man's profile. In the corner of her eye she also noticed the back seat which seemed to be bathed in a deep, very dark shadow.

At that precise moment her mind did not process this information. It merely recorded it into her sub-consciousness.

Later, as Tamara pulled out of the northbound travel lane on I-93 and into the passing lane, her eyes routinely checked the rearview mirror. She spotted what seemed like the same car she had passed earlier on her neighborhood street. As she settled into the passing lane she looked into the mirror once more.

The car pulled in behind her, keeping pace with her car. It took about three seconds before a flash memory hit her. It was the patient she had seen last week whom she had to tell that he had Type II diabetes. He was the truck driver guy who needed his license renewed. She recalled him with complete clarity as a man with intense anger and who had rattled her.

Could he be the one who was following her now?

She couldn't know for sure but the very thought gave her a nervous jolt. Her stomach tightened considerably with the awareness that the angry patient appeared to be stalking her.

While she continued the drive to work her mind began to surge with all sorts of concerns.

The man was following her now. He was obviously stalking her but to what end? *What could she do about this? Did she dare confront the man herself? She could pull his file and get his address. Perhaps she could confront him up and tell him she was wise to him. What if he turned violent? Should she tell somebody? Who?* She didn't have any proof. She needed to do something, anything.

Her hands were sweating and her heart was pounding as she pulled into the parking lot at the Manchester Dartmouth-Hitchcock Clinic. She hurriedly locked her car. As she turned to rush to the relative safety of the building she glanced around for the car which had been following her. She didn't see it anywhere.

Could she be mistaken?

After she entered the building she stood in the shadows of the double doors and looked back once more into the parking lot.

The very same small car slowly cruised past the rear of her car. The driver seemed to be looking right at the doorway where she stood. She felt a chill seize her.

The mysterious car drove away.

PA Sacha hurried to the ladies room.

She stepped into a stall, lifted the toilet seat and promptly threw up.

"Do you think she's on to us?" asked the shadow one.

"Probably," answered Stanley.

"That's not good, you lose the element of surprise."

"I want her to worry, to sweat, and to lose sleep. I want her so damn scared she can't do her damn job."

"Why do you want that? Let's just kill her and move on."

"No."

"Why not?" inquired the inky figure.

"Because when I do kill her, she is going to see it coming. She is going to have time to think about it. The terror alone makes it all worthwhile for her having screwed up my life."

"So, what do you have in mind?"

"I'm still working it out."

"Want to tell me?"

"What, and ruin the surprise?"

Stanley continued driving to work.

When Stanley arrived at work there was a message taped to the screen of his computer.

The owner of the company wanted to see him.

Stanley had a feeling the meeting might be about his stalking the woman. She probably looked up his records, found out where he worked and decided to call in a complaint.

Stanley walked to the owner's office and knocked on the door.

"Come on in," said the man's voice.

The present owner of the trucking business was the 44 year old grandson of the founder of the company. His name was Fred Hilliard. He was a bookish looking man who was starting to lose some hair even though he combed it back as best he could in order to disguise his thinning hair. Up until now he was harmless enough. He had never driven a truck for a living like his father and grandfather had. This guy had a business degree. He was business smart, Stanley would give him that, but he wasn't road smart.

Stanley opened the door and walked into the office.

"Stanley thanks for coming in. Have a seat."

Stanley sat down in the armchair in front of the desk.

Situated in the front edge of the desk was a tin model of one of the company's trucks from the early 1920's era. The model truck had sat in the same place on this very same desk for over ninety years.

"Stanley, I heard you had your physical the other day. The insurance company sent me a follow-up letter. They say you have diabetes. Is that correct?"

"Yeah, I guess so. It ain't nothing. I just have to watch what I eat, maybe get a little more exercise. I'm already on it."

"Well diabetes isn't something to mess with. Did you know my dad had it and I think my grandfather did to? The last couple of years of my dad's life he had to have kidney dialysis every couple of weeks. He didn't want anyone to know. Big tough guy didn't want folks to think he needed treatments."

"I didn't know."

"Yeah, well anyway, as you know the feds will not let the state renew your CDLA license. Not to worry though. You really don't need it for your job. I just want you to know, all I care about is that you take good care of yourself. Whatever you need to do, you know, like take time for doctor appointments, stuff like that, you just go ahead and take the time. Fair enough?"

"Yes, sir, it is and thanks."

"Don't mention it."

"I guess I'll get back to work."

"Sure and remember, Stanley, whatever you need from this company you can count on it. You have been a damn good employee over the years and as dad preached to me, our employees are like family and family takes care of one another."

Stanley nodded his agreement as he stood up and left the owner's office.

He hadn't really paid much attention to what the man said.

Once he knew the meeting wasn't directly about the bitch Sacha, all he could think about was her and devising a plan to kill her in the most painful way possible.

Chapter 44
Home of retired FBI Profiler, Kit Baylor
Island Pond, Vermont
August 18

Kit had called and left a message with his buddy, P. J. Lincoln, at the FBI Washington, DC Field Office. The two went way back together. They had joined the FBI together. Their careers intersected many times during the course of numerous investigations. Larry was heading towards retirement at the end of this year. Kit knew he could count on Larry to lend him a hand, and most of all, he would be discreet about it.

His phone message gave no hint about the purpose of the call.

Finally, just before noon time Kit's phone rang.

Kit picked it up on the first ring.

"Kit you old dog, how in the hell are you?"

"Larry, great to hear your voice. I'm hanging in there. Getting old really sucks. Don't put off your retirement a minute longer than you planned, that's all I have to say."

"Seriously, are you okay? It sounds like you have some issues. And how about your mom, how's she doing?"

"Larry, I don't have time to go into my medical issues. Let me just say, there's a cloud hanging over me. My mom's doing okay considering, but she's getting up in years too."

"Well, whatever it is you're having to deal with, you know you can call on me for anything. I mean it too. Please give your mom my best. Now you called me and I'm sure it wasn't to pass the breeze. That just isn't your style. So what's up? What do you need?"

Kit filled him in over the next five minutes. Kit was careful in choosing his words. He wanted to impress his friend with the urgency and importance of what he was asking for while not revealing too much. He didn't want his friend to be put in the position of possibly interfering with the ongoing FBI investigation in New Hampshire.

"I can handle this for you. If I push it I might be able to get back to you in a few days. I presume you want this one kept under the radar?"

"You got that right. If anything you dig up for me proves hot I will brief you on the whole picture, until then I need to keep this quiet. I have my reasons."

"This doesn't sound like you are completely retired. I just knew you would find a way to get back in the game."

"Not quite my friend, I wasn't looking to get back into anything. But there are some really good investigators up this way struggling with a difficult case. They thought I could help them out. You could say the game found me."

"I hear you. Okay, I'll get on it right away. Get the bad guy, my friend."

"Yeah, you too, get the bad guy."

The call ended.

Kit felt drained from the call. He reached over and picked up the tall glass and took a sip of the protein drink. His insides revolted from the attempt to fortify himself. He had an immediate need to rush to the bathroom.

He barely made it.

Twenty minutes later a physically drained Kit walked slowly back to the rear porch. He eased down into the wicker love seat. His mother had taken up her usual seat in the wicker rocker.

She watched him with the careful eye only a mother possesses.

Their lives had come to this - both of them were in a race to meet their maker. She had always thought it would be her fate to go first but now she was no longer sure and the thought troubled her deeply. She was always good at hiding her emotions and this time in her life was no exception.

"I couldn't help but hear your earlier phone call. The one you are helping to hunt, he sounds evil."

"Serial killers are especially evil, deeply evil. As for this one, let me just say he's especially hard to figure out."

"I will pray you and the others find a way to stop him."

"I'm afraid we are going to need more than prayers for this perp."

"Prayers and hard work will be rewarded. That's what your father would always say."

Kit stared off into the backyard and beyond. The air was warm but not too warm. The insects and various bird noises provided soothing auditory stimulation.

His mother's words kept repeating in his mind, "Prayers and hard work."

Then it hit him. He had been so distracted by his illness he had overlooked the one thing he had always relied upon to enable him to help break a case. It was hard work that always did the trick. So far he had relied upon the work of the other investigators in reading him into the cases. He needed to see the case files himself. He needed to read the CCU records, the interviews, see the crime scene photos for all the cases, etc. He was the one with the trained profiler eye and a long career of finely sharpened instincts.

He reached for the phone sitting on the small table beside his mother.

"Thanks, Mom. You have been a big help."

His mother smiled at her son as she slowly rocked back and forth. Prayers she could provide and her son would provide the hard work. Each in their own way needed this to help them get through what was ahead.

She started right in on the prayers.

Chapter 45
Office of Vermont CCU Investigator Doug Wetstone
Montpelier, Vermont
August 19

Doug hung up the phone.

He had been talking with his friend, Crosby "Kit" Baylor.

Kit had just asked for all the files on the cold cases suspected to be part of the multi-state serial killer investigation. Doug agreed to drive up to Island Pond with the Vermont files. He had also agreed to contact Mark Atkinson in New Hampshire to see if Mark could send up their files and the same for Alice Poindexter in Maine with their records.

Doug called Mark first.

He had to leave a message for Mark and for Alice.

Doug decided he would pack up his Vermont files and drive to Island Pond this very afternoon.

Mark reached him on his cell phone while he was on route to Kit's place. Doug explained Kit wanted to pour over the records himself. After a short discussion Mark agreed to arrange with the state police to drive the records up to Vermont if Doug could help arrange for Vermont Sate Police to take the hand off of the records and deliver them to Kit.

"I don't see a problem with that. Get me the details from your state police on where and when to meet. I'll have our guys take it from there," said Doug.

"Will do, as soon as I finish this interview with one of the driver's on my list I'll set things up and get right back to you. How are your interviews going?" asked Mark.

"I have got to tell you, I'm not getting much. Only one guy mentioned something about some guy he thought was a New Hampshire driver. It seems my guy thinks this other driver was an ex-green beret type who was a mean son-of-a-bitch. He says nobody liked the guy. He couldn't offer anything specific but said this other guy was the only one who gave him the creeps."

"That's not much help."

"I know."

"Got to keep plugging," said Doug.

"We need something to break and soon. I sure don't want another death on our hands," said Mark.

"I hear you Mark. Listen, I've got to go. Alice is calling."

Doug ended his call with Mark and began another with Alice.

She also quickly agreed to share her files with Kit. She would have her intern, Bruce Wyte, drive the records over. She added that Bruce wanted to meet Kit.

Alice reported her interviews were striking out as well. It seemed the truck driving community in northern New England was a closed mouth bunch.

Doug passed along what he had learned from his interviews and the little Mark could report.

Doug wrapped up the call. He continued his drive on to Kit's house. In Doug's mind Kit was the key. Kit had the training, the experience, and the instincts which could find the break they all needed in this fog. Doug was buoyed by Kit's renewed interest in digging into this case. Doug was prepared to do all that was necessary to help Kit out with this. This case was pulling Doug in. He so very much wanted to get this killer. For the first time in a long time, he was having trouble sleeping at night. All he could think about was this case.

Forty minutes later Doug pulled into Kit's driveway.

After checking in with Kit, Doug unloaded his boxes from his car.

Kit invited him to stay for dinner but Doug declined. He had an interview set up for first thing in the morning. He wanted to get back to the office to clear up a couple of things before the day ended. Before he left he mentioned the information one driver had offered up about another driver he knew who disturbed him. Kit listened carefully and took notes.

"My guy inside the FBI is looking into the military records angle. I hope to have something from him early next week."

Kit immediately began to dig into the files.

Doug headed to his car and began the drive back to his office in Montpelier.

Kit was soon buried in the case records.

He took many notes.

His mother called to him from the rear porch.

"Kit, could you bring me some tea?"

"Sure," responded Kit.

He brewed the tea and brought the cup and saucer out to his mother.

"Can I get you anything else?"

"No dear, this is just fine. Thank you. You know you should try and eat something. You need your strength."

"I know. I'll get something later."

She recognized that look in his eyes.

She would have to remind him to eat later on because he was surely going to forget his promise once he returned to the files Doug had brought.

Kit's mom sipped her tea and continued her prayers. She was deeply religious in a private way and for her, prayers always served her well. She prayed daily, offering her thanks for the creator's blessings. Occasionally she also prayed for the healing of others. Now her prayers were being offered up for her son's continued welfare so he could help solve this heinous crime spree.

She would do her part through prayer.

Chapter 46
Home of Physician's Assistant Tamara Sacha
Londonderry, New Hampshire
August 22

For the past week Tamara's emotions were on edge. She was constantly looking over her shoulder. She would jump at the sound of the phone ringing or a door slamming shut. She snapped at her husband and children. She wasn't sleeping well at all.

At work she lived in complete fear. Each day, her drive in and return home had her strung out. She was anxious whenever she was alone with a patient. Even her co-workers noticed the change in her behavior.

P.A. Sacha was certain she had seen Stanley Bolinski stalking her on several occasions only to later question herself.

This morning she made breakfast for her family. While working in the kitchen she found herself frequently walking past the kitchen window which looked out onto the street in front of her home. Each time she passed by she would pause and anxiously glance in each direction, up and down the street, looking for the small dark car which had been following her for the past week.

Her heart rate was high and her blood pressure was too. She felt light headed.

Tamara elected not to discuss her fear with her husband. She believed he would likely dismiss her feelings which would only add to her increasing sense of isolation. At least for now, she would bear this burden alone.

Late yesterday evening she had taken a small folding knife out of her husband's bureau. It was a sentimental piece he had kept since his days as a Boy Scout.

Tamara slipped the knife into her purse. Although she had practiced opening and closing the knife while locked in their master bathroom, she more often fumbled with it rather than develop a smooth and swift opening.

The presence of the knife in her purse gave her a small measure of comfort. She refused to consider using a handgun. Her husband didn't own one and she didn't know anyone who did. Even if she did she doubted if someone would merely lend it to her. She had also thought about getting pepper spray or mace. However, she didn't know where to purchase such things. Tamara was afraid to ask anyone for assistance in finding such things out of fear they would want to know why she felt she needed such personal protection.

She kissed her family goodbye and headed to her car. She sat down in her car and placed her purse on the passenger car seat. She opened her purse and felt around for the knife. Her right hand found it.

She removed the knife and slipped it into her lab coat side pocket. She closed her purse and placed it on the floor behind the passenger front seat.

Tamara backed out of the driveway.

She looked up the street and Stanley's car was not in sight.

This allowed her to relax just a bit.

She drove on to work without noticing any sign of Bolinski.

She allowed herself to consider the possibility, *Maybe he's given up*.

Tamara pulled into a parking space in the employees parking area at the clinic. She retrieved her purse and got out of the car. She used the fob with her car keys to remotely lock her car.

Just as she turned to head into the clinic she bumped into the chest of a man standing directly behind her.

Her body froze in a grip of terror.

She raised her eyes and met his.

It was the man of her nightmares.

She took a step backwards.

"You, you stay away from me," said Tamara in a voice breaking with fear.

"This is a public place. I have just as much right to be here as you," said Stanley in a mocking tone.

"No, no you don't, no, this area is for employee parking."

She couldn't believe she was arguing with the man.

Her legs felt weak. Her left hand reached out for the car next to her to steady herself.

Stanley's eyes looked down at her shaking hand reaching for the adjacent car.

He smiled.

"Am I scaring you?"

"Yes, damn it, you are. Look, I was just doing my job. You must know that. Your diabetes is a manageable disease. It's not the end of the world."

"Bitch, you have no idea how much you have screwed things up for me. Now I have to make things right."

"Are you threatening me?" said Tamara as she slipped her right hand inside her lab coatd pocket.

Stanley only smiled and said, "What do you think?"

"I'm armed and I will defend myself if I have to," asserted Tamara as she gripped the knife and pushed it forward inside her pocket.

Stanley looked down at her pocket. The shape could be a gun, although it would have to be a small one at that.

Standing directly behind Stanley was his ever faithful dark terror.

"*She's bluffing. Grab her and let's get this over with,*" demanded his dark shadow.

Glancing over his left shoulder Stanley said, "I'll handle this."

"*Who is he talking to?*" thought Tamara.

Then her eyes began to see a shimmering shadow just behind Stanley.

Her stomach seized up with complete and absolute fear.

"Have a nice day," declared Stanley in an obvious mocking tone before he turned and walked away. She watched him walk over to his car parked in the last space at the end of the row. She noticed Stanley repeatedly gesture as if he was engaged in conversation. The shadowy shimmering effect still disturbed the air around Stanley.

Tamara suddenly took a breath. She hadn't realized she had been half-holding her breath. Her knees felt weak and she was sweating profusely even though the early morning air was cool and there was a steady breeze.

She finally found the strength to head into the clinic. She ran to the doors and slipped inside.

She looked outside and watched Stanley drive away.

She couldn't believe no one else was in the parking lot during her confrontation with Stanley.

Suddenly, the overwhelming tension she had been struggling to control took its toll. Her lightheadedness overtook her which caused her to faint, in the doorway.

Chapter 47
Home of retired FBI Profiler, Kit Baylor
Island Pond, Vermont
August 22

The phone rang.

It was just a few minutes past 8:00 a.m.

Kit answered it right away. He was sipping a weak tea he had brewed a few minutes before. He was trying to keep it down when the phone rang.

"Can I speak with Kit?" asked the caller.

Recognizing the voice Kit said, "Larry, it's me."

The caller was Special Agent, P. J. Lincoln, Kit's longtime friend calling from Washington, DC, FBI Field Office.

"Kit, I just knew you would be up early. You haven't changed much".

"Neither have you, I'm sure."

"So look, I did some digging. I pulled some strings down at the Pentagon too. My guy down there is curious as hell as to what I wanted the info for so I told him, without revealing your name, naturally. If you're okay with it, I said I would let him know the background on this request. I also had the boys here in my office do a computer run for you. Are you ready to hear what I turned up?"

"Larry, if it's okay with you, I will put the phone on speaker so I can take notes."

"Fine with me."

"Okay, I'm ready."

"All right then, I'll start with our office's research. From the list of names you provided we ran them through CODIS and

NDIS. We have DNA on only sixteen of the parties identified. In AFIS we have fingerprints on nineteen of the named individuals. So we don't have DNA and fingerprints on everyone on your list but if one of the crime scenes has either DNA and or fingerprints we can run them to see if we have a match to our data. Once we have a match, we have a name. The other data bases we ran gave us mixed results. ATF's data indicates every one of these individuals have bought guns at one time or another. In fact, one of the guys on your list holds a federal firearms dealer's license. You want me to send the details to you. I can fax it to you or email it. Which way do you want it?"

"I will have you fax it to a friend's machine. He owns a restaurant in town and I can pick it up there. I don't have a fax machine here and I don't want this data emailed here because I want to keep you in the background, for now. You're going to have to trust me on this."

"Okay, that's fine with me. Now, for the Pentagon data, it seems twenty-one of the named individuals served, at one time or another, in the military. Most of them served in Vietnam and a couple stayed in for a few years and later served in the reserves. Eleven received combat medals for injuries or acts of heroism. Three of them were hot shot green berets. None of them have any serious black marks on their military records. Although my guy went out of his way to say that during the Viet Nam era some stuff would sometimes happen and the military would scrub the records for whatever purpose it deemed necessary. I found that odd, but I don't really know the mindset of the Pentagon. After all, I was just a grunt and everyone knows grunts don't have any brains. Ha Ha!"

Larry laughed at his own attempt at humor.

Kit was taking notes at a furious pace and didn't react to the attempt at light hearted humor.

"So that's all I could come up with. Does any of it help you?"

"I can't say for now. I will have to go through my notes again and the stuff you fax up here before I can tell if any of this points us in a useful direction. If I had to guess, I would say yes, this helps. So, when can you fax the stuff up here?"

"As soon as you give me the fax number I will hit the send key and it will be on the way."

Kit gave him the number and told him to make sure the info is transmitted for his eyes only.

The conversation ended.

Kit immediately dialed the Pride and Joy Restaurant and mentioned a fax was going to be coming through for him and he would be coming over to pick it up in a few minutes.

The restaurant owner replied, "The fax machine is already printing out something. It must be your stuff. I will keep an eye on it and set the papers aside until you get here."

"Thanks that would be great," replied Kit.

Chapter 48
Dartmouth – Hitchcock Clinic
Manchester, New Hampshire
August 22

Tamara woke up lying on a bed in the urgent care department of the clinic. A nurse was taking her pulse.

"How are you feeling?"

"Okay, I guess. My head hurts though."

"That's because you struck your head on the floor when you fainted. The doctor will be here in a moment. We drew some blood and sent it to the lab for analysis."

Tamara tried to sit up but the nurse gently pushed down on her shoulders insisting she wait until the doctor had a chance to examine her.

The doctor arrived a moment later and conducted a thorough exam. The physician's name was Dr. Susan Van Otis.

"You can sit up but I recommend you do so slowly. You've received a mild concussion. I want you to get some rest. I also want to see you again before I can clear you to return to work. This is a Workmen's Comp case now. So let's have you see me in three days. I should be able to sign off for you at that time. Is there someone we can call to take you home?"

Tamara's head was lowered to avoid the gaze of the doctor. She shook head slowly.

Tamara didn't put up any resistance to the order to rest. She slipped off the bed and carefully placed her feet on the floor. She swiped her hair behind her ears. Her hands were shaking.

Dr. Van Otis sat on the bed next to her and took her left hand into her right.

"Tamara, what is going on? There isn't any apparent physical reason for the fainting spell. Your hands are shaking and you look like you are a bundle of nerves right now."

Tamara avoided eye contact with her colleague. She kept her eyes down and her head slightly turned away.

"Tamara, is it something at home?"

That provoked a reaction from Tamara.

"No, no, it's really nothing. I just need some time to myself."

She spoke these words without being able to look at Dr. Van Otis. Most of all, she spoke the words without any conviction whatsoever.

"Tamara, please look at me."

Slowly, Tamara raised her head and looked at Dr. Van Otis.

"That's better, now, talk to me. What's going on?"

Tamara emotionally was ready to explode. Her eyes swept back and forth.

"I don't know. I, uh, can handle it. I'll call my mother-in-law to take me home." You call this handling it. C'mon, we both know better. Talk to me girl."

Tamara couldn't go on holding things in. She pulled her hand away from Dr. Van Otis putting her hands over her eyes. She began to sob out a story of being stalked by one of her patients. She recounted the several times he had watched her house and followed her to work. She described the encounter in the employee parking lot.

Dr. Van Otis offered Tamara some tissue to blow her nose.

"Have you reported this guy to security?"

"No, I, I thought I could handle it," she said haltingly. "I, I," she paused, "I didn't think he would keep it up. I know now I was wrong."

"Well, I think you should report him. He sounds like he is not just persistent but he is escalating his stalking behavior. Don't try to handle this alone. Do you want me to call security?"

Tamara lowered her head and silently nodded her agreement.

Minutes later Tamara was being interviewed by the clinic's private security service. The security person, a young man in his mid-twenties, left her to look at the security cameras to verify her story. Sure enough the recording matched her story. The security employee returned and strongly recommended she file a complaint with the Manchester Police Department. She resisted at first but eventually relented.

Shortly before noon, a police officer and his partner took her statement regarding the stalking and threatening behavior of her patient, Stanley Bolinski. They discussed the possiblity she needed to obtain a restraining order. The officers offered also to speak directly with Bolinski.

"Sometimes that can help get guys like him to back off. But I have got to be honest with you, other times it can provoke the stalker into more aggressive behavior," said the younger police officer. "If you want us to talk with him, we will. It's your call."

Tamara's mind kept searching for a way out of this nightmare. From her point of view, no real solutions were forthcoming.

Just then a nurse knocked on the examination room door. She poked her head in. "Sorry to interrupt, Tamara, your mother-in-law is here. I have her settled in the waiting area."

"Thanks," responded Tamara.

Looking at the officers Tamara said, "Thanks for your assistance and advice. I'll think it over and get back to you. I've got to go now."

The taller, senior officer handed her his business card.

She took the card and silently walked out of the examination room.

The two officers looked at one another. The youngest one shrugged while his partner nodded. They left the room not expecting to hear from her until something pushed her to the breaking point.

After calling and checking in with their shift supervisor they decided to visit Mr. Bolinski and let him know the police had been alerted to his "un-welcomed" behavior.

Chapter 49
Dubuque Street, West Side Neighborhood
Manchester, New Hampshire
August 22

It was nearly 6:00 p.m. when Stanley arrived home. On the way into the house he grabbed his mail out of the hallway mail box. He lived on the first floor of a three-decker residential property located on Dubuque Street in a residential Westside neighborhood in the City of Manchester. He was the landlord although he hadn't had a tenant for the second or third floor apartments in over twenty years. The last tenants he had, made the tragic mistake of pissing Stanley off. He had to add them to his kill list.

One single male tenant who rented the third floor unit was terminated twenty-four years ago. A middle-aged couple was dispatched one Christmas Eve, twenty-one years ago. No one came looking for the single male. He had no family and few friends. The middle-aged couple was different. They had only a daughter who lived in Missouri and she filed a missing person's report. The police came by to investigate. Stanley cooperated with them and hinted at peculiar literature in the mail involving sex clubs. He also told the police the couple would often entertain strange acting couples for overnight weekend visits. The police were gullible enough to take the helpful suggestions. Their official report concluded the couple had simply taken off, present whereabouts unknown, and perhaps didn't want to be found.

Stanley had disposed of their cars and most of their personal possessions. Their bodies were buried in shallow unmarked graves alongside the Contoocook River some twenty miles to the North.

New Hampshire Cold Case Unit's case records only listed the couple's case as an unsolved missing person case with the case number of NHMP 91-15.

Stanley's doorbell rang.

He walked over to the front door and looked through the sheer curtain to the front hallway where he saw two Patrol Officers standing in the hallway. Behind them Stanley could see the patrol car parked at his front curb.

Stanley's evil companion lurked behind him.

"What do you think?" asked Stanley.

"*I think that bitch of a doctor turned you in. You'd better be real careful with these two. You don't want to give them a reason to take you to the station.*"

"No shit. I could have figured out that part for myself," said Stanley.

Before he opened the door the dark spirit replied, "*Do you want me to take care of her for you. They won't be able to trace it back to you and we'll set up an airtight alibi.*"

"No, don't you go near her. She's mine."

Stanley turned the deadbolt lock and opened his front door.

"Are you Stanley Bolinski?"

"Yes, yes, I am officer. May I ask what this is about?" said Stanley with a forced look of curiosity.

"Mr. Bolinski, I am officer Deets and this is my partner, Officer Gendron. There's a matter we need to discuss with you. May we come in?"

"Yes, of course please come in." He held the door open and invited the two officers to enter.

"Please sit down," said Stanley as he gestured to the well-furnished living room.

"No thanks," said Officer Deets.

"Mr. Bolinki let me get right to the point." The young police officer pulled out his iPhone and touched the screen." We understand you recently had a health care visit with Physician Assistant Tamara Sacha at the Dartmouth-Hitchcock Clinic off of Roy Drive. Is this correct sir?"

"Yes it is. How is my private medical appointment a police matter? I don't understand how it's now a matter for the police."

"Sir, did you approach Ms. Sacha earlier this morning in the parking lot at the clinic? Did you have a conversation with her at that time?"

"Yes, as a matter of fact I did. I was planning on making a visit to the clinic to go to the business office to discuss a matter in connection with one of the bills they sent me. I spotted her and went over to her to say hello. She's a nice young lady. A bit high strung but a very competent professional, if you ask me." The two police officers glanced briefly at one another.

"We watched the security camera video and frankly sir, it didn't look like a friendly chat. Ms. Sacha reports you have been stalking her ever since your recent exam. She also reports you threatened her this morning."

"Why I'm shocked she would say those things. I can assure you she is wrong. Look, during my physical she told me I could no longer be certified for my commercial truck driver's license. Frankly, I was relieved at the news. Look at me," said Stanley as he extended his arms.

Continuing, in his most sincere performance he went on to say, "I'm an old man getting older by the minute. I don't want to have to drive anymore. In my job I assign other drivers their routes. Sure, once in a while I would have to drive a route. I was the backup driver. But now, with the loss of the CDLA license, I don't have to put my ass inside of an 18 wheeler anymore. As far as I'm concerned, it's nothing but good news for me. This old body doesn't want to have to drive another 10 hour shift."

"Sir that may well be correct, but the fact is, Ms. Sacha wants you to leave her alone. We strongly advise you to steer clear of Ms. Sacha. Don't approach her, don't call her and don't talk with her. Whatever went on has upset her and it would be in your interest to just stay away from her," said the older officer.

Continuing he said, "Just so you know, the clinic is very likely to assign your case to a different clinician. We don't want to have to speak to you again on this matter. Is that clear?"

"Clear enough. Whatever it is that is bothering her is not of my doing and I assure you I will be following your advice.

Poor thing, I do hope she can resolve whatever is bothering her. Thank you both for coming by today. I had no idea she was upset with me. Now that I do, I will be sure to be careful whenever I have a need to visit the clinic."

"Thanks for your time."

The two young officers turned and headed to the front door. Officer Gendron glanced around the place one last time as he followed his partner out the door.

Once the officers had left the building Stanley closed the door. He locked his front door. If the officers had glanced back at this moment they would have seen he was seething.

"That bitch turned these dogs on you. You aren't going to let her get way with that, are you?" demanded his dark partner.

"Just shut up. I need to think and I can't do that with you hissing in my ears. Now leave me alone."

The two officers climbed back into their patrol car.

Officer Deets was the driver. He pulled out his iPhone and called up the email message with the attached video copy of the security scene of Tamara's and Stanley's conversation. The clinic's security person had privately offered to provide a copy to Officer Deets.

"Look again at this video. Look how he leans in on her. You can't see his face because he has his back to the camera but look at her face, her body language. Whatever he's telling her is scaring the crap out of her."

Officer Gendron followed up with, "I see it clear as a bell. The old man is a lying sack-of-shit if you ask me. His place gave me the creeps. It felt like somebody in there was watching us."

"Yeah, I felt that, too. I hope he leaves her alone now but something tells me he won't and we will be back here to arrest his sorry ass."

"Hoc ecce veritas."

"What in the hell does that mean?"

"It's Latin and I think it means this is true or truth. I'm not really sure. "

So why do you quote some Latin phrase when you don't even know what the hell it means? That's so lame."

"Just drive, my brother."

As the patrol car pulled away from the curb, Officer Gendron glanced back at the three-decker residence. For just a brief moment he spotted a huge hulking shadow figure standing behind the left front window blinds. The blinds were parted slightly. The last thing he saw were the slats of some of the blinds dropping back into place. A feeling of dread seized him. He didn't dare speak of this to his partner.

Chapter 50
Home of retired FBI Profiler, Kit Baylor
Island Pond, Vermont
August 23

After picking up the fax messages from his friend and former FBI colleague Special Agent P. J. Lincoln at the Pride and Joy Restaurant, Kit stopped at the local business supply store and bought a white board. Kit hung the white board up in his kitchen. On it, he listed in profiler fashion, what he knew from the information he had considered.

Un-sub is male. He's in his late fifties to late sixties and is also likely a loner. The un-sub has an extensive knowledge of weapons and is proficient in their use. From three murder cases where a knife was used as the weapon, it could be discerned the killer was right handed. There was a strong likelihood the un-sub had a job where he easily moved about the New England area. Next to this point, Kit had added the words "truck driver" with a question mark added for emphasis.

Probable points were also listed on the white board. He noted it was probable the un-sub had been active for over thirty years.

Under the word "Motive" was a brief note that the un-sub appears to act upon perceived slights or arguments.

Under the phrase "MO, Modus Operandi," Kit noted the following point, no pattern in methods of violence. Under the column titled. Evidence, he noted no fingerprints, no footprints, no DNA, no handwriting, no posing of victims, and no communication to press, police or relatives of victims. He also noted off to the side of this list there was no apparent pattern to the selected victims.

Kit stood before his white board and stared at the information. What else did he know but hadn't yet recognized?

Then he hit on something.

Could one man completely unassisted have been so successful and leave no trace of evidence for all these years? The answer was, not very likely. Did this guy have a partner? The answer to this was a highly probable, yes. Was he possibly mentoring a prodigy? This question was more difficult to get his mind around. His gut told him the answer was not likely.

There had to be more. He needed to get some feedback from the CCU investigators on the progress of their interviews with the truck drivers.

"You son-of-bitch, you have slipped up somewhere. Someone knows who you are, I can feel it. If it's the last thing I do, I will get you, I will bring you down."

He went looking for his telephone. He had to call the CCU investigators.

Kit spent close to two hours in a conference call with Doug, Alice and Mark. Not much new was being developed by the investigators. Kit was getting very tired towards the end of the telephone call when Mark made a comment which reignited Kit's energy level.

Mark said, "You know, this guy is so careful and so good at not leaving any clues. Right from the beginning and up to now it has been the same thing, no eyewitnesses, no fingerprints, no DNA, no signature or pattern and no links between the victims. I just can't believe one guy can be that perfect for so long."

Kit immediately locked into what Mark had just stated. His internal hunter instinct kicked into gear.

"Mark, you have just made an excellent point. I made an elementary mistake on this case. I haven't examined his evolution or devolution."

"What in the hell are you saying?" asked Alice.

"Yeah, please explain this evolution or devolution thing," said Doug.

"It is simple really. I haven't compared his earliest cases to his latest cases to see if there is any deviation. From his earliest case until now, is he getting better at covering up his crimes which is evolving or is he showing any signs of slippage, which is devolving?" said Kit.

Kit went on.

"Mark, we agreed we believe he is behind the recent murder of the three teenage boys at the New Hampshire movie complex. Didn't police investigators find a shoe print at the scene?"

"Yeah, that's right they did."

"Then consider for a moment the murder of the Judge. This was a broad daylight murder and in a residential neighborhood. The killer took an enormous risk with the time of day and location. In my opinion, an unnecessary risk and, might I dare say, an uncharacteristically high risk approach. All the other murders were always undertaken at a location and time of day which ensured a low risk of exposure or detection. Unless I am way off base here, I would have to say our killer is beginning to slip up a bit. He's rushing things, becoming more impulsive. This change makes him even more dangerous while at the same time more likely to make a mistake which will lead to his eventual arrest. We are entering a new phase here. His killings have been spread out over a long period of time. But as of now, he appears to be accelerating his pace and concentrating his killings in New Hampshire. There are small indicators he may very likely have an accomplice. I can't say what role this probable accomplice is playing right now but I am confident this un-sub is getting help.

"In addition, I am still analyzing data from my FBI source. I hope to have that finished up today or tomorrow. I believe we're getting closer. We just need one or two more pieces to this puzzle and it will all begin to come together."

Kit wrapped up the call with everyone.

He once again attacked the files of the cold case murders and missing persons with renewed purpose and energy.

He even took time to eat a small amount of food. He had plain Greek style yogurt along with half of a natural peanut butter sandwich. He also faithfully followed his pill regimen. To his surprise he was able to keep this small amount of food down.

Chapter 51
Home of Physician's Assistant Tamara Sacha
Londonderry, New Hampshire
August 26

Tamara pulled into her garage. Before getting out of her car, she remotely lowered the garage door. Her hands were sweating and they ached too. She had been gripping the steering wheel intensely throughout her drive home.

Samara was physically and emotionally exhausted.

Despite being cleared to resume work, her supervisor encouraged her to take today off and more if she needed it.

Tamara declined.

She refused to let her encounter with the maniacal Stanley Bolinski interfere with her commitment to do her job.

She was comforted by the routine of work although she kept a wary eye out for her nemesis. In the back of her mind she half expected him to drop by the clinic. She believed him perfectly capable of such a stunt.

Earlier in the week, she let herself get talked into asking the police to talk with him. Now she was even more terrified their efforts would only provoke him even more.

She looked in the rearview mirror. Her face clearly showed signs of stress. Her eyes were puffy. There were dark lines forming under her eyes. Her makeup was smudged and rubbed off in places.

Tamara unlocked her car and slipped out of the seat and headed inside. She dropped her purse and keys on the kitchen counter and headed directly to the guest bathroom to splash water on her face.

She stood looking in the mirror with water dripping off the center of her chin.

Tamara didn't like what she saw.

The reflection she saw was that of a terrified woman. It was the image of a woman being stalked by a madman.

Tamara vowed she would not involve her family in this nightmare.

Stepping out of the bathroom she made every effort to conduct herself as if her day was like all others, busy and rewarding. But inside she was paying a heavy price. Her stomach was in knots and her nerves were seriously frayed.

At dinner Tamara seemed distant and distracted. She listened to her chatty children talk about their day's adventures and to her husband who told a story about a co-worker. After dinner, while Tamara and her husband cleared the dishes from the dinner table, her husband spoke up.

"Honey, you okay?"

Tamara merely nodded in the affirmative.

"Are you sure, because you don't seem like yourself tonight? You hardly spoke during dinner. That's not really like you."

"I'm okay, really, I am."

"Is something wrong at work?" pressed her husband.

"No!" responded Tamara in a defensive tone.

"It must be something. You took three days off from work this week. This is so unlike you."

"It's been very busy at work lately. I just needed some time to myself. I guess I'm just a little tired. That's all. If it's okay with you I might just turn in early tonight."

"Sure, I'll look after the kids and get them to bed. You just look after you."

Her husband leaned over and kissed her lightly on the cheek.

She returned his kiss with a forced smile.

"I'll finish up loading the dishwasher, you go on now."

"Thanks, I owe you one."

"And you know I will collect." he said playfully.

She leaned in and kissed him on the cheek and said, "That's what I'm counting on."

Tamara headed into the master bedroom and master bath.

She started the hot water in the oversized Jacuzzi.

She poured some relaxing bath salts into the steaming hot water.

While the Jacuzzi was filling up she retrieved her bed clothes. She placed them on the bathroom bench next to the Jacuzzi.

Tamara slipped out of her work clothes. She piled the clothes in the hamper in the bathroom closet.

Tamara adjusted the water temperature in the Jacuzzi, and selected a bath fragrance from a nearby rack of bath oils. She measured out two full caps of oils and poured them into the bathwater. Satisfied the water temperature was just right she turned on the Jacuzzi's pulsating water jets.

The bath water immediately began to bubble and swirl.

Tamara slipped into the water and settled back in the oversized tub. She brought with her a small terry cloth, water-proof headrest. Positioning it comfortably behind her neck she stretched out and began to relax.

She tried to clear her mind of the events of the past few days. It took a while before she could finally suppress the face of Stanley Bolinski from her consciousness. With the assistance of the soothing warm bath water along with the pulsing sounds of the Jucuzzi she drifted off into a half-slumber.

She was no longer aware of the time. Her semi-consciousness mind was fitful as it rebounded through a series of seemingly unconnected images.

Eventually her mind gave way to the inadequately suppressed earlier memory. .

The recollection began to recount the confrontation in the parking lot. It was the same but different at the same time.

She watched herself being approached by Stanley. This time he seemed different somehow. She wrestled with her mind trying to hear or see what was different. Then it happened.

She found herself starring into his eyes, those menacing eyes. Suddenly his eyes began to change. The pupils began to darken and darken until they were completely black. The blackness was so deep. There was no shiny reflection in those eyes. The darkness instead seemed to be a deep and never ending pool of blackness. Then the eyes changed once more. This time the darkness seemed to open to reveal a swirling mass of burning redness. Tamara sensed the menacing eyes radiated madness.

Her perspective pulled back so that she was once again seeing the whole of her stalking nemesis.

Standing beside Stanley was a black smoky hulk of a human-like figure. This figure appeared to be controlling Stanley as if the man was merely a ventriloquist's dummy.

As her mind's-eye focused upon the two, the dark evil figure appeared to remove his arm from inside Stanley's back.

Stanley's mouth was forming a word as he tried to speak but instead his figure collapsed to the ground into a fleshy heap. It was as if all the bones in his body had been suddenly removed. The fleshy form of what was once Stanly Bolinski was now just a pile of human mush spreading out on the ground.

LOOK AT ME, demanded the evil, smoky, dark figure.

Tamara heard the commanding words shouting at her but she resisted looking directly at the menacing figure.

I SAID, LOOK AT ME! LOOK AT ME, OR I WILL RIP OUT YOUR EYES!

In this nightmare Tamara was shaking with fear.

HE'S NOT THE ONE YOU NEED TO FEAR. I'M THE ONE YOU NEED TO BE AFRAID OF.

"Why me?"

BECAUSE YOU ARE WEAK AND I DESPISE WEAK, USELESS HUMANS! growled the evil shape.

"I am not weak. I don't deserve this. Leave me alone," said a suddenly defiant dream-state Tamara.

LEAVE YOU ALONE? THAT'S FUNNY. I'M JUST GETTING STARTED. KNOW THIS - FIRST, I WILL KILL YOUR HUSBAND. THEN I WILL KILL YOUR CHILDREN RIGHT BEFORE YOUR EYES. NEXT I WILL HAVE YOU IN WAYS YOU CAN NOT IMAGINE. YOU WILL BEG FOR DEATH OVER AND OVER. ONLY I WILL BE THE ONLY ONE WHO CAN GRANT YOU YOUR REQUEST. MAYBE I WILL OR JUST MAYBE, I WILL FIND A BETTER USE FOR YOU.

The dark evil figure laughed a throaty laugh. Tamara could see a large maw forming in the place where a mouth should be.

The figure reached out and put its icy cold black hands on her shoulders and pushed down. She fought with all her strength against its efforts to force her down onto her knees. Somehow it didn't seem content with just forcing her to her knees. Powerful arms drove her down lower and lower. She reached up with her own hands and arms and flailed at the powerful death grip this menacing figure had on her. The evil figure now shifted his hands from pushing down on her shoulders to slipping around her neck.

Its grip began to tighten and tighten.

Tamara struggled against the powerful chocking grip. Her efforts were useless.

She felt coldness seize her entire body. She needed to draw a breath but couldn't.

Her mind screamed at her.

"Breathe, breathe, breathe damn it!"

She felt she was drawing her last breath when the evil figure's face seemed to be thrust right up against her own. *Not now, not here, but soon,* growled the shape.

Tamara suddenly awoke from her nightmare. She was underwater. In a panic she pushed frantically against the slippery sides of the Jacuzzi until she could push herself into a sitting position. She gasped for air. Chocking on water she had ingested she climbed out of the frigid Jacuzzi. She turned off the water jets.

Her entire body quaked with fear and from the cold.

The bathroom mirror had steamed up. When she reached up and touched it the surface was icy cold. It wasn't steam clouding the mirror it was a thin layer of ice.

Tamara wrapped a bath towel around her. She couldn't stop shaking as her teeth suddenly began to chatter. She removed the towel and slipped into her cold bed clothes and equally chilly bathrobe.

She could see her breath in the humid air of the bathroom.

She felt cold, violated and watched, all at the same time.

Then she began to feel angry. The anger began to help raise her body temperature.

She picked up her watch and looked at the time.

According to her watch she had been in the bathroom for seventeen minutes, yet it felt to her as if she had been in the bathroom, immersed in that horrifying nightmare, for hours.

Even though she could not detect anyone in the room with her, she still felt a presence of some kind.

"You leave my family alone. Don't you even think of coming after my family. I don't know how right now, but I will fight you. I will find a way to stop you. Now get out of my house, **NOW!**" shouted and angry Tamara.

In the amount of time it takes one to snap their fingers, the air in the bathroom returned to normal.

Even though things had seemingly returned to normal Tamara still found herself quaking from both the cold and the dark experience.

Later she sat up in bed and tried reading a book.

When her husband joined her in bed for the night he reached over and kissed her goodnight.

He immediately noticed how cold and waxen her lips felt.

"Honey, are coming down with something?" asked her husband.

"No, I don't think so."

He decided to let it go for now. He would check on her in the morning.

He rolled over and turned off the light on his nightstand. Tamara continued to try and read. Eventually she gave up and put the book on the nightstand on her side of the bed. She turned off her nightstand light. She slipped beneath the covers and pulled the blankets up under her chin.

Tamara didn't sleep at all. She was simply too terrified to close her eyes. She was deeply afraid of what waited for her if she fell asleep.

232

Chapter 52
East Coast Trucking
Office of Stanley Bolinski
Manchester, New Hampshire
August 24

Stanley was busy this morning.

He had been in touch with all of his drivers lining up their schedules for the next few days. He ended up having to call in four of his part-timers to fill in some gaps.

One of the office women entered his office and dropped off a pile of new trip orders.

The pace of work for long distance truck haulers had been picking up lately as the overall economy continued its recovery from one of the longest economic slumps in modern history. Stanley looked at the pile of new trip orders and smiled. His drivers would be happy with the increased work. It would boost their income which would be a welcome relief.

The woman lingered in front of his desk as he thumbed through the pile of paper she had just deposited in his in-basket.

"What is it Marge?"

"Did you see those two men in Fred's office?"

"What are you talking about?"

"Two men in business suits are in with Fred. They have been meeting with him since 8:00 o'clock this morning. Shortly after the men entered his office he came out and told me he doesn't want to be disturbed. He even closed the blinds to his office."

"So he's meeting with two guys, no big deal." said Stanley with a shrug of his shoulders.

"Stanley, I tell you, something is up. I can feel it. One of those guys had a huge brief case like lawyers have, you know, the kind which looks like a piece of luggage. They didn't have an appointment either." she said with emphasis.

"Okay, Marge I can see this has your curiosity seriously ramped up."

"What do you think they're talking about?"

"How should I know?"

"Do you think the company is in trouble? Do you think Fred is looking into filing for bankruptcy?"

"No and no, enough already! Look, you just handed me a pile of new trip orders. We're close to running at maximum now. If things keep up we may well have to take on some additional drivers. I seriously doubt the company is in trouble. Now get out of here. I have a lot of work to do."

He waved her away.

Before she left his office she turned and said, "Mark my words Stanley, something is going on. You'll see."

She turned and left his office.

Soon after she left Stanley stood up and closed his office door.

He didn't like being interrupted and he didn't like wasting time on office gossip. He preferred being focused only on the things that mattered to him.

Right now the one thing which mattered to him was planning the murder of PA Tamara Sacha.

His dark and evil partner was pacing the floor in Stanley's office.

So, have you decided how you're going to handle her?

"No, not yet. I'm not in any hurry on this. I need to keep away from her for a while so the police don't automatically suspect me. I don't want or need their attention. You already know that."

Yeah I do, but if that's all you're worried about, I can take of it for you while you set up a solid alibi. That should take care of your cop problem.

"Not necessarily, you know cops are suspicious by nature. They may still spend too much time linking me to her murder.

Who knows what they might stumble on? I don't want to risk it right now. Don't worry, she's on my list and she will be destroyed by me when I am good and ready. End of discussion."

Stanley's evil companion wasn't happy with him. Leaving her alone for however long it might be wasn't satisfying for the evil one. He decided he would continue to press Stanley until Tamara Sacha was dead.

Just then Marge returned. She knocked insistently on Stanley's door.

Stanley pushed himself up from his office chair and went to his office door. He unlocked the door and peered at Marge. He held the door open just a crack refusing to open the door and invite her back into his office.

"What is it now?" he demanded.

"I just want you to know Fred cancelled all of his calls and meetings for the rest of the day. He left his office and said he didn't expect to be back today. He even locked his office door. He told me to tell you he had to leave and if you need to reach him you can leave a message on his cell phone. And, the two men in suits left with him."

Marge raised her eyebrows while tilting her head upward at Stanley.

"In all the years I have worked here he's never done anything like this. I'm telling you, something is going on."

Marge pushed her black butterfly rimmed glasses back up the bridge of her nose while she slightly shook her curly, shoulder length, auburn hair.

Without another word she turned and walked away with the air of someone who had just scored a personal point in an ongoing battle of wits.

Score one for Marge.

Stanley closed his office door and hurried to his computer. He decided he wanted to check his computer to see if the company owner, Fred Hillard, had sent him an email which might reveal what was going on.

Stanley would never admit it openly but he had to agree Marge was right. Something was happening and Stanley needed to know what it was. He didn't like surprises.

Stanley sat down at his desk and entered his password. He logged into his office email account. There were four messages, none of which were from the company owner.

Stanley's curiosity ramped up to maximum speed. He didn't like this feeling. Fred's unexplained behavior and accompanying secrecy had all the hallmarks of something big happening.

Stanley decided to put his dark and menacing partner into action.

He commanded the smoky, shadowy figure to find out what Fred Hilliard was up to.

With an electric crackling sound, his partner disappeared. This assignment was one of things he did best.

Chapter 53
Home of retired FBI Profiler, Kit Baylor
Island Pond, Vermont
August 24

Kit rubbed both of his eyes with the backs of his hands. He was extremely tired. He had only three hours of fitful sleep last night.

The case was wearing on him. Shortly after noon today he developed a low grade fever. He was keeping it in check with large doses of Tylenol. So far the fever had stayed at a steady 100 degrees. Still it affected his concentration and now he began to battle a heavy sense of fatigue.

Kit poured over the information his friend at the FBI had turned up. Nothing stood out there either.

Kit sat back in the chair and folded his hands behind his head.

Whenever he was stymied with a profile he would often reverse his role as the FBI Profiler to that of the un-sub.

His thoughts began to pour out in a tide of questions. *What would the un-sub need to know to commit the crimes? What special skills would be needed? How were these skills acquired? Where would one go to acquire such skills? How were the victims selected? How does the killer escape? If the killer had help, who is a likely helper? What role does the killer require the helper to play? Has the killer tutored anyone to succeed him?*

Kit's mind worked through these and many other questions as he searched for the most likely answers which best matched the record of kills he had been intensely studying for over two straight days.

Trust your instincts, he thought with a constancy developed through years of discipline as a hunter of serial killers.

Slowly his keen mind began to piece together shapes which led his mind to whittle away at these amorphous hidden thoughts until he felt the certainty of conviction overtake him.

The first thing to emerge from his complicated roundabout analysis was a vision this killer or killers probably started out killing at a very early age. Early on, this killer must have honed his craft with an impulsive killing or two. His mind then locked onto the notion there really was only one killer. Perhaps someone else is involved but not necessarily a co-equal killer, maybe a coach, a teacher or even a guardian. Kit's mind continued its own unique analysis and concluded the killer, after the first couple of murders, would have begun to try and control its murderous urges. He would have recognized straight away that by carrying on with impulsive killings, he would surely be caught.

Yes that's it, thought Kit as he hurriedly made notes in his notebook. The killer's a male with a keen mind, with practiced self-control. For the longest time he was learning from each murder but now things were different. He was becoming impatient.

Kit's mind kept at it, kept grinding away.

His highly trained mind continued to run its own internal analysis.

This killer has been very methodical for a very long time. His killings have involved several types of weapons. He's used guns of different caliber. He's also used knifes, blunt instruments and garrotes as well. He has been able to get close to his victims. In some cases it appears the killer was able to sneak up to his victims, unseen. Yet in other instances it appeared he must have had face to face encounters and even likely conversations with his victims before he took their lives.

Kit began to write once more in his notebook.

His newest entry simply said, "Highly trained killer with excellent knowledge of several weapons and killing techniques. Killer also demonstrates likely clandestine stalking techniques and possible use of disguises to keep victims at ease until killing is executed."

He reviewed his latest notes.

"Damn, it reads like a want ad for a killer," said Kit to no one.

Then he added another note to his last entry. The notation simply said, "Military Training."

What evidence suggested the aid of an accomplice?

That was a tough one. There was scant evidence on that point but for one obvious thing. The recent murder of the three young boys at the movie complex suggested the likely use of an accomplice. To be able to kill one boy at a time strongly suggested somehow two boys were subdued or restrained while their friend was killed before their very eyes. Then the process was repeated between the remaining boys. Yet the police and medical examiner had not found any signs of physical restraint such as rope burns or stun gun marks. The toxicology data did not reveal the use of any drugs or alcohol which might have been used to impair the boys or diminish their reactions.

This all pointed to someone else, someone who could intimidate two boys and then one boy into complete silence while watching their friends die and without fleeing for their own life or raising an alarm. Such an incredible set of circumstances. Yet Kit's instinct needle was way to the right on this one. There had to be an accomplice, someone with the overwhelming power to terrorize the victim to a near point of paralysis. This accomplice didn't just happen on the scene of this one crime. Someone with that type of ability would have been very useful at some of the other crime scenes too.

In Kits' mind he was certain the un-sub has a partner with an incredible ability to terrorize and intimidate. Either the size or appearance of this other un-sub must play a role in these crimes.

What else could there be? thought Kit.

Kit unfolded his entwined fingers from behind his head.

His arms felt heavy and weak. His mind suddenly felt drained. *Dying sucks*, he thought.

Chapter 54
New Hampshire State Police
Cold Case Unit
Concord, New Hampshire
August 24

Mark Atkinson couldn't stay seated. He paced the floor of his office much like a lion in a cage. His eyes kept glancing back to the large victim board he had propped up on the top of his antique office credenza.

The victim board had a time line along the top edge. Beneath the time line and pinned to the board were copies of photos of the victims from the cold case unit files of Maine, New Hampshire and Vermont. These were the unsolved murders or missing person cases which were likely murders fitting the original theory Mark had developed on the un-sub now at the epicenter of this multi-state investigation. Below each image was a 3x5 card with the date of the murder or date of when the likely victim was first reported missing. Finally beneath the index cards were other index cards filled with bullet points about each case. These cards contained the key details of each case.

The time line went back nearly forty years to 1973. It carried forward to include the recent murders of three teenage boys at a Hooksett, New Hampshire, movie theater complex on the "possibility" the case might be related. Mark had a strong hunch the triple murder did connect.

Mark needed the visual aid of the victim board to help him think. He also needed the board to help him stay focused on the details. In this particular case there were many facts, but also too many gaps of the sort of critical pieces police usually depended upon to help them break a case open.

On Mark's desk was a map of New England with dark red spots all over the three northern states. The dark red spots represented the places where victim's bodies were found or where other victims went missing. Yellow highlighter lines were drawn along major roadways connecting these red dots. The highlighted roadways Mark felt were the routes taken by the unsub to move between locations to either escape from the crime or to hunt his next victim.

The map looked like a spider web.

Mark felt a heavy burden from all of this.

He always personalized his investigations. Once he took on a case, Mark felt he owed the victim justice and closure. He would speak for the victim. The victim was his until he solved the case. But now, the sheer size of this investigation was pressing down on him and he was feeling emotionally drained. Every morning since this case first took hold of him he would look in the morning mirror and vow to see it through.

Looking into his bathroom mirror he would speak a daily variation of these words, "I will not let you down. I swear I will hunt down the bastard and that's a promise."

Mark paced the floor when suddenly his phone rang.

He pounced on the desk phone.

It was Kit Baylor.

"Mark is that you?" asked Kit in a voice barely above a whisper.

"Yeah, Kit it's me. What's up? You sound tired. Are you okay?"

"Yeah, I'm tired and I don't feel too good either. My temperature is spiking. Right now, it's 102 degrees. Listen, I am going to have someone take me to the hospital in Burlington. I called my doctor and he wants me to come in right away. I wanted to call you first because I have a couple of ideas which might help on this case."

"Wait let me sit down and take some notes." Mark swung himself back behind his desk and grabbed a notebook and a pen. "Okay, I'm ready."

Mark heard Kit laborious breathing through the phone.

"First, thing, is this. I strongly believe our killer has committed murders before our timeline. His killing had to have begun at a much earlier age. We need to look for murders before the timeline we have been looking at. These murders or even missing person cases would very likely be clustered together both in time and location. I know CCU records don't go back that far. I also know our killer might have gotten his start outside of New England, but right now I doubt that. My instincts tell me he started here and has been hunting here all this time."

"I'll see what I can find. Doug and Alice can work their files and I will work mine. Is there anything else?"

Kit let out a deep sigh before resuming.

"I also believe our un-sub has had extensive military training. He is way too proficient with a wide array of weapons and killing techniques to have picked this up on his own. We have three on our truck driver list who have the right kind of military training which would fit this profile point. These three were green berets. I recommend you move these three to the top of your list. I will send you, by fax today, the military backgrounds on our truck drivers. The last thing I came up with is this guy has had a partner for a very long time. This partner only rarely and directly involves himself in the actual murder, but he is a player, count on it. What is strange about this partner is he can intimidate and control some of the vics without laying a hand on them. I can see it clearly in the killings at the movie complex. This suggests to me this other un-sub is one powerful and scary individual. When you guys are running your analysis and interviews keep a look out for a close friend, a possible relative, someone who is close and scary as hell."

"Okay, I got all that," said Mark. "Is that it?"

"Yeah, for now. Look, I have got to go, my ride just pulled up. If I can think of anything else I'll give you a call."

"Kit. Take care brother, we need you. Our vics need you, too."

"I know Mark, believe me I know. I'll be in touch."

The phone connection ended with a click and then a dial tone.

Mark held the phone close to his ear a bit longer. He imagined himself still talking with Kit. He could still hear his voice and see him in his mind's eye. Mark slowly replaced the telephone on the phone console.

He was deeply worried for Kit. For just a fleeting moment he wondered whether he would ever see him again.

Mark's next move was to call Doug and Alice. He filled them in on what Kit had passed along.

Before Kit left the Town of Island Pond, he had his friend stop by the Pride and Joy Restaurant to ask the owner to fax the military information to Mark.

Kit stayed in the car while his friend went inside.

Kit reached into his right side jacket pocket for a container of pills. He shook out the pills into his left hand. He pushed through the pills until he had found the Tylenol ones. He slipped the other pills into the container. Kit tossed back the Tylenol tablets before swallowing some water from the water bottle he had brought along for the nearly two hour ride.

It was only seventy-two degrees today and very cloudy with a strong westerly breeze. To Kit, it felt like it was in the high nineties with high humidity. He was burning up with fever.

He knew the fever was not a good sign for him. He silently prayed he would make it to the hospital in time.

Chapter 55
New Hampshire State Police
Cold Case Unit
Concord, New Hampshire
Late in the Afternoon of August 24

Mark heard the fax machine's familiar dial-up tone. He hurried over to the machine and waited.

Once the complete message had come through he went back inside his office and sat down to look over the information.

It didn't take him long to pick out the three individuals who once were Green Berets.

One was a man named Jack Peters. His current address placed him in Brattleboro, Vermont. The second Green Beret was someone with the name of Oscar Tilton who apparently lived in Deering, New Hampshire. The remaining Green Beret was someone named Stanley Bolinski. This last guy lived in Manchester, New Hampshire.

For now these three would become the focus of the investigation until such time as they could be ruled out.

Mark's gut told him he was getting close.

He immediately called Doug back and filled him in about Jack Peters of Brattleboro, Vermont. Mark decided to fire off a short email message to Alice telling her that for now, she didn't have a Green Beret suspect in Maine to chase down.

Mark used his access to computer data mining programs to dig out everything he could about his two New Hampshire suspects, Oscar Tilton and Stanley Bolinski.

It was getting late.

In fact it was so late, Mark was the only one left in the office.

He pulled out everything he could on each man he was looking at.

Mark had their motor vehicle records along with their individual driving records. He also obtained the vehicle registrations. Mark pulled marriage records. It looked like Oscar was divorced long ago and hadn't remarried. As for Stanley, he had never married. He had also obtained copies of the suspect's tax records. There was nothing of any consequence in this particular data. It seemed Oscar held a Federal Firearms Dealer License. He had been dealing in guns for over twenty years.

Both Oscar and Stanley had sought local permission to carry a concealed forearm. Permission had been granted by their respective local Police Chiefs.

Oscar had both hunting and fishing licenses while Stanley did not.

Both men were current on their local taxes.

Finally, both men had no police records of any consequence. Oscar had never received any police citations, nor had he ever been charged with any crimes. There was no record of any complaints either. The records also revealed Oscar Tilton once reported a burglary at his home back in 2002.

Stanley had a clean record as well. His only apparent contact with local police involved being questioned about missing persons many years ago. The missing persons were apparently tenants who rented from Bolinski.

Both guys were looking like model citizens.

Mark stood up from his desk and stretched out his chair-weary body.

He grabbed his jacket off the coat rack and headed out of the office. He would start again in the morning. He called up his girlfriend to grab a late dinner somewhere. His mind was filled to the point of overload. He had to get away from all of this for a few hours just to recharge.

During the drive to pick up his girlfriend, he thought about Kit Baylor, the retired FBI Profiler. He was deeply concerned about Kit's battle with pancreatic cancer. Kit was living with a death sentence, yet he was still willing to join in the hunt to capture this serial killer. There was no doubt in Mark's mind that Kit's days were numbered. He prayed the end wouldn't come until after this serial killer was found and arrested. Mark felt Kit needed to know his exceptional talents had once again contributed in a huge way in bringing this serial killer to justice.

In a very short period of time Mark had developed a huge amount of admiration and respect for Kit. He considered Kit a friend. His first impression of Kit had quickly evaporated and was replaced by a powerful bond Mark cherished.

Would Kit have enough time? thought Mark.

If asked, just then, for his opinion Mark would have answered, "I don't know" and that unknown was becoming a powerful emotional force deep inside of this investigator.

Chapter 56
Dubuque Street, West Side Neighborhood
Manchester, New Hampshire
Home of Stanley Bolinski
Evening of August 24

Stanley was in an absolute rage. He stormed about in his residence wanting very much to destroy everything in his sight.

His deeply evil partner returned to him on his drive home from work.

Stanley had not considered the possibility his partner revealed. The news came as a sucker punch to the explosive Bolinski.

Those guys he met with earlier today are trying to buy the company. They are representatives from some large Illinois trucking company. Their offer to buy Fred's company came as a surprise to him. The reason he left the office in such a hurry was because he was headed to his accountant's office to discuss the offer and the tax consequences. Apparently he's tired of the business and welcomes the buyout offer. From what I heard him say to his accountant, several people would likely lose their jobs if he sells the company. Your job is one of those which would be eliminated.

"First, I have this damn diabetes. Then, that bitch Tamara sets me up to lose my CDLA driver's license and now this shit has to happen. What in the hell is going on here?"

Stanley prowled his kitchen. Explosively he decided to kick the garbage can across the kitchen. Garbage flew everywhere. The overturned kitchen garbage can careened off of a small wall which separated the kitchen from the dining room. The heavily dented can spun to a stop against the dining room antique sideboard.

Stanley ignored the trash, stomping through it all while he moved into the living room.

Slamming his right fist into his left palm he growled, "That son-of-a-bitch, Fred, just punched his own ticket. Now I have to kill him too. Will killing him stop the sale of the company?" asked Stanley.

I doubt it. His family is even more likely to want to sell.

A fuming Stanley shouted, "**Damn it all to hell!**"

Then he suddenly turned to his dark and evil partner and demanded an answer to his next question.

"Is there a way to persuade him not to sell? I need this job just as much as I need my CDLA license. If I lose both I will never have a chance to be on the road. I need to be on the road. I just need to be."

"Stan, my man, you can always be on the road. We can go out anytime you want. We just take your car and we go. It will be just you and me on the road. What a team, a dream team."

"You don't understand. A car won't work. People remember cars. They remember color, type and they can usually get a good look at the driver. It's different with a big rig. To most people, big rigs more or less look alike. They don't see color or type, all they see is big. Shit they seldom can remember the company name. They sure as shit can't recall what the driver looks like. It's been my cover for all these years. I need to drive a rig and that's all there is to say. So, can he be persuaded to change his mind or not?"

All right my friend I see your point. To stop him from selling you have three possible choices. One, you can try and buy the company yourself. That won't work because everyone knows you don't have the money to pull that off. If we had more time perhaps we could get our hands on enough but I doubt we have enough time to pull that off. The second choice is to kill the guy who is trying to buy the company. I could do that if you want me to. Or the third approach is this, either you or I threaten to kill his family if he tries to sell the company. From what I know of this guy, he's hung up on his family. If you threaten him then he would have something on you and that knowledge could become dangerous. If I pay him a visit and scare the shit out of him he won't be able to connect me to you. So, do you want me to take care of this? I would love to do this Stanley. Just say the word, my brother.

Stanley didn't answer his dark angel. He needed time to think things through.

"Boom, Boom, Boom, …..Boom, Boom."

Stanley rushed to the front of the living room and looked out onto the street in front of his building.

A small black car with deeply tinted side and back windows drove slowly up Dubuque Street. The heavily amped up bass notes thumping from the car's oversized stereo speakers caused the glass in the windows of Stanley's property to rattle.

In his agitated state of mind he became instantly enraged at the disturbance caused by the neighborhood punks. He threw open his front door and shouted at the top of his lungs "**turn down the fucking radio.**"

At first it seemed like the occupants of the small car hadn't heard him.

Then just before reaching the street corner the car stopped and slowly backed up before stopping directly in front of Stanley's property.

The driver's darkly tinted window slowly lowered. The driver of the car was a young street tough Stanley had seen many times before. The young man smiled at Stanley and said, "Hey old man, you have something to say?"

"Yeah I do. I don't care what crap you want to listen to in that shit box you call a car. But I don't want to have to hear your shit music inside my house. So do yourself a favor and dial it down."

The young punk turned around and said something inside of the car to his friends and laughter erupted from inside the car. The punk returned his gaze back to Stanley and slowly began to turn up the volume until it was much louder than before.

Other neighbors looked on from the relative safety of their homes or apartments at the brewing confrontation.

The punk sat in his car and smirked at Stanley.

Stanley stared back at the driver.

The driver put his car in gear and slowly pulled away. He and his three friends raised their hands out the car's windows and collectively gave Stanley the finger.

Stanley glanced around at his neighbors who swiftly pulled away from gazing out their windows.

He headed back inside his house.

"I want you to go to Fred tomorrow and set him straight, if he chooses to sell the company both he and his family will die. Tell him he will get to watch them die before you kill him. Then tomorrow night you and I are going to pay a visit to those street assholes who just drove by. It's past time someone teaches them some manners."

Chapter 57
Home of Fred Hilliard
Bedford, New Hampshire
Late morning of August 25

Fred had just enjoyed a morning round of lovemaking with his wife. He felt exhilarated by the offer to buy his company, East Coast Trucking. He and his wife agreed it would be the best thing overall for the family. Fred had college bound teenagers still in high school and with the sale of the company he would have the money to pay for college tuition and much, much more. The offer was for just over 6 million dollars for the hard assets of the company. The five year fuel contract he had bought into last year added another 1.5 million and then the business accounts added another 4.3 million for a total of 11.8 million. His accountant estimated that after taxes he would net around 7.5 million. If invested conservatively he could expect to gross over $400,000 per year with most of that, tax free income.

The clincher was he would have to sign a non-competition agreement whereby he would agree not to go into a similar business for a period of not less than seven years. He was eager to sign that for sure. He would be free of the business, the daily grind, the responsibility and everything which went with it.

He had asked if he could have the weekend to think it over. The representatives of the Illinois buyer had agreed. They made it quite clear, they required his answer by 11:00 a.m. Monday the 25th.

Fred was standing in the shower soaping up. The water was turned up to the high temperature he preferred. He began to hum a favorite tune as the hot water ran down over his head.

He had his back turned to the rear of the oversized shower. He began to scrub his back with a soapy brush.

After two strokes with the bath brush the hand holding the brush was seized by a large and powerful hand.

He couldn't break free. He was about to say something when a second and equally powerful hand wrapped around his mouth. His body was pulled tight against someone who was evidently much taller and certainly more powerful than he.

He struggled to break free but the more he did so the tighter the grip seemed to get.

Then he heard the voice.

"Fred, I've come to pay you a personal visit. You see, I have some advice you're going to want to hear before you make that business call on Monday. You know the one where you sell off your old man's business, you sack of shit."

The voice wasn't spoken out loud, it emanated from inside his own mind.

The voice was threatening in ways Fred didn't yet understand. His mind was in overdrive trying to figure out who had managed to sneak up on him, *in his own goddamn shower. Who in the hell sent this asshole?*

The threatening voice continued, *"Fred, don't even think about the money. In fact don't even think about all the exotic trips you could take with your wife or the places you two could get it on. I don't want you to even think about giving up your wonderful life as owner of your own company. You know why? Because I am going to make you an even better offer. This offer you will not refuse. In fact you will quickly agree it is a more superior and well thought out alternative to the one you already have."*

Fred was confused. This was some strange way to make a business offer. For now, all he could do was listen.

"Fred, my offer is this. Are you listening carefully? I am only going to say this once and I don't want any unfortunate misunderstandings. If you accept the other offer your family will die. I will come back, I will find you and make you watch as I kill your children first then your wife and finally I will kill you. Don't even think you can hide from me. No amount of protection can save you from this."

Fred's heart began to thunder in his chest. His head felt like it was about to explode. Fred's kidneys suddenly failed him too.

"Now Fred, if you do as I ask, everything can continue as it is. You would have your business and you would still have your beautiful family. I'm sure you now see my offer is a fair and generous one. Don't you agree?"

The evil shadow threw Fred out of the shower and onto the bathroom floor. Fred slammed into the bathroom vanity. Slipping and sliding on the wet tiled bathroom floor, he scampered to turn around and look at his assailant. What he saw terrified him. He let out a blood curdling scream.

The dark angel towered over Fred. He stepped away from the oversized shower and bent down so that his face was directly in front of Fred.

Fred was mumbling something.

Elsewhere in the house, Fred's wife called out to him.

"So my wet and soiled friend, what is your answer?"

The evil one allowed his piercing red eyes to be revealed from deep in the smoky countenance of his face.

Fred cringed further at the sight of those menacing eyes.

He stammered, "I, I, will not sell my company. Please, please you have got to believe me. I won't sell. Don't hurt my family."

"Now, that is great news. I suggest you go and round up that lovely wife of yours and share it with her before you screw her again."

The ink black shadow stood up and laughed a deep and throaty laugh before evaporating into the steamy bathroom air.

Fred struggled to his feet and turned off the shower just as his wife burst through the bathroom door.

Her husband Fred was standing there naked in front of her. Water was everywhere.

"Fred, what happened in here?"

Fred didn't answer her right then. He simply collapsed onto the closed toilet seat and began to sob with his head in his hands.

He rocked back and forth shuddering while pouring out a painful wail that deeply unsettled and frightened his wife.

Chapter 58
Dubuque Street, West Side Neighborhood
Manchester, New Hampshire
Home of Stanley Bolinski
Evening of August 25

Stanley had been elated all day long with the news his dark angel delivered to him concerning the morning visit he had with Stanley's boss, Fred Hilliard.

"You, my friend, are a genius when it comes to scaring the shit out of somebody. I mean it. So do you really think he's going to abandon his plan to sell the trucking company?"

"*I would bet his wife and kids on it,*" laughed his evil companion.

"This is so damn incredible. Now all that is left for us to do today is take care of a little neighborhood business. I want to show those punks they can't screw with me. Tonight we hunt."

"*Isn't this a little too close to home? Someone might connect you to them, you know, because of yesterday. They might whisper your name to the police.*"

"You don't have to worry about this? I have it all figured out. Nobody will connect me to this, you'll see."

"*Okay, so when do we do this?*"

"We follow them tonight and wait for the right time and location. Then we swoop in and take care of business."

"*I am sooooooooooooooooooooo ready!*" sung the dark shadow figure.

That put a smile on Stanley's face.

Things were righting themselves as far as Stanley was concerned. Lately his life was just one long roller coaster ride, a thrill a minute if you asked him.

Chapter 59
Home of retired FBI Profiler, Kit Baylor
Island Pond, Vermont
August 25

Kit gave a small wave to his friend as he drove away.

His oncologist kept him in the hospital overnight for observation. He suspected Kit had contracted an infection which would account for his fever.

He had been given antibiotics intravenously. They seemed to work well enough. Kit's fever was gone. His oncologist released him from the hospital

Kit was free to return home.

This time a different friend had driven from Island Pond to Burlington to retrieve Kit and take him back home. His friend this time around was the owner and head cook of Island Pond's favorite restaurant, the Pride and Joy.

The conversation was lively and varied as one would expect. Kit's friend actually did most of the talking and Kit held up his end by doing most of the listening.

He dragged himself into his house. It was nearly 9:30 in the evening.

Kit was heading to his mother's bedroom to check in on her when he noticed her sitting in the living room. She was sitting in a Queen Anne style chair with a nearby table lamp turned on. She was busily engaged in knitting what appeared to be a sweater.

"Ma, were you waiting up for me?"

"Of course dear. That's what mother's do, you know."

"There is no need to stay up now that I am home. You can go to bed."

"Now Crosby Baylor, Don't you go telling me when I must go to bed. I'm old enough to know when I need to be in bed. Now sit yourself down and tell me all about it. Would you like me to fix you some tea?"

"I'll make the tea. I'll be back in a couple of minutes."

Kit turned around and headed back to the kitchen to make some tea for the two of them.

Hearing his mother playfully scold him actually gave him reassurance and comfort. No matter how he felt he always worried about his mother and she in turn did likewise.

He returned moments later with two tea cups, tea bags and saucers. He retrieved some vanilla wafers from the kitchen along with a teapot of hot water. He poured the water for his mother and himself. He returned the teapot to the kitchen, shuffled back to the living room and sat down in a matching chair next to hers.

Kit began talking about his visit to the hospital and what everyone told him. He reassured his mother he was feeling fine although that was a half-truth. He was actually feeling weak. For now, he couldn't feel warm enough.

"So now that you have brought me up to date on this hospital visit how about you tell me where things are with this mysterious killer you and the others are hunting?"

"Mom, it is getting late for both of us. We can talk about this tomorrow."

"I am not tired in the least. So unless you are heading to bed I suggest you begin."

His mother never even looked at him as she spoke. Her fingers were flying with the movement of yarn and the clicking of the knitting needles she deftly held in her delicate and nearly translucent hands.

Kit began to tell his mother the latest insights he had developed and the progress of the CCU investigators.

His mother was a very good listener and rarely interrupted.

She kept at her knitting only occasionally shifting herself in the chair.

As Kit was winding down she finally interrupted him with a question.

"You mentioned something earlier about how this killer must have begun at a very early age."

"Yes, that is when he would have begun to evolve as a killer from killing on impulse to killing with control."

"I see. And you also think these early murders would have happened close together and near to one another. What was that word you used, oh yes, I remember it now. The word was cluster."

"That's right. Why do you ask?"

"Oh, I was just thinking."

"Thinking about what?"

"I was thinking about a time many years ago when I was a teacher. You do remember I was a High School Teacher once. You were in grammar school back then. We moved to Maryland the year you would have been a freshman. I gave up teaching and took on a job with that law firm. Anyway I remember when I was a teacher we had a young boy in school who went missing. Many in the community thought he was the victim of foul play."

"Go on," said Kit with a degree of curiosity.

"Well, it wasn't long after that when another odd thing happened. A young couple from school died in a terrible car accident."

"Your point is?"

"There was a boy in school who was involved with both situations. In the first instance he was bullied by the boy. This bully had many victims, but still."

"This other kid, was he friends with the couple?"

"Oh dear. No, not at all, you see there was an incident in school where the girl asked the other boy to the Sadie Hawkins dance and he refused. He thought she was trying to mock him. He thought she would dump him at the dance or something like that. As I recall the girl's boyfriend and this boy argued over this too."

"Do you remember this boy's name?"

"No, dear. I'm sure someone at the school might or maybe someone in town might recall this boy's name."

"We moved around a lot when I was young. What town was this all happening in?"

"It was St. Johnsbury, Vermont, not far from here. I taught English at the high school. The school is called the St. Johnsbury Academy."

"Okay, ma that might help. I'll try and make some calls on Monday."

"Oh, and dear, and there is one other thing I remember about that boy. Right after we moved one of our neighbors back then dropped me a note to see how things were. That's what friends do. Anyway, inside her note she sent along a newspaper article about this boy. The news story described a horrible fire at his home. It seems both his mother and father died in the fire."

Kit's curiosity now kicked into overdrive.

He left his chair in the living room to retrieve his case book he used for jotting his notes in.

For the next several minutes Kit pumped his mother for anything and everything she could recall about this boy.

Could he allow himself to think that somehow he had stumbled upon the genesis phase of the serial killer he was now hunting? His mother, of all people, may have held the key to this case. It was almost too incredible to believe. Yet, he did allow himself to believe, just a tiny bit.

He knew, from his many years of police work, knowledge, skill and resources were the important factors in solving cases. But, once in while it also took some luck, or as some would say, divine intervention, to help break a case open.

Perhaps this would be one of those times.

Chapter 60
Manchester, New Hampshire
Kimball Street
Kelley Falls Housing Development
August 26

Stanley Bolinski slowly rolled his car up the short, steep hill on Kimball Street. It was 3:30 in the darkness of a moonlit night with hardly any clouds in the dark sky. The overhead moon would be full in just two days.

As his car crested the rise of the hill he spotted the now familiar taillights of the car he had been following for the past two hours. He had kept his own car lights off while tailing his next victims.

The small car he was following took a right turn. It was apparently going to cruise the backside of the low income family housing development alongside the part that abutted Rimmon Park.

Stanley moved his car cautiously forward.

He noticed the car he was following had come to a stop. Its taillights flashed bright red.

Stanley stopped his own car.

He could see, in the moonlight, four young men get out of the car and stroll towards the adjacent park. Two of the young men were noticeably smoking. In the still night air he could hear them laughing and talking.

They hopped the chain link fence and passed a bag over as they did so.

Stanley looked at the housing development. No lights were on in any of the apartments.

This seemed like the perfect place and perfect moment.

Stanley reached up and disabled the interior light of his own car.

He slipped out of the car. He inserted the Smith and Wesson 40 caliber handgun into his left side waistband underneath his belt. From there he could draw the gun quickly and effectively. The gun clip held 14 rounds of hollow point ammunition. He was ready for business. He decided against using a silencer. This time, loud noise would be his friend. It would scare off any good Samaritans should they consider becoming involved.

Stanley noticed the moon would be at his back as he approached the young punks. This would help too. With the light at his back his targets would find it difficult to pick up his features before it was too late.

Stanley whispered to his partner, the evil one, to circle around the punks and come at them from behind. Stanley trusted his fiendish helpmate to wait for just the right moment to spring into action.

The four young men sat next to one of the park soccer fields. They had parked their own car in one of the slots reserved for tenants. This way any cops patrolling the development wouldn't think to look for anyone in the park. Stanley had done the same.

The men were splitting up the proceeds from an armed robbery they had committed earlier. They had robbed a neighborhood market on the Southside of the city. They had managed to get away and were giddy with their success.

"Yo, did you see that bitch piss her pants when I showed her El Diablo? She was like, you know, all tense and shit. When she saw the gun she just freaked out and pissed herself."

"Yeah, and yo, she was like so fucking nervous she couldn't open the cash drawer, man."

"What about that dude, man, you know the customer guy who came on? We beat his ass real good."

"Yeah, so how much did we get?"

"Hold your weeny bro, the bills are like all messed up. I'm trying to count them so just shut that trap of yours up bro."

The young men hadn't noticed Stanley until he climbed over the chain link fence.

Instantly all four guys leaped to their feet.

One pulled out a gun while the other three brandished knives.

"I didn't think you assholes knew how to count," said the mystery man as he slowly walked toward them.

They couldn't make out his face. His voice was familiar but for now, nothing clicked.

Adrenaline was juicing through their veins. Their hearts were pumping to the max.

They moved to loosely form a v-shaped wedge with the driver of the car, their leader, taking point.

Stanley stopped just ten feet away.

He kept his hands at his side, at the ready.

He was relaxed even though he too felt a surge of the familiar rush of adrenaline.

"Yo, old man, you don't have any business here. Why don't you go home and screw your dog or old your lady, whichever one is uglier."

The young man's remark elicited laughter from his partners.

"See, that's why I don't like you. You don't show respect. You don't respect your elders, your neighbors and you don't show me any respect. Now that isn't right. Not right at all. So I'm here to school your sorry asses and teach you the true meaning of respect."

"You have that all wrong motherfucker. We are your teachers and we are going to take you to school. Yeah, I know who you are. You're that old shit head who mouthed off to us. You live on Dubuque Street. Hey homies, look who has come to our little party. He thinks he has the tools to take us to school. Yo, its' time we teach this old fucker to respect us."

Stanley held up his left hand, signaling to hold on."

"Wait up. There is someone I want to introduce you too. You can call him my teaching assistant."

Stanley gestured to the area behind the four young men.

"He's bluffing," said their leader.

One of the young men turned his head to look over his shoulder and what he saw paralyzed him with terror. The fiery red eyes pierced the darkness as did a massive hand that gripped the boy's hand which held a knife. In one swift move Stanley's partner guided the terrified boy's hand to slit the throat of his friend standing to his left. Then the boy's arm was forced into the back of the boy standing in front of him.

The stabbed boy wheeled around, as he cried out, "What the ….. did you do?"

He tried to reach the knife stuck deep into the upper center of his back but he couldn't reach it. His fingers felt sticky with his own blood, his own life dripping out of him. He half stumbled and fell into the young man Stanley's dark angel was holding fast. The wounded man's own knife now struck deep into the belly of the other man.

The man's stomach was ripped open from the stabbing. The two boys fell into each other's arms in a deathly embrace as they slowly collapsed to the ground.

While these orchestrated attacks took place the young men's leader stole a glance over his shoulder just in time to see his two friends collapse dead to the ground. The third man in his posse was standing rigidly with his back to his leader. The young man's fingers were clawing at his own throat. In a flash he spotted two fiery red eyes fix on him. The eyes were emanating from an ink black form. The evilness released his grip dropping the breathless boy into a heap.

Before the leader could react Stanley moved in.

Stanley covered the small distance with quickness which surprised the young man. Stanley grabbed the young man's arm which held the pistol. Instead of forcing him to drop his weapon, which Stanley could have easily done, he chose to quickly force the man's arm up so the pistol was now pointing at the young man's own head.

"Sorry about your homies you useless sack of shit! They're all dead because of you. So I guess this means you're really busted up over this. You know, most guys would be so despondent they would have to take their own life."

"Pluheeeze" mumbled the deeply terrified young man. "Can't we work something out man? I, I…… am sorry I dissed you."

"Do you hear that? I think he is learning some respect after all. What do you think we should do with him?" asked Stanley.

The shadowy figure moved to stand right next to Stanley. His piercing red eyes zeroed in on the horrified young man.

I think he should do the honorable thing and join his friends. The voice of the evil thing resonated inside the man's head.

The young man still had the gun in his grip. His own fingers were wrapped around the gun handle and his trigger finger was still gripping the trigger.

The gun cocked.

The sound of the gun cocking seized the young man's attention. His bulging eyes swept a sideways look at his trembling hand. Huge beads of sweat ran down his face.

"No, no don't do this. I beg you!"

Stanley released his grip on the man's arm. He stepped back three paces. The young man still held the gun at his own head.

"Yes, yes, and don't beg. It offends me. Oh, I see you have pissed yourself. How fitting, wouldn't you say?"

The gun went off with a single shot. The bullet passed through the man's head entering on the right side just below his right ear before ripping through his brain and then exploding out the left side of his skull just above his left eye socket.

He didn't collapse to the ground. Instead the dead man was held up by Stanley's shadowy friend who helped him empty the gun on the remaining boy who was terrorized and frozen, huddled on the ground.

While these shots were being fired Stanley climbed over the chain link fence and strolled away to his car.

Unknown to Stanley, peering out on the murderous scene from an upstairs window was a young woman by the name of Keisha Mfume. She had gotten up to breast feed her two month old son. She had been feeding him while she sat in a rocker in the darkened bedroom. The sounds of voices coming from the direction of the nearby soccer field had drawn her attention. She listened, transfixed by the snippets of conversation she could pick out. The bedroom window was open just a few inches. She dared not try and open it further.

Keisha now sat, horrified, in the dark shadows of the bedroom. She had seen the muzzle flash of the gun firing again and again. Now she saw just one man walking across the grassy areas next to the parking lot as he headed towards his car. He was walking towards the moonlight.

From above, Keisha got a good look at the man.

It was a face she could not forget.

The man was smiling.

Chapter 61
Manchester, New Hampshire
Kimball Street
Kelley Falls Housing Development
August 26

Keisha Mfume held her infant son close to her chest. She was quaking with fear. She couldn't control her shaking.

Her son was asleep in her arms. She looked down on him as tears rained down from her eyes and dripped off her chin onto the baby's blanket.

It was nearly 4:00 a.m.

She was sure she had just witnessed multiple murders. She also had managed to get a good look at what she assumed to be the killer.

Alone in her apartment with her baby she didn't dare try and sneak outside and see for herself. It was still too dark to see anything. She walked the bedroom floor while holding her son in her arms, waiting for the first rays of morning light.

Her eyes kept stealing glances out the window. She was certain the man she believed to be the killer had not seen her. She had not turned on a light in the bedroom so there was no interior illumination source which might have revealed her. She heard dogs barking outside the window from just beyond the chain link fence which separated the housing development property from the adjacent expansive city park.

By eight o'clock this morning dozens of children, along with their parents and coaches, would begin to arrive for a full day of soccer matches.

She had to do something before people began to arrive but what could she do.

She didn't want to get dragged into a police investigation. She was terrified of authority almost as much as she was terrified by the killer she knew she could identify.

Finally the cloudless sky began to brighten in the East. She still kept pacing the floor. She could have put her son back in his crib to sleep but she just couldn't let go of him. Holding on to him was the only thing keeping her from losing control.

Her eyes began to adjust to the early morning light and that was when she spotted the four bodies lying in the grass behind a soccer goal just on the other side of the chain link fence.

Keisha made up her mind. She hurried to the kitchen and pulled her house keys out of her purse. She grabbed some loose change and dumped several coins into her pocket. Still in her bathrobe and wearing heavily worn sandals she slipped out of her apartment and left the building still carrying her son.

Once out of the building she turned left and walked as quickly as she dared towards a small neighborhood market located at the corner of the housing development. She was heading to the store hoping to place a call to the police by using the payphone which was bolted to the outside of the front of the store. It was one of the few places in the city which still had a working pay phone.

When she turned the corner to the front side of the store someone was already there using the phone. Keisha began to pace on the sidewalk in front of the store while glancing at the older woman using the phone.

Two minutes later the woman caller hung up the phone.

"It's all yours honey," said the woman as she walked away.

Keisha rushed up to the phone. Balancing her son in her left arm she removed the receiver and wedged it to her right ear and right shoulder. She was about to pull out some coins from her bathrobe pocket when she noticed a sticker on the pay phone change box.

The sticker read, In emergencies dial 9-1-1. Please remove the phone from the cradle and dial the numbers. You will be immediately connected to the nearest 9-1-1 operator.

Keisha dialed 9-1-1 and waited.

The phone began to ring.

"9-1-1 operator; what is the nature of your emergency?" said a woman in a monotone voice.

Keisha spoke quickly and in a hushed voice just barely above a whisper.

"There are four dead people in the park where they play soccer. I saw their bodies. You have got to send the police before the children begin to come here to play."

"Ma'am we are going to need an address or specific location. What park are you referring to?"

"It is the big one on the West side. I don't know its name. Please, hurry."

Keisha's baby began to stir.

The 9-1-1 operator asked, "Do you mean Rimmon Park just off of Kimball Street?"

"Yes, yes, that is the one," responded a relieved Keisha who now recalled the name.

"All right then, now listen to me, I am sending out a squad car now. I need you to stay on the line with me so I can direct the officers to your location."

Keisha hung up the phone and hurried back to her apartment.

She wanted no part of the police.

Her baby was now wide awake and was working hard to fill his little diaper.

Chapter 62
Manchester, New Hampshire
Kimball Street
Kelley Falls Housing Development
August 26

Lieutenant Pete Burlingame pulled his unmarked police car up next to several marked cruisers already on the scene. Another homicide detective had arrived before him and had already begun securing the crime scene.

Pete walked over to his friend and fellow homicide detective, William Karatzas, known to all in the law enforcement community as Big Willy. He stood 6 feet 6 inches tall. He was a little heavy at 265 pounds. He shaved his head bald and sported a neatly trimmed mustache which was well on its way from black to gray. His suits never seemed to hang quite right on his somewhat lumpy frame. He was constantly tucking his white dress shirt tail back in. The man had just turned forty years old. His previous stint with the Manchester Police Department had been in undercover work with the narcotics unit. He left for a short time and worked for a police department in Arizona until his divorce. He moved back to New Hampshire and rejoined the Manchester Police force. As of now he was a nine year veteran of homicide. This man loved his job almost as much as his partner did.

The two detectives exchanged looks with a nod of recognition.

Pete strolled over to the crime scene. He squatted down and took in the scene. His eyes slowly panned left to right. He repeated this sweep once more before standing back up and walking over to his partner.

"DA and AG are on the way. The state police's major crime unit van is inbound. I also rang up Terry with the gang unit. He said he would be right over. Two of the vics are wearing colors. I figure Terry might have something on who these guys hung around with or who might have a beef with them."

"Good work, Willy."

Pete noticed a crowd of adults and children had begun to gather near the back street and the parking lot of the adjacent housing development. They had come to see the bodies.

Pete gestured for one of the uniform officers to get those people out of there. The area they were milling about may yet be part of the crime scene. He didn't want to take any chances with evidence being disturbed or worse yet turning up missing.

The uniformed officer grabbed a couple of other officers. They headed in the direction of the crowd. Before long, the crowd dispersed.

Over the next several minutes all sorts of vehicles began to arrive.

When Pete had a moment he took out his cell phone and dialed Mark Atkinson's personal number. Pete had a hunch Mark might need to see this one. He might also have something to contribute to this investigation. It was a cop's hunch.

Mark's cell phone vibrated on his nightstand next to his bed. It vibrated five times and was on the verge of vibrating itself clear off the stand and onto the floor when Mark grabbed the phone, with a thumb swipe he opened his new smart phone.

It was just beginning to take a message. He had missed the call.

He put the phone back on the nightstand. He climbed out of bed and padded off to the bathroom. When he returned he checked the phone. The display screen indicated he had one new voicemail message. He swiped the menu icon and checked his messages. He listened to the brief digital recording. He quickly selected the return call button

Five minutes later Mark was flying out of his front door running to his car. He had hurriedly dressed and grabbed a cup of coffee from his Keurig Coffee Maker. He was on his way to Rimmon Park to a murder scene with four bodies. Lieutenant

Burlingame thought he needed to see the crime scene before the techs completely worked the scene and certainly before the bodies were moved.

Chapter 63
Pleasant Cove Retirement Center
Laconia , New Hampshire
August 26

Father Daniel G. Linwood was visited in his room by a Eucharistic Minister from the local Catholic parish. The woman kindly delivered Communion to the disabled priest, Father Woody. They briefly exchanged small pleasantries until she excused herself and headed off to deliver the sacrament to other patients who requested the weekly service.

It was nearing lunch time and after lunch he would have himself wheeled to Roger Gamache's room where the two old men would take in the Sunday football game. Woody would catch the game by listening to the announcers while Roger would repeatedly mutter about the "damn officials ruining the game" and the "damn commercials" which he equally despised.

Father Woody found himself wheeled into place in the dining room. He was seated at his usual table with four women.

He generally enjoyed their company and conversation. Much of the time however was usually taken up by discourse on who was going to the doctor's in the coming week, or who had been to the doctor's or hospital the week before. All the intimate details were shared with everyone at the table, without exception, and naturally were also repeated all too often.

Lunch today was roast beef medallions with gravy, on a toasted piece of bread. Carrots were the vegetable of the day which dominated the menu four out of seven days with peas taking up the rest. Today, the lunch had an extra treat with a wedge of sweet potato thrown in. Dessert was a choice between chocolate chip cookies, or a small bowl of butterscotch pudding.

Father Woody had become rather skillful at feeding himself since he had lost his vision. The rehabilitation specialist who worked with him taught him how to hold his plate and utensils as well as being able to locate the food on his plate. He also quickly picked up the use of a spoon as his all-around utensil.

Conversation today at the luncheon table turned out to be livelier than usual.

One of the elderly women, known by all as Mimi Campbell, was beginning to tell a story about the high point of her week.

It seems that Mimi had received a visit from her youngest daughter just this morning.

The daughter brought her some long awaited good news.

Mimi reported that many years ago a man was married to Mimi's youngest daughter and by all accounts they had a happy marriage and had a daughter together.

The man was a traveling salesman who worked for a flooring company out of Lowell, Massachusetts. His job was to service the commercial accounts in northern New England. One day his body was found sitting in his car alongside a road leading into Biddeford, Maine. He had been shot in the chest three times.

His murder, now over twenty years old, was recently solved. It seems the New Hampshire Cold Case investigators, working in collaboration with counterparts in Maine, had found new and important evidence. It was some sort of evidence Mimi couldn't quite remember. Nevertheless, she did remember the fact the police ended up arresting a man from New Hampshire for her son-in-law's murder.

During her retelling of this momentous news Mimi kept mentioning the name of a very nice man with the New Hampshire Cold Case office whose name was Mark something-or-other. He had even come to interview Mimi several months ago. She was very impressed with the determination of the investigator.

"He was a very bright young man and very handsome, girls. Easy on the eyes in all the right places, if you know what I mean. Sorry, Father."

"No need to say you are sorry, Mimi. You know what they say. Just because there is snow on the roof doesn't mean there isn't a fire in the furnace."

The women giggled at his obvious innuendo.

While the women continued on with their various stories Father Woody kept repeating to himself, "Mark, Mark is the name," along with "Cold Case Unit."

When it came time to wheel him off to his usual Sunday afternoon football session he asked the attendant to jot a note down on piece of paper for him and to give him the note. The woman accommodated his request.

Father Woody slipped the note into his pants pocket.

All through the football game he kept checking to see if the note was still there.

On Monday morning he would see if someone could help him place a call to this investigator named Mark something-or-other.

Chapter 64
Manchester, New Hampshire
Kimball Street
Kelley Falls Housing Development
August 26

Mark Atkinson badged his way past uniform patrol officers blocking the roadway leading into Rimmon Park. He drove his car up the short, but steep hill only to be stopped and checked once more by another uniformed officer. This officer radioed Lieutenant Burlingame who told the officer to have Investigator Atkinson park his car. He also told the officer to have the Investigator continue the rest of the way to the crime scene on foot.

Mark followed the officer's direction and found himself walking the dusty, sandy Rimmon Park parking area. Up ahead he could see a collapsible tent had been erected over what was likely the bodies of the four young men the lieutenant had mentioned. Three tall white tarps were waving gently in the morning air as they hung on portable privacy barriers the police crime scene investigators had erected to prevent media and curiosity seekers from looking in on the police as they worked the scene.

Lieutenant Burlingame broke away from a couple of guys he was talking with and walked over to Mark. They shook hands.

The lieutenant deliberately didn't introduce Mark around. For the moment he wanted to be able to speak candidly and privately with the cold case unit investigator without having anyone leaping to conclusions.

Pete and Mark walked over to the crime scene. Pete began to point out things to Mark. They spoke for a couple of minutes when Pete's radio went off.

The radio report was from two uniformed officers. One of the neighbors in the housing development had pointed out a car which didn't belong to anyone he knew in that building. The officers ran a check on the license plate. They ran a DMV check on the owner and pulled his license. A copy of the license was sent to the lieutenant's cell phone. After looking at the picture Pete passed his phone over to Mark. Both agreed the DMV registry photo bore a strong resemblance to one of the victims.

"Here's what I don't understand Mark. I see four tough guys who appear to have turned on one another. Somehow they fight and kill each other. The knife wounds which were inflicted are each lethal. Yet, each also has bullet wounds probably from the one gun we found here at the scene. Only one bullet wound appears to be lethal, that one there. He's also the apparent owner of the nearby vehicle. My gang unit guy tells me these four deceased individuals are just posers, you know, gang wannabees. Tough talkers but no real balls for the hard stuff gangs are into."

"Then, there's all this money rolling around in the grass. None of this adds up for me. I don't see them fighting with each other over the chump change we found here. I don't see them sticking one another with fatal blows with the first stick. Nobody is that good. Then why does one guy empty his pistol on his buddies before he obviously takes one of his own in the head. This is just one big fucking mystery. The state police major crime unit guys will be here any minute now. Before they roll in I wanted you to take a look around and see what you think. You've seen some strange stuff, so what do you think?"

Mark looked down at the soft, patchy ground.

He had learned a great deal from working with the retired FBI Profiler, Kit Baylor. Mark's mind was open to seeing evidence in a way he hadn't before. Mark's senses were also focused in new ways as he took in the details of this crime scene.

"I don't see you turning up any useful footprints here. I agree with you. It looks to me like this whole thing was staged. Not posed but staged. Given the fact all the bodies are clustered so close together suggest to me there was no fight, no one tried to run away. It was nighttime when this apparently went down. It would have been easy to run off in the field, to the woods beyond if one wanted to get away. But from the looks of this, no one tried to get away. This has a similar feel to the recent Hooksett murder at the movie complex. If you ask me, someone else was here for this. Someone organized all this. He wants us to think it was just some punks offing one another. But this killer had to have help. He had to have someone else here keeping these guys cornered. Then somehow the un-sub gets them to off one another. It would work if he actually was able to manipulate them like they were sort of human puppets. He's pulling the strings getting one guy to stab the other and so on. Forensics and the ME will be able to sort out sequence and who did what. The "how part" is going to be toughest to figure out. My gut tells me the Hooksett murders are linked to this case somehow. I see two un-subs at work here. How they did this, I can't figure out yet. But I just know there has to be at least two. That's the minimum if you're trying to kill so many vics like those kids at the movie theater complex and especially here with four armed men."

"What you're telling me then is we may have a pair of very skilled serial killers on the loose and perhaps on a killing spree."

"Yup, I am, and if I am not mistaken, they have been doing this for a very long time."

"Damn!"

Chapter 65
Home of retired FBI Profiler, Kit Baylor
Island Pond, Vermont
August 27

Kit rose early. He made breakfast for his mother. Kit wasn't hungry but managed to force down some tea and a slice of toast along with the several different pills his doctor required him to take.

At 7:30 in the morning he placed a call to St. Johnsbury, Academy. This was the school his mother had once taught at many years ago. It was also the school she had talked about last evening when she described a cluster of missing persons and deaths. It appeared all of the tragedies seemed connected in varying ways to one young boy whose name Kit's mother was not able to recall.

This was Monday morning and the first week of school here in Vermont.

The school phone number was busy.

Kit dialed again.

The number was still busy.

He ended up dialing the school number several more times before he finally got through. The woman who answered the phone sounded a bit harried. She had only been working at the school for three years. Therefore, she certainly didn't have any direct knowledge of students and events from many years before.

She kept putting Kit on hold as she tried to juggle the flood of incoming calls.

Kit ended up being on the line for over thirty minutes with only about three minutes of actual conversation time. In the end he asked to speak to the school Principal. The young lady indicated the Principal was busy at this time but she could transfer Kit to the man's voice mail.

Kit left an urgent message and hung up the phone.

Next he dialed the Town of St. Johnsbury library. He spoke with an assistant who gladly tracked down the Head Librarian.

Kit carefully explained he was with the FBI, not revealing he was retired FBI. Kit explained he needed the confidential assistance of the Librarian to track down some very important information.

Kit asked if the library maintained copies of past editions of the local newspaper.

"Why certainly we have access to that kind of information. All newspapers in Vermont are digitally stored and centrally maintained by the State library in Montpelier. Just a few years ago a large project was undertaken statewide to scan or digitally photograph all past editions physically stored in local libraries. Now everyone can access the information online. Would you like the internet link information?"

Kit eagerly copied down the web address. He thanked the woman for her assistance and ended his call by asking the librarian to keep this conversation privileged for the time being. She agreed.

Kit hung up the phone. He was about to head to his computer to go online and initiate an internet search when his phone rang.

"Kit."

"Hello Mark," answered Kit, "I'm really glad you called. I have some important news to pass along. I'm tracking a possible lead on our un-sub's roots."

"Yeah, well I called you because I have something important too. Something happened down my way which I'm pretty sure connects to our serial killer. It seems he struck again, killing four armed young men."

Mark paused on the phone as Kit did the same.

The pause was broken when Kit said, "Tell me everything and don't leave out any details."

The two talked for over an hour.

Kit agreed with Mark's initial observation that these latest killings were most likely linked to the deadly trail they all have been analyzing.

From Mark's perspective, he was excited with Kit's news that he may have found the starting point for this long trail of death. Best of all, this lead might lead them to a name, the name of the one they all were hunting.

They needed this breakthrough. They were getting close and both men knew it.

Their call ended with promises to connect as soon as any new information turned up. Mark promised to call Alice in Maine and Doug in Vermont to bring them up to speed on things.

Kit rushed to his computer to try and track down any news story about the things his mother had recalled last evening. He hoped the reports might contain the name of the boy his mother had remembered. He wanted a name, just a name."

Mark rang up Alice. She offered to help in any way she could. Mark thanked her but told her he had things in hand on his end, at least for the moment.

Alice asked, "Have you interviewed the two Green Beret vets on your list yet?"

"Not yet, things have been breaking so fast I haven't gotten to it. I expect to do so today."

"Be careful Mark. Watch yourself ," cautioned Alice.

"Thanks Alice, I will try not to step in it."

They ended their call. Mark called Doug.

Mark caught up with Doug while he was in route to interview the only Vermont ex- Green Beret who was on their list. He estimated he was forty minutes away.

Mark briefed Doug on everything which had recently transpired.

Doug was excited with the progress being made. He was getting increasingly frustrated and now he was also angry this killer was still on the loose and had apparently struck again.

Mark and Doug agreed to check in with one another later in the day. Mark hoped to have completed both of his interviews by then.

Mark's next call was to former Green Beret, Oscar Tilton.

The man didn't answer the phone at his business so Mark had to leave a message. Mark tried the man's cell phone too. The results were the same. Tilton apparently did not have a home phone.

Mark dialed the other former Green Beret, Stanley Bolinski's home number. No answer. Once again Mark left a message to please call him.

The message Mark was leaving was always the same. He left his name, his telephone number and he described himself as an investigator with New Hampshire Cold Case Unit. He also mentioned he needed to briefly meet with them to conduct a brief interview in order to complete a fact check on some information they may be able to help with.

Next, Mark called Stanley's work number.

The phone number rang a few times before it went to voice mail function.

On a hunch Mark punched in the number "0" for operator. His call was forwarded to another number. A perky sounding woman answered the phone. Mark asked for Stanley. The woman reported Stanley wasn't in yet. She mentioned he had called in to say he had some kind of early morning appointment and expected to be in by 11:00 a.m. She offered to take a message for him or to send Mark back to Stanley's voice mail.

Mark declined both options.

He decided to pay a cold call visit to Oscar Tilton and then drive on over to East Coast Trucking to meet up with Stanley Bolinski.

He would simply surprise both men.

Mark got up and took his notebook with him as he headed out of the office.

Just after he left the office his office phone began to ring.

He had an incoming call. The caller would just have to leave a message, or, if they followed his voice mail message, they could call his cell phone number.

Unfortunately, so distracted from all the things going on, Mark hadn't realized his cell phone needed charging. The phone battery was dead.

Chapter 66
Pleasant Cove Retirement Center
Laconia, New Hampshire
August 27

With the help of one of the retirement center's Patient Aides, Father "Woody" Linwoood was able to track down a telephone number for the New Hampshire Cold Case Unit located in the New Hampshire Attorney General's Office. With the help of the aide, Woody now had the telephone number for Investigator Mark Atkinson.

The aide dialed the number for Woody and handed him the phone. After a few rings the phone went to voice mail. The recorded message directed the caller to leave a brief message or, if the call was an emergency, the caller could call Mark's cell phone number which followed.

Father Woody memorized the cell phone number. He asked the aide to redial the office number once more. He wanted to leave a message for Mark on his office phone before trying his cell phone. Father Woody gave the aide the cell phone number. Woody waited for the number to connect. After two rings a telephone systems message came through.

"The number you have dialed is not in service at this time. Please hang up and try again at a later time."

Disappointed Father Woody returned the phone to the aide.

"Father Woody, what do want to do now? I can take you to the recreation room. There's a class today on making greeting cards. I bet you would find that a lot of fun. Want to give it a try?"

The blind priest's face provided his response.

His countenance displayed an obvious frown.

"Listen, Margaret, its Margaret right?"

"Yes, I'm Margaret."

"Okay Margaret, I need some really special help. I need to be taken to Concord to see this guy I just called. How can I get a ride there? Who do I have to talk to?"

"Well, we could talk with Thelma, the Director of Resident Services. Is that what you want?"

"Yeah, I want that more than anything. Take me to see her right away."

"If she's busy you may have to wait for a while. I could check first and come and get you when she is available."

"Don't you worry about my possibly having to wait, after all, I have nothing but time on my hands. Let's go!"

Father Woody began to say a prayer he could catch a ride down to Concord, NH, to meet this investigator. After hearing thousands of confessions it was going to be his turn to confess. He needed to unburden himself with the knowledge he has carried around for many, many years. He was now more certain than ever. As chaplain, he had known a special killer, an evil killing machine and he had failed to stop him back in the jungles of Viet Nam. The evil soldier's success was no doubt aided by the dark and evil force which accompanied him.

Father Woody knew what Stanley Bolinski was and he also knew about his dark angel too. The deadly duo would surely have continued killing beyond the time in the Vietnam War. Father Linwood felt deep remorse he hadn't been able to stop Stanley back in Vietnam. Now he felt an even heavier burden with the knowledge the killings very likely continued after the war.

Father Linwood was experiencing a growing certainty the murdering duo were still active somehow and somewhere. Before he died, Father Linwood wanted them stopped at whatever the cost. The knowledge that all the deaths since Vietnam could have been prevented if only he had pushed harder or fought more courageously wore heavily upon his conscience. Father

Woody also prayed for his own soul. He hoped his failure to stop the evil duo was a sin which God could forgive. He hoped and he prayed.

Chapter 67
Residence of Oscar Tilton
Deering, New Hampshire
August 27

Mark Atkinson pulled his car into the gravel driveway of a beaten down house, which outwardly appeared to be more of a cabin or summer camp than a year-around residence.

In the front yard was a rusty, faded Volkswagen bus sitting atop cinder blocks. All the wheels were missing.

Cords of wood were loosely piled in neat stacks along the left side of the building.

The aluminum front door appeared to be sprung. The door was hanging open and at an odd angle. One of the three front windows was cracked and held together with strips of duct tape.

Along the right side of the house were two vehicles. Closest to Mark was a jeep with a rag top which had seen better days. Behind the front seat of the jeep was a gun rack with two rifles sitting in their slings.

In front of the jeep was an older model van. It appeared to be outfitted with a lift for a wheelchair.

Mark took note of both vehicles.

He jotted down numbers of the license plates. He would run a check on them later.

Mark walked up to the front door. He pried open the aluminum door which creaked and screeched with every inch of movement.

Not seeing a doorbell Mark knocked three times and waited for a response.

Somewhere to the right side of the house a dog began to bark. In a moment a black, mixed breed dog appeared at the corner of the house. The dog had a black-going-to-grey muzzle which indicated the dog was getting up in years. The dog stood guard at the corner of the house and kept barking.

Suddenly a voice could be heard above the dog's insistent barking.

"C'mon out back. I'm in the barn. Don't mind the dog. He won't bite unless you're an IRS agent. Just kidding."

Mark looked up and spotted a speaker crudely hanging on a j-hook screwed into the overhang.

Following the advice and invitation Mark headed to the rear of the house.

"Patton, come here. Heel, Patton, Heel," shouted what had to be Oscar Tilton.

The dog dropped his head. Wagging its tail, the dog turned and led the way back to the barn.

A hand painted sign hung across the open doors. The sign announced, "Live Free or Die, Guns and Taxidermy."

The inside of the barn was well lit.

Standing at a work bench was a tall and very thin man sporting a handle bar mustache. He was bald and wore a light blue long sleeve work shirt with heavily worn jeans and work boots. He also wore a khaki hunter's vest.

On the far side of the work bench, sitting in a chair was a man Mark recognized from the DMV photos. It was Oscar Tilton.

Tilton wore a red and black checkered chambray shirt. He had a pair of eyeglasses positioned high up his bald head. There was a scar running along the left side of his head starting just past the eye and continuing back over the top edge of his ear before turning downward out of sight.

"Hi, you must be Oscar Tilton," said Mark as he approached the work bench and held out his hand.

Oscar didn't extend his hand in return.

Oscar Tilton took a moment to eye Mark.

The other man did likewise.

Feeling a little bit put off by the lack of a greeting Mark turned away for a moment to assess the contents of the barn. It was filled with dozens of rifles sitting in locked cabinets. Posters were tacked to the walls. There were two large gun safes in the far rear of the barn. Mark also spotted an assortment of bows, arrows and targets. There were two glass cases filled with an assortment of hand guns and knives. Scattered everywhere were examples of taxidermy ranging from trophy fish to small animals like squirrels, rabbits, skunks, and even a fisher cat. There was a large stuffed upright black bear along with an excellent trophy quality 14 point white tailed deer over in the deep left corner.

"I didn't catch your name," said Oscar.

"I'm Mark Atkinson. I have been looking for you for a while. I was hoping I could talk with you. I could use your help with something I'm looking into."

With an upward nod Oscar asked, "You a cop?"

"Sort of, I am an investigator with the Cold Case Unit. We work to try and solve old cases."

Mark pulled out a business card.

Without breaking eye contact Oscar took the card and set it aside on the nearby work table.

The other man grunted and said, "I'm gonna git going. I'll bring you the deposit on that 308 later today."

Oscar looked over at the man and said, "Sure enough Smitty, I ain't going anywhere."

Oscar looked back at Mark to see if Mark had any reaction.

There was none.

There were no chairs in the barn except for the one Oscar was sitting in.

This was an obvious way to discourage visitors from overstaying their welcome.

"So mister big shot investigator, what brings you all the way to the Town of Deering to talk with me? I warn you, don't bull shit me or you can take your sorry ass off my property, cause the next time we talk you had better bring a search warrant or an arrest warrant."

Mark was sure the man meant every word he had just spoken. He hoped the direct approach would work.

"Okay, Mr. Tilton, here's the deal. I've been working the better part of the summer on a bunch of unsolved homicides in Maine, New Hampshire and Vermont. These cases appear to be linked to someone who has driven long distance rigs for the years the crimes occurred. We are trying to interview all the truck drivers who have held valid CDLA licenses during the right period. We think one or more of the drivers may have seen something or heard something which might point us in the right direction. If I run the dates and places by you could you see if you have any ideas?"

Oscar squinted a bit and then said, "For sure there's more to this than you're tellin'. I can smell you spinning a tale to get me to loosen up, sure enough to make me want to do the good citizen thing. Truth is, you think I'm a suspect, all the drivers are suspects to you. Am I right?"

"We are not at the point where anyone can be considered a suspect and that's the truth. Right now what we need is help." Mark returned the man's fixed gaze.

This meeting was beginning to feel like a staring contest.

"Sorry, I can't help you. This conversation is over."

Mark was knocked back by the abruptness of Oscar's comment.

"Look, these murders have taken at least twenty-five lives that we know of. More than that, there more than twenty-five families who've lost someone they loved, someone they depended on. C'mon man, work with me here. I am not leaving, until I get some answers."

Oscar considered the measure of the man standing before him. There was something solid about this guy. Oscar sensed the man was all about doing the right thing. This investigator was one righteous man. If there was one thing Oscar respected, was a man who stood up for what he believed in."

Oscar stood up and steadied himself before he reached behind his chair. He pulled out a pair of crutches. He slipped the upper arm braces in place and then gripped the crutches. He swung his hips around and swiftly went over to the bear.

"Come over here. Grab the chair behind Patton and set it up near the bench. Git yourself a bottle of water out of the cooler under the bench. I'll be right back. I have to take a piss. We'll do some talking when I get back."

Mark pulled the folding chair out.

While he was setting it in place Oscar headed out of the barn to relieve himself.

Mark took the opportunity to check his DMV records on this guy again. Sure enough, there was no mention of the man's disability.

"How in the hell had that happened?" he wondered.

Moments later Oscar returned. He settled himself back in his chair. He pulled a dog biscuit out of his pants pocket and tossed it over to the dog. It landed right in front of the dog. With well-practiced technique, the dog named Patton simply turned his head slightly, flicked his tongue and swiped the biscuit into his mouth.

The two men began to talk and talk they did for over two hours.

Mark learned Oscar had been in a bad accident driving his rig one night during a snow storm along I-95 in Maine. The accident had severely damaged his spine. He went through four months of rehabilitation and then gave up. His employer generously modified one of the smaller trucks in the fleet to accommodate Oscar's special needs. Oscar loved the man for doing that when he didn't need to. Oscar somehow managed to keep his license current all these years. DMV folks had coded his driver's license to note his handicap status but somehow a computer glitch kept rejecting the code. He gave up trying to get it corrected after three separate long visits to DMV headquarters. He figured it was their problem not his.

He ramped up his gun dealing and taxidermy efforts to supplant his income. What was just a hobby soon blossomed into a small, successful business. Oscar retired from the truck driving business earlier this year. He was planning on letting his CDLA license expire when it came due for renewal later this year. He frankly admitted he wasn't impressed or happy with the added burdens Homeland Security was placing on long distance truck drivers.

"In the old days all we had to deal with were the needle dicks at Fed DOT and State DOT crawling up our asses. State and local police were generally okay. But those Homeland Security jerks take the fucking cake. They're clueless. Let's just leave it at that."

Mark finished off the bottle of water he had been nursing for the past couple of hours.

"So where is the bathroom?"

"I have an outhouse in back of the barn. Help yourself."

Mark's take on Oscar was he was not likely to be the unsub they were all looking for. Even though Oscar, no doubt, had plenty of friends whom he could easily have used to partner with, Mark couldn't see this man as being cold enough to have committed all those murders. Mark was ready to move his name down the suspect list.

When Mark returned he decided he would ask a couple of final questions.

"Oscar, talk to me about your Vietnam experience."

"Not much to say. I saw a lot of good people die. I saw friends blown to bits and others who survived who wished they hadn't. That was one big cluster fuck if you ask me. I try not to think about it. Nothing good can come from reliving that long mother-of-a-nightmare."

Mark wrote down a short note in his notebook.

On a chance that Oscar knew or had served in combat with Stanley Bolinski, Mark asked, "Ever hear about a fellow trucker and Green Beret by the name of Stanley Bolinski?"

Oscar sat back in his chair.

"Yeah, I heard of him. I never went into combat with him. From what I heard that was a good thing."

"Can you explain that?"

"Word was, wherever he went, death followed. It was like there was some sort of dark cloud traveling with that soldier. Sure, he won a bunch of medals, racked up a bunch of kills, but the men around him took heavy casualties too. This guy came out of Nam with hardly a scratch. I'm telling you, right there, it ain't normal. Everybody came out of Nam with something."

Mark scribbled some notes and closed his notebook.

He stood up and once again offered his hand to Oscar.

This time the men shook hands.

Mark turned around and left.

His next stop would be to see Stanley Bolinski.

Chapter 68
Home of retired FBI Profiler, Kit Baylor
Island Pond, Vermont
August 27

Kit's eyes were getting tired.

He had spent the past two and a half hours searching the online newspaper data system established by Vermont. The compilation had some useful search tools but Kit opted for the "do-it-the-old-fashion" way. He was reading every single issue of the Caledonia-St. Johnsbury Record for the year his mother believed most closely corresponded with the events she recalled.

So far the news record was thin.

All he had managed to come across so far were the names of the young high school couple who had died tragically in an automobile accident. In addition, buried in one of the letters to the editor, was a reference to another classmate of theirs. The letter to the editor indicated this boy had vanished a couple of years before. The boy's full name wasn't mentioned in the letter. The letter was meant to honor the anniversary of the day he had disappeared.

Kit read on.

While heavily invested in the online research he began to feel his body cramping up. He left the computer on. He stood up from the desk and tried walking around. He noticed he was feeling weak and light headed.

He went to kitchen to look for something to eat. It would have to be something light and easily digestible. While prowling the refrigerator he came across some ice cream. He managed to scrape out a couple of small scoops of ice cream. He also checked with his mother to see if she wanted any. She declined.

Moments later he was back at the computer searching for the one elusive clue he hoped would turn up in the newspaper archives.

Fifty minutes later he found what he was searching for. The front page of the newspaper had a black and white photo of the Town of St. Johnsbury firefighters battling a fire at a single family household.

The bold type oversized headline read, "Mother, Father Die in House Fire."

The accompanying article described the heroic effort of local firefighters in battling an out of control blaze. The article described the victims as a local long distance truck driver and his stay at home wife. The family was described by neighbors as quiet and of the sort which kept to themselves. The family name was Bolinski.

The Bolinski's had only one child, a son who was a recent high school graduate named Stanley.

For a brief moment Kit stopped breathing. His eyes were locked onto the name on his computer screen, Stanley Bolinski.

Kit grabbed his cell phone and immediately called Mark's cell phone.

Moments later he had to put down his cell phone.

Mark's cell phone was not in service.

Kit looked for Mark's office telephone number. He dialed the number and quickly discovered he needed to leave a telephone message.

Reluctantly he left a message for Mark to call him right away. He had a name.

"Mark, Kit here. Listen, we have a breakthrough. I think I've found the genesis of our serial killer. The cluster I spoke to you about yesterday orbits around a teenage boy. His name is Stanley Bolinski. That's the name of one of the Green Berets on our truck driver list. This could be our guy. In fact, I would bet on it. Call me ASAP."

Kit hung up the phone and decided to place a call to the New Hampshire Cold Case Unit's main telephone number. After making inquiry he learned there was no other way to reach Mark except to wait for him to return his call.

So Kit waited.

His mother looked in on him as he sat with his hands folded in front of the computer with his cell phone nearby, within arm's reach.

She recognized that look on his face. It was the same look her late husband had whenever he had been vexed by a perplexing problem and had uncovered a solution.

She was very proud of her son. He had accomplished so much in his life. It pained her to think his life would end soon. He was a fighter and would go out fighting, fighting not only the dreaded disease of pancreatic cancer but fighting to stop a monstrous serial killer.

She passed by Kit and shuffled herself to the kitchen.

Chapter 69
Pleasant Cove Retirement Center
Laconia, New Hampshire
August 27

Father Linwood had to wait thirty minutes until he could speak with the Center's Director. He charmed and pressed Mrs. Sonja Starr, who ran the Retirement Center to please arrange for him to be taken to Concord to the offices of the Attorney General and its Cold Case Unit.

"Mrs. Starr, you and your staff know me well. I'm not suffering from senility or dementia or any other mental disorder. I am not a raving senior looking for attention. I assure you I have some urgent information which is of some importance to that office. I am certain it is literally a matter of life or death. I am prepared to even pay for a cab if necessary."

Finally relenting, she put up her hands in protest and said, "Okay Father I will see what I can arrange for you. I would rather arrange your transportation with one of our volunteer angels. I think Scott Rutledge might be available. Let me give him a call."

Moments later Father Linwood was appropriately dressed and wheeled to the front doors of the Pleasant Cove Retirement Center.

Scott Rutledge arrived and parked his car in the visitor parking area. He came inside and signed out one of the two wheelchair accessible vans.

It was just past lunchtime. To his great relief, Father Linwood was about to be on his way to meet with CCU Investigator Mark Atkinson.

Scott was a delightful volunteer driver who freely gave of his time to help transport residents of Pleasant Cove to doctor appointments, shopping and the occasional special transportation request which applied in this instance.

"So how long do you think this meeting will last?"

"I don't know."

"You don't know."

"That's right."

"But usually folks make an appointment to start at a certain time and end at a certain time. So how did you leave it with this guy?" asked Scott.

"I didn't exactly talk with him personally."

"You didn't," responded Scott.

"No, I left him a message on his answering machine."

"If I hear you correctly, if this guy hasn't checked his voice mail he might not even know you're coming down for a meeting. I'm beginning to think this trip isn't a good idea. I'm going to turn around and take you back. When you have a firm meeting set up I will be glad to drive you to a meeting."

Even though he was blind Father Linwood reached out and gently touched the right arm of his volunteer driver.

"Look, you have every right to want to go back but I will just call a cab. I need to speak with him as soon as possible. I assure you it is a matter of life or death. I can't let another day pass without doing something. Please, I would appreciate it very much if you take me to his office. I will get a ride back or take a cab if necessary. You have my word all that I say is true."

Scott Rutledge looked over at the priest and after a small sigh he said, "Okay Padre, I'll take you there. But I'm not going to leave you there. I'll wait however long it may take so I can drive you back. Take it or leave it."

The priest broke into a broad smile and said, "I'll take it Scott. Thank you very much."

They arrived at the state capitol and found handicap parking near the Attorney General's office.

Scott helped Father Woody out of the van. He wheeled him inside of the impressive, large granite building. Moments later they arrived at the Attorney General's Office. There they learned the cold case office was a part of the state police whose headquarters located in the Meldrim Thompson, State Office Park on the city's east side. They got back in the van and drove to the Headquarters. After inquiring with the lobby receptionist they learned Mark was out of the office. He hadn't called in from the field yet. The woman who answered their questions told them Mark almost always came back to the office late in the day but she couldn't guarantee it.

Father Woody insisted he would take his chances and wait. He told Scott he could leave him but Scott wouldn't hear of it. It was settled, they would wait together.

Chapter 70
Headquarters of East Coast Trucking
Manchester, New Hampshire
August 27

Stanley made it into work around 10:30 in the morning. He glanced over at the office of Fred Hilliard, the owner of the company. The offices were empty. Stanley learned that Fred still hadn't made it into work.

He wasn't worried. If Fred decided to proceed with the sale of the company than all the pain he and his family would endure would be on him.

The office was in a buzz over the weekend story of the four murdered men on the West side of the City.

A couple of employees tried to get a reaction out of Stanley, "You live near there? Do the killings make you feel less safe?"

He didn't take up the challenge. He simply shrugged off their questions and headed into his office. He closed the door to his office and proceeded to immerse himself in the backlog of paper work. He busied himself with changes to his assignment list for his drivers for the week ahead. Someone was always falling behind, jobs needed to be added and of course, there was always the unexpected breakdown.

At ten minutes before three o'clock Mark Atkinson arrived at the offices of East Coast Trucking.

Walking in behind him was the owner Fred Hilliard.

All eyes in the office turned to look at the owner.

At first Mark thought everyone was looking at him.

He soon realized he was mistaken when one of the women in the office rushed past him to speak with the man he belatedly noted was behind him.

"Fred, we were worried about you. We hadn't heard from you. Is everything all right? Is the family okay?"

Mark glanced over at the man who seemed to be behaving like he was in some sort of daze. His eyes were red and puffy. There were dark circles under his eyes. He appeared to be sweating and his clothes were badly wrinkled.

Fred Hilliard didn't answer any questions. He waved off everyone as he shuffled to his office. He went inside, closed the office interior window blinds shutting himself off from his employees.

Including Stanley and Fred, there were eight other employees in the office. They all began to whisper with one another over the troubled state of their boss.

Mark had to finally reach out to a guy passing by to inquire about Stanley Bolinski.

Stanley watched the goings on from behind his own partially closed office blinds. He was simply giddy with the highly stressed state of the company's owner.

From the corner of his office came the voice of his smoky and evil angel.

"See that other guy who came in with Fred. He's here to talk with you. He has the look of a cop."

"Yeah, he does look like a cop. Don't worry, I'll be cool. He's probably checking with people who live in the neighborhood. The cops have nothing to connect us to those killings. He can ask all the questions he wants."

Stanley watched the outer office out of the corner of his eye.

He saw one of the other office workers gesture in Stanley's direction.

The stranger was heading towards Stanley's office.

The man knocked on Stanley's office door before he opened the door and poked his head inside.

"Mr. Bolinski, could you spare me a few minutes of your time?"

"That depends, if you're a salesman you can just turn around. I'm too busy to listen to some sales pitch."

Easing himself inside the open office door Mark smiled and said, "I assure you I'm not a salesman. Here's my business card."

Mark was prepared to show Bolinski his credentials if he asked.

Bolinski looked at the business card and showed no reaction.

After a moment he gestured for Mark to take a seat.

Mark sat down and waited for some kind of reaction. His career in law enforcement taught him to wait out the person being interviewed. Let them talk. Periods of silence only added to the pressure some felt. They invariably would begin talking to relieve their tension. This often led to a slip up, an error where one statement would contradict another. This typically became a wedge a skilled interviewer could use to pry out a useful piece of information.

Bolinski waited on Mark as well.

He would not offer up anything but would only answer direct questions with short and simple answers.

Finally Mark elected to break the silence.

"As you can see from my card I'm an investigator in the New Hampshire Cold Case Unit. I have been working all summer on some of our cold case murders. I sure could use some help. It seems to our team…"

They have a team, thought Stanley. *This must mean it's a big case. Interesting.*

"Our team has uncovered a pattern of unsolved murders which go back close to 30 years or more. These murders appear to have occurred in close proximity to well-travelled roadways used by long distance truckers."

He said, "We are interviewing all the drivers we can find who have worked northern New England during the period in question. We are hoping someone might have seen something or heard something that seemed out of place."

Mark paused. He was watching Stanley's body language for any telltale signs of deception. He did this with everyone he interviewed even during his earlier interview with Oscar Tilton.

Stanley sat back in his chair and folded his hands behind his he

He wanted to convey how relaxed he was, how he didn't feel threatened.

To Mark's trained eye, Stanley's gesture conveyed the opposite. The casual gesture appeared to be forced. It was often used by someone undergoing a police interview to hide the nervousness they felt. They didn't want to show shaky hands or nervous hand gestures and so they would try and hide their hands behind their head as Stanley was doing now or they would put their hands below the surface of the desk.

Stanley said, "I don't drive big rigs anymore. I've been largely out of the driving side of the business for years. My job is to assign drivers to delivery routes. I'm sorry I can't be of any help."

Mark noted immediately Stanley was uncomfortable and was trying to rush him out the door. Mark decided to increase the level of discomfort a bit to see what kind of reaction he could get out Stanley.

Mark sat forward in his chair and placed his folded arms on Stanley's desk. He was deliberately trying to crowd Stanley's space.

He noticed his movement had provoked a reaction. Stanley's breathing rate was accelerating.

"Mr. Bolinski. I really could use your help. Anything, anything at all which you can remember from the days when you were driving could help us. You know sometimes people see or hear something they don't think is important when it is. Maybe you heard something from other drivers. Maybe you saw something. Perhaps there was something which didn't fit, didn't feel right to you. Think about it will you? We're looking at over twenty-five murders over what looks like up to 30 years. Those victims and their families need closure, they need justice and I intend to give it to them. We're already making progress on this investigation. We've interviewed numerous other drivers. I have to tell you those guys were sure eager to help. Many of them have a keen eye, excellent recall. How about I check back with you in a couple of days? I wouldn't mind coming back here to meet with you or you can come to my offices. We're located in the Headquarters Office of the state police. Anyway, thanks for your time today."

Mark stood up and extended his hand to shake Stanley's.

Stanley unfolded his hands from behind his head and reached out to shake Mark's hand. Stanley stood up and was now eye-to-eye with Mark.

"I'll give it some thought. Who knows what I might have heard or seen? You're right, those families need answers."

Mark nodded, turned and left Stanley standing at his desk.

Stanley watched him leave.

Mark was clever. He had boxed Stanley in. By suggesting other drivers were cooperating and maybe providing helpful information he had Stanley in the position thinking he would be making himself a target if he didn't cooperate. If he cooperated, Stanley might also think he could feed false information to the investigators or he might even learn what they knew and who the other witnesses might be?

Why did Mark set this trap? Simple, from his perspective, Stanley might as well have been holding up a sign announcing he was guilty of something. Guilty of what?

Mark was going with his gut on this ploy. It was based purely on feel, from Mark's experience, a cop's gut feeling is seldom wrong.

Stanley wiped his sweaty hand on his pants.

"Fuck, now I have to deal with this old bullshit. Why is everything so screwed up lately?"

His evil partner spoke out, *"I don't know. Do you want me to follow him, see what he's up to? I'm ready to make him go away. Just say the word, my man."*

"You stay the fuck away from him. I need time to think about this. We do nothing until I say so, you hear me."

"You're making a big mistake."

"You let me worry about that."

Chapter 71
Manchester, New Hampshire
Kimball Street
Kelley Falls Housing Development
August 27

Keisha Mfume sat at the kitchen table breast feeding her baby. All day long she had watched the comings and goings of the police and investigators from the relative safety of her apartment windows. A few of her neighbors had dropped in to visit with her. They too, found themselves looking out the windows.

"Damn girl, you got yourself front row seats to them murders. Tell me woman, I won't tell nobody. Did you see them fight? Did you see them kill each other? Did you hear anything?" pressed her neighbor from across the hall.

"Nah, I didn't hear anything," replied Keisha. "My baby was fussy last night. I had to tend to him. You know how a baby can get?"

"I sure do, honey, I sure do."

It began at mid-afternoon. Several police officers began going door to door canvassing everyone who might have been in the building last night. They were looking for anyone who might have seen or heard anything.

As talkative as everyone in the building was with one another they were just the opposite with the police.

No one wanted to get dragged into the investigation. They were especially fearful if this was some sort of gang killing. The tenants didn't want to be labeled as cooperating with the police.

They all feared it would easily translate into a death sentence for them.

Keisha held her baby and rocked him in her arms. He was done feeding and had fallen to sleep. She couldn't bring herself to put him down in his crib. She needed to have him in her arms.

Keisha could hear the police knocking on doors in her hallway. It was just a matter of time before they would be knocking on her door.

They had to know a woman had called 9-1-1.

She felt certain they were looking for that woman.

Keisha nerves were deeply frayed.

Twenty minutes later there was a loud knock on her apartment door.

"Hello, who is it?" asked Keisha in a small voice.

"It's the Manchester Police ma'am. We would like to speak with you."

Keisha looked through the apartment door peephole. She saw two men in suits standing in front of her door.

"Can I see some identification please?"

One of the men held up his badge to the peephole while the other held up his credentials.

It was two detectives.

Keisha was still holding her infant son. She shifted him in her arms so she was able to work the locks.

She pulled the door open and the two men stepped inside.

After introductions she offered the men to sit at her tiny kitchen table. She sat down across from the men.

The older man pulled out a small notebook.

The questioning began.

"For the record, what is your name?"

"Keisha Mfume.

"And your child's name please."

"I don't see why you need his name. He's only two months old."

"It's just routine police procedure ma'am. We need to gather the names of everyone in this building. Now the name is?"

"His name is Devon Randall Mfume, Jr. He's named after his father."

"Does his father live here?"

"No, he died before Devon was born. His father was in the Marines. He died in Afghanistan."

The two detectives looked at one another.

"We're deeply sorry for your loss. He was a Marine, damn such a loss. I was a Marine too."

"Thanks."

"Are you aware there were four men murdered in the field across from this building last night?"

Keisha nodded.

"Ma'am did you hear anything unusual last night?"

The man not asking questions nor taking notes stood up. He asked to use her bathroom.

She pointed to the small door off the kitchen.

He disappeared into the bathroom for a few moments.

"Ma'am, did you hear anything?"

Keisha said, "Let me put the baby down."

She stood up and headed into the bedroom. The detective who used her bathroom followed her to the bedroom. He stood in the doorway and spotted the chair next to the window.

"That window has a perfect view of the crime scene."

Their eyes met.

She placed her son in the crib and left the bedroom with the detective following close behind.

She sat back down at the table and crossed her arms holding them closely to her chest.

"Her bedroom window looks right across at the crime scene. There's a chair up against the window too," said one detective to his partner who was taking notes on this interview.

Keisha's eyes began to water up. Tears began to slip away and run down her cheeks.

She wiped them with the back of her left hand.

"Mrs. Mfume, what did you see last night?" said the note taking detective.

Keisha thought of her dead husband taken from her and her son before they could even begin to build a life together. She thought of Devon, Junior. She wanted him to grow up happy and safe. Would that be possible?

Taking a deep breath she wiped the tears from her face for the last time.

She began, "I saw them last night. I saw it all from my bedroom window. I was up feeding Devon."

Backtracking a bit she went on, "I didn't actually see the murders. They were out in the field. They were out in the darkness. There was some moonlight but not enough to see the fight or whatever it was. I heard voices and parts of their conversation. I heard a gunshot maybe more than one, I'm not sure. Then later I saw him, one old guy walking away. He was alone. At first he walked towards the building. With moonlight I could see him. Then when he got closer the outside security lights helped some more. I could clearly see him. He was smiling, no wait not smiling, it was more of a grin. That's it, a big grin."

"I don't know if he saw me. I was sitting in the darkness so maybe he didn't see me. He did look around before I lost sight of him. He was walking to the South end of the parking lot."

The detective taking notes wrote furiously trying to keep up.

The other detective said, "Go on."

"I didn't dare go outside. I had Devon to look after. So, I waited until the sun came up. That's when I saw the bodies. I took Devon and went down the street to the market and called 9-1-1."

"That was you?" said the detective taking notes.

"Yessir, I was the one who called."

"I don't want that man to know about me or to find me. I'm really, really scared."

"Listen, we will keep your name out of this for as long as possible. I can speak to the DA and we can set up protection for you and Devon. I promise you as a Marine, I'm not letting anybody mess with you." said the detective in a tone which conveyed his firm resolve.

His note taking partner nodded his agreement.

The former Marine asked, "Did you see anyone else?"

"No I didn't."

"Okay, let's go over this again if you don't mind." said the note taking detective.

Meanwhile, his partner stood up, removed his cell phone from his suit coat pocket. He stepped away from the kitchen area and walked into the living room.

In a hushed voice he placed a call to the command center. He looked over twice at his partner and Keisha while he spoke on the phone.

Keisha went through her story once more for the two detectives. She recalled more details of what she had witnessed while not contradicting the key points of her first statement. She was proving to be a very good witness.

Within ten minutes several more officers arrived in her apartment. The DA had authorized her protection. They made plans to move her to a safe location where she and Devon would be under guard 24/7. Before they did they brought in a police sketch artist to work with her. The police wanted to put together a composite image of the older man she had witnessed leaving the scene of the murders.

Once the police sketch work was done a woman police officer and two uniform officers helped her gather up some things from the apartment. She changed Devon's diaper and was whisked away to a secret location.

State police major crime scene techs began working her apartment. Several photos were taken from the bedroom window looking out over the crime scene. They would return to the apartment later on during the night, to take photos of the scene from the window, while taking into account the nighttime lighting situation. Fortunately, for the investigators, tonight the sky would be cloud free once more with a nearly full moon, very much like the conditions of the previous night when the murders went down.

Finding Keisha was huge break for this active investigation.

Chapter 72
New Hampshire State Police
Cold Case Unit
Concord, New Hampshire
August 27

Father Daniel G. Linwood sat patiently in his wheelchair. Sitting across from him was his volunteer driver, Scott Rutledge. Scott had just returned with a couple cups of coffee and two protein snack bars.

The people in the cold case unit office explained, to no avail, Mark was out for the day no doubt conducting interviews on a big case he had been working on.

They repeated that he might return to the office later in the day but there was no guarantee he would.

Father Woody would hear nothing of it. He wasn't leaving and that was it.

As the afternoon passed Woody was growing anxious. He so wanted this to be over with. He just had to speak with the investigator. But if the man didn't come back to his office Woody knew he certainly couldn't spend the night there. He had already taken too much of Scott's time.

"Look, Scott, this guy may not come back until it's very late. Hell, he might not come back at all today. You really should be heading back to the Center. They're probably putting out a police call for the two of us by now. I'll wait until 6:30 and then if he hasn't come by then I will call for a cab. I can get to the elevators good enough and I am sure I can make my way out of the building too."

"Look Woody, I signed on for this adventure of yours so don't you worry about me. I already called the Center when I went out for coffee. They are not too happy about this but they'll get over it. I tell you what. Like you said, we'll wait until 6:30 and if he hasn't shown up by then I'll take you back to the Center. If you want to try again tomorrow I would be happy to drive you back."

"Scott you are very nice to help me with this. I won't forget this."

"Just say an extra prayer for me now and then, that'll be payback enough for me."

Just then Mark walked into the Cold Case Unit.

One of the staff introduced Mark to the two men waiting for him.

They shook hands all around.

Mark said, "Listen guys I will gladly meet with you right after I check my phone messages. I've had a full day and I haven't returned a single call all day. I am sure I have quite a few backed up. Why don't you come on in while I do that. It shouldn't take very long."

They all moved into Mark's office.

Mark sat down and pulled out his cell phone. The battery was dead. He needed to recharge the phone. He pulled out the charging adapter and plugged his phone in. The phone powered up and indicated he had fourteen messages waiting.

Mark set the cell phone down to finish charging up.

Mark checked his office phone. He had eleven messages in the message queue.

Damn, he thought. *It will take me an hour to go through all those messages.*

Mark put that thought in the back of his mind as he turned his attention to the two men sitting in front of him.

A blind man in a wheelchair and another man, I wonder what they could have to say to have spent the better part of this afternoon waiting for me, thought Mark.

"Well gentlemen, what can I do for the two of you?"

"Father Linwood, perhaps you want me to wait outside in the other office while you talk in private with Investigator Atkinson," offered Scott Rutledge.

"No, Scott you can listen too. My secret has to be told, the sooner the better."

"So you're some kind of a priest?" asked Mark.

"I'm a retired priest. I lost my vision and my two feet to diabetes last year and now I live in a retirement home in Laconia."

"I'm listening," said Mark.

The old priest leaned forward in his wheelchair before he spoke.

"I want you to know my mind is sound and my memory is crystal clear. I am not some old coot who's lost his mind and is dreaming up stories to get attention."

"I'm still listening. Something is eating at you. I can see that. So what is it?"

"I want you to find someone and stop him from killing anyone else. The man is a killing machine. I knew him when I was a chaplain back in Vietnam. I tried to stop him then but I failed. For years I thought I would find him but never quite saw it through. I wanted to find him, to expose him for what he was; a completely evil man. But a part of me didn't want to have to confront him again. I guess I'm afraid of him. I know you investigate old murder cases. That's why I am here. I'm hoping you might have come across this man during your investigations."

"What's his name?"

"Stanley - his name is Stanley Bolinski."

Mark's heart skipped a beat.

"Bolinsky was in the Green Berets in Nam. Do you mean that Stanley Bolinski," said an obviously excited Mark Atkinson.

"Why yes, he was a Green Beret, but how do you know this?"

"This is freaking incredible," said Mark."

"It sounds like you're familiar with him," said a wide eyed Scott.

"I just left his office less than an hour ago."

Father Woody made the sign of the cross.

"He is in New Hampshire and you are looking at him for something. It's a miracle."

"All right, listen Father, you're going to have to start from the beginning because I need to know everything there is to know about this guy. If you don't mind, I'm going to record this conversation. It will be better than my taking notes. It will be smoother and easier."

"I don't mind. That's why I came here today. I have lived too long with the fear this man may still be killing people. I prayed you might help me find him and stop him and his partner."

"Whoa, hold on. You're saying he has a partner. What's his partner's name?" asked Mark as he set up the digital voice recorder.

"He doesn't have a name that I know of. I am sure he has one, I just don't know it. His partner is pure evil, of that I am sure. You're going to think I'm losing it but I swear to you it is true. His partner isn't human. He's a shape, a smoky, ink black shape. He is constantly with Stanley. He's like some sort of dark angel."

Mark's mouth hung open.

He had never, ever heard of such a thing.

"How do you know this?" asked Mark.

"Because this thing spoke to me and threatened to kill me if I tried to stop Stanley, to stop the two of them."

"Are you sure?"

"I'm certain. If you want me to take a lie detector test to prove I am telling you the truth, I will gladly do so."

Mark ran his fingers through his hair.

This news stunned him. It was beyond anything he could get his mind around.

Instead of moving on to record the interview he decided he needed to bring in Alice, Doug and, most of all, Kit.

"Would you mind if I set up conference call with some other investigators? I want them to hear everything you have to say and to ask any questions they might have. We're all under a tight deadline and your information may help turn a case for us all."

"Whatever you think is necessary is fine by me."

Scott Rutledge hurriedly nodded his agreement.

Chapter 73
Home of Physician Assistant Tamara Sacha
Londonderry, New Hampshire
August 27

Tamara arrived home from work exhausted. She wasn't tired from the work itself. She was drained by the tension which consumed her.

Her stomach was in knots. It had been this way since the parking lot confrontation with Bolinski and made worse by the appearance in her home by the dark, evil force he had obviously sent to terrorize her.

All day long she felt light headed. Her pulse was racing, her blood pressure was high and she was jumpy.

She couldn't stand anyone being behind her. Any unexpected noise caused her to shriek. Twice during the day she broke down in tears for no apparent reason.

I can't go on living like this. I can't, she thought.

In her mind Stanley or his evil minion were simply waiting before they sprang some sort of trap on her. She was convinced the two of them were plotting and planning her death, maybe even the deaths of those she loved.

All of this was bottled up inside of Tamara.

The worst of it was the feeling of powerlessness.

There was nothing the police could do. They were not usually successful with stopping violence. She was all too familiar with that from the abused women cases she had handled.

From her point of view, the police were good at coming in after the woman was maimed or dead. They would do their investigation and later arrest the perpetrator. The bad guy was usually the husband or the boyfriend who would profess some sort of twisted love for the victim.

The darker side of love was then exposed for what it was. The dark side was an excuse to toss out "cherish one another" and replace it with "fists, knifes," or whatever was handy to control and destroy the supposed object of their dark love.

Stanley wasn't a secret lover, not by a long shot. She knew full well what he was. He was someone so filled with hate the only way he could feed that hate was to destroy whatever stood for that hate. Right now Tamara believed Stanley couldn't, and wouldn't stop, until she was dead.

Gradually her mind was coming around to a plan to fight back.

She began to see her only salvation was to kill him first.

That was her answer to the terrorized state she was in thanks to the *bastard Stanley Bolinski and his freaky friend, the smoky, dark bastard*, thought Tamara. Her mind was beginning to unravel.

She would absolutely not tell her family anything about this war she was about to engage in. This was her fight and she was going to bring it.

She didn't have any details worked out yet. The only thing she had settled on was the certainty she would find the means to destroy Bolinski and his evil minion or die trying. At least it would be better than waiting.

Chapter 74
Home of retired FBI Profiler, Kit Baylor
Island Pond, Vermont
August 27

It was late in the afternoon nearing dinner time.

Kit had spent the entire day anxiously waiting for a call back from Mark.

He had important news he needed to discuss with Mark. For him, finding the genesis point for the un-sub helped bring some things in this case into perspective.

The house phone rang. Kit hurried to pick up the telephone extension while sliding into the chair at his computer desk.

"Mark is that you, did you get my message?"

"Yeah Kit, it's me. I haven't gotten to my phone messages today. I've been out of the office all day conducting interviews. I didn't notice my damn cell phone battery was drained."

Before Mark could continue, Kit interjected, "Mark listen to me. Before you go any further I need to tell we've had a breakthrough. Thanks to my mom, I found the genesis of our killer. Everything fits the profile. I'm convinced we are no longer looking at an un-sub we are looking at ...."

Before he could finish what he was going to say Mark finished it for him.

"Our suspect is Stanley Bolinski."

But you said you hadn't had a chance to check your phone messages. How did you get on to Bolinski?"

"There's a story which goes along with this. I need you to hold on for a few more moments. I'm trying to get Alice and

Doug on the line for a conference call. I'm going to put you on hold for moment. Hold tight and I will be right back with you."

The telephone went silent.

Kit was not surprised Mark had reached the same conclusion he had. Things were beginning to fall in place. Everything was now pointing at the ex-Green Beret, unmarried long-time interstate truck driver, Stanley Bolinski. It had taken some time to dig, to analyze, to piece things together. Good old fashion police work was beginning to pay dividends. This is what fed the soul of Kit.

Meanwhile back at Mark's office, he turned to Scott Rutledge and said, "Mr. Rutledge I'm afraid I'm going to have to ask you to wait in the outer office during this conference call. What we are going to be discussing is sensitive and privileged. I hope you understand."

"Of course I do."

Scott stood up and left the room, closing the office door behind him.

Mark turned to Father Linwood.

Listen Father, I need to have you stick around and tell your story. After that you and Mr. Rutledge are free to go. I do ask that what we discuss here today be kept in the strictest of confidence. This is still an active and ongoing investigation and we cannot afford to compromise it in anyway. Do you understand and agree to what I have just said?"

"I do, young man, I most certainly do."

In a few moments Mark had been able to track down Alice on her cell phone. She was on the highway. Alice said she needed to pull off the roadway and find a place to safely park for this call.

Mark put her on hold and then dialed Doug. He was lucky. Doug was still in his office.

Mark brought Kit on the line and then the two of them waited until Alice was safely situated.

Mark led off the conference call by introducing Father Linwood.

"I'm going to put the phone on speaker so Father Linwood can speak to everyone. Before we report on whatever else we have uncovered I want you all to listen to the priest's story. We will continue our internal discussion afterwards. Father Linwood will not be a part of that discussion."

Mark said, "Okay, it's on speaker phone now. Father Linwood you may begin by telling everyone what brought you to my office today."

The old priest rolled his wheelchair right up against Mark's desk.

"First of all, please call me Woody."

"Okay Woody, please tell everyone what you told me earlier," said Mark.

"I have been carrying a heavy burden for many years. I served six and a half years in Vietnam. I was a chaplain during the war and I spent most of my time with front line forces. Those young men, most of them boys, really saw and did some pretty horrible things. Don't let anybody tell you differently, war is hell on earth. Anyway, while I was there, I kept hearing about this one Green Beret who was becoming a sort of legend with the troops. This guy had incredible instincts. He seemed to know what Charlie was up to before Charlie did. He racked up some impressive kill numbers while hardly getting more than a scratch. To be completely truthful, he saved a lot of lives too and while doing so, earned himself a bunch of medals."

"He was a tough son-of-a-bitch and a loner. Part of my job was to talk it up with the troops to see if I could help them with the pressure, the nightmares, their consciences and yes, to minister to their souls when they would let me. With most guys I could find a way to reach them, you know, to get them to open up. There was one guy who went out of his way to avoid me. His name was Stanley Bolinski. I made it a point to watch him, keep up on him. Something about this guy made me uncomfortable. He was cold and distant about the killings. Whenever I pressed him to speak with me he pushed me away. That in and of itself was not unusual, other soldiers did the same. Eventually though, they came around, but not this guy."

"He became proficient at killing the enemy in many different ways. It was almost like he was in training for the Olympics or something. He took chances which usually got men killed, but not him. Then one day I pressed him hard and he became really pissed at me. I backed off, but then, later in the day, I was paid a visit by his partner."

The old priest rubbed his forehead. He was tired but pressed on.

"This partner was not human. I know you may well think I am crazy but I assure you I am not. His partner was a dark, ink black figure much bigger than I was. I had sensed for a while that something evil resided in Stanley. I thought it was the hardness of his heart, his sinfulness in taking joy and comfort from his prowess at killing the enemy. I never, ever considered he might be protected by a dark angel. This dark angel visited me that day. It was an evil spirit who was both a guardian and mentor to Stanley. This dark force spoke to me. I was warned to stay away from Stanley or I would be killed in a most horrendous fashion. I didn't fear death. I still don't. But what I feared was I would be killed and Stanley would go on killing and killing."

Drawing a deep breath the tired priest continued his story while everyone listened carefully to what he had to say.

"I know what I am telling you sounds like some sort of horror fiction right out of some sort of graphic novel, but let me assure you it is not fiction. I went to the base commander and others to try and get them to do something about Stanley. I couldn't come right out and tell them I had been threatened by Stanley's dark angel. I would have been discharged under Section 8 as being unfit to serve. I tried repeatedly to no avail. Later when I was discharged I tried keeping tabs on Stanley. I wanted to go to the authorities and tell them how dangerous he was but I also knew no one would believe me. I needed to find some way to get some evidence on him. It would have to be something where he was suspect in a murder. Unfortunately I lost track of him and frankly, the more I thought about his evil partner the more I became intimidated. But now, here I am. I've lost my feet and my eyesight thanks to adult diabetes. I don't have much time left. I needed to tell someone. I overheard at the retirement home a fellow resident speaking highly about Investigator Atkinson. It was then I had an idea. I decided to come here to see him and tell him my story. I need to know someone else knows about this man. I believe he has continued to kill even after the war.

I can't prove this mind you, but I just know it. It was my hope Investigator Atkinson, in working on so many murder cases, perhaps he might have run across Stanley and my information might help bring him down. That's my story."

Doug spoke first.

"Woody, you're to be thanked for bringing this to us. It's just incredible, man."

"Thanks, Father Woody," said Alice.

"I have some questions," said Kit.

"That figures," said Doug with a chuckle.

"I do too," said Mark. "You go first, Kit."

The interview with Father Daniel G. Linwood continued for nearly an hour longer.

During a brief break Mark fetched some coffee for the priest and offered some to Scott as well.

The biggest area of discussion evolved around the mysterious dark smoky creature. Kit and Alice were deeply skeptical while Doug was coming around. Mark was more easily convinced. After all, he was sitting there with the Woody. He could see firsthand the pain and fear which ebbed and flowed on the face of the man. Mark came to an easy conclusion, the man was truthful not just because he was a priest but because he was reporting on everything with absolute confidence and with no deviation to his story.

Father Linwood explained the origin of such a creature. This dark angel figure existed in the Old Testament, the New Testament and throughout all of human history. The evil creature never sought to possess its companion. Its purpose was principally to serve, to bend and to lead its human companion to the dark side. Once its human partner embraced the dark side, the possibilities were endless for evilness, mayhem and destruction. The person wasn't a puppet being manipulated by evil, on the contrary explained Woody.

"Make no mistake here. Stanley has been in complete control of this creature. He's the true puppet master. He is the one making all the decisions. His evil helpmate is more than willing to assist, perhaps even to enhance Stanley's efforts and outcomes. But Stanley is the more dangerous of the two."

"So if we arrest Stanley and get a conviction this killing spree will end," said Doug.

"I don't think so. Stanley still will have his partner to direct. He can use him as an instrument of vengeance and revenge. In my opinion, Stanley will send his partner out to do his bidding, killing whomever angers him. Stanley has been harboring a huge amount of anger his whole life. Whenever someone pisses him off they most surely will die."

"So we not only have to lock up Stanley we have to find a way to get rid of this creature," said Mark. "How do you suggest we do that?"

Woody bowed his head and paused before answering.

"I don't have an answer for that. Exorcising Stanley would be a useless gesture. His creature isn't internal to him so there isn't someone or something to drive out. The creature doesn't occupy a place so you can cleanse the space and banish it from returning. I just don't know how to get rid of it. Perhaps if I could do some research, but damn it, I am blind. I'm sorry."

Tears streamed down his face. Mark reached across his desk and touched the priest's hand and said, "This isn't all on you to handle. We'll find a way. You've given us a great deal of helpful information."

Pulling back Mark continued, "Look everyone, Woody's had it for today. We can talk with him again if we need to. I'm going to send him home. Stay on the line. I'll be right back."

Chapter 75
Dubuque Street, West Side Neighborhood
Manchester, New Hampshire
Home of Stanley Bolinski
Evening of August 27

Stanley couldn't eat. He couldn't sit. He couldn't stay still.

He paced around his apartment without purpose.

His anger had never, ever been more intense. He was developing a major headache from his rising anger and the stress which fueled it.

Everything was always under control for Stanley ever since his grandfather had given him his dark angel. Stanley always had the upper hand, the way out of any and all situations. Now was different somehow. He couldn't quite put his finger on it; but he just somehow knew something was in play, something he couldn't, as of yet, figure out.

"Stanley, why don't we take out the Sacha woman? C'mon man, let's do this. She's a chip this Mark bastard could pick up and use against you. You don't want that."

"I know. But if she is taken out now it could work against me. It would add to his suspicion if he links her to me. Leaving her alive could help. It would show him I'm not a good suspect since the pattern is off, I'm not someone who simply kills people who pissed me off. It might be just enough to keep him off balance. Right now I need to come up with something to feed him. I want to give him something to make it look like I'm cooperating with his investigation. If I play this right maybe I can pick up on what he knows."

"I still think you should kill her or at least let me do it for you."

"Okay, here's something you can do. Visit her, visit her tonight and deliver a message. The message is this. Don't even think of trying to fuck with me. Otherwise she will find out the hard way. I always collect what's due. Now leave me alone. I have to think and I can't do that with you always interrupting me."

Chapter 76
Manchester Police Headquarters
Evening of August 27

The police sketch artist's composite drawing was handed out to all on duty personnel. The details provided by the witness, Keisha Mfume were very helpful to the sketch artist. The unsub depicted in the sketch was described as someone authorities wanted to speak with, a person of interest in police speak. He was described as someone who may have important information relevant to the ongoing investigation into the murders at Manchester's Rimmon Park next to the Kelly Falls Housing Development.

Off duty officers and staff would receive their copies when they arrived for duty. The state police were circulating the composite drawing to all law enforcement authorities throughout New Hampshire.

Print and electronic media were provided a copy of the sketch during a brief news conference conducted outside the Valley Street Headquarters of the Manchester Police Department.

Lieutenant Burlingame tried to call Mark Atkinson at the NH CCU Offices in Concord. His office phone was busy. The lieutenant tried calling Mark's cell phone number. The call went directly to voice mail. He left Mark a message to call him back ASAP. He mentioned they had a possible suspect in the recent quadruple homicide and he would email Mark a copy of the unsub's composite sketch developed from details provided by an eyewitness.

He tried Mark's office phone once more and it was still busy.

This meant he was still in the office. Lieutenant Burlingame sent an email message to Mark with the police sketch attached to the message. His email message asked Mark to get back to him ASAP.

He would just have to wait to speak with Mark.

Meanwhile in Mark's office the telephone conference call was ongoing and robust.

Kit described the tip provided by, of all people, his own mom. That tip led him to try and find someone who could fill him in on the events from long ago. He tried the school and then the local library to no particular avail. It was when he researched the newspaper archives maintained on line by the Vermont State Library that he struck gold. His review of the Caledonia Record, the daily newspaper of the Town of St. Johnsbury turned up key information. His mother's tip panned out and was confirmed by the information in the news stories he read. The most important detail, he uncovered in his search for information about what he suspected was the genesis or starting point of the multi-decade long serial killings, was the name of a high school aged boy, Stanley Bolinski.

The early events around Stanley Bolinski fell neatly into the genesis profile. He was at the epicenter of two unexpected deaths for certain and closely connected to at least three others. Kit reported he had managed to track down the name of the former Police Chief. He expected to receive confirmation that Stanley was either a suspect in the other cases or at least was questioned as a possible witness.

Doug spoke up next and said his interview of the once Green Beret from their list who resided in Vermont was not productive.

"The guy is homeless most of the time. He has a severe mental health problem and is addicted to painkillers too. He's lived on the street more or less for the past twenty years. He managed to pick up driving for independent haulers throughout the years. Usually he was fired after a couple of runs. Still he managed to keep his CDLA although he won't any longer. I will be reporting him to our State DOT and DMV folks first thing in the morning. Believe me, his driving days are over."

Alice had nothing to add so it was Mark's turn.

He began by reporting the first Green Beret he interviewed at first looked good as possibly a person of interest. As the interview went on his answers and body language suggested very strongly that the man empathized with the victims. The clincher was the fact the man got around with the use of crutches.

"I say we move him down our list and concentrate on the next guy I interviewed. This afternoon I met with Stanley Bolinski. Yup, he's the one whose name Kit turned up during his research into the possible beginnings of our profiled unknown suspect and is connected to the Viet Nam stories provided by Father Woody. This suspect is slick. He was very careful not to tell me anything I could use to possibly pry him open a little bit. His body language suggested deeply controlled anger. While we've been talking, I've been thinking about the visit a bit more. I also see him as arrogant, maybe overconfident even though I think I rattled him a bit. I strongly hinted we were interviewing a large number of his fellow truckers and that several were proving to be very helpful. I left things open ended with him. I told him I could really use his help. Should he manage to recall anything he thought we could use he should call me. I said I would be willing to come back to his place or he can come here."

"Good move Mark," said Kit. He will want to be helpful to get the bull's eye off of his back. He'll want to try and steer things away from himself. He will also very likely want to try to learn what you know. He's in a box now and I bet he's sweating over it."

"Did you see or feel his evil partner?" inquired Alice.

"I can't say that I did. I will say this. The man is creepy for sure but my gut tells me his confidence resembles someone playing poker holding an unbeatable hand. Maybe his Ace-in-the-hole is this dark thing. I really can't say if it was nearby somewhere listening in on the conversation."

"Mark, since you are the only one who has had face time with the bastard you need to be on the highest alert. If everything we heard tonight is true he's one dangerous man when he's pissed off. Right now he must be beyond pissed off. Be very, very careful," said Kit.

"I will. Why don't we take a short bathroom break, say five minutes?"

Everyone agreed.

Mark rushed off to the bathroom.

Moments later as he was heading back to his office he checked his cell phone messages.

He thumbed through a couple when he spied a message from Lt. Burlingame. He opened the message. After scanning the message he double tapped the attachment. A sketched image filled his telephone screen. He was staring at a strong likeness of the man whose name Kit had identified, Father Woody had reported and whom he had interviewed a couple of hours ago. It was a dead on likeness of one Stanley Bolinski.

Chapter 77
Dubuque Street, West Side Neighborhood
Home of Stanley Bolinski
Evening of August 27

Stanley was all alone.

He had sent off his evil companion.

Things were finally quiet.

He needed to think things through. He needed a strategy to deal with the cold case unit investigator.

I need to get inside of this guy, thought Stanley.

"He's a smart one. I can tell. I can't just dazzle him with double talk," said Stanley out loud in the solitude of his home.

"I need to come up with something plausible for him to chew on for a while. There has to be somebody I can set up as a suspect for a couple of the cases he's working. Gotta think here. Let's see, in order to figure who I can use I first need to know what he's looking at. What are the cases he is working on, yeah that's the key."

Stanley slowly began to regain his composure and confidence. With a plan he felt more in control.

"I can go to him and say if I knew the cases I might be able to come up with something. I could tell him I could run the cases through my truck route database to see if there were any drivers who might have been in the area. He might go for that. Maybe they heard something, maybe they saw something. I can offer to talk to them, trucker to trucker, to get them to open up. Maybe I can build a story around some guy, better if he's already dead, yeah dead, so there's a dead end to this investigation. Yeah, I like this approach. I might even use someone still driving, then get my pal to off him. That would mess things up for that wise ass investigator. I'm beginning to like this."

Talking out loud helped him find his center, his balance.

Stanley had calmed down to the point he actually felt hungry.

He decided to call in an order to a local sandwich shop.

Yessir, as always, old Stanley is going to come out on top, thought Stanley.

Chapter 78
Home of Physician's Assistant Tamara Sacha
Londonderry, New Hampshire
August 27

After dinner Tamara's mind was still reeling with flashes of Stanley Bolinski and his dark and evil partner.

The mental and emotional pressure she was under was nothing short of intense.

She tried to steady herself by doing things to keep busy.

She went around the house and gathered up everything possible which needed washing. She striped all the beds in the house of their sheets and pillow cases and even searched for all the family's summer clothes on the pretense the clothes needed to be washed before being stored.

Tamara had her back to the laundry room door as she pulled the first load out of the dryer. She dumped the tumbled pile of sheets and pillow cases onto the folding table.

She was in the middle of folding the items when she heard the e laundry room door softly "click" shut as its latch engaged.

Tamara didn't turn around to see how or why the door had closed.

She sensed it was the smoky demon who had decided to pay her another visit.

The temperature in the small room plummeted. She could see her breath as she nervously exhaled.

"Tamara, can I call you Tammy?" said the demon in its low and audible vulgar voice.

"Go to hell," responded Tamara.

"That is not very creative Tammy - no, not creative at all. Surely you must know hell is my home. Going there would only please me."

"Leave me alone," demanded Tamara. She stopped trying to fold anything. Her hands were now tightly formed fists.

"Tamara, we are acquaintances now. Can't I come over for a visit now and then? If you play your cards right I might even take you home with me some time, you know I could show you around. I might even introduce you to the boss."

Tamara turned around to face the dark beast. She needed to confront her fear. The dark smoky shape shifted and swirled in place. In places she could see through the shape and then the darkness would deepen, then all she could see was a dense, thick inkiness.

The eyes were the only feature which revealed any life in the inhuman form. The eyes pulsed with a burning redness. The intensity of its glare emitted a heat she could actually feel.

Summoning up what little courage she still retained, Tamara spoke up.

"What do you want from me?"

"Tammy, Tammy, Tammy," said the evil one in a condescending voice. *"You're likely to be approached by the authorities in a matter which concerns my friend. Now we can't have you stirring things up. You have already caused enough trouble. This time, you are going to say it was just a misunderstanding and things are fine, just fine."*

"I would rather say nothing than lie for you or that bastard."

"Tammy, you don't seem to understand. You don't have a choice in this."

The smoky shape lifted up its right arm and seemed to snap its fingers. With the "snap" sound there came a loud "boom" from somewhere else in the house then a scream and crying. It was one of her children.

Tamara showing sudden courage rushed past the dark angel and pulled at the laundry room door knob. It wouldn't turn, it wouldn't budge.

She pounded on the door with her fists. She screamed, "**Let me out of here!**"

The dark one began to chuckle at her frantic and desperate efforts.

"No one can hear you. You're not going anywhere until we have an understanding **BITCH***!"* said the dark shape as it growled out the last word.

"Okay, okay I will do what you want, just leave my family alone. Leave them alone or I swear, I will find a way to destroy you."

The shape moved in close, closer than close. She could feel his heat, smell his fetid breath, and experience his threats washing over her like some sort of hot, sticky tar.

"Don't think you can screw with my man Stanley or me. If you try anything, anything at all, if you even sneeze the wrong way, ***I WILL COME BACK AND DESTROY EVERYTHING THAT YOU LOVE. I WILL INTRODUCE YOU TO LEVELS OF PAIN YOU CAN'T EVEN BEGIN TO IMAGINE. I PROMISE YOU THIS. I CAN MAKE IT LAST FOR A VERY LONG TIME."***

Tamara was shaking now.

She closed her eyes, trying not to let the terrible images inside her head of her family being destroyed at the hands of this dark fiend. She managed somehow to get on top of her terror which had filled her throat with foul tasting bile. She choked back the hideous taste and slowly opened her eyes once more.

It was gone. The laundry room door stood open.

Tamara bolted from the room to rush to the aid of her children.

As she ran past the living room she slid to a stop in the hallway. Her husband and two children were sitting peacefully in the living room. Her husband was reading a book while the two children, a four year old boy and a seven your old girl, played with a pile of Lego blocks scattered around the living room carpet.

This whole nightmare thing was a big joke with that bastard, thought Tamara.

She turned around and walked slowly towards the laundry room. She felt herself swept up into a sort of trance. Her mind was in one place while her body was in another.

She went back inside of the laundry room, closed the door and leaned back against it. She slid down the inside of the door until she was sitting on the floor leaning up against the door. She pulled her knees up against her chest and locked her arms around her knees. Laying her head down on her knees she began to cry, then, her cry turned to sobs until her gut ached from the pain of crying.

She sat there for nearly an hour all the while her desperate mind searched for a way out.

Chapter 79
New Hampshire State Police
Cold Case Unit
Concord, New Hampshire
August 27

Mark came back on the conference call line. Doug and Alice were talking.

"Is everyone back?" asked Mark.

"I don't think Kit's back on," said Alice.

"Okay, I guess we'll just wait then," responded Mark.

He was eager to report to everyone about the fax he held in his hands.

"I'm back," said Kit slightly out of breath. "I needed to take some meds. It takes a while because I need to have something to drink and something to eat when I take them. Sorry about holding things up."

"No big deal, Kit," said Doug.

Mark spoke up.

"Listen everyone, I just opened up an email message and it just about floored me. The email message had an attachment. The attached document is a composite sketch image of a person wanted for questioning in the quadruple murders this past weekend in Manchester. The image fits our target, Stanley, dead on. One of the homicide detectives working the case emailed it to me and wants me to call him ASAP.

"Do you know what this means? If our target, Bolinski, is behind those murders and they are now hunting him he might bolt along with his partner. They could disappear and turn up somewhere else and just carry on as before," said Kit. "Mark, you have got to get to this detective and get him to hold up. This guy can't be allowed to slip through everyone's fingers. Damn it! Look, I'll call some of my friends in the FBI and see if I can call in some chips on this. Other than the priest and the four of us no one else knows about this evil angel thing. If we bring that up the investigative team on this will kick us to the curb as a bunch of loonies. I know I would if I were them. Nobody is going to believe us. Somehow we have to work our way inside on this and fast. Mark, you're our man for this. You have got to go to your Attorney General immediately and tell him this same guy is your suspect on multiple cold cases you are on the verge of solving. Tell him you need access to the Task Force or Investigative team, whatever they're calling it. Doug, you and Alice need to do the same thing and I mean now. Doug, I need you to pick me up ASAP. We're going to New Hampshire. Mark is going to need our help. Alice I suggest you do the same."

Finally Kit paused and took a breath.

"Damn, I am sorry, Mark. This is your case, you started the ball rolling on this whole thing and here I am acting like I am the one in charge. I was way out of line.'

"Kit, no big deal, seriously, I'm okay with it. You're right on with everything you said. I agree completely. I do have one question though, what about the priest?" asked Mark.

"Good catch. We're going to need him. We can figure out some cover for having him in on this, like he's known our suspect since back in the day, you know, back when he tuned up his killing skills. It will have to be something like that."

"Okay, I'll arrange to have him brought in after I return a call to the Manchester Homicide Detective and after I meet with the Attorney General. I'll have to clear that with my boss. He'll back me up. He's solid like that."

"Okay boys, so where will we meet?" asked Alice.

"Let's meet first at Mark's offices and then we need to get down to Manchester right after that. Stay in touch by cell and make sure your phones are fully charged and available for calls."

Mark felt a bit guilty about his own bad habit of letting his cell phone battery drain down or leaving it turned off.

The call ended moments later with everyone having important things to do. The hunt was about to begin.

Chapter 80
New Hampshire State Police
Cold Case Unit
Concord, New Hampshire
Very Late in the Evening of August 27

Mark called his contact in the Manchester Police Department.

After just two rings Lieutenant Peter Burlingame came on the line.

"Burlingame here."

"Pete it's me. Listen thanks for the email on the man wanted for questioning. How solid is this?"

"Solid as it can be. Our witness watched this fucker walk away from the scene with a big old grin on his fucking face. We have her in protective custody. So what do you think? Does any of this link up to your cases?"

"That's why I am calling Pete. It links up in a big way."

"For real?" asked the lieutenant.

"I even interviewed the son of a bitch this afternoon?"

"Holy shit!" said Pete.

"Have your guys found him yet. Are you picking him up?"

"No, we don't even have a name to work with yet. It's just a matter of time though. By now his composite is in the hands of just about every law enforcement person in the State. Give me his name and we can roll on this."

"I can't right now. Pete, I'm giving you a heads up on this. I'm going to the Attorney General right after I'm done here to ask him to let us in on this. Pete, this is the guy that Maine, Vermont and I have been hunting for the past few months. He's a suspect in over thirty murders. There is even more to this case than I can discuss right now especially over the phone. Pete I need you to get to the DA and anybody else you can reach quickly and tell them to wait up a bit until they hear something from the AG's office. After I meet with the AG, I promise you this, you and everyone else will have his name. We just need to be very careful with this bastard. We don't want to have him get a sniff we're closing in so he can bolt. I damn well don't want him dying in some crazy shootout. I want this wacko alive so we can question him. We need to nail him to these open cases, we owe that to his victims and their families. There could easily be even more murders than we think we can pin on him. Please Pete, I need you to hold things together for me for a little while longer. Can I count on you?"

"I'm with you Mark. I'll be with you all the way on this. I can't wait to get his name and to hear your story. I bet it is a pisser for sure."

"Thanks Pete. I'll fill you in on all of this when it's over."

Their call ended.

Before calling up his boss. Tom Sisti, the CCU Investigator-In-Charge for the NH CCU, Mark called the Pleasant Cove Retirement Center to get in touch with Father Linwood.

The person who answered the phone at the retirement center at first protested it was not appropriate to call and disturb the residents after 9:00 p.m. She insisted this was a firm policy.

Mark had no patience to do the polite dance with this person and so he went all official on her.

"Listen, Ms. Tentas. Let me make this perfectly clear. In a couple of minutes I am going to call the state police and make arrangements for them to come over to your office and pick up Father Linwood. He is needed to assist us in a very important and urgent investigation. I want him dressed and ready to leave within 15 minutes. If he isn't ready and waiting to leave by the time the officers arrive, I will authorize them to arrest you for police interference. Now, have I made myself perfectly clear?"

The young Ms. Tentas swallowed hard and whispered, "Yes, sir."

"Good."

With that done Mark hung up the phone. He called the state police office and put in a request for an immediate pick up of a material witness. He explained the man was disabled and used a wheelchair. The dispatcher told Mark they would handle it and asked where to take the witness.

"I need him brought to Concord, the Attorney General's Office."

"Consider it done."

Mark called his boss, Tom Sisti.

Tom had just finished tucking his son in bed when his cell phone vibrated.

He recognized the caller ID as Mark's. Tom answered his phone.

"What's up?"

"Tom, you know that string of cases I have been working all summer? Well, I've just had a huge break and things are moving real quick. I need your help. We need to take this to the AG tonight. I need you to be with me to help get the AG lined up."

"You're going to have to give me more Mark."

"Tom, my suspect, actually correct that, the suspect wanted by CCU's in Maine and Vermont and here, is connected to over 30 murders, maybe more. This same guy is now wanted in connection with the quadruple murder this past weekend in Manchester. The PD in Manchester and the State Major Crime Unit Task Force has a composite out on our suspect. I'm afraid this guy might get wind of this and bolt or worse yet decide to go down fighting and die in a police shootout. Believe me Tom, he is one sick and immensely dangerous man, the likes of which no one around here has ever encountered before. I want this guy captured alive so we can question him and nail him to these unsolved cases and any others he might be connected to. There are a whole lot of victims and their families that need us on this. I can't let them down."

"Mark you had me when you said over thirty unsolved murders might be tied to your guy. I trust your judgement. Give me thirty minutes and I'll be there."

"Thanks Tom."

Tom had already hung up the phone and didn't hear Mark's expression of gratitude. As Tom left his house he used his cell phone and speed dialed the Attorney General's private number.

Chapter 81
Dubuque Street, West Side Neighborhood
Manchester, New Hampshire
Home of Stanley Bolinski
Late in the Evening of August 27

Stanley's evil partner returned to Stanley's side.

"So, how did it go with the doctor bitch?" inquired Stanley.

"*I don't think she will be any trouble. I messed her up real good. She is so twisted she is starting to imagine things.*"

"**BUT WILL SHE TALK TO THE COPS? THAT'S WHAT I WANT TO KNOW!**" the increased tension and volume in Stanley's voice revealed his increased anxiousness.

"*My man, dial it down. I seriously doubt she will. She knows the price for screwing with us. I told her it would cost her entire family and then her in that order. I'm telling you she's not willing to pay that price. Even if she tried, her mind is going downhill. The cops would have a hard time taking her seriously.*"

"That will have to do for now. But I warn you if she screws us, all we have and all we have left to do will go wrong sided."

"*Don't worry, I will keep an eye on her. I will keep her in line. You can always count on me.*"

Stanley stopped pacing, headed to his refrigerator and grabbed a beer.

"Time for the late news. Let's see what the cops are up to."

Stanley sat down in his well-worn recliner. He tilted it back and took a long pull on the bottle of beer.

Picking up the television remote he turned on the television and selected the local channel for its 11:00 p.m. newscast.

The screen came to life on his television set.

Chapter 82
Valley Street
Manchester Police Headquarters

Homicide Detective Peter Burlingame had pleaded his case with the assembled officers working the Rimmon Park murders. The task force consisted of state police major crime unit staff which ran the task force and Manchester Police Department Homicide staff along with two representatives of the DA's office and a Deputy Attorney General.

"Are you sure about this Pete?" asked Deputy Attorney General, Deirdre Bishop.

"Look, Mark's one of us. He knows what's riding on this. He says he knows who this guy is, where he is, and that he is a flight risk or a death-by-cop candidate. I believe him. He is getting close to nailing this guy for a long string of murders going back many years. I say we should let him have his shot with the AG. If the AG turns him down, then we would have our green light to grab this guy and Mark will give us his name and location. If the AG buys into what Mark is selling then we work together to grab this guy as peacefully as possible. There are over thirty victims and their family's grief riding on this."

The room was quiet for a moment as everyone looked at each other. The decision to wait would be in the Deputy AG's hands.

Deirdre Bishop, a small woman in her mid-thirties, looked tired. Her shoulder length, jet-black hair was pulled back and tied off. Her gray business suit was wrinkled. She had been working this Rimmon Park Murder case straight through without sleep ever since she took the call on this case. This was the third major case in a row; first the Judge Ambrose murder, then the three young boys at the Hooksett Movie Complex and now the Rimmon Park murders.

All eyes were on Deirdre.

"Okay, Pete we'll wait for the final word from the AG. We need to call all media outlets and ask them to hold off running the composite. It's now five minutes to eleven. I'll call WMUR and NECN. Pete, you call WBIN and anyone else you can think of. Then we work the newspapers. Let's go. We don't have much time."

The calls were made. Local and regional news outlets agreed to hold off until the morning news cycle only, unless they heard otherwise and directly from the AG.

The newscasts had already begun and the news anchors and news directors were advised during the news cast through their respective ear pieces not to show or mention the composite.

At six minutes past eleven the news anchor for the late news show for New England Cable Network known as NECN handed off the story about the Rimmon Park Murders to his on the scene reporter.

"In Manchester, NH we have on the scene, Sue Carlisle. Sue, do you have an update for us?"

"Thank you, Frank. Indeed there has been an update. I just spoke with sources before this broadcast tonight. I can confirm there has been a very important break in the case. Police now have a witness they aren't yet identifying who observed a person leaving the scene around the time of the murders. This person is working with the police. The witness is providing a detailed description of individual who undoubtedly is now a person of interest in this terrible crime."

The television camera showed a nervous news anchor. The reporter had not walked the thin line the Deputy AG had drawn but had trampled it. Frank Baker, once a longtime veteran reporter, knew this report would create unknown consequences which could compromise the ongoing investigation. Too late to take it back now.

Stanley was not watching NECN. Instead he had tuned into the WMUR late night news cast. He was not a channel surfer.

He seldom watched television except to follow coverage of the murders he committed. The WMUR report didn't offer much new information on the case. They had agreed to hold back and had kept their word. For now, their cooperation would help keep Stanley in the dark about the impending storm cloud. The full force of State and local law enforcement would soon come crashing down on him.

Chapter 83
New Hampshire Sate Police
Cold Case Unit
Concord, NH
Early morning of August 28

Tom sat down across from Mark in Mark's office.

It was almost 12:30 a.m. Tom emptied his coffee mug.

"The Attorney General is coming in for a meeting. She'll be here around 1:30. She's asked for her Deputy, Deirdre, to sit in on this meeting. I told her it was fine with us. I hope this priest you have told me about gets here soon."

"He will. I received a call confirming he had been picked up just before you arrived."

Just then the elevator bell for their floor "dinged." Mark stood up and went to see who was arriving. Father Linwood was rolled off the elevator by a burly veteran state police officer.

"Thanks, Simon, for picking up Father Linwood for us," said Mark.

"Not a problem. do you want me to stick around and take him home?"

"That won't be necessary, Simon. Woody here, is going to be staying with us for a while. We have a couple meetings we need him for."

With a tip of his hat Simon returned to the elevator and was soon gone.

Tom stood up and introduced himself. He greeted the old priest with a firm handshake.

"Just call me Woody and please, Mark, don't talk about me as if I am not here or completely deaf. Damn, I hate that."

"Fair enough. Want some coffee?"

"Damn right I do, and a donut too, if you have any. Waking up in the middle of the night has made me hungry. I thought I gave you everything I had on Stanley."

"Yeah, you did give us a great deal and its helped, believe me. But now there's been a huge break in this case," observed Mark.

Half listening the priest replied. "Did you just say you have a break? Did you catch him? Is he being charged? "

"Whoa, partner, slow down. Belinsky isn't under arrest yet. But he will be and soon we expect," said Mark.

Continuing he asked. "How do you take your coffee?"

"Black, just plain old black. I developed a liking for it that way from my days in Southeast Asia. Damn that's good news. I want to see him pay for his crimes."

Woody sipped his coffee and polished off two glazed donuts while the questions flew at him from Tom. Tom wanted to be ready for the AG who would naturally have his own questions.

Woody licked his fingers clean from the donut glaze.

"From the sound in your voice it appears to me you aren't sold on how dangerous Bolinski really is," said Woody.

"I'm sold enough. If Mark says he has the bastard in his sights then I have his back on this. Just so we're all clear on this. It is the Attorney General who will need convincing. I will support this all the way. In the end it's his call to make."

"Tom, about the meeting with the AG - I need to mention something else."

"I have a feeling I am not going to like this am I?"

"That part I don't know but you need to know the AG's in Maine and Vermont are also being briefed on this by their CCU Offices. Those AG's will be calling our AG probably before our own meeting with him."

"Shit," said Tom Sisti.

If there is anything a Department Head hates, it's hearing about things in their Department from someone outside the Department. The cardinal rule is to always give the boss the first heads up. There should be no surprises, ever.

In this instance that standard and important rule was not just violated but shattered.

"Look, I know this may look bad but this investigation has been moving on three co-equal lines ever since it got started. I couldn't tell my counterparts to hold off while I gave our AG veto power over all of this. They have just as much of a stake in this as we do."

"I hear you. If anyone is to blame here it's me. I should have kept up with this more closely and as necessary read the AG into this so she had a working knowledge of what we were up to. Don't worry, Mark, I'll handle this."

Mark nodded but he was worried. In his experience the top of the organizational chart can be real tight ass on things like this. How this AG reacts could, and would, make all the difference in this case.

"Tom, there is one more thing."

Tom rubbed his temples with his left hand and said with a cringe, "Let's have it."

"The CCU investigators from Maine and Vermont left their offices earlier and are on their way here. We need to work together on this case all the way to the goal line. The retired FBI profiler we've been working with is also coming along. I told you about this guy. Anyway, apart from the help we received from Woody here, Kit Baylor has been the key guy on this case. He has been able to point us in the right direction each and every step of the way. Besides he is ex-FBI and could help with that angle."

"Mark, is there anything else I need to know before we go into the meeting with the AG? Anything at all, anything that might cast doubt on this investigation, you know what I mean? Is there anything, that if it comes to light later, that could blow up our work on this? If there is, now is the time to tell me."

Mark told a lie.

"No Tom, you have it all."

Father Linwood outwardly said nothing. Privately he said a prayer of forgiveness for Mark's lie.

Tom's cell phone buzzed. It was a text message from the AG. She was ready for them. Tom looked at the priest and Mark. "She's ready for us. Let's go!"

Chapter 84
Office of NH Attorney General
Concord, NH
Early morning of August 28

It was approaching 2:00 a.m. when Tom, Mark and Woody entered the office of the NH Attorney General.

The Attorney General had held the job for the past three and a half years. The current Governor, Vivian Post, had appointed her soon after taking office during the Governor's first term and had kept her on during her second term. Since the current Governor wasn't seeking reelection rumors swirled that the AG would end up with a Federal Judgeship or an important job in the US Justice Department.

Attorney General Constance Fuller-Morton was, in fact, not an ambitious person whatsoever. Opportunities were presented to her because of her keen legal mind, her fairness and common sense, and because she refused to play partisan political games. Connie, to her many, friends was in her mid-forties. She was athletically built at five foot five inches tall. She had played point guard forward for her college basketball team at Harvard. She had also served six years in the US Army in the Adjutant General's Office. She loved to ski and hike. She was married to her college sweetheart, Dr. David Morton. They had two children, one of which was autistic. Her staff knew her to be a tireless worker and a boss who supported her people.

AG Fuller-Morton had slightly graying hair and a warm easy smile.

She wasn't smiling when the three men arrived.

"Tom, Mark, please be seated. And this is?"

Mark introduced Father Linwood. The AG took the blind priest's hand shaking it vigorously.

"I'm happy you would give up your sleep to lend us a hand, Father."

"Anything I can do to help bring an end to this man's carnage is all I live for now," said Father Linwood with a voice and conviction he no doubt had successfully used on many occasions from a pulpit.

AG Fuller-Morton turned to his two CCU unit Investigators. "Tom, Mark, I just got off the phone with the AGs in Maine and Vermont."

Her voice and body language didn't reveal how she felt hearing about this case from her peers in two nearby states.

"We had a good discussion. They both sang your praises, Mark. It seems you have put together quite a case on this suspect. I need to hear it from both of you. I want it all. I need to know everything you know. But before we continue, I want you to know we are waiting on the Deputy AG to arrive. I want her in on this. I also am aware CCU Investigators from Maine and Vermont are on their way here. We need to wait up for them as well. No need to have to repeat ourselves. But before others arrive let me say I was most uncomfortable learning about this from my peers. Tom, you know this is not how we work around here. I understand there may have been some exigencies which required keeping things close, but ultimately I am the person who has your backs. I can't do my job very well and provide cover when needed if I'm kept in the dark. This cannot and will not happen again. Am I clear?"

Tom spoke up first. "You're completely correct, Madam AG. I take full responsibility for this communication snafu. I assure you it won't be repeated."

Mark interjected his views. "Look, everyone, it is really all on me for this screw up. I didn't want to run this up the chain of command until I was certain we had enough to move on. Tom only really learned of most of this tonight when I read him in on what has happened and where things are at this time."

AG Fuller-Morton looked over at the priest. "Father, what should I do with these two?"

"I'll forgive them their sins and you can promote them."

Everyone broke out into a hearty laugh.

Just then Deputy AG Deirdre Bishop walked into the room. "Did I miss the punch line?"

Everyone laughed once more.

Mark spoke up.

"Ma'am, you need to know the Vermont CCU Investigator is bringing along a retired FBI Profiler. His name is Crosby K. Taylor. He prefers to be called Kit. The guy has been very helpful to our investigation. We wouldn't even be this close were it not for him."

"I know. I also received a call from the FBI. They told me he is one of the best. I told them I already knew of his reputation. I once took one of his seminars when I was in the Army's AG Office. I had to go to FBI Quantico for the seminar. The man is brilliant and has a gift for profiling that's for sure. I signed up for another seminar but never quite made it. It looks like we are all going to be favored with his keen mind. I'm certainly looking forward to meeting him again although he probably won't remember me."

Mark spent the next hour providing a general outline of the case from the beginning. He laid out all the work he had done in NH and the coordination with the other two States.

Then Mark dropped the bombshell on everyone.

"I think, and our consulting profiler agrees, our suspect is the likely killer of Judge Ambrose along with the three young boys in Hooksett. We also believe he is behind the case of the missing girls which is linked to the Hooksett Movie Theater murders. Then there are the recent murders in Rimmon Park. We believe he is the one who committed those murders as well."

The AG and his Deputy AG looked at one another and then they turned to look at Mark.

The AG leaned forward in her chair and put her elbows upon her knees while folding her hands into a prayerful pose. She kept her two index fingers together pointing upward while she rested her chin on the tips of her index fingers.

"That is incredible. How confident are you about all this?"

Mark looked around the room slowly before he spoke once more.

"We have been studying this man through the prism of our cold cases. We didn't immediately see a connection to the recent cases because, after all, they hadn't come to us yet."

"But a Manchester Homicide Detective, on a pure hunch, brought to me copies of case records on Judge Ambrose's murder. It didn't take long to see the same pattern in that case which we were seeing in our cold cases. Then the same thing happened with the movie theater murders in Hooksett."

Pausing, Mark looked around once more before continuing.

"He's beginning to make mistakes. For the longest time we haven't have a lead on who our suspect was. We only had a probability all the crimes were committed by the same person, but we had no real proof, only professional supposition. That would not be enough to bring to you. Then in the past 48 hours or so everything began to break for us in this investigation. We got a lead on the possible genesis of his crime spree, his origins. Then we had a walk-in with Father Woody here. He brought to us some incredible information which confirmed some information on one of our profiled targets of interest."

Mark continued, "I actually interviewed this target, yesterday afternoon in connection with our ongoing cold case breakthrough. Then late last evening, or rather a few hours ago, we received an email from our MPD Homicide Detective with a composite of the man they were looking at for the Rimmon Park murders. It was the very same man. Sir, for us that became the clincher. Now our multi-State team decided we had enough probable cause to grab this guy. Our concern is that we nail him not only for the recent murders but that we tie him to as many of our unsolved cases as circumstances and evidence may warrant. From my interview with him I strongly believe he is a flight risk or worse yet, a death-by-cop candidate. Too many victims and too many families have been destroyed by this man. We want to lay it all on him to bring closure for them. We are the only ones who can stand for those he destroyed."

Father Linwood spoke up.

"Look I know that all I am is an old, disabled priest. But you should know something else. This guy may have been a hero in Vietnam as far as the Defense Department is concerned, and I no doubt believe at times, he performed heroically. But there were many other times, too many, if you ask me where he killed when it wasn't necessary. The worst of it though was that he enjoyed it. He embraced his job. He couldn't wait to go out on another mission. He volunteered for everything he could. He never rested or relaxed. He never showed any remorse or regret. He long ago crossed the thin line between killing out of necessity, to killing for pleasure. I stand for those he immorally killed in that horrible war. I'm their voice and I want them to be heard, too."

AG Constance Fuller-Morton solemnly nodded her head in recognition of the priest's statement.

Just then one of the security guard's for the building escorted Alice Poindexter, State of Maine CCU Investigator and her intern Bruce Wyte, into the AG's office.

They were accompanied by Doug Wetstone, State of Vermont CCU Investigator and Kit Baylor, retired FBI profiler. They had met up in the parking area.

Everyone was together.

Chapter 85
Home of Physician's Assistant Tamara Sacha
Londonderry, New Hampshire
Early in the Morning - August 28

Tamara slipped out of bed.

It was nearly 4:30 in the morning. She slowly and quietly moved across the bedroom floor. She looked back over her right shoulder to be sure her husband was still asleep. She carefully pulled open the top drawer of his dresser. She slipped her right hand inside and slowly searched for the lanyard with gun cabinet key.

It took her a moment before her fingers found the desired prize.

She made her way quietly down the stairs to the first floor. Tamara continued on into the cellar and turned on the overhead light in the work room. There, in the far corner, was her husband's gun safe. She hurried over to it and inserted the key into the lock cylinder. With a turn to the right, the door to the safe was unlocked. Tamara opened the latch and peered inside.

In the left corner, she found what she was looking for, her husband's 22 caliber semi-automatic pistol settled inside a carrying case. She opened the case and there it was. The pistol was inside the case. It used a fifteen-shot clip. There were two fully loaded clips sitting beside it, nestled in the cut-out grey foam liner.

Tamara picked up the pistol and one loaded clip. The pistol had been stored with its slide open revealing there were no bullets in the chamber. She examined the gun clip. The metal felt cool to her skin but it soon warmed to her touch. She slid the clip in the gun, pulled the chamber slide all the way back, then released it. It slammed forward loading one bullet into the chamber. She flipped the gun's safety into the on position.

She closed the gun case and then closed the gun safe. Outwardly everything appeared as it should. Tamara carefully made her way back to the first floor. She stopped at the mudroom closet and opened the door. She inserted the pistol deep inside her purse. With that done, she headed back upstairs. She reentered the bedroom and put the lanyard and key back inside of her husband's top dresser drawer. She slowly slid the drawer closed.

All that remained was for her to climb back into bed.

Before she did she looked around the darkened room. It was quiet except for the heavy breathing of her husband. He was in deep sleep enjoying a dream he would never remember.

Tamara took in the quiet and the enveloping darkness. She had never before feared the darkness, never before until Stanley and his Dark Angel entered her life. She wanted to reclaim the darkness. She wanted it as before when darkness meant sleep, dreams and the recharging of her energy.

A deep sadness overtook her. Her life, her world, her everything would never be as it was, never again. Hopelessness poured generously over sadness and became a deeply dark comforter which could not provide its possessor with any escape.

Only one thing could bring her freedom from the living hell visited upon her by Stanley's evil partner. She had to make a stand, she had to fight back. She had to take back her freedom. She had to destroy Stanley and his Dark Angel. She didn't know how or when, but she felt certain she was meant to bring an end to this oppressive evilness.

It was this one powerful thought which kept her going. It fed her hope and gave comfort to her need for revenge.

Chapter 86
Office of NH Attorney General
Concord, NH
Early morning of August 28

With the arrival of everyone who was central to the case, which was building up against Stanley, introductions were exchanged while additional chairs were rounded up from adjoining offices. The AG preferred meeting in her personal office rather than the nearby conference room.

The AG noted she had already received a preliminary briefing from Mark Atkinson, Tom Sisti, and Father Linwood. She wanted to hear what the other investigators had to report. Alice and Bruce reported on things from the Maine's perspective. They mentioned their AG wanted assurance their office would be kept abreast of events as they unfolded. NH's AG agreed.

Doug followed up with an accounting of things from his office's perspective. He also reported his AG wanted to have a chance to prosecute Stanley on any cases which originated in Vermont. Alice added that her AG also expected the same.

NH's AG Constance Fuller-Morton responded she would have expected nothing less.

"You can assure your respective AG's they will be kept in the information loop. My Deputy AG will coordinate this case for the Vermont and Maine AG offices. Secondly, once NH has finished with our prosecution efforts regarding this Mr. Bolinski we would be happy to agree to any requests from Maine and Vermont for extradition for the purpose of prosecution for crimes committed in your respective States. NH reserves the right to prosecute first and to impose whatever penalties our judicial system may require. To our friends in Maine and Vermont, please note NH still has a death penalty on our books while your States do not. I intend to prosecute this man to the fullest extent possible for all crimes for which we have sufficient evidence to support our charges. Further, I reserve the right to ask for the imposition of the death penalty if warranted by the evidence."

"Now, we haven't heard yet from retired FBI Profiler, Mr. Baylor. Before you begin, let me say I once had the pleasure of attending one of your seminars back in the day when I was with the Army's Adjutant General's Office. The seminar was in Quantico."

"I remember you. You sat in the third row to my left. You sat in the aisle seat as I recall. I believe you asked several excellent questions, too. I seem to also recall that after the seminar you approached me with a question about a case your office was handling."

AG Fuller-Morton was impressed with Kit's recall.

Kit continued, "It would appear to me there is enough probable cause to make an arrest of the subject Bolinski for the recent quadruple murders in the park."

Kit continued, "As to the other cases, I am of the opinion there is insufficient evidence at this time to proceed. However once in custody and after more investigative work it should be then possible to add charges for the other recent murders and perhaps some of the cold cases as well."

At this time, Deputy AG Deirdre Bishop interjected, "I will secure search warrants for his place of work, his car, and his home. I agree, other evidence may turn up as a result of our searches which would implicate him in the other murders. As a result, those cases will only get stronger."

"Perhaps, although I doubt such a search will yield much. This man is way too careful. His crimes scenes appear to have been thoroughly scrubbed of any incriminating evidence. There are no eye witnesses, there is nothing. In addition, a smart defense lawyer would easily get such evidence tossed since your search warrant can't be so broad as to seek evidence on crimes for which we haven't a scintilla of probable cause, let alone hard evidence. Initially, I suggest your request for a search warrant should be confined to only evidence which connects this guy to the murder of those four young men," said Kit.

AG Fuller-Morton then replied. "I agree with Kit on this. For now we have to keep our focus upon this recent case. We need to nail him on this one, then we can work the other cases while he sits in prison for the Rimmon Park murders."

Kit continued, "This guy is arrogant and super-confident. He has built up a huge reservoir of confidence over not being caught throughout all these years and all these crimes. He knows he has been careful. He would have to know we have not picked up anything on him before now. I frankly see the interrogation of Stanley as the key to unlocking more evidence on all the other murders."

"Why would he simply incriminate himself in an interrogation, if he is as smart and careful as you make him out to be?" questioned NH's AG.

"Because of two things; one, his genesis or beginning crimes reveal the origin of his rage which can be used against him, to pry him open, and two; his rage is what fuels his urge to murder. Once he is locked up he will have no way to release his rage, to vent his fury, to strike out and kill the object of his rage. That object must be the interrogator. The interrogator will need to expose the raw nerve of Stanley's beginnings, even his devolvement while serving in Vietnam. In the end, he will give us the proverbial rope to hang him with. I'm sure of it."

"Whom do you suggest we use for the interrogator?"

"It should be me! I know, I know," he said with his hands up in a defensive pose. "I know what you are thinking. It's your case and one of you should be doing the digging on this one. But this case isn't about prosecutorial territory or who has the biggest balls, excuse my English. It's about getting a conviction and about getting justice. Am I right?"

"But Kit, what about your health?" blurted out Doug.

"My health won't be an issue. For those who don't know, I need to make a candid disclosure. I have pancreatic cancer. I have already had over half of my digestive system removed. I've decided I don't want to go through the radiation and chemotherapy procedures. My oncologist told me he thinks I have just a few weeks or months left to live. I accept that. I'm okay with it. But what I am not okay with is letting this guy get away with all the death and pain he has inflicted. We may only get one shot at him to try and break him down. I believe I'm the best qualified person for the job. I'm the one who found his genesis point admittedly thanks to a little bit of luck. Still, I have studied his beginnings and I am convinced I know what makes this guy tick. I know what buttons of his to push. Thanks to Mark, Alice and Doug and Padre over there, I am fully up to speed on the rest of his career. I am one hundred percent certain I can crack him open!"

AG Fuller-Morton along with everyone else in the room sat there in silence as they absorbed all Kit Baylor had just said.

"Kit, I will promise you only this! I will speak with the state police investigators and with Manchester PD along with our local DA's in Hillsborough and Merrimack counties. I will listen to what they have to say and then I will make the decision on who takes the lead in the interrogation."

"Thank you," said Kit.

"Don't thank me yet. Now, let's get down to the business of how do we execute the arrest? Deirdre, I want you to get started on swearing out an arrest warrant for Stanley Bolinski for the murders in Rimmon Park. Use your assistant Paul Simpson to work on the search warrants. Make sure they are as specific and limited as possible."

"So does anyone have an idea how we grab this guy?" inquired Deridre.

Mark spoke up first.

"The way I left things with him when I visited him at work I indicated I may have a need for some follow up. I told him I might need to stop in and see him or that he might have to come here. I left open the possibility that if he had any information he wanted to pass along he could give me a call and either I go to him or he could come here for a follow-up interview. I told him I was working him as a possible source. I believe he might be tempted to steer our attention away from him. The best way to do that would be for him to feed us info. I suspect he's very anxious to learn what we know. I could pay him a visit at his workplace and spring an arrest on him there."

"Too risky Mark, there are too many civilians that work there. The risk of collateral injuries is too high for me. I also doubt we could easily extract those people without arousing his suspicion and thus create a greater risk to you," said AG Fuller-Morton.

"What if I bring along a partner?" asked Mark.

"That only lowers the risk, but not enough to suit me!" responded the NH AG.

Deputy AG Bishop spoke up. "What about bringing him to your office? We could fill the workspace with state police. We could have state police work undercover in the building so that we have a secure corridor for him to pass through while on his way up to see Mark. We can have our people keep everyone else back. Once he sets foot inside of the CCU we nab him."

Kit reacted to that suggestion immediately.

"That could work, but I would respectfully suggest you keep the state police out of sight while having them work the perimeter to the building. This guy is sharp. Even with all the precautions he is likely to spot them and quickly think we are on to him. To keep this area of the building cordoned off will arouse his suspicions too. No, what we need is to dangle such a hugely tempting reason for him to want to rush here. We want him so focused on coming here that the closer he gets the more he lets down his natural defensive instincts."

"All right, just what do we draw him in with?" asked the AG.

"You draw him with me," was Kit's answer.

"Mark could tell him he's brought in an FBI Profiler who just happens to be in his office. If Stanley could make it up to the CCU Office he might get a chance to meet the profiler and pass along whatever he had to offer directly to the profiler. You can't get more tempting than that. He would see it as an opportunity to learn about the identity of one of the key people in the investigation. Perhaps Stanley would see this as a recon opportunity to later kill the profiler and set back the overall investigation. The more likely scenario however, is that Stanley would see the chance to meet the profiler as an excellent opportunity to steer the investigation away from himself. I believe he would jump at the chance to match wits with the FBI and to confound the investigation by his feeding bogus info to the FBI. This guy's ego is simply too big to let this chance slip through his fingers. He'll come here all right, you can take that one to the bank!"

CCU Investigator Mark Atkinson picked up his office telephone and dialed Stanley Bolinski's Office.

Listening in on the call in an adjacent office, through the use of a speaker phone was CCU Investigator-in-Charge, Tom Sisti, retired FBI Profiler Kit Baylor along with several others. The call was being recorded.

After four rings Stanley answered the phone.

"East Coast Trucking, Stanley here. Who's calling?"

"Mr. Bolinski, hi, this is NH Cold Case Investigator Atkinson calling. Do you have a minute?"

After a pause, Stanley responded. "Yeah sure, as long as we keep its short. I'm pretty busy!"

"I understand. I just wanted to follow up with you after our recent meeting. Have you thought over what we discussed? I'm hoping you might have some information which could help us with these cold cases."

"Yeah, I thought about it over the weekend. I may have heard a thing or two. I don't know how helpful it might be, but yeah. I heard some things!"

"That's great news, as I told you we need all the help we can get on this. By the way, we also caught a lucky break with a couple of other interviews too. Our consulting FBI profiler is coming to my office this afternoon to review what we have developed so far. It sure would help us if you could come up to

Concord and tell us what you heard, or may have observed. This way you could meet this guy. He's really good. It would also give him a chance to ask you follow-up questions, if he has any, without having to use me as a go-between. You know how things can get screwed up when retelling the story."

"I don't know if I can spare the time. My boss isn't feeling too good lately. So I have to handle things around here."

"I sure hope you'll reconsider. The FBI Profiler will only be here from three this afternoon until maybe five. He's pretty busy too but thankfully he recently helped us narrow down our suspect list to just a few people. We're getting closer thanks to help from several truckers. Our FBI guy is real good at helping some of our interviewees to remember some stuff they didn't think would be useful. Anyway, I won't keep you any longer. I hope you can make it!"

Cautiously Stanley said, "I can't make any promises, but I will see what I can do!"

"Thanks Mr. Bolinski. I'll keep my fingers crossed!"

The call ended.

Everyone sitting in on the call in the Concord Offices of the CCU waited for a moment before reacting to the call.

Kit smiled and put his right index finger inside his mouth and pulled against his right cheek in a symbol of having just hooked a fish. Everyone broke out in a cautions cheer. Kit gave Mark two thumbs up. Tom Sisti patted Mark on the back.

The arrest warrant was ready. Now all they needed to do was implement the plan outlined by Kit earlier that morning.

A state police undercover officer was assigned to stake out the headquarters of East Coast Trucking. His job was to remain out of sight but in position to let them know of the comings and goings of Stanley Bolinski. The officer took a beat-up older-model Ford Mustang out of the undercover vehicle storage lot. He drove to Tony's Does-It-All auto repair shop which was located directly across the street from East Coast Trucking. He spoke with the owner and asked them if they could handle an emergency job for him. The police officer's story was that he needed to get the car washed, vacuumed, polished and have a couple of dents pounded out. He said the car belonged to his brother who had been serving with the Marine's in Afghanistan. According to the cover story, his brother had called last night to say he was on his way home early from his tour-of-duty. Since he had been asked to look after the car for his brother he wanted to surprise him by picking him up at the airport with the car looking as good as possible.

The auto repair shop owner hesitated at first then decided he would fit the job in to his busy workday. He explained his own daughter was serving overseas. She was in the Navy.

With the car getting a first class cleaning, the state police undercover officer had a perfect vantage point to keep an eye on the comings and goings at nearby East Coast Trucking.

Meanwhile at the NH CCU Office it was decided Tom Sisti would work in the outer office next to Mark's. He would be on the phone and in the adjacent conference room. Two state police detectives would be pretending to go over case records. Tom's call would also be connected with the AG's conference room where the AG, his Deputy, and Father Linwood would be listening. In addition, Doug from Vermont's CCU Office would be there as well, along with Alice and Bruce from Maine's CCU Office. The call would be recorded. A state police technician set up three digital cameras. One would record the approach to the CCU Offices. The second camera would record the inner office of CCU which would include Tom's location. The third and final camera would be set up in Mark's office.

As the technicians prepositioned things Mark took the time to pull Kit and Father Woody aside.

"We all know about this wild card, the dark shape, his dark angel. Father what can we expect when he arrives and when we arrest him? Is this thing going to go off on us?"

"Frankly I don't know," said the priest. "My general sense is that this thing takes his cues from Stanley. If Stanley wants his partner to strike out and destroy this place I suppose he would. In my opinion this dark force is perfectly capable of killing both of you two and anyone else he perceives as a direct threat. I don't mind telling both of you I'm worried. Stanley isn't about to submit to being arrested." "I'm counting on him doing just that."

"How so?" asked the worried priest.

"It's just my gut on this, but I believe Stanley actually will welcome being arrested. He will want to use his arrest to throw off suspicion on him as the serial killer. He will send his partner out to kill someone else while Stanley himself is in custody. I expect Stanley will use the interrogation as a means to extract from us information which he can pass on to his evil partner. This is going to be a high stakes chess match. Stanley fully expects to win and to discredit us in the process. Later, in his mind, he can come back on us all and destroy us when it best suits him."

Mark exhaled and said, "Kit, a hell of a lot is riding on this. I sure hope you're right about this because we're going to get only one swing of the bat!"

Everyone nodded then Father Woody made the sign of the cross and reached out to Mark and Kit.

"I will pray for your success and your safety."

Mark said, "Thanks Father Woody."

Kit remarked, "Thanks Padre and could you say a prayer for my mom too. "The priest nodded his agreement.

A little over two and a half hours later, Tom's office phone rang.

It was the undercover state police officer calling in.

It was 2:40 p.m.

"Heads up everyone, our subject just entered his car and is now pulling out of the parking lot. He's turned to the right heading in the direction which will take him to the entrance ramp for I-293."

"Thanks," responded Tom ending the brief conversation.

One earlier precaution was added thirty minutes ago.

Monitoring the state police calls, with a call from his cell phone Tom Sisti put into action a second stage to the operation to report on Stanley's movement. An undercover car was pulled over by a marked state police cruiser two miles north on I-293. The two police officers went through the motions of the unmarked car's driver receiving a ticket for a motor vehicle violation.

Nine minutes after the first call came through to Tom a second call came in.

"Subject just passed our location and is heading north on I-293."

"Roger and out," said Tom.

Chapter 88
Stanley's Car
Heading North on I-293
Mid-Afternoon of August 28

"Stanley, I really think this is a bad idea. You can never, ever, trust cops," protested his evil partner.

Keeping his eyes on the road Stanley responded.

"I know that. Do you think I'm some kind'a fool? This investigator thinks he's smarter than us. Well, I have news for him, he's friggin wrong. I know this a trap. Anybody with even shit for brains can see that. Let them arrest me. They haven't got a thing on me. They'll play their mind games and try to screw with me. Meanwhile, I still have you as my ace-in-the-hole. When they haul me off to jail we will surprise them when you kill someone else. How are they going to explain that, eh? They won't be able to. I'll have my lawyer rub their damn noses in it. He'll tell them they have the wrong guy and if they don't release me he'll threaten to go the press and tell everyone the cops are incompetent and have the wrong guy. After that, I'm telling you the DA or AG won't want to touch me because their whole investigation will be suspect. It won't be long before they have to release me and then I will be completely arrest proof. They won't want to come anywhere near me. Then we can do a couple more murders and throw suspicion on some other hapless dumbass, end of story!"

"I hope you're right," responded Stanley's dark angel.

"Hope has nothing to do with this. Being smarter than the other assholes is the key and having you in my pocket trumps everything else. There ain't no way I can lose!" said Stanley with an air of complete confidence.

His dark partner studied his charge, Stanley. He had reached the place all his other human partners had arrived at. Like the many others he had served throughout time, sooner or later they each began to think of themselves as invincible, even godlike. As the dark demon he had served a stone mason in Mayan times and he had served a Pharaoh in ancient Egypt. He had also served a Persian Princess and an ancient Chinese warlord. He had been a helpmate to a Greek Philosopher, and he once sailed with ancient explorers. He had helped plan the sacking of Carthage and the burning of Rome. Stanley's dark one had been at the side of one of the most feared Visigoths of ancient times. He had been a partner with a healer in medieval times and a seer in the days of Babylon. There had been so many roles, so many human partners, he couldn't recall each and every one.

Stanley had no idea his lifelong companion was once known as Apep, in ancient Egypt as the Serpent of the Nile. In Hindi he was known as Vritha, the Enveloper. His Greek name was Diabolos, the Accuser.

The Hebrews knew him as Samael, or the Angel of Death. The Danes even had a name for him as well. He was called Tjernobog or the Black God. His personal favorite was Angra Mainyu, or simply the Evil Spirit.

There was nothing the dark angel could do to change Stanley's mind. He wouldn't even try.

At this point he was resigned to do whatever was asked of him. His eternal role was to assist, to guide, to help fulfill, and to help develop the evil traits and skills of his human partner. He had perfected his craft over the centuries. Stanley was nothing more than one of many willing evil partners. There was so many more who would welcome and willingly accept a partner such as him in order to deliver their own special brand of pain and suffering.

In due time Stanley will pass him along to another and his eternal journey would continue, as it has and as it should.

Stanley arrived in Concord at 3:15 p.m.

He parked his car in the designated visitor parking area. He casually looked around. He didn't immediately notice any police. Stanley felt so confident he had to actively work to restrain himself from laughing out loud.

"Look, over near the visitor center, the man and woman talking are speaking into radios. Your name has already been reported to those waiting for you inside," reported his evil partner.

"Good, I was beginning to think I might have misjudged this guy. My faith has been restored. He's as predictable as they come."

Stanley hitched up his pants before walking briskly to the building and going inside. His smoky companion was at his side, every step of the way.

Stanley exited the elevator and turned left down the hallway. The heels of his shoes softly clicked against the polished stone floor. The tall, oversized, dark mahogany door had a frosted glass center pane. The words, State of New Hampshire, New Hampshire State Police, Cold Case Unit was stenciled in a gold colored paint in an arched position at eye level.

Stanley turned the door knob and entered the office.

The small office he was standing in was noticeably unoccupied.

He heard a voice in the adjoining room. Stanley peered into the room. He caught the attention of a man who was sitting at one of two desks talking on the phone. He had gestured to Stanley to wait a moment. Stanley nodded his acknowledgement.

Moments later the man hurried into the room.

"Sorry about that - I'm on a call with one of my victim's parents. I put her on hold for a moment. My name is Tom, how can I help you?"

He shook Stanley's hand.

Stanley sized him up.

He's all cop, that's for sure, thought Stanley.

"I'm here to see Investigator Mark Atkinson. Is he here?"

"Yes, yes he is. He's in a meeting. Can I tell him your name?"

"Sure, I'm Stanley Bolinski. I believe he'll want to see me," said Stanley as he sardonically smiled at Tom.

"I'll be right back."

Tom left the room and went deeper into the labyrinth of offices. He returned and gestured for Stanley to follow.

Stanley had to chuckle at the charade being played out for his benefit. When you have dodged law enforcement for over four decades it becomes too easy to see police as bumblers and fools. That's just how the now amped up Stanley saw the upcoming mind game, a battle, no a skirmish with Stanley as the talented killer once again evading and avoiding confused and incompetent law enforcement personnel.

Stanley was ushered into Mark's office. Sitting in a chair in front of Mark's desk with his back to Stanley and his dark angel was Kit Baylor.

Tom left the room.

Mark shook Stanley's hand and then introduced him to Kit.

Mark gestured to Stanley to take a seat next to Kit. He easily slid into the seat.

"So gentlemen, I'm under the impression you're eager to hear what I have to say. Am I correct?"

Mark and Kit nodded.

"As I recall you indicated the investigation into a series of most unfortunate unsolved murders are the work of what you believe to be a serial killer, perhaps someone connected to the long distance trucking business. Somehow my name has come up in the course of your investigation and now you claim to be interested in anything I may be able to contribute to this ongoing investigation. How am I doing so far?"

"Fine, Mr. Bolinski, just fine. Keep going." said Mark.

Kit said nothing, he simply watched Stanley's every move and listened very carefully to every word, every nuance.

"I know you both aren't interested in anything I may know about other drivers, I believe you think I did it and I think you want to arrest me!"

Mark feigned surprise at Stanley's statement.

Finally Kit spoke.

"Why would you say that?"

"Because it's true," said Stanley

"What do you base this on?" said Mark.

"Let's just say a little bird told me," said Stanley as Tom walked into Mark's office followed by a couple of state police officers.

"Okay, no more games Mr. Bolinsky."

Mark stood up. "Stanley Bolinski, you're under arrest for the murder of ......"

He rattled off the names of the four young men killed just a couple of days ago in Rimmon Park in Manchester.

Mark delivered the standard Miranda Warning as Stanley was stood up and handcuffed by the two burly state police officers. Now in custody, he was turned around and led away to one of the interrogation rooms located at the other end of the building. After the initial interrogation he would be processed by the state police in the normal fashion. He would be photographed and finger printed. After the initial interrogation the AG had decided Stanley would be held at the Merrimack County prison before his arraignment.

Stanley offered no resistance while he was led away.

After Stanley left, Tom looked over at Mark and Kit. "I thought that went very well, don't you?"

"I don't know. I don't trust the guy. It almost felt like he was setting us up, not the other way around. That was way too easy!" replied Mark.

They both looked at Kit for a reaction.

Kit's expression hadn't changed from the moment Stanley had come into the office.

Finally Kit stood up slowly, as if he was in pain, which he was.

Kit looked at Mark and Tom. "He's playing us. He thinks this is all a game of cards and he's holding all the aces. He is way beyond dangerous. Tom, make sure you double the guards around this guy and no one, I repeat no one is to be allowed to speak with him other than Mark or I or his lawyer if he asks for one, which I doubt he will, at least for now."

Tom looked at Mark who nodded his agreement. Tom left the room.

Mark leaned over and said in a whisper, "What's going on Kit?"

Kit sat down and doubled over for a moment before straightening.

Suddenly he was visibly sweating.

He spoke softly.

"He's got some kind of plan. I can't quite figure it out right now. He's going to spring something on us and try to turn our investigation upside down. When and how I don't know, but we have to be ready for whatever comes next." Pausing, he wiped his forehead with the backside of his left hand before continuing. "I could use some water, warm water, nothing cold. I need to take some medication that's all, and then I'll be fine. I promise."

Mark hurried off to get some room temperature water for Kit.

Kit sat there in the most intense pain he had yet experienced. He closed his eyes, gripped the chair arms and tried to focus upon an image of his mother.

Chapter 89
Dartmouth Hitchcock Clinic
Manchester, New Hampshire
August 28

Physician's Assistant, Tamara Sacha, clapped with all the other physicians, PAs nurses, and staff after singing Happy Birthday to the ever popular, Dr. Kimberly Jones. Those who could spare a minute had quickly snuck into the Internal Medicine Department Conference Room for the impromptu and very brief birthday celebration complete with cake and balloons. The celebration was over in less than a few minutes as staff hurried back to the examination rooms or their work stations to assist the never ending stream of patients.

Tamara melted away from the gathering even before the cake had been cut.

Outwardly she appeared normal in every respect. She smiled, conversed freely and otherwise carried out her duties as she had always done. There were, however, two differences. The first was her internal emotional and psychological state. She was wound up so tight that, at times, she had to work to just take a breath. It seemed all her senses were on the high alert. The second difference was this. She was carrying her husband's gun. She wore it underneath her physicians smock, wedged underneath the belt of her slacks, against her back.

Just the feel of it pressing against her body gave her just enough courage to work through the day's activities.

After work, she quickly exited the building. Before she headed out to the parking lot she slipped the gun from behind her back and moved it to the side pocket of her smock. She was careful to do so while not being seen by others.

Tamara headed to her car, unlocked the door and quickly climbed inside. She started up her car and headed off to the grocery store to pick up a few things before proceeding home.

While walking through the grocery store she barely heard the clatter of the shoppers or the everyday business noise of the store. She went through the check-out line like an automaton.

Before approaching her car with her groceries she carefully scanned the crowded parking lot. Satisfied that she had a safe and clear route to her car she made a bee-line for it. She remotely unlocked the trunk. Tamara unloaded the several bags of groceries from the grocery cart to her trunk. Just as she unloaded the final bag she caught sight of a long shadow on the parking lot pavement.

The shadow indicated a figure was approaching and rapidly closing the distance to her location.

She carefully began to turn to face the threat. Tamara dropped her purse into the trunk while at the same time inserting her right hand into her side. Her hand closed around the gun grip just as she turned to face the expected approaching threat.

An elderly man was hastily approaching her with a gait which betrayed a limp due to a failing hip. He had a warm smile on his heavily lined face framed by a neatly groomed white goatee. While it was unusually warm weather he wore a blue button down sweater over a casual shirt. He also wore thin gold colored metal framed glasses.

"Miss, I would be happy to take the carriage for you."

He extended his right hand towards Tamara's grocery cart.

Tamara's nervous eyes quickly scanned the threat. She caught the sight of a small elderly lady clinging to her handbag and also wearing a sweater while she obviously waited for her husband to return to her with Tamara's carriage. The lady was standing next to a small car across the parking row.

Tamara' released her grip on the pistol and with a nervous smile she released the carriage to the man who expressed his gratitude.

The man turned and headed off with the carriage towards his wife.

Tamara picked up her purse and closed her trunk. She slipped behind the wheel and within minutes she was on the highway heading home.

Just as she pulled into her driveway, her radio show was interrupted by a late-afternoon news flash. The news break announcer reported the New Hampshire Attorney General had indicated during a hastily called news conference that State authorities had made an arrest in the recent multiple murders at Rimmon Park in Manchester. The announcer went on to say that sources indicated Manchester resident, Stanley Bolinski, was the person arrested. The reporter ended the announcement by saying the investigation was still active and underway.

Tamara Sacha sat in her car for a moment after the radio news break. Her mind was trying to get itself wrapped around this news. *What did it mean to her? Could he somehow evade prosecution? How does this affect his dark and evil partner?*

This last question troubled her.

If this guy, Stanley, feels the need to clean up any trouble in his past which might expose him to prosecution she would be, had to be, at the top of his list. She was certain of that.

His arrest didn't end the pressure on Tamara it only served to ramp it up even further.

Somehow, she needed to ensure Bolinski is crushed by the criminal justice system or she would need to take things into her own hands.

Her mind began to grasp and amplify an image of a serpent slithering towards her. The serpent was large and seemed hungry. It was slithering back and forth as its tongue lashed out of its oversized mouth searching the air for a hint of a life it could consume.

Suddenly, in her mind's eye she could see herself swinging the large curved blade of a sword. The air rippled with the swishing sound of the blade as it sliced through the body of the snake while removing its head from the still slithering, animated body.

Remove the head, kill the snake, thought Tamara.

Chapter 90
State Police Headquarters
Concord, New Hampshire
August 28

Inside of the interrogation room number 2 sat Stanley. He looked uncomfortable while sitting on a battleship-gray, steel chair. His arms were handcuffed to the arms of the chair while his legs were shackled to the legs of the chair. The chair itself was bolted to the floor.

Directly in front of him was a mismatched gray steel table. It was not bolted to the floor. On the other side of the table were two empty folding chairs. The room was unusually large as interrogation rooms go. It measured out to 12 feet by 16 feet. It was painted forest green. The wall directly across from Stanley had a large one way mirror. The room also had a two way communication system and was set up with state-of-the-art digital audio and video recording capabilities.

Waiting in the room on the other side of the mirror was the Attorney General and her Deputy. In addition, other occupants of the room included the DA for Hillsborough County, the commander of the state police, Alice and Bruce from Maine's CCU, Doug from Vermont's CCU along with Father Linwood, Tom Sisti and Mark Atkinson from New Hampshire's CCU. Kit Baylor, retired FBI Profiler stood silently off to the side. His eyes were transfixed and his arms were folded. Above all, Kit was deep in thought as he soaked up everything about the suspect, Walter Bolinski. Kit watched the man's eyes. He counted the number of times the man's eyelids blinked in a minute, in two minutes then three. He was paying close attention to the man's eye movement.

Stanley offered nothing. He sat perfectly still. His eyes were fixed upon the table. Then it happened, a slight turn of his head. It was so slight the untrained eye would not have noticed. Kit Baylor had a highly trained set of skills and he immediately noticed. To Kit, the slight tilt of the suspect's head suggested the man was listening to someone, someone close by, listening as if a message was being delivered as it were, by a mere whisper.

Mark and Kit were assigned the task of interrogating Bolinski. The others eagerly wanted to watch. Extra folding chairs and office chairs were brought in so everyone else could watch. Special arrangements were made to provide a live feed to the AG's Offices in Maine and Vermont. Everything was in place for the interrogation to begin.

Mark and Kit had held a brief private discussion out of earshot of the others prior to entering the observation room.

They mutually agreed to not bring up any mention of Stanley's dark angel. If Stanley brought it up they would go along as if he is spinning a delusional point.

It was now time for Mark and Kit to initiate the interrogation.

The two men each received numerous words of encouragement along with a few pats on the back from the others gathered in the observation room before they entered the room holding Stanley Bolinski.

As they entered the room, Mark announced their arrival for the record.

"The date is August 28th, 2016. The time is 16:40. Now entering the main interrogation room of the New Hampshire State Police Headquarters, Concord, New Hampshire, is Mark Atkinson, investigator with the New Hampshire Cold Case Office in the office of State Police and working under the supervision of the New Hampshire Attorney General. Accompanying this investigator is Crosby K. Baylor, retired profiler for the Federal Bureau of Investigation. Mr. Baylor is assisting as an expert consultant to the New Hampshire Cold Case Unit."

"Also present is Mr. Stanley Bolinski, current known address Dubuque Street, Manchester, New Hampshire. Let the record show Mr. Bolinski is restrained at the wrists and ankles to his chair which is also secured to the floor."

Mark continued, "For the record, Mr. Bolinski was read his Miranda warning at the time of his arrest. He acknowledged his receipt of the warning and his right to counsel. At this time I am going to repeat the warning."

Mark repeated the Miranda warning.

"Mr. Bolinski, we are here to ask you some questions. If at any time you request counsel the interview will cease and your counsel will be summoned."

Following the reading of his rights, Mark asked, "Mr. Bolinski, do you understand your rights as I have read them to you and do you wish to exercise your right to counsel at this time?"

"Yeah, I understand my rights and no I don't want my attorney at this time. I would like a cup of coffee, light on the cream and one sugar."

Knowing someone in the adjacent room would be getting the requested coffee ready for the prisoner Mark continued. "Mr. Bolinski, at this time, the State of New Hampshire, under the authority of duly authorized search warrants, is conducting a search of your house, your office and your car."

"Big deal," said Stanley.

"Mr. Bolinski where were you on August 26th, 2016 between the hours of 2:00 a.m. and 6:00 a.m.?"

"I was home sleeping, but I suppose you aren't going to buy that. Am I right?"

"Is it your statement you were at your residence sleeping? Is there anyone who can confirm your statement?"

"Are you shitting me? Do all you numb nuts really talk that way?"

"Is that a yes or a no?" asked Mark.

Kit sat in his chair with his arms folded studying Stanley and in part keeping his senses alert for the presence of Stanley's alleged dark and evil partner.

Nothing had occurred as of yet.

"I was alone. I'm always alone. Everybody knows I don't have a wife, or some slut girlfriend."

"Mr. Bolinski, what would you say if I told you we have a witness who places you at Rimmon Park during the date and time in question? That same witness also observed you leaving the scene of multiple murders."

A state police officer entered the room and placed a paper cup filled with the coffee that Stanley had requested.

Kit leaned forward and slowly slid the cup just within reach of the chain restraints Bolinski was shackled with.

Stanley fixed his eyes on Kit and bore down on him with a stare that conveyed his seething anger. Kit offered no reaction to the stare down.

Stanley's manacles barely allowed him to reach the cup. He picked up the cup and took a careful sip of the coffee enjoying the warm liquid as it passed his lips. He put the cup carefully down and returned his gaze to Mark.

"I would say this witness of yours is full of shit."

Mark opened a folder from a pile of papers he had brought into the interrogation room. He turned the sheet of paper around and showed it to Stanley. It was a photocopy of the composite sketch made with the information provided by the witness.

The sketch was a very good likeness of Stanley. He could clearly see that.

Son-of-a-bitch, thought Stanley.

His Dark Angel responded by whispering his thoughts to Stanley.

"Stanley, this is a big problem. Do you want me to find this witness? I can kill the witness in no time flat. I won't let you down. Then they'll have nothing!"

Stanley didn't respond. His ego, his twisted evil mind, was redlining at the moment. Over the years Stanley had acquired a sense of invincibility. This was the fuel which, at the moment, propelled his conscious and subconscious mind. If he was ever to prove his superior intellect and skills he would need to shed the dark partner who was so much a part of his life. Stanley had considered this nuclear option before, several times in fact, but somehow he always fell back to relying upon his partner in crime, suffering and death.

Mark waited for a couple of minutes expecting some sort of response out of Stanley. None was forthcoming so he decided to lay out some more information. Pulling the crime scene photos of Rimmon Park murders out of a large manila envelope, he laid them out on the table next to the composite sketch of Stanley's likeness.

"Recognize these young men?"

"Before or after?" asked Stanley as he chuckled over his own sense of humor.

Mark leaned forward and folded his hands on the table while staring directly into Stanley's eyes. Stanley stared right back. He was starting to really enjoy these mental games. Stanley was convinced he was winning handily.

I could do this all day long, thought the supremely confident Stanley.

"What I would like to hear is your story. What were these guys to you? Did you buy drugs from these punks? Did they work for you? Was it some kind of drug deal gone wrong? Tell us, we want to understand what went down," said Mark.

Stanley picked up the paper coffee cup and drank slowly from it while still looking directly at Mark. He emptied the cup and worked on a small belch.

In a flash Stanley knew just what he wanted to do. He wanted respect, recognition and appreciation. Three things he never, ever felt before. Throughout his whole life all his success came as a result of his partnership with the evil one, his dark and mysterious minion. Stanley was bored with his life. He had lived alone, he had no real normal friends, no girlfriends and no contact with whatever was left of his distant family. His buddy, his partner in crime, was the only companionship he knew. In one brief instant his destiny was flashing before his mind's eye. He needed, no wanted, to shout out a claim to any and all who would listen. He was a killer, a true and unapologetic killing machine. Stanley suddenly wanted what other notorious serial killers had enjoyed, eternal recognition for their work.

And so a righteously angry Stanley elected to have his coming out moment right here and right now.

"You really want to know. I'll tell you. They pissed me off, that's all! These piss ants thought they owned the neighborhood. They acted like everybody owed their punk asses' big time respect. Somebody had to put these dogs down before they really hurt somebody. Consider it community service. I did you guys a favor taking them out."

There it was. A full and clear admission he had killed the four young men in Rimmon Park. Mark was shocked at how easy it was to obtain the unambiguous admission. On the other hand, Kit wasn't ready to call it a day, not yet.

"So how did it go down?" asked Mark.

"Trade secrets, Mr. Big Time Investigator, you haven't earned my respect yet. I have more secrets than you can shake a stick at," said Stanley with a small wink at Mark and Kit.

The interview went on for another forty minutes. Nothing new was forthcoming from Stanley. The verbal jousting was devolving into a circle of questions with no clear answers.

Mark and Kit took a ten-minute break. Stanley was asking to go to the bathroom but Mark and Kit were holding off in an effort to put some added pressure on him.

The Deputy AG Deirdre Bishop approached Mark and Kit. "You pulled out of him a confession on the Rimmon case. That'll go a long ways. The witness is another big score on this case as well. If our team, executing the search warrants, finds anything else it will add another nail in it for him."

Her phone vibrated. "If you'll excuse me, I have a call."

She turned away to take the cell phone call. Mark and Kit headed off to the men's room.

They returned moments later and stood together watching Stanley through the one way glass.

Kit suddenly became excited.

"Turn it up, turn up the speaker!" demanded Kit. "Shhhhhhhh; everyone; Quiet!"

Kit even tapped Deputy Attorney General Bishop on the shoulder and shoed her out of the observation room so she could continue her phone conversation. With the room finally settled, they could barely make out Stanley's voice. He was trying not to move his lips but his voice was clearly coming through. It was a one way conversation.

376

"Don't argue with me. I want you to go now. Look, I can handle myself. By the time I'm done with them they will be so screwed up they won't know what hit them."

"Yeah, yeah, that would work. It has to be spectacular. I want that bitch's prints all over this one."

"No, you leave him alone. He's already messed up."

"I'm sending you to her. You're hers to keep. You're not mine, anymore! If you do this right, I will be home free and you can move on. Yeah, that's what I want. Yeah, I know. It's final, I'm telling you. Look, stop friggin arguing with me. That's it, now get the hell out of here before they come back."

The others in the observation room looked at each other and began whispering conversations of what was Stanley up to.

Mark and Kit had an idea but even they were not completely sure. Only one person might be able to shed some light on what they all had just heard. Father Linwood may well hold the key to unlocking this new twist to the unfolding story of one Stanley Bolinski.

Mark and Kit went looking for the disabled priest.

Chapter 91
Manchester, NH Police Headquarters
Valley Street
August 28

Tamara Sacha parked her car in the parking lot of the Valley Street Shopping center, a half-block away from Manchester's Police Department. She exited her car and locked it remotely.

Tamara slung her purse over her left shoulder and settled her right hand inside of the right side pocket of her three-quarter length overcoat. The temperature was dropping. The late summer evening air felt cool and so the coat seemed appropriate.

Her right hand felt the reassuring texture of the pistol grip on the weapon sitting heavily inside the side coat pocket.

Nervously, but still determined, she walked in the direction of the Manchester Police Department. Her objective was to ask about the murder suspect, Stanley Bolinski. She certainly had personal information which would be of some value to investigators regarding that freak, Bolinski. However, Tamara's motive wasn't altogether altruistic. Her true motive was to try and learn where he was being held. It would be better yet if she could learn when and where he might be moved. She wanted to get close to him. Close enough so he would see her and know she had evolved. Tamara was now a vengeful instrument wholly devoted to taking him down.

Tamara's ever-changing mission grew bolder. She wanted to get close enough to him to kill him.

"To kill the snake, cut off the head," she whispered again and again, as she climbed the steps of the Headquarters of the Manchester Police Department.

She pulled open the heavy glass door with her right hand and then slipped inside the lobby. There were over a dozen people milling about or sitting on the few chairs and benches in the lobby. Two uniform police officers were talking with an elderly couple seeking information about their grandson who had been arrested earlier in the evening. Two heavyset women were speaking with raised voices, having some sort of argument.

Standing at a glass window labeled "Information" were two men wearing baggy pants along with a young woman. They were arguing with a police official who was standing at a desk on the other side of the bullet proof glass enclosure.

Tamara moved to stand behind the three people.

The din in the waiting room would annoy just about anyone, yet Tamara stood perfectly still. She waited patiently with her right hand gripping the loaded weapon in her pocket.

Suddenly, in her left ear, she heard the too familiar and dreaded voice of the dark angel.

"Tamara, my sweet Tamara, what do you think you are doing?"

She tensed up.

"You have your husband's gun in your pocket. Are you considering using it here, right now perhaps? That would be spectacular. I would love to help. Just tell me what you want me to do. I am yours to command."

Tamara looked over her shoulder. No one was visibly standing beside her.

In a whispered voice Tamara replied, "Leave me alone."

"I can't do that anymore. You see, our mutual friend Stanley; he just gave me to you. I'm a gift to you for life. No returns allowed. I am your humble servant. You have to just say the word, whomever you hate, despise, or simply dislike, I can destroy them for you. Surely there must be someone we can destroy. Anyone at work perhaps, or even here. If you ask me, those two women sitting on that bench over there arguing, are just too bitchy! What do you say we take that gun of yours and put a bullet into their useless heads? C'mon, it will be fun!"

"Leave me the alone," said Tamara in a raised voice that drew the attention of some of the people in the lobby.

A uniform officer exited a side door and went over to the two women sitting on the bench.

They stopped arguing with each other and now directed their angry voices at the young officer.

"Tamara, I will be at your side from now on. Give me a chance to prove myself to you?"

"Okay, kill Stanley for me. Better yet, tell me where he is and I will kill him myself."

"I can't do that. That's just not permitted. It would break the rules."

"What damn rules, you bastard?" she asserted in a heavy whisper.

"That's just the way things are."

"I'll tell you what. If you belong to me now then get these three punks out of my way so I can get down to business finding out where Bolinski is being held."

Her new evil partner accepted the order and proceeded only as he knew best.

He let himself be seen by the three young people.

The girl shrieked and the two young men let out a string of expletives as all three began to shuffle back from the glass window.

They bumped into Tamara and one of the young men shoved her out of the way.

Just as this was unfolding the young police officer which had arrived moments before turned around. He spotted Tamara and immediately recognized her as the woman he and his partner had interviewed in connection with a stalking complaint involving Stanley Bolinski. The young officer had moments ago reported to his shift commander he had some information on this Bolinski guy who had been picked up earlier today in connection with the Rimmon Park multi-murder case. After he finished up with the two women in the lobby he was going to return to his watch commander and brief him on the Bolinski connection.

He raised a hand to gesture to Tamara.

When the young man bumped into her it caused her right hand to come out of her coat pocket with the pistol firmly in the grip of her hand.

The young officer along with the other two officers working the lobby instantly spied her pulling out the gun. The officer behind the glass window hit a button on the edge of the desk which triggered a building wide alarm.

The three uniformed officers drew their weapons while shouting at everyone to get down. People began screaming and moving in several directions.

The dark angel was trying to get Tamara to listen to him but it was hopeless under the rapidly changing conditions.

Tamara's eyes were bulging with terror. She knew in that instant there would be only one way to end this living hell. She gripped the pistol with two hands trying to find the dark angel. She swirled around quickly in search of the smoky figure.

"**Put the gun down, put it down now,**" shouted one of the lobby officers.

The young officer who recognized her shouted, "**Don't do this lady, don't.**"

Tamara gave up in a flash. She pressed the pistol to her temple and pulled the trigger.

A millisecond before the bullet left the gun, the dark angel knew his rein on earth was about to be over. The only way to possibly destroy him was to destroy the one he was given to with one's own hand.

To kill the snake, cut of the head, thought Tamara.

She died instantly.

Chapter 92
State Police Headquarters
Concord, New Hampshire
August 28

The Deputy AG and the AG approached Mark and Kit.

"What was that about?" asked the AG.

Kit spoke up first. "It's possible he was trying to set the groundwork for a later insanity plea. Or he's just having a conversation with himself which is not unusual in serial killers. It happens more than one would think."

"Well, listen guys, our investigators have uncovered his cache of weapons. One of them is sure to match our murder weapon. But get this, they also found a small flip notebook tucked inside of a hidden compartment in his car's glove box. It seems this notebook's cover has a title of some sort. On the cover he appears to have written, "Kill List." The book is filled with individual pages; there are names, dates, and in some instances weapons, and get this, even the time of death. The notebook is on its way here. I thought you guys could use it."

Mark and Kit both felt exhilarated with this news.

A few minutes later a state police officer came in carrying a clear plastic evidence bag. Inside of it was a small, spiral bound flip notebook. The officer was told to hand it over to Kit and Mark. Kit took possession of the evidence bag while Mark filled out the chain of evidence paperwork. Kit asked the officer if he could remain around for a while in order to transport the key evidence back to the investigators. He agreed to wait as long as necessary.

Mark handed Kit a pair of white evidence rubber gloves while he took out a pair for himself. They put the gloves on and then opened the bag. They slowly flipped through the pages. It contained critical information on every murder Stanley had a hand in before and after his tours of Vietnam.

They both paused when they saw the notes regarding Judge Ambrose's murder. They paused again when they reached the page with the murder details of the three teenage boys at the Hooksett movie complex.

They put the book back inside of the evidence bag. They turned around and reentered the interview room to find Stanley had worked himself into a fit.

"Where in the hell have you been? I have to take a leak. If you don't let me take a piss I'll just piss right here."

Stanley's eyes suddenly fixed on the evidence bag. His body language betrayed his reaction. For a man who had developed an immense ego, he was now clearly rattled.

He looked away.

"Stanley, look what we found. It's your Kill List," said Mark as he dropped the evidence bag on the table outside of the reach of Stanley.

"C'mon, man, don't stop talking now. Why don't you take a walk down memory lane for us, then you can have your bathroom break, right Kit?"

"Sure, sounds right to me."

Now Kit leaned in and propped his arms on the table.

He raised his right hand and pointed his index finger at Stanley. "I'm know you killed three kids when you were back in school. I figure you were angry, yeah, you were pissed at them for whatever reason, but you weren't yet the monster you've become. No, no, that happened when you decided to kill off your parents. God only knows what they did to you. But after that, you, you Stanley Bolinski, you became a killing machine. You killed anyone and everyone who got in your way. You know it and now we know it, too."

Stanley started rocking in his chair. While he did so Mark began to pull out of a manila folder photo after photo of the Stanley's victims that had turned up on the CCU lists in Maine,

New Hampshire and Vermont. He began to spread them out on the table.

Stanley's eyes raced back and forth among them.

Suddenly the interview room door opened and the Deputy AG came into the room. She whispered to Kit. Kit stood up and left the room with the Deputy AG. Mark kept placing photos on the table. He stood up and began to pace the room, carefully watching Stanley's reaction.

Stanley was becoming more and more agitated with each passing moment.

Suddenly the door to the interview room opened once more. Father Linwood was wheeled into the interview room with Kit.

Kit stopped the wheelchair next to the gray metal table.

"Stanley, I believe you remember Father Linwood from back in the day when you were in Vietnam. It seems he knows a great deal about you."

"Yeah, I remember you, Stanley. I've never forgotten you. I vowed I would see you brought to justice someday and now I am here. God has truly blessed me."

"Shut your mouth you piece of shit. You were useless in Nam. While guys like me were laying our lives on the lines every day you were satisfied to just lay the guilt trip on us guys. You fucked up some of them real good, old man!"

"Whatever sins I have committed I have prayed every day for forgiveness. What about you? Do you want forgiveness?"

"Hmph, me I just want to rip your heart out, that's what I want."

"By the way, Stanley, your Kill List isn't finished. We just received a message about a horrible shooting in Manchester at Police Headquarters" said Kit.

Here it comes, my dark angel has worked his magic. Now here's the case that'll screw up this investigation, thought the delusional Stanley Bolinski.

Stanley was sweating from the strain of holding his kidneys. Nevertheless he couldn't wait to hear what had happened.

Kit began, "It seems there was a Physician Assistant by the name of Tamara Sacha. She had gone to the police station for some, as of yet, unknown reason. We just learned she had spoken with the police several days ago complaining about you stalking her. Well, Stanley, it seems the poor woman apparently committed suicide less then thirty minutes ago."

"NO, NO, NO, NO way. Noooooooooooooooooooo!" screamed Stanley as he explosively fought against his restraints.

He thrashed about violently to the point he had to be held down by four police officers.

Mark, Kit and Father Woody's work was done here.

Epilogue

The number of unsolved cold cases in Maine, New Hampshire, and Vermont which were tied back to Stanley Bolinski number close to slightly more than forty. The number of victims totaled over fifty. No one could or would ever know about the number of murdered in Vietnam during his tours of duty. No one would pursue this part of his life to sift through the fuzzy military records and the fading memories of his comrades in arms. His recent and localized string of murders, Judge Ambrose, the boys at the movie theater, the four gang-bang wannabes were linked to Stanley, too. Nothing definitive linked him to the three missing girls even though investigators strongly believed he had a hand in their disappearance and likely deaths.

As for Stanley, he remained combative throughout his arraignment and his trial. He refused to plead out.

He fought with his attorney and shouted out so much he was removed from the courtroom twice during his trail. Later, he was forced to watch the proceedings via close circuit television.

The jury was unanimous. They announced their verdict of guilty after only four hours of deliberation. One week later, at the sentencing hearing, Stanley was sentenced to death in the matter of the four young men he murdered in Manchester's Rimmon Park.

He was now only the second person in modern times in New Hampshire history to be sentenced to death. It was expected his lawyers would file numerous appeals which, given his age, would ensure the likelihood he would eventually die in prison.

In the unlikely event Stanley's lawyers would win an appeal and possibly get him out on some unforeseen technicality authorities in Maine and Vermont were waiting to extradite Stanley and prosecute him in their respective states for murders committed in their jurisdiction. After all, there is no statute of limitations on murder.

The day after Stanley's sentencing, retired FBI Criminal Profiler, Crosby K. Baylor, better known as Kit, died from pancreatic cancer.

The retired priest, Father Linwood suffered a stroke two days later. Shortly thereafter he was admitted into hospice care. He died less than a week later.

Vermont cold case Detective Doug Wetstone cleared the Bolinski murders from his backlog of cases. The files were moved to the active files of the State's Attorney General. He also met with the families of the victims to bring them up to date and to hopefully provide them with some closure.

Maine's cold case Detective Alice Poindexter did pretty much the same as Doug. After it was all over, she took an extended vacation using up some of her accumulated vacation days.

Mark Atkinson, New Hampshire cold case Detective, like his colleagues, met with the victim's families. Mark received compliments from many but never felt comfortable with the numerous "well dones" and pats on the back. His case files linked to Bolinski were also transferred to the active files of the State's Attorney General.

Mark eventually began to dabble in writing a book to retell the Bolinsky story but abandoned it after several month's work. It didn't feel right to him.

It wasn't long before other writer's begun to hound him for his insights into the case. He turned them all down. Even Hollywood got into the act with two separate producers pitching a movie to him. Each one offered him the opportunity to be their "technical consultant" which would have earned him some serious money as well as on screen credit.

He turned them down even though his superiors had signaled their approval for a film to be produced covering this case.

Mark's career at the state's cold case office would go on as it had before. He showed up for work each day and opened yet one more file. Each folder was one more case for which there weren't any answers, at least not yet.

The dark companion, the evil force which was omni-present throughout Stanley's murderous lifelong career no longer existed, a least as far as anyone could tell. But they were wrong.

Nearly a full month had passed since the sentencing of Stanley Bolinski.

On the streets of Boston, on Symphony Road, a homeless runaway teenager was busy panhandling without success. He had bounced from foster home to foster home for the past two years. Before that he lived with his drug-addicted father. He never knew his mother. She died when he was just three years old while trying to give birth to another boy.

The teenager's name was David Lymon. He hadn't been on the streets long enough to have earned a street name.

While the long string of being passed along to one partner after another had come to an unexpected end, the smoky and deadly force was now ready to start up a whole new sequence of companions. The first was always special since it was one he alone got to choose. This young man would do just fine.

For the moment he simply watched the teenager being rejected again and again. This was good. Rejection of one desperate human being by another eventually leads to a hardened heart. A heart, cold and empty just waiting for someone to fill it up, fill it to the brim with rage!

"*Yessir, Davey Lymon, you will do just fine!*"

***

Stanley Bolinski, a.k.a. New Hampshire State Prison inmate number 389448-2 sat in his cell settled deep in thought. His eyes flitted from side to side as his mind worked over the problem.

From the prisoner's unique perspective his sole problem was his damn lawyer, the no-good-son-of-a-bitch, Walter D. Gifford the 3rd, had insulted him today during their client-lawyer meeting. It seems Attorney Gifford had pronounced that Walter should submit himself to yet one more psychological exam. He hadn't come right out and said Walter was a bit off, but that's what he meant.

Walter picked up on the signals, the subtle vibes his lawyer was giving off. It was the tone in his voice, his hooded eyes, his body language and his damn bow tie.

Killing him would be so easy, so invigorating, so fulfilling. The problem was how and when. For Walter, the how and when was the best part. Deep inside he clung to the notion of killing the present target of his rage. The how, when, and where were his paintbrush, his palette, and he was the excited artist.

"I need a notebook," said Walter to the emptiness in his cell. "Yes, that's exactly what I need to do. I need to get my hands on a small notebook. It ain't over until I say it's over. They are all going to have to learn the hard way, a man ain't dead until he's really dead!"

From the Author

This story is an obvious fictional account of a cold blooded serial killer. I elected to portray the main character, the killer, as someone who was not inherently born evil but certainly devolved into evilness with the help of his weak and deeply flawed parents and of course, the deathbed gift from his grandfather. The gift was an evil wraith who existed solely to bringing out the very worst in the assigned human partner and to help fulfill his true potential.

Setting the above aside, it is important to see past the evilness in the story and to recognize the tireless and oftentimes thankless task of trying to solve cold cases, to speak for the dead as well as their families and friends.

At present, in Maine, New Hampshire and Vermont there are over 500 open and as of yet unsolved murders. These are crimes which, in some instances, go back decades. These cases don't even include the hundreds of missing person cases which in turn could yet become another unsolved murder case or simply lack sufficient information to be moved to the murder side of the ledger. Each and every day these lists grow.

I can't begin to fathom the pain deep and sense of loss which weighs upon the families and friends of those murdered or long missing. None of us can.

Across our nation the numbers are evermore staggering so let this book be <u>dedicated to the investigators</u> of cold cases and missing person's cases and <u>to the families and friends of dead or missing persons</u>.

Each unsolved murder case must not be forgotten. Investigations are ongoing, seeking the one piece of evidence to break open the case. The missing person cases need to be resolved as well. Only one thing can possibly bring resolution to these and it is evidence, solid, actionable evidence.

Let us pray that someone, anyone, who may know something about any unsolved murder or missing person case, we pray for them to come forward and **do the right thing and do it now**!

NH Department of Justice
Office of the Attorney General - NH Major Crime Unit
33 Hazen Drive
Concord, NH 03305
603-271-2663

Vermont State Police Headquarters
45 State Drive
Waterbury, VT 05671-1300
802-244-8781

Maine State Police
42 State House Station
45 Commerce Drive
Augusta, Maine 04333-0042
207-624-7200

Acknowledgments

My deepest appreciation for all her support and encourage goes to my wife and very best friend, Anne. Without her wisdom and prodding my life's many achievements would still be dreams. She is uniquely talented in many ways which serves as a challenge to my own creativity.

My sons, daughter-in-law, granddaughters and extended family members all contribute their own special support. My deceased parents and deceased parents-in-law were and still are foundations of inspiration which I still draw upon.

Nothing is more valuable, more cherished to an author than readers. I can't tell you how very much you have contributed to my work and my life. Your ongoing and growing support serves as a vast reservoir of inspiration to me.

The list of authors who have inspired me is long and prominent. At the very top of this list is Steven King. He is the one writer whose style serves me as a steady beacon of excellence.

No acknowledgement could or would be complete without my tribute to my publisher, friend and writing stylist extraordinaire, Cathy Teets, President of Headline Books, Inc. Cathy and her gifted staff extract the best from all those who contribute material to her. Bless them one and all!